Praise for ... *it!*

"Warmth, wit, an[d] ... [o]n every
page . . . With a ... die for,
How to Dance with a Duke is a romance to remember."
—Bestselling author Julie Anne Long

"Sexy, thrilling, and romantic—whether she's writing
of the mysteries of the heart or of the shady underworld
of Egyptian relic smuggling, Manda Collins makes her
Regency world a place any reader would want to dwell."
—*New York Times* bestselling author Kieran Kramer

"Manda Collins writes sexy and smart historical romance,
with a big dash of fun. Romance readers will adore *How to
Dance with a Duke*!" —*Booklist* New Stars of Historical
Romance author Vanessa Kelly

"Regency lovers have a new author to add to their dance
cards! Manda Collins heats up the ballroom and writes
romance to melt even the frostiest duke's heart. With spar-
kling Regency wit, a dash of mystery, and just the right
amount of steam, *How to Dance with a Duke* is an enchant-
ing debut, sure to sweep readers off their feet!" —Tessa Dare

How to
Dance
Duke
with a

Manda Collins

St. Martin's Paperbacks

This is a work of fiction. All of the characters, organizations, and events portrayed in this novel are either products of the author's imagination or are used fictitiously.

HOW TO DANCE WITH A DUKE

Copyright © 2012 by Manda Collins.
Excerpt from *How to Romance a Rake* copyright © 2012 by Manda Collins.

For information address St. Martin's Press, 175 Fifth Avenue, New York, NY 10010.

ISBN: 978-0-312-54924-4

Printed in the United States of America

St. Martin's Paperbacks edition / February 2012

St. Martin's Paperbacks are published by St. Martin's Press, 175 Fifth Avenue, New York, NY 10010.

10 9 8 7 6 5 4 3 2 1

For the ones who are no longer here to read this:

Mama, Daddy, Papaw, Kirby, Robbie, and Alida.

I would blush, but I wish you were here

to celebrate with me all the same.

Acknowledgments

Thank you to my editor, Holly Blanck, who has made this a better book with her thoughtful editorial suggestions, her savvy oversight of the production process, and her general fabulousness.

To everyone at St. Martin's Press, especially the art department, for giving me a cover that raises envy in the hearts of my fellow authors.

To my brilliant agent, Holly Root, who saw something in my writing that made her want to read more and who has been a joy to work with from day one. And who does not flee in terror when I send her my quarterly career freak-out e-mail.

To the Bon Bons, the Vanettes, and the Romance Vagabonds for support, laughter, and general mayhem.

To Janga for loving my writing from the get-go and reading every WIP—no matter how unpolished. To Lindsey for being the voice of reason and for late-night plotting sessions. To Julianne and Santa for keeping me positive and making me laugh.

To my GCCRWA chapter-mates for continued support and encouragement. Especially Cindy and Katie, who are always up for career-focused chat and talk of hot doctors.

To Fred and Maria for understanding missed phone calls and get-togethers when I was deeply entrenched in deadline mode. To Finley and Neal for being almost as excited about this whole publication thing as I am and who always welcome me into their family with open arms. To Laura, who plotted another book entirely with me on one long-ago New Year's Day.

To Christina Cannon Banker, for sharing a love of Nancy Drew with me that eventually led to this series concept.

To my sister, Jessie, for reading for me even when she'd rather be sleeping and for sharing every squee-worthy moment even when she wasn't quite sure what she was squeeing for. Love you.

And finally to the Moody Family for love and support and for coming to my rescue more times than I can remember.

One

$\mathcal{M}$iss Cecily Hurston battered her ivory-tipped parasol against the hulking footman who none too gently thrust her through the doors of Number 13 Bruton Street.

"You cannot do this!" She elbowed him to emphasize her point, and smiled in satisfaction at his grunt of pain. "My father was a founding member of this club! I demand you let me in at once!"

"He's the one whot made the rule," the beefy man said, putting her down and fending off further attacks with one arm as he backed inside and shut the door.

Cecily stood gaping at the closed door. "He . . . he . . . what?"

"You heard me!" The shout was just audible through the heavy door.

She tried again. "Surely in this particular situation you would be willing to bend the rules a bit . . ."

But after a couple of minutes with no response, she heaved an exasperated sigh, and gave the door one last aggravated kick. The heavy boots she'd worn for today's visit protected her toes, but did little to protect her wounded pride.

She had hoped, considering the circumstances, that the members of the Egyptian Explorer's Club would waive their ridiculous no-unmarried-females rule. After all, none of them had considered that Lord Hurston would suffer an apoplexy on the return trip from his most recent expedition. She was an unmarried lady, true, but she was also—despite her father's best efforts to discourage her scholarly pursuits—one of the only people in England capable of translating his idiosyncratic form of hieroglyphics, which he used for all his travel writings in an effort to deter would-be thieves. Without her help, the tale of her father's final Egyptian tour would be told, for the first time in his illustrious career, in someone else's words.

And then there were the rumors. She knew his notebooks held the key to disproving the rumors surrounding her father since his return to London.

Now she would be forced to go to the Duke of Winterson. His brother, Mr. William Dalton, had served as Lord Hurston's personal secretary on the journey and might have kept his own records of the trip. Unfortunately, in another bit of bad luck for the expedition, that gentleman had gone missing during the trip, and had not been seen or heard from since. It would not be the same as her father's account, but Mr. Dalton's notes would surely be more reliable than those of any other man who had accompanied them to Alexandria. Still, the thought of using anything other than her father's words was disheartening.

Defeated, Cecily took a calming breath and straightened her hat, which had been knocked askew in the scuffle. Smoothing her dark hair back from her brow, adjusting her gloves, and yanking her pelisse firmly into place, she turned to face down the front steps to the street below.

Unfortunately her ejection from the club had not gone unnoticed.

His exquisitely fitted attire and gleaming, silver-topped walking stick marked the man gazing up at her as a gentleman. And he was handsome enough to give her pause. Bright blue eyes surveyed her from a face that might well have been stolen from a classical statue, aquiline nose and all. While not normally one to have her head turned by a pretty face—in her experience handsome men, like her cousin, were a selfish breed—even Cecily felt her breath momentarily stop at the sheer elegance of the gentleman below.

But when he raised his beaver hat to reveal a head full of closely cropped dark curls, she had the uncanny sense that he laughed at her.

"Are they not accepting visitors today?" he inquired politely—as if he hadn't watched Cecily's forcible removal from the establishment moments earlier.

On her guard, she tried to determine his intent. Was he laughing? Or was he merely obtuse? Probably the latter, she thought to herself. In her experience handsome gentlemen were also lacking in common sense.

As if reading her thoughts, he raised a gloved hand. "I assure you, madam, that my query is sincere. I thought perhaps your . . ." He cleared his throat, as if trying to determine what to call what had just occurred at the door behind her. "Exit," he settled upon, "was due to the club's closure."

"No," she responded, making her way down the first few steps leading to the street below. "They are closed only to me." She paused at the next to last step, and looked the gentleman up and down, in a rude gesture that would have earned her a boxed ear from her old governess, Miss Milton. "I feel quite sure that someone of your . . ."

"Sophistication?" he suggested, making no move to ascend the stairs, and effectively blocking her descent.

She took one step down, bringing her to eye level with the stranger. He did not look like the sort of man who would have business with the club.

Perhaps reading her expression, his sharpened gaze was replaced with a look of playful challenge. "Breeding? Looks?" he inquired.

Tired of their game, and if truth be told a bit unnerved by his attentions, she pushed past him into the street below.

"Sex," she said, stalking away.

But, to her dismay, the gentleman followed her.

"I beg your pardon," he said, shaking his head as if to clear it. "I think I misheard you."

The man was wits-to-let, however appealing his dimples might be, Cecily decided. Pausing, she looked him squarely in the eye and repeated, "I said that I feel quite sure someone of your sex should have no difficulty gaining entrance to the Egyptian Explorer's Club. Now, if you will please excuse me, sir."

She continued on her way and was annoyed, but not surprised, to find him trotting along at her side, though a slight limp in his left leg slowed him down a bit.

"Of course that's what you meant," her unwanted companion said. "I had not realized that the club was not open to females."

"Yes, technically, that is correct," Cecily said tersely. "If you would excuse me, sir . . ."

"Indeed, I am quite certain ladies *are* allowed into the club because my sister-in-law has mentioned several times that she has attended lectures here."

His conversational tone indicated that he had no intention of leaving her to go on about her business. With a sigh of surrender, she kept walking. By the time she reached her waiting carriage, she decided, he would likely have given up and left her side.

"Then your sister-in-law must be married to a member," she replied, deciding to keep her tone brisk to discourage further conversation.

"That is true," he said companionably. "My brother was a member so that probably explains it."

When they had walked several hundred feet in silence, however, Cecily could stand it no more.

"Sir," she said, stopping, "I do not know who you are, but as you can see I am in a bit of a hurry, and as we have not been properly introduced it is highly irregular for you to escort me down Bruton Street."

She did not add that if she were to return to her carriage with a strange gentleman accompanying her, she had little doubt that her maid would carry the tale back to her stepmama. A circumstance she desperately wished to avoid.

"You disappoint me," the gentleman said, shaking his head. "Surely the Amazon who kicked both the footman and the door of the Egyptian Explorer's Club is not concerned with a matter as conventional as the proprieties."

"Yes, well, the Amazon was overcome by pique outside the Egyptian Explorer's Club," she said tartly, resuming her brisk pace. She did not add that it was all very well for a *man* to ignore the proprieties. He did not have to rely on the goodwill of a distant cousin and a stepmama to keep a roof over *his* head.

"Your irritation was understandable," her escort responded. "But you are not overcome by annoyance now, and yet if I were not here, you would be walking unescorted down Bruton Street for all the scandalmongers of London to see. So you are hardly a reliable source for what does and does not constitute proper behavior."

Cecily opened her mouth to object, but he interrupted before she could speak.

"However, if you are so concerned about our lack of proper introduction, then let us by all means dispense with that nonsense."

He halted, and out of habit Cecily stopped as well. He made her an elegant bow and Cecily dropped into a curtsy. Which felt exceedingly foolish in the middle of Bruton Street, but then this entire day had devolved into a series of foolish vignettes, one more insane than the last.

"Winterson, at your service, madam," he said curtly, as if he did not like revealing his name to her.

She looked up abruptly.

"Winterson?" she asked. "The Duke of Winterson? Why on earth didn't you say so before?"

Lucas should have known better. The first lady he'd encountered since his return to London with more than a passing acquaintance with her own brain, and she turned out to be just like every other woman he'd met since coming into the dukedom.

Title hungry.

It shouldn't have mattered so much, but it did. As Major Lucas Dalton he had certainly never hurt for female company—though he acknowledged that the scarlet uniform did its part—but once his uncle and cousin had died, leaving him to assume the title, he had found himself the object of an unseemly amount of female attention.

Discovering that his fiery Amazon was just another avaricious harpy was a disappointment, but hardly surprising given his recent interactions with the fairer sex. A different sort of man might have embraced his sudden popularity with enthusiasm, but Lucas had never aspired to more than the life of a military officer. Though there were some parallels between serving as an officer and serving as a peer of the realm, the differences at moments like these were as vast as an ocean.

"Indeed, I am Winterson." He cast one last look at her shapely form, and mink-colored curls, and suiting his actions to his words, turned to walk away. "Now, if you will excuse me, I have just remembered a pressing appointment with—"

A firm hand on his upper arm stayed him. He cast a speaking look, one even his raw recruits would recognize, at the place where her fingers gripped his coat.

Flustered, as he had intended, she let go of him at once. "Please, Your Grace, I beg your pardon. But do not go. I have been looking forward to making your acquaintance for some time."

I'll just bet you have, darling.

Aloud, he said, "Yes, well, I am in a bit of a hurry, miss." And without waiting to hear what she said, he stalked back the way they had come, aware that his limp was more pronounced when he hurried, but not really giving a hang.

"But wait." She followed after him. "Your Grace, pray do not run away—"

He halted abruptly, and dammit if she did not grip his arm again.

"I am not running away," he said between clenched teeth. "As I told you a moment ago, I have a previously forgotten appointment. And stop gripping me by the arm!"

"If you are not running away, then why will you not stop a moment and allow me to introduce myself?" she snapped, her cheeks flushing and her bosom heaving in a show of temper that was, if truth were told, quite becoming.

Perhaps her reasons for ignoring the proprieties were less

about ignoring convention and more about where she stood on the social ladder. He took a moment to examine her attire, and noting her plain hat and the drab color of her gown, he decided that she might be an impoverished widow. His mood brightened considerably at the thought. An unmarried miss might want him for his title, but a widow might be willing to accept a less permanent arrangement.

Another few minutes to hear the lady out would hurt no one, he thought.

At his continued silence, however, the lady lost patience. Throwing up her hands in disgust, she began to walk away.

"I had thought perhaps you and I were after the same thing, but at this point it doesn't matter. You may have your arm back, Your Grace. I will importune you no longer."

Ah. So he was right. She had been importuning him. But not for marriage—that was the important thing.

Now he was the one rushing after her, and even with his injury, his stride was so much longer than hers that he was able to overtake her quite easily.

"I beg your pardon for my boorish behavior, Miss . . . or Mrs. . . . ?" His voice rose with the question as he mentally crossed his fingers that she would fall into the latter group.

Stopping, she once more dropped into a curtsy, and extended her hand to him. "Miss Cecily Hurston."

Dammit.

Lucas closed his eyes. When he opened them, she was still there.

"Of course you are," he said wearily. "The daughter of Viscount Hurston, no doubt?" He had been trying to arrange a meeting with that gentleman for weeks now. The family claimed the viscount had lost the power of speech, but Lucas wouldn't believe it until he saw the man for himself.

"Indeed," she returned. "Now you see why I was so eager to stay you, Your Grace. We have much to discuss."

Even as he considered using her to get to her father, he dismissed the idea. She would have no influence over the man. Look at the reception his friends at the Egyptian Club had given her.

"I am afraid, Miss Hurston," he said calmly, "you are mistaken. What could I possibly have to discuss with the daughter of the man who will not even grant me the courtesy of a face-to-face meeting about the disappearance of my brother?"

His momentary flight of fancy over, for the first time in his adult life, Lucas Dalton, Duke of Winterson, dismissed common courtesy completely, turned on his heel, and walked away.

To his relief, Miss Cecily Hurston did not follow.

Cecily felt a dull ache in her temples as she returned to the carriage bearing the insignia of the Viscount Hurston. She'd asked the coachman to wait for her several blocks away from the Egyptian Club, and after the duke's abrupt dismissal in Bruton Street she'd almost given in to the childish urge to run in order to get there. Letting the driver hand her into the carriage, she settled in and leaned her head back against the heavy cushion.

Though she had spent the majority of their encounter attempting to be rid of him, once she knew that her handsome interloper was the Duke of Winterson, Cecily had hoped the man might wish to discuss the circumstances of his brother's disappearance from her father's latest expedition to Egypt. Not only had her father taken ill on the voyage back, the rumormongers of the *ton* had begun circulating a rumor that he was responsible for William Dalton's death. That he had become crazed as a result of some nonsensical curse that plagued those who tampered with the ancient dead.

The curse, Cecily knew, was merely a figment of the lurid imaginings of an ignorant populace who failed to understand the customs of any culture but their own. But the allegations that Lord Hurston had killed Will Dalton were unconscionable given that her father was unable to defend himself.

Though she had hoped the Egyptian Club would help her prove that her father had no hand in Will Dalton's disappearance, its members had been strangely distant since her father's return. Not a single member had visited her father since news of his illness had spread through town. Thinking to ask for the club's help directly, she and her stepmama, Violet, had called on Lord Fortenbury, the president now that her father was unable to perform his duties, but his welcome had been lukewarm. When they beseeched him to speak out against the rumors, Fortenbury had refused, saying he did not wish to involve the club in scandal. Directly addressing the rumors, he said, would merely give credence to them.

Never one to sit by and wait for things to happen, Cecily, who already wanted her father's journals to transcribe them, suspected they also held clues that would clear her father's name. But to her consternation, they were nowhere to be found. Not in his rooms and not in the library of Hurston House. Which left two options: the Egyptian Club, and the bags of his secretary, Will Dalton.

She and Violet and their other friends would do what they could to stifle the gossip, but for real proof that her father was innocent of causing harm to his secretary, she needed those journals. And to get the journals she needed to get into the Egyptian Club.

Having the Duke of Winterson attach blame to her for her father's actions was hurtful, but having him accuse her father of murder was worse. If she had not been so overset by her ejection from the club, she might have been better prepared to deal with his accusations. She was used to being ridiculed for her bluestocking tendencies, which was a badge she wore proudly since it implied she had more on her mind than flounces and ruffles. But the whispers about her father were still a new enough occurrence to sting. Outright accusations were rare, but, as this morning's encounter had proven, infinitely more cutting. Especially given her sometimes tumultuous relationship with her father.

From her earliest years, Cecily had pestered her father to teach her to read Latin and Greek as he did. But fearful that she would become obsessed with the subject he blamed for her mother's death when Cecily was only a small child, Lord Hurston had attempted to dissuade her from her intellectual pursuits.

Though she had little recollection of the event herself, Cecily knew that her mother had been quite a gifted scholar in her own right when she'd been found dead on the moors surrounding the Hurston country house. Speaking about the incident had been discouraged, but from what Cecily gathered from the servants' gossip, the first Lady Hurston had been struggling with her own translation of Homer's *Odyssey* at the time, and it was speculated that she had developed a brain fever from the overstimulation.

The only reason she knew anything at all about Egyptology, or Latin and Greek for that matter, was thanks to her godmother, Lady Entwhistle, who had been a great friend of Cecily's mother, and who had endowed the motherless girl with a thirst for knowledge equal to her own. Now Cecily was able to speak and read several languages with ease, and in addition had a remarkable facility for unraveling codes and ciphers.

It was odd, she supposed, given the number of times Lord Hurston had discouraged her interest in his travels, that she even considered ensuring that his accounts of his final voyage were included as part of his legacy as a scholar. But for all of their arguments and difficulties, Cecily loved the man. Their relationship, aside from his feelings about her scholarly activities, was a strong one. And, intellectually at least, she understood just why he did not want her to become involved in his work. His fears that her interests would turn into the kind of obsession that had precipitated her mother's death were unfounded, but came from a place of love. And there was something about seeing him now, a shrunken shadow of his former self, which made her long for one last conversation to set things right between them. Because there was little hope of that, she would settle for ensuring that the account of his final expedition was told, truthfully and in his own words.

Then there was the matter of Will.

If she could get her hands on the journals themselves, she would prove that her father had nothing to do with his disappearance. She was sure of it. But how to get them? That the Egyptian Club did not allow female visitors to examine their library was a hurdle, one she had hoped to avoid this morning by explaining the situation. But clearly, as the guard's actions had shown, the club was adhering to the rule her own father had imposed. If she could not break the rule, she would be forced to go around it.

As she had told Winterson that morning, there was one particular set of ladies who *were* allowed into the club: the wives of club members.

She thought about her cousin Rufus and his vile wife, who were even now encamped in Hurston House in hopes that Rufus would soon be the new Lord Hurston. She thought of what her life would be like if her father died, and she was forced to live on the crumbs of their charity. And how much worse it would be should he die without being exonerated of William Dalton's murder.

It was a sobering notion.

Being whispered about because of one's intellectual pursuits was an entirely different thing from being blackballed because one's father was a killer.

Cecily had hoped she would be able to avoid marriage. The one time she had considered it, it had ended badly. Very badly.

But she was older now. And, she hoped, stronger. And perhaps marriage would not be so very difficult. Though her brief engagement had never afforded her more than a few kisses, she had read enough ancient texts to know that the marriage bed could offer pleasure.

Unbidden, the image of the Duke of Winterson locking eyes with her when she stepped out of the club rose in Cecily's mind. Her stomach gave a little flip as she recalled how exhilarated she'd been for that one glorious moment.

Focus, she told herself. The duke wasn't even a member of the club. And even though marriage to him might give her access to Mr. Dalton's papers, the thought of seducing his brother to get them was more mercenary than she would consider. Much better to arrange a marriage of convenience to a club member. She had skills and connections to bring to such a match that would make it—on the surface at least—equitable. She doubted the Duke of Winterson had a pressing need for Greek or Latin translations, and he certainly could do better on the marriage mart than a viscount's daughter with bluestocking tendencies.

Closing her mind to the tantalizing duke, she gave a brief knock on the ceiling of the carriage, alerting the coachman that she needed to speak with him. Enticing a member of the Egyptian Club to marry her would take serious planning with the fashionable equivalent of Wellington. Her stepmother fit that description, but before she could approach Violet, she needed to sound out her scheme with someone who knew the workings of the *ton* from the edges of the dance floor, where she spent most of her time.

She needed her cousins Madeline and Juliet.

The Ugly Ducklings.

Two

Lucas returned to Winterson House in a foul mood, still berating himself over his flight from Miss Hurston in front of the Egyptian Club.

He was a bloody soldier, for pity's sake. And he'd tucked tail and run from her like a damned raw recruit in his first battle. It was galling.

His temper was not improved when he found his sister-in-law waiting for him in his study. Uncomfortable with the opulence of the Winterson town house, Lucas had been relieved to find that the study, at least, had escaped the interfering hand of whoever had furnished the rest of the house. It was still richly appointed, true, but its polished wood paneling and darker tones were a relief to a man who had spent the better part of ten years living in a military encampment.

Mrs. William Dalton's presence in the room could have been no more jarring if Prinny had popped over in the night and had had the place remodeled in the image of his pavilion in Brighton.

"Clarissa," he said, noting the teapot at her elbow that indicated she'd been seated here for quite some time. "I take it you wish to speak to me." It had never been clear to Lucas why his brother had married Miss Clarissa Livingston. She was passably pretty but of a cool disposition that brought to mind icebergs and snowdrifts. Certainly she was not the sort of woman who inspired passion. He'd sooner embrace one of Elgin's marbles. But Will had ever danced to his own piper, and by the time he'd introduced Miss Livingston to the family, they were already betrothed.

Clarissa stood and curtsied as he entered the room, her cherry-colored morning gown striking a festive note, out of keeping with the household's somber tone since Will's disappearance. She might follow the rules of etiquette, but always to the rule rather than the spirit.

If anyone could make a curtsy insolent, Clarissa could. "Yes, I do have a matter to discuss with you, Your Grace," she said, her thin lips pursed so tightly they all but disappeared.

Lucas stepped behind the massive mahogany desk, and waited for her to be seated before he sank into his chair, thankful that she hadn't insisted upon standing. His leg hurt like the devil after this morning's brisk walk.

"So, what is it you wish to say?" he asked her, knowing it was not something he wished to hear. Clarissa always manipulated situations to suit her need for control. And bearding the lion in his den was a classic maneuver.

"It has been nearly three months since William's disappearance," she began, her gaze firm, no glimmer of sorrow in her eyes. "I believe it is time for us to conclude that he will not be coming back."

He could hardly be surprised by her words, or her lack of emotion. There had been no indication, even from the first, that his sister-in-law felt anything at all about his brother's disappearance.

Her arrival on the doorstep of Winterson House, her belongings in tow, had come hard on the heels of Lucas's elevation to the dukedom. She had assumed, she told him, that he would not wish, as the duke, to see his brother's wife living in squalor in a questionable area of London. The questionable area of London was actually a quite respectable street in Bloomsbury, but he had chosen not to point that out. As the head of the family, he did feel a responsibility to look after his mother and sister-in-law. And though he had never really warmed to Clarissa, he had promised Will to look out for her before his younger brother departed for what might turn out to be his final trip ever.

"We have had this discussion before," he said, his voice even despite his anger. "And I do not believe I have indicated that my opinion on the matter has changed in the interim. My investigator has not yet reported back from Alexandria, and until I hear more from him, we will continue with the assumption that William is still living, but was separated from his party before they departed for England."

His tone was harsh, but he was damned tired of Clarissa's fight to declare dead the little brother he'd taught to fish and ride and flirt with pretty girls.

Either not noticing or not caring how he received her words, Clarissa pressed on.

"No one has heard from him," she persisted. "He has not been in touch with anyone from the expedition. The British consulate have conducted their own search and come up with nothing. There is no reason for us to believe that William will come back. Ever."

Lucas had requested help from the Foreign Office as soon as he learned of his brother's disappearance, but they were just as flummoxed by the situation as everyone else was. He'd even applied to Lord Henry Shelby, who, coincidentally, was both Lord Hurston's brother-in-law, and a top official in the Foreign Office. He had no reason to expect the truth from Shelby, but he was the next in line to the foreign secretary, and had to be consulted—if for no other reason than to gauge his sincerity. But upon meeting the diplomat he was confident the man was telling the truth when he claimed to have no further information. He'd learned to read people in the army and was seldom wrong. Which left Will's loved ones with exactly nothing.

Even so, Lucas was not prepared to simply give up. He knew from his own experience that there were times when you had no choice, when the odds were simply too great to overcome. But he did not yet think this was one of those times.

No matter what this brother's not-so-grieving wife said.

Clarissa's expression was hard, her cheeks flushed with

anger, as she defied him to contradict her assertions regarding Will's death.

"Why are you so determined to stop the search for your husband, Clarissa? Are you so eager to be a widow that you would abandon the fight prematurely? Perhaps to leave him, if he is injured or ill, to die before we have an opportunity to save him?"

She flinched at his accusation. It would appear that even she was not immune to all emotion. Good, he thought, let her feel what the rest of us do.

"Pray tell me, madam," he continued, "because I have endured your constant pessimism these past weeks with the understanding that your dire predictions stemmed from a fear that they might come true. Now, however, I begin to suspect you are indeed wishful of seeing William return to England in a wooden box."

If eyes could fling knives, Lucas would be sporting several holes in his chest.

"How dare you!" Clarissa hissed, her back ramrod straight with anger. "I am merely being levelheaded in the face of hardship. I would welcome his return. But I do know that he loved that godless, lawless foreign land and all its heathen trinkets far more than he ever loved me. If he died in a mistress's arms it could not be more shameful to me than knowing he chose to abandon me time and time again for that fiendish place."

Lucas had known Clarissa bore some resentment for William's dedication to Lord Hurston's work, but he'd never known how deeply she despised and even disapproved of it. Like the Dalton brothers, she'd been raised in a country vicarage, but now Lucas had some idea of how different their respective fathers' sermons must have been. Despite her appreciation for material wealth—he had the modiste bills to prove it—she harbored an almost puritanical disgust for anything that might smack of idolatry.

"However you might dislike my brother's occupation, Mrs. Dalton," he ground out, "as the head of this family I will choose when we give up the search for William. So I will thank you not to come to me again with this request."

Clarissa's chin came up in defiance. "I see now that you are just as stubborn as your brother. Rest assured that I will trouble you no further in this regard."

Not even bothering to bow, much less curtsy, she bid him good day, and left the room, closing the door with a resounding thud.

With a sigh of frustration, he rose gingerly on his wounded leg and poured himself a glass of claret from the decanter on the sideboard. He'd just returned to his chair when a brisk knock sounded on the door. Steeling himself for another round with his sister-in-law, he bade the visitor enter, and was relieved to see not Clarissa but his mother.

He stood, careful to hide his fatigue. "Come in, Mama, but I warn you that I am not in the best of tempers, so do so at your own risk."

"Never let it be said, my dear," his mother said, closing the door behind her, "that I am such a wilting flower that I cannot endure a temper tantrum from one of my boys."

Still handsome in her mid-fifties, Lady Michael Dalton had managed the vicarage on the Winterson estate with the same determination and good humor that infused all of her endeavors. When her husband, the Reverend Lord Michael Dalton, had succumbed to a putrid fever while Lucas was still up at Oxford, she had overseen their removal from the home where she had spent the whole of her married life to a cottage on the Winterson estate. She had made no complaints about their reduced circumstances, but had answered all of her brother-in-law's, the duke's, little slights with a quiet dignity that put her husband's family to shame. His admiration of her notwithstanding, Lucas found her tendency to make him feel like a lad in the schoolroom more than a little disconcerting.

"A grown man of my advanced years does not indulge in tantrums, Mama," he reminded her, gesturing for her to take the chair recently vacated by Clarissa. "Though it is dashed difficult to remember that when you are forever making me feel like I'm still in short coats."

"I am sorry, Your Grace," she said, a rare twinkle in her blue eyes so like his own. "But it is difficult to remember that you are a war hero and a peer of the realm when I can still remember your dear little baby voice asking for another sweet."

"Pray, do not say that outside this room. If word of *that* gets out, no amount of bravery will save me from the scandal sheets."

Their shared laugh faded when she turned her attention back to her reasons for seeking him out.

"I couldn't help but overhear your conversation with Clarissa," Lady Michael said neutrally. "You are very hard on her."

Lucas heaved a sigh and thrust a hand through his hair in frustration. "She wishes to call off the search for him. Which is something I am not yet willing to do. It's as if she's already decided he'll never come back and just wishes to begin her life without him."

His mother smiled sadly, the wrinkles around her eyes more prominent now. "Lucas, I know it is difficult for you to understand, but you must remember that Clarissa and William, though they have been married for five years, have spent more time apart than they have spent together. She never shared your brother's enthusiasm for Egypt, and the idea that he might have done the unthinkable and chosen Egypt over her is a worse fate for her to contemplate than the notion that he might have died there.

"It is a hard thing for a woman to compete with an abstraction, another culture, another land."

"You speak as if you've done so as well," he said, trying to imagine his parents' marriage as something other than the idyll he'd always fancied it to be. "Surely you never had to compete for Father's affections with an 'abstract idea,' as you call it."

She bit back a laugh. "What do you suppose the Church of England might be called?" Lady Michael stared off into the distance as if seeing another place, another time. "There were days when I would cheerfully have marched to London and challenged the Archbishop of Canterbury to a duel, I was so fed up with the demands he made on your papa. There was always some other family, some other mother, some other child who seemed to need him more than we did."

"But you were always so busy yourself, so dedicated to the needs of the parish."

"That was later," she said, smiling ruefully. "After the first few years I realized that I was not only making your father miserable, but myself as well. So I began to do what I could to assist him when he helped those needy families in the parish, and before long we were happy again and I was surprised to realize that I had found my own calling as well. But the difference between your father and I and William and Clarissa is that William's work takes him farther away than just the next village. And even if she were to take an interest in Egyptology, it would do her no good. He would still be gone more often than he is home."

"I still don't understand why they married in the first place," Lucas said.

"You were away with the army," Lady Michael said, "but at the time, William had just taken his post with Lord Hurston. I don't think he realized that his position would require as much travel it did. And, like most men, William has been known on occasion to lose his senses in the presence of a pretty face."

He shook his head. "No matter what she says, I won't give up the search, Mama."

"I don't believe she really expects you to, my dear." She leaned forward to squeeze his hand. The touch was brief but comforting. "But she desperately needs someone to rail at and as head of the family you are a convenient target.

"Now." Lady Michael's tone was brisk. "Let's speak of happier matters. What measures have you taken to find a bride for yourself?"

"Good Lord, I'm hardly eager to marry with my brother's example to warn me away from it."

"What of the example your father and I set for you?"

"I'd always supposed that you were the model of a happy marriage, but your revelation today makes me doubt myself."

"Oh," she said chidingly. "Those were the early years. It takes a little time after the novelty wears off for a couple to hit their stride. And your papa and I were gloriously happy. Make no mistake." Her eyes softened. "There is not a day that passes when I do not wish to share some bit of news or some observation with him, and then I am heartbroken all over again to find him gone."

Lucas wished there were something more substantial than words to comfort her with. "I miss him too."

"He would be so proud of you, my love. Never doubt that."

They sat in comfortable silence for a moment, both lost in their own thoughts.

"Now, about this bride of yours," she began again. "We are to attend the Duchess of Bewle's ball this evening. I do hope you will not spend the whole evening in the card room. Though your leg prevents you from dancing, you are permitted to stroll about the room with young ladies, you know."

Will's disappearance, though it cast a pall on their entertainments, did not prevent the family from attending the various *ton* social functions. And Lucas had made a habit of late to go to those events where he expected to see members of the Egyptian Club in attendance. His leg did ache, but he needed to attend, if only to apologize to Miss Hurston. It was a meeting he looked forward to with anticipation.

Unbidden, an image of Miss Hurston, her cheeks flushed in agitation, her curves accentuated by a revealing evening gown, rose in his mind. Perhaps seeing her again wouldn't be so unpleasant after all.

"I will stroll with at least one young lady this evening," he said, careful not to let his thoughts show on his face lest his mother jump to unfounded conclusions and start planning a wedding. "I promise you, Mama." Perhaps his leg was feeling a bit better after all.

* * *

"You met the Duke of Winterson?" Lady Madeline Essex, a pretty, petite blonde, nearly dropped her teacup in her excitement. "Is he as handsome as everyone says? Does he appear rakish? I have heard that he exudes a delicious air of danger wherever he goes. Does he, do you think?"

"She can hardly tell you if you keep peppering her with questions, Maddie." Miss Juliet Shelby, eminently sensible despite her flame-red hair, leaned forward to move a stack of sheet music from the nearest chair.

It was hard to remain indifferent to news about the only unwed duke in England who still had all of his own teeth accosting her cousin in the street.

Before approaching her stepmama about her newfound need to become fashionable, Cecily had directed the coachman to the Grosvenor Square address of Lord Shelby, where she found her cousins, Madeline and Juliet, tucked into Juliet's little sitting room bickering over which musician to invite to the next meeting of their Salon for the Edification of Ladies. All discussion of which was dropped as soon as Cecily informed them of her encounter with the Duke of Winterson that morning. They might be scholarly, but they were not dead, after all.

"I will tell you everything if you will pour me a cup of tea, Maddie." Cecily had skipped breakfast and she reached eagerly for a ginger biscuit before collapsing into the chair opposite her cousins.

They interacted with the ease of friendship and long acquaintance, each seated in her own place at what they'd dubbed the Talking Table, in honor of their usual activity when they were all three seated around it. Theirs was the sort of affection that can only be forged through shared hardship.

When Violet had married her father when Cecily was still quite small, the girl had had no inkling of just what ripples their match had sent forth into the social world. Unknown to the young Cecily, her stepmama was one of the Fabulous Featherstone sisters, whose arrival in London in the season of 1799 had set the *ton* on its proverbial ear. Though their origins, as the daughters of an obscure country parson in the wilds of Yorkshire, were hardly impressive, Violet, Rose, and Poppy had something stronger: beauty, grace, and cunning. Before they were in town for more than a week every hostess in the Beau Monde was clamoring to have them in attendance. Brummell declared them to be originals, and the Prince of Wales was rumored to be dangling after all three of them, albeit not with marriage in mind. Thus were the Fabulous Featherstones made.

When the newly widowed Lord Hurston had married the eldest sister, Violet, St. George's Hanover Square had been full to bursting with guests. In short order, Rose had married Lord Shelby, famous for his diplomatic endeavors, and Poppy had tamed the wild Earl of Essex. When their daughters had arrived, Cecily had been pleased to have playmates for the family gatherings that are a staple of any large family. By the time they made their own social debuts, the three had become the best of friends.

Unfortunately, being the daughters of such famed beauties had created expectations in the *ton* that were unrealistic. And as is often the case with celebrity, by the time the cousins made their debuts, backlash had set in. They were hardly antidotes, but in the time-honored tradition of asinine wags everywhere, one such wit had dubbed the cousins the Ugly Ducklings as a play on the Fabulous Featherstones. Nevermind that the duckling in the fairy tale turned into a swan. Society being what it was, there was little chance for the three young ladies to redeem themselves, much less point out the error.

Which was all the same to the cousins. Cecily had little interest in social affairs—except when they afforded her an opportunity to discuss her intellectual pursuits. Juliet would just as soon spend her evening practicing on the pianoforte or working on her own compositions—especially given that a childhood injury had left her unable to dance. And Madeline was far too outspoken to make it through an evening's entertainment without inadvertently offending someone, so she often used her time with the dowagers and wallflowers gathering fodder for the novel she was writing.

They might not be the most fashionable of young ladies, Cecily reflected, but they were by far the most interesting.

"So," Juliet prodded, "tell us all. It is not every day that an Ugly Duckling gets the opportunity to meet a handsome prince. Or duke."

Cecily frowned. "Well, he was hardly princelike. When he discovered who I was he practically ran as fast as he could in the opposite direction."

"That's hardly fair." Maddie's blond brows drew together. "You weren't even on the expedition where his brother disappeared."

"Since when do gentlemen operate based on the concept of fairness?" Juliet bit into a ginger biscuit. "Especially gentlemen with newly inherited dukedoms."

"Given that his brother is missing, I cannot hold his coldness against him," Cecily said with a sigh. "Though I would have thought he would agree to help me since Papa is in such dire straits now."

Both of Cecily's cousins sobered at the mention of Lord Hurston.

"How is he today?" Juliet asked, reaching out to squeeze Cecily's hand.

"The same." Cecily could not keep the slight tremor from her voice. "He is still unable to speak, and I am convinced that the bleeding and purgatives that Dr. Fairfax prescribed are doing him more harm than good. He is getting weaker and shows no signs of improvement."

"Dearest," Maddie said, "what can we do? How can we help?"

Cecily sighed. "That is just it. There is nothing to be done. We are simply forced to wait it out. There have been some cases where an almost full recovery has been achieved. But there are others . . ."

She did not say it, but her cousins knew what outcome she spoke of. It was what they all feared.

"In the meantime," Cecily said in what she hoped was a bracing tone, "I will try to get my hands on Papa's diaries for his latest trip and clear his name of these ridiculous allegations that he killed William Dalton."

"I am appalled that anyone who knows Uncle Hurston even entertains such ludicrous notions." Maddie shook her head in disgust, sending her already messy blond chignon into further disarray. "It's almost as vile as the curse rumors."

Juliet echoed the sentiment. "But how can you use the journals to prove his innocence if the club refuses to let you see them? You can hardly break in and steal them."

"Oh, I shall have them," Cecily said with conviction. "And I will do so by using the club's own rules against it."

Quickly she told them about the rule her father had put in place that would only allow the wives of current members to enter the club.

"When he created the rule, of course," Cecily went on, "Papa assumed that I would be marrying David soon. It could never have occurred to him that we would dissolve our engagement and I'd be barred from the club."

"Yet another thing to blame David for," Juliet said, her auburn brows bunching together in a frown. Neither Juliet nor Madeline were overly fond of Cecily's faithless fiancé, who had been found in a compromising position with another young lady and had been forced to wed her instead of Cecily.

He wasn't Cecily's favorite person, either.

Still, she didn't want to get sidetracked by rehashing their old grievances against her erstwhile betrothed.

"At any rate, the rule is in place now and there is nothing we can do to have it changed. I have no doubt that Papa's illness has been seen as a blessing by some club members, who have been waiting for the right moment to unseat him from his leadership position. They will hardly countenance having his daughter run tame there. Besides, I have asked Lord Fortenbury to return the journals and he insists that he doesn't have them. Which is, of course, a lie."

"So, how will you get in?" Madeline leaned forward, as if she wished to break down the door herself.

"I'll marry a club member, of course."

"Good Lord, Cecily." Juliet laughed. "I believed you for a moment, you goose."

"Oh, I am deadly serious," Cecily said, taking a sip of tea.

"What?" Madeline gaped. "You would marry just to get into the club? Surely there is an easier way."

"One that would not involve matrimony," Juliet added.

"I think I would enjoy the freedoms that come with being a married woman."

"But what of the restrictions?" Juliet asked with a frown. "You can hardly expect to marry someone who will let you do as you please. I doubt there is a man alive who is that easygoing."

"So long as he allows me to continue my work with the Ladies' Egyptological Society, I don't care what sort of temperament he has."

"But how can you set about it in such a cold-blooded fashion?" Madeline demanded. "Even after what happened with David, don't you wish to find someone you can love? Or for whom you hold some kind of affection?"

"Love is the last thing I am interested in," Cecily said baldly. "I had quite enough of that from David Lawrence and all it got me was a broken heart. No, I will be quite content with a marriage of convenience. And if I choose wisely, I might even be able to find someone with whom I share a love of scholarship."

"It all sounds so . . ." Juliet paused, as if she were trying her best to spare Cecily's feelings.

Cecily felt a rush of affection for her cousins. She took them both by the hand.

"Don't fret," she told them with a grin. "I won't enter into any match lightly. But if I am to retrieve my father's journals it is the only way. And if Papa should die of his illness, then my marrying will remove a burden from Violet's shoulders. I certainly don't wish to live with Cousin Rufus."

"When compared with a life lived with Rufus and his toadying wife, marriage does seem like a sensible option," Juliet said, brushing biscuit crumbs from her hands.

"So, what next?" Maddie asked. "If you intend to

husband-hunt you won't be able to do it from between the chaperones and the wallflowers."

"No, I won't," Cecily agreed. "Isn't it lucky for me that I have one of the loveliest, most socially savvy ladies in the Beau Monde as my stepmother?"

Upon her return to Hurston House, Cecily found her step-mother working on her embroidery in the sitting room attached to her husband's sickroom. Even in the midst of all this drama Lady Hurston was stunning. Her dark hair, which shone blue-black in the sunlight, was arranged simply in a tasteful chignon, and her royal-blue morning gown high-lighted the porcelain of her complexion and the blue of her eyes. Her forty-one years showed only around her eyes, which since Lord Hurston's illness had grown more disheartened as time passed.

Seeing Cecily enter the room, Violet stood. "Darling, how was your visit with the girls? Have you had luncheon? Tea? I'll ring for some."

Nodding her assent, Cecily sat in the chair opposite where Violet had been. It was chilly for spring and the warmth of the fire felt good after her carriage ride.

"Juliet and Madeline send their love," she said. Then sobering, she asked, "How is Father? Any better?"

There was a slight pause as Violet thought about her response.

"He is no worse," she said carefully, as if speaking of her husband's condition would bring on further troubles. "But he is also no better. In fact, I believe since his last cupping he is weaker."

It had been thus ever since a litter bearing the stricken man had arrived at the front door of the Hurston town house. The knowledge that Hurston was ill had been difficult, of course, but realizing the extent to which his apoplectic fit had affected his brain was devastating to those who knew just how keen his mind had always been. In the months since, his lack of progress and the hours both Violet and

Cecily spent at his bedside, seeing him in such suffering, had taken its toll.

Knowing it would divert Violet's mind from the gravity of Lord Hurston's condition, Cecily changed the subject.

"What would you say if I asked you to assist me with another matter?" Not waiting for an answer, she pressed on before she could change her mind. "I need your help refurbishing my wardrobe."

Violet's blue eyes went wide. Quickly, she hopped up, took Cecily by the arm and ushered her through the connecting door to her dressing room. Safely out of the sickroom, she let out a muffled squeal. "Huzzah! My dear girl, whatever has caused you to change your mind?"

Cecily bit her lip. She was torn between revealing her real reason for wanting to transform herself, and simply fobbing off her stepmother with a tale of nursing a *tendre* for some likely gentleman. The image of Winterson's handsome face invaded her imagination, but she ruthlessly suppressed it. He was far too handsome for his own good. And his military background likely meant he was used to giving orders. Which made him the last man on earth she'd ever wish to marry.

In the end, she decided a half-truth would be enough to whet Violet's matchmaking appetite though it meant acknowledging a possibility neither of them relished. "I have decided that since Cousin Rufus has all but taken a measuring tape to the drawing room window coverings, it would be prudent of me to ensure that I have some means of looking after myself should . . ."—she paused here with very real emotion—"something happen to Papa."

Violet's eyes swelled with unshed tears. Cecily did not like to dwell on such an unhappy topic, but it was something Dr. Fairfax had warned them about since Lord Hurston had first been carried off the ship and into his sickbed. It was an unfortunate truth that victims of apoplexy were liable to follow any number of paths in the course of their illness. And many of them ended with the same dire result. Though the physician was one of the most reputable in Harley Street, he could do no more than ensure that the prescribed therapy of cupping and purging was carried out with astonishing, and often alarming, regularity. And since there had been little change in Lord Hurston, despite the added application of ice water to his forehead every afternoon, both Cecily and Violet had been forced to consider just what they would do in the event that the unthinkable happened and Lord Hurston succumbed to his illness.

"Oh, how I hate to hear you speak of it, dearest," Violet said, taking Cecily's hand in hers and leading her to the sitting area in her rooms. "But I do think you are wise to have made this decision. While it is certainly possible that your father will improve, I do know that he would not wish for you to go on for very long without having some gentleman to whom you could turn for guidance and protection. And I am afraid that your father does not hold your cousin Rufus in very high esteem in that regard."

Lord Hurston despised Cousin Rufus for the grasping, rackety fellow he was, Cecily thought to herself. And though it gave her a small prick of annoyance to hear Violet parrot her father's views on the need for every young lady to have a strong man to guide her, she did agree that her papa would not wish for his daughter or even his wife to be very long under the protection of such a rapscallion as Rufus Hurston.

"Yes," she said aloud. "And though you know I have been opposed to marrying as a general rule, I daresay I would find marriage to a man of my choosing infinitely preferable to marriage to someone of Cousin Rufus's choosing. Or for that matter to living out my days in the former household of my father and being forced into unpaid domestic slavery."

Violet nodded. "I do understand. I do not know what I shall do if, God forbid, the worst should happen to your papa. My marriage portion would allow me to live very frugally." She gave a sad smile. "But you know that frugality has never been one of my virtues. And I do not wish to be a burden to my own family. I shall simply have to pray very hard for your father to improve.

"But," she continued, her expression lightening, "you cannot imagine how pleased I am to know that you have decided at last to allow the gentlemen of the *ton* to see what a lovely woman lurks beneath the dull gowns and unflattering hats you insist on wearing. I should think we will be able to find you a suitable husband even before the fortnight is out!"

Cecily stifled a laugh. She knew Violet was an optimist, but surely she did not believe any such nonsense was even possible. It was one thing to hope for Cecily to make a viable match. But within a two-week span was asking for a bit much, even for someone of Violet's considerable matchmaking prowess.

"My gowns are serviceable. And I choose them for comfort, not for beauty," she defended herself. "Though even I must admit to wishing for something a little more daring from time to time."

"Well, I will send out for Madame d'Auberge at once. She will have an entire new wardrobe ready in the space of three days, I should imagine!"

Cecily shook her head at the notion. But if anyone could wheedle the modiste to do her bidding it was Violet. "I don't suppose she'd be able to make something up for me to wear to the Duchess of Bewle's ball tonight?"

Violet considered for a moment. "I suspect she will have something already made up that could be altered for you. Though you are rather tall, so she might need to add a flounce to the hem."

She rose and tugged on the bellpull. "I don't suppose you would consent to have Monsieur LeBlanc cut your hair?"

Pushing back the tickle of unease she felt in giving up control of her appearance, Cecily gave a brisk nod. "If it were done, then 'tis well it were done quickly," she said, paraphrasing Macbeth. "I give myself into your hands, Lady Hurston."

Violet clapped her hands like a giddy schoolgirl, and despite her earlier misgivings, Cecily was glad to have given her stepmother this means of taking her mind off her ailing husband.

Even if it was to help Cecily ensnare a member of the
Egyptian Club in her matrimonial trap.

Determined to spend her evening scouring the ballroom for
single members of the Egyptian Club, Cecily arrived at the
Duchess of Bewle's ball wearing the sort of gown she had
been avoiding her entire adult life. Its puffed sleeves were
the latest fashion, and the buttery color lent a warm creamy
glow to her skin. And it drew attention to her bosom in a
manner that made her feel as if she were standing in public
in only her chemise. In fact, the whole ensemble drew the
eye, which would in the past have been her chief complaint
about it. But for her current purpose, it suited admirably. It
would simply take a bit of time for her personality to catch
up with her desire to find a husband.

That being said, her first stop after she and Violet made
it through the receiving line was her usual position on the
edge of the ballroom. "I love it," Madeline cried, clapping
her hands at the sight of Cecily's transformation. "The color
is perfect!"

"It's wonderful," Juliet agreed, stepping back to see the
full effect.

Her own gown was a deep green silk that was elegant but
modest. It was the sort of costume that would allow her to
blend into her surroundings. Pretty, but not striking enough
to call attention to her. Her ankle injury prevented her from
dancing, and Juliet claimed to prefer watching society from
the safety of the fringes. Though there were times when
Cecily suspected she was not quite so sanguine about her
position as she claimed.

"Never say you did that yourself?"Juliet said, reaching
out to touch the pretty cerise ribbon threaded through her
cousin's dark brown curls.

Cecily held back an unladylike snort. "Hardly. Violet's maid
Meg is responsible for the hair. And Violet chose the gown.
After a consultation with Madame d'Auberge, of course."

Maddie nodded approvingly. Her own pale pink gown had come from Madame d'Auberge's establishment. Of the three cousins, she was the one who most appreciated fashionable gowns. Cecily dressed because she had to. Juliet liked a pretty frock, but would on the whole much rather have the latest sheet music from the Continent. But Madeline had a true weakness for pretty clothes. She also harbored burning envy for Cecily's height. Which was just as well, since Cecily envied her petite stature. As was the way with the rest of the world, they each wanted the opposite from what they had.

"It almost makes me want to ask Mama for assistance with my wardrobe," Juliet said wistfully. Her mother, the middle Featherstone sister, Rose, Lady Shelby, was the vainest of the trio. Which made Juliet's shyness all the more annoying to her. What good was it to have a daughter when she chose to dress modestly and preferred to watch society rather than participate in it? "Almost, but not quite. Though it might be worth it to see her astonishment."

"Well, I'm sure Violet would be happy to help," Cecily said, grateful that her father had married Violet Featherstone rather than Rose. At the thought of her father, she sobered, adding, "I don't think I've seen her this pleased since Papa returned from Egypt."

Madeline squeezed Cecily's hand in sympathy.

"How is . . . ?" Juliet started to say, then broke off when Lady Hurston approached.

"Doesn't she look marvelous, girls?" Lady Hurston asked, kissing the air over the cheeks of her nieces. "You really do look lovely, Cecily. I hope you will actually do some dancing tonight and forget about that silly talk of a curse."

"I'm more worried about the talk of Papa being a murderer," Cecily said once Violet had left them. "Though they dared not say it to our faces, I could tell that Lady Taunton and Mrs. Fowler-Monk were thinking of it. Their eyes positively glowed with spite."

"You should definitely avoid Amelia Snowe, then," Maddie said with a frown. "Before you arrived she and Felicia

Downes were compiling a list of who was likely to be stricken down next. I am sorry to say that most of her little coterie of suitors joined in."

"Wonderful," Cecily said. "All I need to make my attempt to find a husband as painful as possible is the addition of Amelia Snowe adding to the curse rumors. Though I suppose I should be grateful she hasn't got wind of Winterson's grievances."

Maddie shook her head in disgust. "Well, at least she's qualified to talk about curses, since it seems as if she signed a pact with the devil to trick every gentleman in London into thinking she's a sweet little thing."

"The only pact Amelia Snowe has made is with herself," Juliet said firmly. "She is the most conceited person I've ever met."

"Matters of Amelia's character aside," Cecily said, lowering her voice so they wouldn't be overheard and squaring her shoulders, "I need to entice a member of the Egyptian Club and I don't intend to let her spoil my efforts. Not with rumors, not with curses. Now, if you ladies will excuse me, I must away to the retiring room to check my hair."

"Good luck!" Maddie called after her, trying to see over the heads of the dancers blocking her view.

"She'll need it if she intends to compete with Amelia Snowe," Juliet said. "Even Aunt Violet isn't powerful enough to best Amelia alone."

"No," Maddie said. "But she has us. We might not be the most fashionable ladies in the Beau Monde, but we are certainly the most determined."

"Are you sure this gown shows my figure to the best advantage?" Miss Amelia Snowe asked, turning this way and that before the pier glass set up in the Duchess of Bewle's retiring room.

From her position on the other side of the chamber, where she was fluffing a curl that had fallen, Cecily knew the blond beauty was not asking for her opinion. Instead the question was addressed to Miss Felicia Downes, who was Amelia's dearest friend.

Still, even Cecily had to admit that Amelia looked lovely in the ice-blue watered-silk confection she wore that evening, with its puffed sleeves and sweetheart neckline.

"I am quite sure my bosom would have looked better in the pink," Amelia continued, not waiting for her friend to answer. Adjusting her ample cleavage so that more creamy skin peeked out from the expertly cut bodice, she frowned at her reflection.

"Don't be ridiculous, Amelia," Felicia said. "You are beautiful as always. I would not be at all surprised if you brought Winterson up to scratch this evening on the strength of your bust alone."

At a raised brow from Amelia, the other girl winced. "You know what I mean."

The mention of Winterson's name startled Cecily, though why, she could not say. It was hardly remarkable that a man of his looks and title would search for a bride of equally stunning looks. And though he could not have been back in London for very long, she supposed he and Amelia might have met one another at some *ton* gathering from which she herself had been excluded. Besides, she needed to worry about catching the eye of Egyptian Club members tonight. Winterson was entirely beside the point.

"What are you staring at, Cecily Hurston?" Felicia sneered, interrupting the other girl's reverie.

"I'm sure I don't know." Cecily did not bother to look her in the eye, but turned her own gaze back to the mirror, and made a show of straightening the ribbon laced through her hair. "Perhaps if you are concerned about being overheard you should conduct your conversation in a less public venue."

Before Felicia could stalk to Cecily's side—no doubt to pinch her ear as she had once done at a birthday party when they were still in the nursery—Amelia called her hound to heel.

"Felicia," she said in the cool tone she adopted when displeased. "Do remember why we are here."

Felicia scowled, but stayed where she was. "Of course, Amelia. I believe you were inquiring about the fit of your gown."

Tucking a golden tress behind her delicately curved ear, Amelia smiled benignly. "Yes, of course."

Then, perhaps because she wished to prove to Cecily that she did not care what she thought of her, she smiled with just a hint of triumph. "You know, just between ourselves, Felicia, I think Winterson will propose any day now." Cecily had no doubt that Amelia meant for her to hear every word. "Just last evening he had this look about him that seemed to indicate he was thinking deeply about our future together."

Cecily stifled a snort. She doubted the man she'd encountered that morning thought any such thing.

Unfortunately, she had not stifled herself enough. Amelia turned from her self-admiration and cast a disapproving eye on Cecily. "Oh, Cecily. I'd forgotten you were there."

And after that blatant lie, Miss Snowe surveyed Cecily from head to toe.

"Really, my dear, one would imagine that your stepmama would be able to dress you better than that. I don't believe I've seen that style gown since the summer my sister Veronica debuted. And that was nearly five years ago. Though I suppose with all that bother about your father her attentions were needed elsewhere." The beauty's clear blue eyes held no particular ill will. She would have needed to care to feel animosity. And sadly, Amelia had not the least bit of fellow-feeling.

Cecily stiffened at the mention of her father. But she refused to let Amelia know that her barb had found its mark. Instead she stood tall, daring the blond beauty to say something else. For one brief moment she imagined what it would be like to have the freedom to shun truly unpleasant people like these two.

What a delightful existence that would be.

"It must be very trying to find clothing suitable for one of your Amazonian proportions. I daresay the cost for extra fabric is nearly prohibitive. Still, it is good to see you have at least made an effort this evening. Even Amazons must wash the dirt of the jungle from themselves and venture out every now and again."

"Better an Amazon than an elf," Cecily said, unable to stop herself.

"Oh, you mustn't let your jealousy turn your temper waspish," Miss Snowe said kindly, though her smile did not reach her eyes. "Waspishness is simply reviled in a spinster."

"Amelia," Cecily said, her gaze cold. She was pleased to see a flicker of something—fear?—behind them. "Why don't you go back out into the ballroom and ply your . . . ahem . . . wiles on the Duke of Winterson? I feel sure if he is as enamored as you say he is, the man must simply be aching to catch a glimpse of you."

Amelia stood her ground for a few seconds more, then with a little shrug she stepped away from the pier glass and headed for the door.

"Come, Felicia," she snapped, beckoning her companion to follow her from the room. Suddenly restless, when they were well and truly gone, Cecily rose and began to pace.

Encounters with people like Amelia made her want to run until her body was aching from exhaustion. Of course, ladies didn't run, Cecily thought grimly, *but I wonder if Amazons do?* She flounced into the chair Amelia had just abandoned . . . and promptly hopped up again when she felt something sharp in the seat.

Rubbing her smarting backside, she looked down at the damask cushion and saw a smallish gold object twinkling in the candlelight. Plucking it up, she turned it over in her hand, and realized she'd found someone's dance card.

No doubt it was Amelia's.

Cunningly fashioned in the shape of a fan, either end was made of gilt-edged ivory with a tiny pencil attached with a string to the bottom. Each fan petal, made of ivory, offered a place for a gentleman to write his name.

Cecily unfurled the little fan and was unsurprised to see the hastily scrawled names of one *ton* eligible after another lined up on the ivory petals.

What must it be like, she wondered with a sigh, to be the lady who never sat out a set? Before tonight it hadn't bothered her so much. She had her translation work to keep her occupied, after all. But being here tonight in a new dress, a new hairstyle, for the first time in her life she felt as sure of the fit of her gown as she did about her ability to conjugate irregular Latin verbs. It had never really occurred to her that there was another position for her to play in polite society than Lord Hurston's odd, bluestocking daughter.

If only Madame d'Auberge sold dance cards like Amelia's, where all the hard work of finding partners to dance with was already done.

She couldn't buy a prefilled dance card from Madame d'Auberge, but she did have Amelia's card. Which was already filled out. And . . .

She stopped. Then broke out in a broad grin as she looked more closely at the names. All but two were members of the Egyptian Club.

Tucking the dance card into the reticule hanging from her wrist, she hurried back out to the ballroom to find her cousins.

Three

Cecily returned to her cousins just in time to see Amelia and Felicia approaching. She held her reticule tightly against her side, praying the other girl hadn't realized her dance card was missing. But it was clear as soon as they reached the cousins that Amelia and Felicia were there for the entertainment value rather than to ask for help finding a misplaced dance card.

"Oh, look." Amelia sneered. "It's three little ducklings waiting by the side of the pond. How sad that they are afraid to dip their widdle toes into the water."

"La," Felicia responded before any of the cousins could make a retort. "I do believe the water in this pond is far too deep for such . . . ahem . . ." Even Felicia was reluctant to call them "ugly" to their faces. "Too deep for such weak specimens. I have no doubt they'd drown should they venture out among the swans."

"Indeed." Amelia nodded at her protégée with approval. "Let's leave them here to muddle along. I've a sudden wish to have my lovely feathers stroked," she said, giggling behind her tiny, gloved hand.

"Spiteful cat," Madeline spat out. "I hope she sprains an ankle and is unable to dance for the rest of the season."

Or at least the rest of the evening, Cecily thought.

"Girls," she said to her cousins, lowering her voice so that they wouldn't be overhead. "What if I told you I had found Amelia's dance card?"

"What do you mean you found it?" Juliet demanded.

Cecily explained how she'd stumbled upon the dance card in the withdrawing room, being sure to include Amelia and Felicia's hateful words lest her cousins forget their hatefulness.

"It's a sign!" Madeline hissed with excitement. "You came here tonight in a new gown, looking prettier than I've ever seen you, declaring you were on the hunt for a husband, and now you've found Amelia's dance card. Right after she was hateful to you. Cecily, this is a gift from the gods, and if you don't use this opportunity, I will."

Cecily nodded, her mind returning to good omens. She *had* come here tonight hoping to attract a member of the Egyptian Club. And here in her hand she clutched the means to do it. Even she, with her skeptical nature, was tempted to believe some fate had intervened on her behalf.

If everyone was so intent on there being a curse, why couldn't there also be a blessing?

"It would be nice to get the upper hand over Amelia just this once . . ." she said aloud.

"Wait," Juliet cut in, her eyes wary. "I'm all for teaching Amelia a lesson, but what makes you think that you'll be able to pass Amelia's dance card off as your own? And even if you do, I hardly think a few dances will necessarily lead to marriage."

"I don't really see a few dances doing the trick," Cecily said, giving the issue some thought. "But we all know how difficult it is to change the *ton*'s perception once you've been rolled up and stuffed into a pigeonhole. What if all it takes to change things is a couple of dances with some of the more popular gentlemen? The sort who dance with Amelia? Gentlemen are so easily led. If I dance with a few of Amelia's regular partners, the others will see it and they'll dance with me too because they've seen other men doing it."

"It is true," Madeline said. "Once my sister Letitia became engaged it was as if every man in London had decided that she must be desirable. If they see someone else wants you, then they all want you too. It is the nature of men."

Juliet nodded. "You're right," she said, glancing up at Madeline, who clapped her hands. "But if you are to convince these men tonight to dance with you, we'll need to do something to get Amelia out of the way."

"Nothing too terrible," Cecily insisted. Even though Amelia was unpleasant, she didn't want to see her hurt. "No sprained ankles," she said to Madeline.

"Don't worry," her cousin said, giving Cecily a mischievous smile. "I've got the perfect idea . . ."

She was hovering behind a pillar on the other side of the ballroom ten minutes later when she heard the commotion from the refreshment area.

"My gown!" she heard Amelia squeal, a red punch stain expanding across the front of her light blue ensemble. "You imbecile!"

Cecily could not hear what Madeline said in return, but bit back a grin as she saw her cousin dab ineffectually at the stain with a handkerchief. She must remember to give Madeline a wonderful gift for her birthday this year.

When she had at last seen Amelia and Felicia escorted from the ballroom by their clucking mamas, Cecily decided it was time to put her plan into action. Suppressing a flutter of excitement in her belly, she made her way toward the side of the ballroom where the single young gentlemen lingered.

Her first victim was deep in conversation with two other men, all dressed in varying degrees of splendor. One wore a cravat tied in such an intricate design that Cecily suspected he'd run through at least ten of the starched neckcloths before achieving the perfect knot. The next, a shorter man, also sported an impressive cravat, but it was his peacock-colored waistcoat that drew the eye. But the third man, her quarry, was by far the most impressive of the trio. His high shirt points hinted that he was a dandy, but the lace that fell from his wrists erased any lingering doubts.

Cecily stood watching for a moment, swamped with self-doubt as she compared her own attire with theirs. How could she possibly compete with such sartorial grace? Taking a deep breath, she looked at her target again.

What would Amelia do?

Thinking back to all the times she'd seen Amelia charm unwitting gentlemen, she stared down at the dance card in her hand, and absently thumbed the edge of a petal that had come loose. Before it could fall away, she grabbed it. Only to see that on the back of the ivory petal were written three phrases:

Smile.

Bat your lashes.

Tilt your head.

What on earth? She checked the next petal to see if it had any writing on the back, but it was blank.

What could this mean? Was it some sort of code?

Before she could retreat back to her cousins, she looked up and saw a familiar face across the room. In boots and breeches he had been handsome, but in evening dress the Duke of Winterson was magnificent. His clothes weren't showy like those of the dandies. They were elegant. His black coat was offset by a silver waistcoat, its embroidered threads echoing the glinting ruby in his cravat. In deference to his injury, he leaned on an ebony walking stick, its head topped with a silver ornament.

As if sensing her eyes on him, he looked up and their eyes met. Just as she had that morning. Cecily felt a thrill low in her belly. Annoyed by the blush rising in her cheeks, Cecily looked at her hands, and saw the three words on the dance card. *Smile. Bat. Tilt.*

Of course! It was a primer for flirtation.

Cautiously, like a toddler taking her first steps, she repeated the words in her head before putting them to use. She smiled, though it felt like more of a grimace. Maintaining the expression, she blinked. Rapidly. Then, still smiling, she tilted her head to the side, just as she had seen Amelia do countless times.

Her quarry stared for a moment. Then, a hint of amusement on his lips, he raised one black brow, and lowered his head in a slight bow. Not enough to draw attention to himself, but certainly enough for her to see.

It worked! Sort of.

Their little scene was ended when a pair of simpering debutantes crossed in front of her, blocking her view. Just as well, Cecily thought. She wasn't quite sure what came after "tilt."

Still, she was eager to try out the technique on the dandies. Squaring her shoulders, she stepped forward.

"Dear me," lisped he of the peacock vest. "I feel as if I should know you, my dear, but I'm da . . . er, dashed if I can remember where we've met. I can't imagine I would forget a f—a face like yours. Lord Marcus Fulton, at your service."

He executed a perfect bow and kissed the air above her hand before she even knew she'd extended it.

"Pay no attention to this blackguard, m'dear," said the chestnut-haired gentleman with the splendid cravat. "I believe it is I you came to slay with your expressive eyes." He took her hand and elbowed Fulton none too gently out of the way.

"Sir Thomas Ashcroft," he crooned, making sure to meet her eyes as he hovered over her hand. "The pleasure is all mine, my lady."

Cecily was momentarily at a loss for words. Being at the center of such scrutiny was both exhilarating and unsettling. But remembering the three little words, she smiled, batted, and tilted and was gratified to see that they seemed pleased with the effort.

"Pay these two fools no heed, Miss Hurston," the third gentleman—he of the golden hair and lacy cuffs—said, stepping forward. "They haven't the combined manners of a pair of pigeons."

Without appearing to do so, he somehow managed to cut out his two friends, and before she could even wonder how he'd known her identity, he had taken her gloved hand in his. "I'm sure you don't remember me, Miss Hurston, but I'm Lord Alec Deveril. We met at the Symington musicale several weeks ago."

Of course she remembered him, Cecily thought with an inward laugh. He was one of the most handsome men in the *ton*. And if that hadn't been enough, Juliet had been enamored of the man ever since he rescued her from a horse that had gotten away from its rider in the park some weeks back. She could speak of little else for weeks afterward.

But the most salient reason Cecily had for remembering Lord Alec Deveril had nothing to do with his handsome looks or his kindness to Juliet. He was, in fact, the first name penciled onto the pilfered dance card, and a prominent member of the Egyptian Club.

She smiled, batted, and tilted.

He smiled back. Lovely!

"Of course I haven't forgotten you, Lord Deveril," she said. A sudden fear that she'd not be able to carry out her ruse gripped her. There was no reason on earth for Deveril to forget he'd promised the first dance to Amelia Snowe; he seemed perfectly sober. Still, this was her only means of getting her father's journals, and she was not willing to give up. Even if it meant a little embarrassment.

"Indeed, my lord. I was hoping you'd remembered me from our conversation earlier when you requested the first dance this evening?"

She ended the statement with a questioning air, with just the right hint of tentative diffidence. She hoped.

Maybe she needed to SBT again.

But Deveril's brow furrowed, and to Cecily's profound relief, he seemed to relax and he smiled.

"That must have been right when I came in, Miss Hurston," he said apologetically. "It was a bit of a madhouse for those first few minutes and I remember signing someone's dance card, but I hadn't realized it was you at the time."

Though he professed not to remember, Cecily thought she saw a flash of understanding in his eyes. As if he knew she had appropriated Amelia's dance card. But in a moment the look was gone, and for whatever reason, he chose not to take issue with her little deception.

Deveril smiled down at her and tucked her hand into the crook of his arm. "Shall we?"

Lucas leaned against a pillar in the Bewle ballroom and watched in silence as Miss Cecily Hurston sailed by on the arm of Lord Alec Deveril for the second time. He'd watched her dance with a veritable parade of eligibles in the past two hours.

Her dark curls, hidden beneath her ugly bonnet that afternoon, now were threaded prettily with a bit of ribbon, accentuating her wide green eyes and high cheekbones. Gone too was the drab gray dress she'd worn to the Egyptian Club, and in its place she wore a high-waisted yellow evening gown that suited her curvy figure. Only a eunuch could ignore the expanse of creamy white bosom on display above that prim bodice.

And he was certainly no eunuch.

He smiled, recalling her bout of flirtatiousness earlier in the evening. Perhaps he'd been too harsh with her that morning.

Almost as soon as he stalked away from her in Bruton Street, he had regretted his outburst.

She was not her father, after all, and probably had no idea about the circumstances that had led to his brother's disappearance during Hurston's last expedition.

No, he thought, watching Miss Hurston laugh at something Deveril said, unless she had stowed away on the expedition herself, there was no way that she could know what really happened to Will.

Lucas swirled his cup of overly sweet punch and stared into it as if he could read its shadows like tea leaves. But the drink was just as incomprehensible as the strange words his brother crossed and recrossed in his letters home from Egypt.

There was something about the scribbled lines, something in the way his brother had chosen to include them in
letters to their mother of all people—who had no more
knowledge of foreign languages than she had of Napoleon's
bathwater—that niggled at him.

Those letters, in fact, had been the sole reason for his trip
to the Egyptian Club earlier today. He had hoped they might
direct him to a scholar with knowledge of such things, but
like Cecily he had not been able to get past the front door.
"Members only" the guard had told him, and they were not
currently accepting new members. When he had inquired as
to when that happy event might occur, he had been told that
such information was not available to the public. Even his
title had carried no weight with the man—a first in Lucas's
experience since inheriting the dukedom.

"Why the devil are you glaring at the dancers as if you
are deciding on which one of them you wish to plant a facer
first?"

The duke glanced up. Colonel Lord Christian Monteith
stood at his side, one blond brow lifted in inquiry.

"Who precisely are we glaring at?" Monteith continued,
leaning against the other side of Lucas's pillar, and sipping
his own cup of the wretched punch.

"I'm not glaring," Lucas said, glaring. "Not on purpose,
anyway. I am merely watching the dancers."

"Ah." Christian took another sip of punch, pulling a face
as he did so. "Any dancers in particular?"

Lucas evaded the question. "What brings you here? I
thought you'd rather be run through with a dull sword than
attend another ball this season."

Christian shrugged.

"I told m'sister I would attend so she'll have the assurance
that at least one of her dance partners won't step on her toes. I
gather she had a bad time of it with Wolsey last week."

Lucas winced in commiseration for Miss Monteith's toes.
John Wolsey was a notoriously bad dancer and a great bull
of a man to boot.

"What about you?" Christian asked, turning the question

back on his friend. "I thought you were bent on learning something about Will's Egyptian expedition. Somehow the Bewle ballroom does not seem the appropriate venue for that."

"You'd be surprised," Lucas said, keeping his eyes fixed on Cecily's twirling form.

Christian followed his friend's gaze and let out a low whistle.

"Aha," he said with a nod of appreciation. "Well done. It's quite sensible of you to focus on Hurston's daughter. She should be able to learn something from her father."

"The man's been ill since he got back," Lucas said. "And besides that, he is apparently not keen on her interest in Egyptology. I've asked around and it's said that he refuses to discuss anything of his expeditions with her."

"Doesn't mean he did so this time. People are liable to behave strangely when they know they will soon be shuffling off this mortal coil. Hurston might have confessed all to his daughter in an effort to mend fences.

"Families are a dashed complicated business," Christian continued. "Though I still think it's a canny move on your part to concentrate your energies on the daughter. Not only does she seem to be rather intelligent for a female, but she's also a ripe little piece. Who would have guessed at the curves hidden under those—"

Monteith broke off his assessment of Miss Hurston's charms at Winterson's low growl.

"You will not speak in such a disrespectful manner of Miss Hurston again," the duke ground out, his jaw clenched. "Understood?"

"Absolutely," Christian responded, raising a hand in appeasement.

The two stood glaring at one another in awkward silence until Lucas backed down, and stared back out at the dance floor.

"What was that?" Christian demanded. "We haven't tussled over a female since Eton, at least. I had no idea you even knew the lady," he continued, rubbing a hand over his jaw, as if in contemplation of the uppercut his friend would have delivered. "I meant no disrespect."

At Lucas's raised brow, Monteith shrugged. "Perhaps I meant a little disrespect. But I assure you it was well intentioned. I was simply marking my surprise at her . . . er . . ."

"Her beauty?"

"Indeed." Christian clutched at the life rope his friend offered. "I've never seen her look so radiant. She's transformed."

Lucas declined to mention the head tilt. Perhaps it was a fluke.

"I am less interested in the results of her transformation," he said, "than in the reason for it. Why on earth would a bluestocking who has spent three years firmly on the shelf develop a taste for fashion and a desire to waltz with the most eligible gentlemen of the *ton*? It makes no sense."

"I wasn't aware you'd made such a study of Miss Hurston's habits," Christian said. "Perhaps she tired of sitting out every dance. I know I'd be driven to drink if I had to spend all my time in conversation with the current crop of wallflowers. And don't get me started on the chaperones. Ghastly."

Lucas acknowledged that his friend had a point.

"But why tonight?" he asked. "I am not ashamed to admit I've never even noticed her before today. I suspect that's been her goal, to remain unnoticed. She was ejected from the Egyptian Club this morning," the duke continued, "and this evening she appears at the Bewle's ball with a fashionable gown and a new hairstyle. Somehow the two are connected."

"Look at her dance partners," Christian said, eyeing Miss Hurston as she curtsied to Deveril before taking young Lord Pennington's hand. "With a couple of exceptions, they all seem to be in the Egyptian Club. Could she be searching for something with regard to her father in the same way you are?"

Lucas stared, arrested by the notion of what Christian suggested. "Who has she danced with?" He began to tick them off on his fingers. "Deveril, Sydnam, Ashcroft, Fortenbury, Deveril again, and now Pennington."

"All prominent members of the *ton,* all bachelors . . ."

"And all members of the bloody Egyptian Club," Lucas finished, his voice low but intense.

"I'd say you've got a dance in your future, Winterson," Christian said.

The other man gestured to his walking stick and grimaced in the general direction of his injured leg.

"Dammit, I forgot. Sorry, old fellow." Brightening, Monteith grinned. "I don't suppose you'd care for me to do the pretty in your stead?"

"Are you fond of your head, Monteith? Or shall I remove it for you?" Lucas's tone was friendly, but there was no mistaking the steel behind it. "Watch and learn, my friend, how not to dance with a lady."

When Lucas arrived at Miss Hurston's side, she was giggling at some nonsense Pennington had just said, her head tilted, her eyes blinking.

Two could play at that gesture game, he thought.

He raised his brow and lifted his quizzing glass.

"You are in fine looks this evening, Miss Hurston," he drawled, enjoying the blush that rose from her chest to her cheeks.

She glanced down, but it was no act. Miss Hurston was genuinely flummoxed by his arrival. He felt a tightening in his chest at the thought.

"Your Grace," she said, sinking into a deep curtsy. A curtsy that gave him an excellent view of her excellent bosom. Christian had been right. She had been hiding some delectable curves beneath those ugly gowns.

When he looked up, he saw that he wasn't the only one enjoying the view of Miss Hurston's charms. Pennington was looking his fill, the insolent puppy. Lucas resisted the urge to throw her over his shoulder and carry her from the room.

A raised brow and a meaningful gesture of his chin had the younger man scurrying away like a frightened rabbit. Before the lady knew what had happened, her hand was tucked into the crook of Lucas's elbow and he was leading her toward the Duchess of Bewle's torch-lit terrace.

"That was very handily done," Cecily said dryly, following along at Winterson's side until they reached a brightly lit bench.

It was the first time she'd ventured out onto a balcony with a gentleman since her ill-fated engagement to David, and she was more grateful than ever that they'd kept that engagement a secret. If anyone in the ballroom had known of it, they would have taken far greater interest in her than they currently did. A bluestocking taking the air with a duke was newsworthy, of course, but a bluestocking who had been thrown over once before taking the air with a duke was infinitely more interesting. She could see the lines in the gossip sheets now: *"At the B——— ball the Duke of W——— was seen taking the air with that bluest of stockings, Miss H———, who was very happy indeed to be seen in the company of a gentleman for the first time since Mr. D——— L——— broke their engagement. One hopes she holds on to this gander more tightly than the last!"*

Their bench was far enough away from the other couples taking the air that they might speak freely. Even so, Cecily felt a bit of a thrill to be on the arm of such a handsome man. And the sound of her gown brushing against his breeches mixed with the warmth of his arm beneath her gloved fingers was intoxicating. It would be so easy to imagine that they were here together because they liked one another. Not because he thought her father had murdered his brother.

That thought stifling any illusions she might have about their relationship, she spoke first. "To what does the daughter of the man responsible for your brother's disappearance owe this great honor?"

Cecily turned to gauge his reaction and was pleased to see Winterson wince. Let him hear his own words thrown back at him and know how foolish they sound, she thought.

Even so, he continued, his voice as calm as she was agitated. "I have heard that you are frequently at loggerheads with your father over your scholarly pursuits. Surely it comes as no surprise to you that others might share your ill opinion of him."

Cecily removed her arm from his, and turned to face him, her temper lending her a measure of coolness she did not feel.

"I do not deny that my relationship with my father has often been a difficult one, Your Grace," she said. "But that relationship is my business. Not yours. If you have brought me here to continue your treatise on the manner in which my father has wronged you, then you will simply have to find a more suitable audience.

"On the other hand," she continued, turning away, grateful not to be facing him so that she might finish her speech without looking him in the eyes. "You wish to know whether I know anything about your brother's disappearance, and I will tell you plainly that I do not. As you have stated, my relationship with my father is not always an easy one. I have certainly never been his confidante on matters relating to his expeditions, given the fact that he has refused to take me with him, but his recent illness has meant that we are unable to speak of even innocuous topics. William's disappearance has been as much a mystery to me as I suppose it is for you."

At the mention of his brother, she saw him tense up. At her denial of having any more information, however, he sighed in frustration. A pang of sympathy ran through her as she thought of how difficult it must be not to know what had happened to his brother. At least she and Violet had Papa here in their care. Having him go missing would have been unimaginable.

Winterson stepped back and handed her down to sit on the bench, then used his walking stick to lower himself to the one opposite.

"I thank you for your candidness, Miss Hurston," he said, his blue eyes meeting hers. She noticed for the first time a tiny network of lines in the skin around them, and more bracketing his mouth. Both, she suspected, remembering his attempts to charm her this morning, were from laughing. Though she had doubts that he'd spent much time in that activity since his brother's disappearance.

"I don't suppose you have access to any of your father's papers from that trip, either?"

"I'm afraid not," she said, hating to dash his hopes again. "Those are what I was looking for this morning at the Egyptian Club."

"Ah," he said, infusing the word with more emotion than should be possible.

"I didn't arrive in time to hear your reason for trying to get in." He grinned. "I was, however, able to see you kick the door in frustration."

Cecily felt her cheeks redden. "Not one of my finer moments," she said, looking at her hands. Then, her sense of humor intervening, she continued, "In my defense it was a most impertinent door."

Their eyes met and held for a moment. Cecily felt the breath rush from her under the intensity of his blue gaze.

"I suspected as much," he said gravely, one dark brow curving upward. "It had that look about it."

Cecily couldn't help herself, giving in to a surprised laugh that punctured the veil of seriousness that had held them. Winterson laughed too, and for a moment, Lord Hurston's illness and Will's disappearance were forgotten in that flash of shared mirth.

Their laughter spent, they sat together smiling until Winterson spoke up.

"Why the transformation this evening?" he asked, waving a hand toward her hair and gown.

It was the last question she'd expected from him. She'd spent so long preparing her set-down for him, it hadn't occurred to her that he would even notice her new gown and new hairstyle.

Well, that was not strictly true, because in a moment of weakness she had imagined how he might see her newer, prettier self and proclaim his undying love while she stepped on his beseeching hands as he knelt before her. But that hardly counted.

Deciding not to make a fuss, she said primly, "I'm sure I don't know what you mean." Just for good measure, she smiled, batted, and tilted.

"Have you got something in your eye?" he asked, frowning in concern.

Cecily'd bet anything that Amelia Snowe was never asked if she had a crick in her neck or a piece of lint in her eye.

Apparently taking her clipped "No" at face value, he pressed on with his questions about her attire. "Come now, Miss Hurston. I may not be able to translate texts in half a dozen languages, but I'm no simpleton. I can tell the difference between a gown that is made for comfort and one meant to entice. And tonight's gown is definitely the latter."

Entice?

"If you are suggesting that our meeting this morning sent me rushing home in search of a new hairstyle and a new gown . . ."

"Pax, Miss Hurston!" He threw up his hands in a gesture of surrender. "That is not what I meant at all."

She eyed him with suspicion, not quite sure what to do with a conciliatory Winterson. She was much more comfortable dealing with the accusatory one. When he behaved himself it was much too easy to notice how very blue his eyes were, and how very good he smelled—like sandalwood and soap.

Perhaps sensing her unease, he added, "Truly, not what I meant at all." Then he smiled in what she supposed was meant to be a reassuring expression, but which merely emphasized his handsomeness and put her back on her guard.

Still, she could hardly fault the man for something so far out of his control as his good looks. "Good," she said finally, "because the change in my appearance has nothing to do with you."

His eyes widened for a fraction of a second. Surely he wasn't disappointed, Cecily thought. Then remembering who she was thinking of, she chided herself. He probably had indigestion from the Duchess of Bewle's crab patties. Still, for all her distrust of him, they did share the common goal of wishing to gain access to the Egyptian Club. And though she disliked admitting it, they both wished to learn whether or not Lord Hurston was involved in Mr. Dalton's disappearance. Albeit for radically different reasons.

Also, he was a gentleman and might have some suggestions for how she might go about persuading one of the club members to see her as a potential fiancée. And perhaps she could do something for him. Perhaps frighten away the matchmaking mamas—weren't all the marriageable gentlemen forever bemoaning the young ladies who schemed to trap them into marriage?

The more she thought of it, the more she recognized the soundness of the plan.

Looking over her shoulder, and around the rest of the terrace to ensure that no one was near enough to hear her, she leaned forward.

"I will tell you my reasons," she whispered conspiratorially, "but you must keep this between the two of us."

The duke leaned forward as well, eyebrows raised in expectation.

"I did it . . ." she hissed, "because I mean to marry a member of the Egyptian Club."

Four

"The devil you will," Lucas said, resisting the urge to take Miss Hurston by the shoulders and shake some sense into her.

The idea of her marrying some prosy scholar with more hair than wit was ridiculous. Not only because she deserved better, but because there had to be a better way for her to get her hands on her father's journals. It had nothing at all to do with the way she looked in the moonlight and the way his eyes kept straying to her mouth.

Unfortunately, Miss Hurston was currently scowling in the moonlight, her delectable mouth pursed in annoyance.

"I'm sure I never asked for your permission, Your Grace," she said, drawing back from him, her arms folding across her chest in the universal posture of affronted females everywhere. "I was simply sharing my plans with you. If you do not agree with them . . ."

Of course he didn't bloody agree with them, he thought, grateful for the military training that had taught him to keep his mouth shut when needed.

"It isn't that I disagree with your plan," he began, though he did disagree with her plan. "It simply seems unnecessary to go to such an extreme to achieve your goal."

But the damage was done. Whatever rapport they'd achieved earlier had vanished in the time it took him to utter an oath.

"Thank you very much for your advice, Your Grace," she said, rising from the bench. "I'm afraid I have to get back to my cousins now."

Her curtsy was perfectly executed. Her expression was serene. But he knew he'd seriously harmed his cause. If he were to convince her to help him search for clues to Will's disappearance, he would need to woo her back to his side.

Odd choice of word, that.

He rose carefully from the bench, the muscles in his leg throbbing, momentarily erasing his thoughts of anything but the red-hot sting of pain. When he could breathe again, his thoughts returned to Miss Hurston.

Cecily.

Surely there was no harm in thinking of her by her given name.

He would have to find some means of dissuading Cecily from her ridiculous plan. Marriages of convenience might be *de rigueur* for the *ton*, but he knew from his brother's marriage that being leg-shackled to someone for whom you felt no affection was soul-crushing. Certainly nothing like the true partnership and genuine love he'd witnessed between his parents.

She might be well versed in Latin and Greek and probably a whole host of other languages, but in this matter, Cecily was woefully ignorant.

He'd simply have to teach her the error of her ways.

It was, he thought, relying on his walking stick the whole way to the French doors, a lesson he was very much looking forward to.

Cecily was finishing up a cup of tea in the breakfast room the next morning when she felt the skin on the back of her neck prickle. Turning, she saw a dark figure looming in the doorway.

She couldn't help it.

She jumped.

Then felt foolish when the dark shadow resolved itself into a very ordinary-looking man of middle years.

"I did not mean to startle you, my dear," Lord Geoffrey Brighton, her father's oldest friend, said, his eyebrows raised. "Never say you've started believing that curse nonsense. I thought you were too sensible for that."

A confirmed bachelor, Lord Geoffrey had run tame in their house for as long as Cecily could remember. And though his hair was turning a bit silvery at the temples, he still looked just as he always had. Comfortable, mussed. He had been a steadfast supporter of Lord Hurston's expeditions to Egypt from the beginning, investing his own fortune heavily in the acquisition and transport of various antiquities back to England. And he had made a tidy profit selling those goods that the Egyptian Club did not always find to be of particularly significant historical value.

And unlike the other members of the club, who had not even bothered to call on her father after that first awful week, Lord Geoffrey was a constant presence in Hurston House. He had even been on hand to calm Lord Hurston a time or two after he had suffered one of the terrible convulsions that still seemed to strike out of nowhere. It had brought Cecily to tears to see her father's oldest friend at his side, speaking to him in a low, patient voice that was surprising in such a robust man.

"Please don't you bring up the curse too," Cecily said with disgust. "Even the *Times* has written of it today. It's like something out of Walpole."

"We are a superstitious people," he said with a shrug, helping himself to bacon from the sideboard and taking his usual seat to the left of her. "It helps to explain things that have no explanation."

Not wishing to dwell on the matter, Cecily changed the subject. "I take it you have been up to see Father? How is he this morning?"

"Well enough," Lord Geoffrey said, taking a sip of tea. "I believe he must have recognized me today. At least, I hope he did. When I spoke to him he squeezed my hand in a manner that up until now he has only done with you or Violet."

His eyes darkened with grief. "I cannot tell you how disheartening it is for me, Cecily, to see your father in such a state. I almost think it would have been better if the apoplexy had carried him off that first day."

An invisible hand gripped Cecily's heart. Though she and Violet had spoken of just such a possibility in the early days of her father's illness, it was jarring to hear her father's dearest friend in the world voice it. Perhaps the public were not the only superstitious ones.

"I do not say that I wish for it to have happened," Brighton went on. "Indeed, I would not wish such a fate on him for anything. But I do know that your father values his mental acuity above all else. And I cannot think that he would ever have imagined himself living in such a condition. Alive, but unable to do any of those things that make life worth living."

"I do understand you," Cecily said, thinking of how vibrant and full of life her father had been before his attack. "I don't know that he would have wished for such a thing, but surely the fact that he still lives gives us hope that one day he will be able to live his life with the same passion he did before."

"You are right, my dear, as always." He reached out to grasp her hand. "I do know this. He would be unspeakably proud to see you now, finally allowing yourself to cast off your cocoon and flap your wings like the glorious butterfly you are."

"Butterfly, indeed." Cecily laughed. "And you know very well that Papa would be heartily displeased at my continued academic pursuits. Though I do believe he would be pleased to see that I've finally accepted Violet's assistance with my wardrobe."

"Oh, I think you do yourself and your father a disservice, Cecily. Your father has always been proud of you. Even when he was railing about your stubbornness. He's terribly proud of you. Just as proud of you as he was of your mother, God rest her soul."

The mention of her mother made Cecily's smile fade. "Yes, I suppose he was proud of her. Though I wish he hadn't taken her death as a sign of why ladies should never pursue any sort of academic activities. It wasn't her translation work that drove her to her death, but a stubborn refusal to rest properly when she was taken ill with the lung infection. Knowing my own restlessness, I suspect that having her books around her would have helped her survive the tedium of the sickbed."

"He took your mother's death hard, my dear," Lord Geoffrey said. "Indeed, there was a time when I feared that he would do the unthinkable . . . but he resisted. For your sake, I think. And eventually he married Violet and all was right again."

But Cecily knew that was only a partial truth. All might have seemed right, but she knew that Lord Hurston had never been the same after her mother's death. And when she had shown the same skill for languages that her mother had possessed, Lord Hurston had tried every means at his disposal to ensure that his daughter would not become as enthralled with her studies as his wife had been.

But Cecily had persisted, and over his objections, with the help of her godmother, she had become a well-regarded scholar in her own right. Or, as much as was possible for a lady of gentle birth.

Knowing that it would do no good to dredge up that ancient history, Cecily simply nodded. "It's true. Violet did change everything."

They chatted for a bit about less upsetting subjects. Cecily's new gowns, Lady Bewle's ball. The latest news from the Royal Society.

Something, however, was clearly bothering him. Cecily gave her honorary uncle a questioning look. It was not like him to mince words.

"What is it?"

Looking a bit sheepish, he said, "My dear, I do not like to bring it up, especially after your earlier comments, but I must. Your father's reputation hangs in the balance."

"I thought we had dismissed the curse as ignorant superstition," she said.

Ever since news had emerged from Bonaparte's explorations in Egypt, and even before, the reading public had been fascinated by the possibility that the ancient people who built the pyramids had sealed them with a curse for those who might disturb their tombs. Each time a worker died, each time an expedition member fell ill, each time a box of cargo was dropped as it was loaded onto the ship bound home from Egypt, it was blamed on a curse.

Never mind that the curses said more about the people who inscribed them onto the tombs than about the people who found them. The newspapers and scandal sheets had told the tales and forever after every expedition member was doomed by a curse.

Cecily had found it tiresome enough to be confronted by whispers every time she ventured out of the house, but she had hoped the breakfast room of Hurston House was safe.

"I do not believe in curses any more than you do, my dear," Lord Geoffrey said. "But I really do believe that something is going on with the members of that expedition. I was there, you know. And there were a good many incidents that happened while we were in Alexandria that in hindsight seem to indicate that there was something amiss with that trip."

This was the first Cecily had heard of anything going wrong during the actual expedition. With the exception of Will Dalton's disappearance.

"Tell me," she said, willing to listen even if she suspected she'd be proved right.

"Well, aside from that nasty business with Dalton," Lord Geoffrey said, "there were many small things that gave us all a bit of unease. Items went missing between the dig site and the storage site at our encampment. A fall rendered one of our guides unable to continue on with us. And one day one of the native men your father hired to assist with the removal of some of the larger items was crushed to death beneath the weight of the sarcophagus he carried."

"Oh, dear," Cecily said, horrified to hear of such an accident befalling the man. Still, this was no more than she had expected to hear. "Surely all of these things are typical of an expedition like that. It is dangerous work. Why attribute such things to a curse rather than simple misfortune?"

Lord Geoffrey fiddled with the lace at his cuff, decidedly uncomfortable. "Because in this instance we were actually warned of a curse just before we opened the doorway into the tomb."

His eyes were troubled as he warmed to his story. "You are acquainted, I think, with our translator, Gilbert Gubar, who has been with us on several previous expeditions?"

Cecily nodded. She and Herr Gubar had corresponded about some Greek texts once or twice. He was a good man, though she envied him his position with the expedition.

"We had been working all day, and already three of the workers had been forced into rest by the heat. But your father was certain that we were close to the entrance. If only we pressed forward. I tried to argue with him, but you are not the only one in your family with a stubborn streak, my dear.

"Finally, as we all looked on, we were there. Everyone crowded back around, ignoring the heat now in their determination to be there when we finally reached our goal.

"Then your father was calling for Gubar to read the inscription on the door, and as he stepped forward we all fell silent. I cannot remember any other unveiling like it.

"In his accented English, Gubar said the words as he sketched them into his notes, though we had no idea what they meant. We all waited there, impatient as the devil, for him to translate them into English. Finally, he read them out word by word.

"*'Whosoever violates this tomb shall cease to exist, his years will diminish, and his house will belong to his enemy.'*

"I can tell you," Lord Geoffrey said with feeling, "there was not one of us who went to bed that night with an easy heart."

"But that curse is nonsense," Cecily said, trying to

maintain her skeptical stance despite the chill Lord Geoffrey's words sent up her spine. "How can one both cease to exist and have his years diminished? Curses are there to deter would-be thieves from taking away the valuables buried with the noble deceased. That is all." Her laugh sounded nervous to her own ears. But her father's friend wasn't laughing with her.

"I know that, Cecily. I have been in more tombs than you've been in ballrooms. And I tell you, this curse—it's different. I have never felt such an air of . . . unease fall over an entire party of people like that. It was one of the most disturbing experiences of my life."

"But even if this curse is real," she persisted, "there is nothing to be done about it. We cannot turn back time and re-seal the tomb."

"No," Lord Geoffrey said, his serious gaze fixed on her. "But what we can do is practice caution. I know you wish to obtain your father's journals from the club."

At Cecily's gasp, he waved a dismissive hand at her. "I am still an active member of the club, you know. Word spreads quickly. And before you ask, I will not retrieve them for you myself. I think the sooner this expedition is forgotten the better. And I will do nothing that would endanger the daughter of my oldest friend. Certainly not anything that would assist you to defy your father's wishes. No matter how altruistic you might think your motives."

"I do wish everyone would stop treating me like a child," she said with pursed lips. "I am perfectly capable of using reason and determining what I should and should not do."

"Well, in this instance, my dear," Lord Geoffrey said with an indulgent smile that made Cecily want to growl, "I beg you to adhere to the wishes of someone who loves you like a daughter. Please follow your father's dictates in this matter and forget about his journals. Nothing good can come of reading them. And I do not think your family could endure it if something happened to you as well as your father."

When he left her a few minutes later, Cecily remained at the table, staring into her quickly cooling tea. It was kind of Lord Geoffrey to look out for her, she supposed. But she would do as she had always done and make up her own mind about what actions she should take. In this case, that meant continuing forward with her plans to retrieve her father's journals.

Rising from the table, she went to dress for her ride in the park with Mr. George Vinson, who had sent round an invitation and a posy of violets that morning. It seemed oddly out of tune to receive violets given her stepmama's name, but she couldn't really fault him for it. Perhaps he didn't know.

There had also been a bouquet of peonies from Winterson in a soft pink, which she tried very hard to ignore. The note had read simply, *"These reminded me of you. Winterson."* It had doubtless been a lucky guess that prompted him to send her her favorite flowers. And because they were her favorites, she told herself, she had her maid put them on her dressing table. It had nothing to do with the butterflies they set to rioting in her stomach every time she looked at them.

Which she vigorously ignored.

She'd danced with Mr. Vinson the evening before and found him to be sweet if rather dim-witted. Still, as a member of the Egyptian Club he was on her mental list of marriage candidates.

Unfortunately for him, Sir Geoffrey's warning had done the opposite of what he wished—it had given her an even more compelling reason to pursue her father's journals than a simple desire to see her father's legacy endure.

Now she had a curse to debunk.

And perhaps Mr. Vinson would give her the means to do it.

After fifteen minutes in Mr. Vinson's company, Cecily was seriously reconsidering his eligibility as a candidate for marriage.

As his curricle crawled at the snail's pace required for seeing and being seen at the fashionable hour in Hyde Park, Cecily tried to engage him in conversation about something other than the sporting pursuits he found so compelling. But that had proved difficult thus far.

While he was just the sort of husband she sought—not overly intelligent, easily managed, and, for reasons she could not quite fathom, a member of the Egyptian Club—he was also a member of the Corinthian set. As such, he talked without ceasing of all manner of things that Cecily was quite sure were improper conversation topics for gently bred young ladies. Not that she was overly concerned with such things, but it made finding out details about his involvement with the club an almost impossible task.

"Do tell me about your other interests, Mr. Vinson," she said, making sure to follow Amelia's directive to smile, blink, tilt. "The Egyptian Club, for example. It must be horribly frightening to see a mummy in real life."

As she had hoped, Vinson's chest puffed out a bit, a sure sign her flattery, and what she was coming to think of as SBT, had hit its mark.

"Oh, I wasn't frightened, Miss Hurston," he said, in an abhorrent patronizing tone.

Why must even cloth-heads like Vinson assume they were superior simply because of their sex?

"A mummy's nothing but some old rags and bandages and a bit of brown stuff underneath it all. Besides, the fellow's dead, so there's no way he's going to jump out of the case thingummy and come after you." Vinson winked.

Good *Lord.* "Have you spent very much time there?" Cecily asked, fighting her frustration. "At the Egyptian Club, I mean. It doesn't seem like the sort of thing a man like you—I mean, one who is so very skilled at other, more sporting types of activities—would be interested in."

"Oh, I've been there a bit," he said, paying careful attention to a turn in the path, expertly maneuvering his horses around the dowager Lady Dalrymple's carriage, which had stopped to allow her to harangue the Misses Henrietta and Eloise Standish, who looked very much as if they wished to sprint away. "It's m'father's doing, really," Mr. Vinson continued. "The membership, I mean. He don't approve of racing and whatnot. So he made me join the Egyptian Club—was hoping it would interest me in something more worldly."

Cecily rather thought he had misunderstood what the term *worldly* meant, but did not tell him so.

"Now I ask you, Miss Hurston, do I seem like the kind of fellow who would spend his time looking at moldy bones and books filled with queer writing?"

He laughed at the notion, and Cecily was hard-pressed to disagree with him. Aloud she said, "Well, you do seem a bit more active than the Egyptian Club would require."

George beamed. "Exactly what I told the pater! And besides, he's the one who likes all that Egyptian rot. If I'm to be my own man, it stands to reason that I'd need a different hobby horse, don't it?"

"Indeed," Cecily replied. There was no denying George would make the perfect sort of husband to fit her needs. He would never appreciate her scholarly bent, but he would also never feel jealousy over her academic accomplishments as David had.

She decided to keep him on the list.

"Mr. Vinson," she began, in preparation to ask how he felt about lady scholars who had their own hobby horses. But before she could speak, the curricle drew to a halt.

"Hullo, Winterson," Mr. Vinson said, welcoming the duke, who had skillfully pulled his own phaeton alongside them. "Tip-top rig you've got there. Are those the bays I saw at Tatt's last week?"

"Miss Hurston." Winterson raised his hat in greeting, his arrival annoying her as much because of its effect on her as because she did not care to be interrupted in her pursuit of Vinson. It really was unfair of him to parade around looking like a Greek god in riding dress. His laughing eyes did not help his cause one whit.

"Yes, these are Knighton's bays," the god told Vinson. "I was in the market and they were really too sweet to pass up."

The two talked horseflesh for a seeming eternity while Cecily seethed inwardly. What had brought Winterson to the park at this hour anyway? According to her sources— i.e., Maddie and Juliet—he was rarely seen engaging in the social whirl. And his stint at the Bewle ball looming at the side of the ballroom floor had proven he had no interest in idle chatter. No, he was clearly here to put a spoke in the wheels of her marriage plans. He'd made his objections clear during their little chat at the Bewle ball the other evening, but she had not thought he'd actually do anything about it.

She suddenly realized Winterston had directed a question her way while she was woolgathering. Unwilling to admit to her lapse of attention, Cecily simply nodded. "Yes, of course."

The broad grin that split Winterson's face stunned her for a moment. If he was handsome when he didn't smile, he was even more so when he did. And it made him seem more approachable. Less . . . dukish. A little shiver of awareness danced down her spine.

Which she promptly tamped down.

"I'll just hand you down then, Miss Hurston," Mr. Vinson said, tossing his reins to the tiger on the seat behind them and leaping to the ground beside the curricle. "I'll expect a full report on the bays," he said with a lopsided grin.

When Cecily realized what she'd just agreed to, she mentally cursed Winterson in six languages.

But for now, she knew that causing a scene might frighten off Vinson, who, while unfrightened by mummies, appeared to be very skittish when it came to marriageable females, so she held her tongue until she was safely in the seat beside Winterson.

The blistering set-down she'd deliver as soon as they were away from the crowd would teach the man not to get between a woman and her goals. After he'd steered the phaeton back onto the path and raised his whip to the brim of his hat in a parting gesture to Vinson, Lucas spoke, keeping his gaze on his cattle. "You're wasting your time there, you know," he said companionably. "Vinson is not, as they say, in the petticoat line. Besides, he's far too young to be thinking about marriage. You'd do much better with Hollingsworth or Pilkingham. At least they're on the hunt for wives."

"And they are also both old enough to be my grandfather.

Pilkingham has already buried two wives—I have no desire to be the third, thank you very much."

He felt her glare as surely as if she'd beaten him over the head with it.

"I'll stick with Vinson, if you don't mind terribly." Her tone implied that she did mind.

Terribly.

Winterson cut his eyes to the side, hoping he didn't get turned into a pillar of salt. Or stone. She seemed angry. But pretty. Definitely no snake-hair like Medusa. His reflection upon the ways in which Cecily, thankfully, did not resemble characters from classical literature was interrupted by the lady herself.

"Are you going to tell me why you interfered with my perfectly lovely outing with Vinson?" Cecily asked, irritation taking her voice up a note. "You cannot mean to mix with the fashionable crowd since you've passed three carriages without sparing them a second glance."

"I am attempting to persuade you that your plan to marry the first member of the club you can wrap around your finger is flawed." He'd said that louder than he'd intended to, Lucas thought. Feeling harassed, he thrust a hand through his hair. Damn her for being so troublesome anyway.

"My 'plan' as you call it," she said with a feminine sort of growl, obviously unconcerned with his irritation, "is most certainly *not* to marry the first club member I can manipulate into doing so." If they'd been standing she would have stamped her foot to emphasize her point.

"Mr. Vinson is a kind and generous young man," she continued, "who asked me to go for a ride in the park with him. I accepted as is often the custom. He would make a most excellent husband for whomever he chooses to marry. And just because he happens to be a bit less . . . clever than you, it does not make it acceptable for you to look down at him over your enormous nose!"

As her voice had risen in both volume and pitch over the

course of this tirade, by the time the word *nose* had left her mouth, Cecily had clapped a gloved hand over her mouth.

By then Lucas had steered the phaeton off the path into a wooded area at the edge of the park, so no one was around to hear her but him. Which was a lucky thing, because he intended them to have a serious talk about her "plan" and just what dangers lay in that direction. He expected that would cause some further raised voices.

But, first there was another small matter.

"My nose is not enormous," he said, struggling not to laugh. "And even if it were, there is no need for personal attacks.

"Though," he reflected gravely, "you know what they say. 'The bigger the nose . . .'"

He raised his brows for emphasis.

She stared at him blankly. "Aren't you going to finish the quotation?" she asked.

He'd stopped the phaeton, and was free to look his fill of her without worrying about running down some stray pedestrian. Cecily's expression of puzzlement was utterly charming and Lucas was struck all at once by her proximity. The scent of rose water coaxed him to lean closer. Her teeth caught her full lower lip as she looked up at him from beneath her lashes.

"Oh," she said, though whether it was because she realized the rest of the quotation, or it was due to something else, he couldn't say. But that one syllable was as eloquent as all the plays of Shakespeare put together.

Their eyes locked, and of its own volition, Lucas's hand slipped firmly behind her neck and pulled her closer. So close that he could see the tiny freckles dotting her nose and cheeks, and the way her eyes widened just before her lashes drifted down. Muttering a curse at his own lack of self-control, he leaned forward and pressed his mouth to hers.

The kiss was gentle. Exploratory. He simply touched his mouth to hers and reveled in the softness, the sweet feel of skin against skin. It wasn't nearly all he wanted, but it was enough for now.

Then slowly, carefully, he opened his mouth for a taste, sliding his tongue along the seam of her lips. It was a silent question, and he was pleased when she answered by letting him inside, her hand stealing up to grab hold of his shoulder, as if she needed him to keep her from sliding to the ground.

A surge of pure male triumph ran through him at her hold, even as he felt her tentatively touch her tongue to his.

The park, the trees, the soft breeze, everything around them receded as he lost himself in the feel of her soft body pressed against his.

Then Knighton's bays, like a pair of equine duennas, tried to bolt.

And all hell broke loose.

When all hell broke loose, Cecily was, to her shame, simply feeling the exquisite pleasure of Winterson's mouth moving over her own.

It had been years since she'd allowed herself the freedom to simply let go. And since she'd been kissed. The heady sensation of his strong arms holding her, coupled with the pressure of his lips against hers, was both a passport to a new world and a homecoming sweeter than any she had ever known. And when he opened his mouth, what was there to do but surrender to the seduction of the heat of him? To respond to the question his lips seemed to ask?

Her arms crept up to pull him closer, to explore with her fingers the surprisingly soft black curls she so admired. She felt the warmth of him through the barrier of their clothes, felt the solidity of his chest pressed against her breasts.

But that was before the carriage jerked, bumping their foreheads together. Hard.

"Damn it," Winterson swore as he reined in the frisky bays, who had pulled them back onto the path toward Rotten Row. With one hand she gripped the side of the carriage, and with the other Cecily firmly held on to her hat.

It was simply bad timing that they were seen by no less than three dragons of the *ton*. Including Juliet's mother,

Lady Shelby, upon whom Cecily could rely to relate the entire story to Violet before the end of the day.

Lovely.

"Hello there!" called the Marchioness Downes, her eyes alight with malicious glee. "Your Grace! Miss Hurston! Pray join us."

Such behavior in a social-climbing cit's wife would have barred the woman from further interaction with the Beau Monde. But since the Downes marquessate could trace its roots back to William the Conqueror, her rudeness was excused as eccentricity.

Winterson, or Lucas as she supposed she could think of him now, swore fluently under his breath. Cecily heartily agreed, though not aloud. She would rather visit the tooth extractor than chat with the group assembled around the Downes open carriage.

"Smile," Lucas said in an undertone, in that close-toothed way one spoke when trying to appear not to be. "And try not to look so . . . kissed."

"I don't believe that is a bell we can unring, Your Grace," she said with some asperity.

"I didn't say I would like to, Cecily," he said, turning to give her a smoldering look. "I just don't want these tattlers minding our business instead of theirs."

She blinked through a shiver as Lucas turned back to face the horses as they neared the other carriage.

Where, to her utter disappointment, she saw Amelia and Felicia watching them with barely concealed pique.

"Cecily," Lady Shelby said sharply, once greetings had been exchanged. "What are you doing here?" *With the Duke of Winterson*, was implied at the end of her aunt's question.

"Yes, Cecily," Amelia echoed with a sweetness that could not conceal her annoyance, her eyes darting from Cecily to Lucas, then back again. "Tell us all why you're here."

A not-very-mature part of her enjoyed seeing Amelia's jealous gaze.

Before she could respond to either question, however,

Lucas replied for her. "I asked Miss Hurston to join me so that we could discuss her father's latest expedition."

Cecily bit back a sigh. Thwarting Amelia had been nice while it lasted.

But Lucas wasn't finished. "I find it so refreshing to chat with a young lady who is both intelligent and lovely. Makes the conversations so much more satisfying."

If his barb found its target, Amelia showed no sign of it. Instead she gave a smile that did not reach her eyes. "Miss Hurston is certainly intelligent," she said, making it sound like a criticism rather than a compliment.

"But how did you come to be here with the duke, Cecily?" Felicia said sweetly. "I could have sworn I saw you with Mr. Vinson earlier."

"Yes," Amelia added. "I am sure that we did."

Perhaps realizing that the two younger ladies scented a possible scandal, something that she did not wish to touch upon her own family, Lady Shelby intervened, though she did not seem particularly pleased to do so. "I daresay you wished to discuss the disappearance of your brother, didn't you, Your Grace?"

Oh, because there is no possible way that he would wish to speak with me for my own sake, Cecily fumed inwardly. How on earth such a vile woman had birthed a genuinely good person like Juliet was beyond her powers of comprehension.

"Indeed," Lucas agreed, with a slight bow. "Now, if you ladies would please excuse us, I must prevail upon Miss Hurston to continue our discussion."

Their good-byes were said, resentful from the Downes carriage, relieved from Winterson's, and Cecily let out a long sigh of relief.

"That," Lucas said with a shake of his head, "was not unlike the first week at Eton when Monteith and I were forced to confront a trio of bullies. Only this time I was more frightened. What on earth have you done to cause such animosity from Miss Snowe and Lady Felicia? Or your aunt, for that matter?"

Cecily shrugged. "My aunt is perhaps easier to explain. She is the most status-conscious of her sisters, and she has long found it perturbing that Juliet, Madeline, and I were unable to repeat the social successes that she and her sisters managed when they first came to London. She is convinced that it is due to the fact that we would prefer to discuss poetry or philosophy rather than the latest *on-dit* or the cut of gowns this season."

"And Miss Snowe and Lady Felicia?" he asked, his tone curious.

She took a deep breath, unsure whether to tell him about David or not. But she didn't need to tell the whole story, she decided. "Amelia has disliked me since our first season when a certain gentleman showed a preference for me over her. He was quite interested in Egyptology and languages. Now I think he was less interested in me than in bolstering his acquaintance with my father, but at the time I was quite flattered.

"I think," Cecily continued, "she holds me responsible for the fact that she is still unwed."

"And what happened to this gentleman?" Lucas asked, turning to look at her, his gaze unreadable.

Cecily was surprised to find that she was able to think of David's betrayal without the usual stab of hurt. "We were engaged, but circumstances forced me to cry off."

"What sort of circumstances?"

"I found that I no longer wished to marry him." An understatement, but the truth.

"You don't strike me as the sort of lady who would change her mind on a whim," Lucas said, his tone implying that he didn't quite believe her tale as she'd just told it. Still, he didn't press her, and Cecily was grateful for it. She disliked thinking about that whole sordid episode, much less speaking about it.

"At any rate," she went on, "Amelia has failed to bring anyone up to scratch since then and she blames me for it. Though I fail to see how, because with the exception of David, we have never shown an interest in the same gentleman again. Indeed, I have steered clear of romantic entanglements altogether."

Until now. The tiny whisper in the back of her brain was enough to bring her up short. Deliberately, she turned the subject back to what they'd been discussing before the horses had bolted.

"And on the subject of entanglements," she said, her voice calm, "I am quite determined to continue my pursuit of possible husbands from the bachelor ranks of the Egyptian Club."

He made a noise of frustration.

"Your scheme," Lucas said, lifting his whip to the brim of his hat to greet someone on the other side of the carriage, "is unsound in the extreme."

Now she was the one to make a noise of disgust.

"I do not think it is wise," he went on, "for you to deliberately seek the attentions of these men simply because they belong to the Egyptian Club. You have no way of knowing what their attitude will be toward your scholarly proclivities and you are just as likely to marry someone with a disgust of your mind as an appreciation for it."

"I thank you for your concern," she said haughtily, "but as I told you last night, the matter is not up for debate."

"Miss Hurston," he said. "Cecily. The men you have singled out for your attentions are not all as dull-witted as poor Vinson, you know." His blue eyes pinned her like a butterfly on a board. "Have you considered what marriage to one of these men will mean? What it will be like after you get your coveted access to your father's journals?"

His voice lowered, and he reached out a gloved hand to touch her lower lip with his thumb. "What it will be like in his bed?"

To her annoyance, she felt a blush creeping up her neck and into her cheeks. Damn him for pressing her this way, she fumed, even as her heart beat faster from his touch. "I have considered it," she said finally, her words clipped as she worked to control her voice. Retreating behind a mask of hauteur, she continued, "And I am prepared to do my duty."

Winterson shook his head, and took her hand in his. "You deserve more than a lifetime of dutiful beddings, Cecily."

Cecily was horrified to feel herself tear up at his words. But though she could not control her blushes, tears were another matter, and she ruthlessly suppressed the urge to bury her face in his strong shoulder.

"I'm afraid the intimate details of my married life, however hypothetical they may be, are not up for discussion," she said, pulling her hand out of his grasp. "Nor," she continued, "is any part of my plans as they relate to obtaining my father's journals."

Lucas cursed himself for frightening her with his frank talk. But the idea of this vibrant Amazon married to some dried-up scholar, or worse, a bacon-brained idiot like Vinson, who lacked the skills or appreciation to handle her, was unthinkable. And there was the matter of that kiss, but he could not think about that now, no matter how much certain of his organs wished to think about it and more. He needed to find a way to dissuade her from her scheme. Or better yet, offer her an alternative one.

"Come down from the boughs, my dear," he said easily, knowing that she'd appreciate friendship over soft words just now. "I have no intention of managing your scheme. It is, of course, entirely up to you to choose a husband, be he a member of the Egyptian Club or not. But it occurs to me that we both have need of the same thing: your father's diaries."

He saw suspicion in her eyes, but at least she was looking at him again rather than staring off into the distance.

"I'm listening," she prompted.

"It may have escaped your notice," he said, giving her the little half smile that he knew would showcase his dimple. "But I am a gentleman."

She raised one dark brow. "I have, perhaps, noted that fact."

"And as a gentleman, I am in a better position than you are to assess the men on your list."

"How so?" Her expression was still wary, but he could see he'd caught her interest.

"When you see men, gentlemen, in the rarefied setting of

the ballroom, or Almack's, or"—he gestured to the crowd of people seeing and being seen along Rotten Row—"the park, you are not seeing them in their natural element. As a lady, you are, in fact, shielded from those places."

He watched with satisfaction as a little frown line appeared between her eyes.

"As a gentleman," he went on, "I have knowledge of these fellows that you, as a lady, are not privy to.

"Did you know, for instance, that Vinson, whom you just allowed to take you up in his curricle, is in a considerable amount of debt? So much so that his father is within a hairbreadth of stopping his allowance and cutting him off altogether? And, since Vinson owes his membership at the Egyptian Club to his father, their estrangement would remove any incentive you might have to marry him."

"That is hardly uncommon knowledge, sir."

But the furrow between her brows told Lucas that his strategy was working.

"Then by all means," he said, "let us continue to the uncommon knowledge. Lord Carrington, with whom you were so eager to dance last evening, has a reputation for enjoying the company of young girls."

Cecily snorted. "That is hardly a great secret. Most men—"

"Very young girls," he interrupted, hating to tell her, and yet desperate to keep her from allying herself with a man like Carrington. "Eleven, twelve, thirteen years old."

The color drained from her face.

"How . . . where?"

"There are certain brothels that cater to such tastes," Lucas said baldly, "And, unfortunately, his tastes are not so uncommon as one would wish."

"But he is quite popular," she said, her outrage beginning to build. "My stepmama is forever going on about what a great man he is."

"That is because such salacious details are not discussed in polite company. But you may be sure that those men who do know are careful not to let their wives and daughters within an inch of him."

Lucas watched the play of emotions cross her face as she came to grips with the knowledge that more secrets lurked beneath the surface of the *ton* than she had previously thought.

"You have convinced me that you are privy to some information that might help me to better assess potential husbands," she said, finally. "But why would you do it?"

"Your knowledge of the people who accompanied your father and my brother on that last expedition is unsurpassed."

"But I am hardly the only one who knows them, Your Grace. Any number of people could assist you in this."

"I think you underestimate the admiration the members of his circle have for your knowledge of the field and the language of the Egyptians."

Her head tilted as she stared at him.

"You must be mistaken," she said, frowning. "His cronies are just as opposed to the idea of a lady Egyptologist as my father is."

Lucas could not help but note that she continued to speak of her father in the present tense, though word in the *ton* had the man's death only a matter of weeks, if not days, away. Then again, the gossip of the *ton* was not known for its accuracy.

"I have read my brother's correspondence to my mother, and he was of the opinion that you were as knowledgeable, if not more so, as your father when it came to translating the ancient words inscribed on the artifacts he brought back with him from Egypt."

In fact, his brother had suggested Lucas seek out her help if anything should happen to him. Knowing Will's propensity to trust too quickly, he had at first exercised his own judgment and ignored his brother's suggestion. Now, however, he wondered if he hadn't misjudged both of them.

Cecily's mouth curved into the ghost of a smile. "Will was always talking nonsense. Though he was kind enough to let me examine certain artifacts they brought back so that I could work on compiling an alphabet of sorts from the inscriptions."

She looked up at him, her eyes troubled. "He is a good man. And I am sorry for whatever happened to him in Alexandria. I know it must be dreadful for your family—the not knowing."

"Then help me find out what happened, Miss Hurston." Lucas took her hand in his again, squeezed it to emphasize his point. "You are the only one who can help me learn what happened to make him disappear. Your father is incapable of speech, and the other men who accompanied them on the expedition are unwilling to talk to someone who is not a part of their inner circle. Whatever your father may have thought of your aspirations to become a scholar in your own right, to these men you are. William admired your intellect, and he made it clear to my mother in his letters that the others did as well.

"Did you know," he continued, desperate now to make her understand, "that they wanted you to come along on that expedition?"

Cecily's surprise was palpable.

"What?"

"It's true," Lucas said, hoping against hope that she would be swayed by the knowledge. "Will said that the translator, Mr. Gubar, the man from the British Museum who accompanied them, was adamant that you should be brought along to help him read the hieroglyphs on the tombs, and had even convinced a couple of the other men, Will included, to approach your father about it, but he was determined that you not be brought along because he didn't think it appropriate for his daughter to undertake such a journey."

She shook her head in disbelief. "I had no idea. None. I know that Mr. Gubar respects my work, of course. We have been quite friendly for years, despite his relationship with my father. But if I'd known they felt that way . . ."

"Miss Hurston," Lucas said. "Cecily, please. If you were ever a friend to my brother, for his own sake if not for mine, help me find out what happened to him. My mother is despondent. And I . . . well . . ." He stopped, unable to continue.

"He was your brother," she finished for him quietly, squeezing his hand this time.

"I will help you, Your Grace," she said firmly, "if you promise to help me with my quest to find a member of the Egyptian Club who would suit me as a husband."

Not wishing to look a gift horse in the mouth, Lucas merely nodded. He had no intention of seeing her sacrifice herself on the altar of marriage to someone she did not hold in affection, but she did not need to know that now. The important thing was that she had agreed to help him.

"Thank you, my dear," he told her, turning to walk the horses back onto Rotten Row. "You won't be sorry."

Five

At Lady Willowbrook's musicale the next evening, Cecily, to her astonishment, found herself surrounded by fashionable young men. Her success at the Bewle ball had apparently lifted some sort of invisibility cloak, which had previously made it impossible for gentlemen of the *ton* to see her among the other wallflowers. In all of her time "out" in London society, she had never dreamed she would be the center of attention as she was now. It was both exciting and overwhelming. And despite her desire to vet these young gentlemen, many of whom were members of the Egyptian Club, as possible husbands, their sheer numbers made it difficult to concentrate. How on earth did someone like Amelia manage this level of attention all the time? If this kept up she would have no need of either Winterson's assistance or Amelia's dance card.

The thought of Winterson and the dance card gave her a pang of guilt. She had neglected to tell him about the dance card, fearing he would refuse to help her if he knew she intended to use false pretenses to go about her husband-hunting scheme. But knowing she had both Winterson and Amelia's dance card to help her, she felt much more secure about her ability to find a member of the Egyptian Club to marry. Besides, tonight there seemed to be no need for either of her secret weapons.

As if to remind her, Lord Ballston interrupted her

thoughts. "Miss Hurston, are you quite comfortable there? Perhaps you'd like to sit here, on the end of the row. I'm sure the view is much better from here."

"Do not be absurd, Ballston," Lord Dareingham interrupted from his seat next to Cecily. "She can see quite well enough from here. Besides, on that side she might catch a draft."

"Miss Hurston, surely you would rather sit up here with me," Lord Fortenbury said, cutting off more talk of drafts from Dareingham. "The view is much better from here, and I have it on the best authority that the pianoforte is best listened to from a more central location."

"Gentlemen, please," a new voice interceded. "I'm afraid you are all doomed to disappointment, for Miss Hurston has already promised herself to me for the evening."

Cecily looked up to find Lucas looming over the group, his height and military bearing making the other men seem like callow youths. Even his black frock coat and snug fawn breeches were dour when compared to the dandyish high shirt points and intricately tied cravats of her coterie of admirers. They were more of an age with Winterson's brother, William.

William, who had gone missing on an expedition headed up by Cecily's father.

Like the basket of a hot air balloon coming into contact with solid ground, the exhilaration generated by her new popularity fell to the earth with a resounding thud.

"Your Grace," she said, rising from her seat between Dareingham and Selby. "I had forgotten our previous agreement. Do forgive me."

The laugh lines around his eyes crinkled at her appropriation of his fictional assignation, though the rest of his expression seemed bland enough.

"My dear lady, there is nothing to forgive," he said, taking her gloved hand in his and bowing over it. "Now, we had best excuse ourselves before the performance begins."

Cecily allowed herself to be guided away to the other side of the room by her new escort, but was not surprised to see

that many of the assembled guests had noted their abandon-
ment of her admirers.

"You have made me the object of talk, you know," she
said as they wound their way through the people who had
not yet taken their seats. "I wonder that you were brave
enough to come retrieve me from my—"

Her brow furrowed.

"What does one call a group of suitors?" she wondered
aloud.

"In the case of that crowd," Winterson said with an expressive roll of his eyes, "nodcocks."

"That is not quite fair," Cecily argued as she allowed him
to hand her into her seat, though she did tend to agree with
him. "They are perhaps not the most intellectually gifted of
men, but having grown up around an intelligent man I can
tell you most assuredly that intellect can be highly over-
rated."

Winterson flipped out the tails of his coat to take his seat
and nodded a greeting to Lady Ashcroft, who boldly surveyed them through her lorgnette.

"Yes," he responded to Cecily, "but there is a world of
difference between nodcock and reasonably intelligent. And
that lot is nowhere near the level of reasonably intelligent.
I doubt they've got enough brains between them to power
the mind of a fourteen-year-old boy."

"Not even a small one?" Cecily asked, amused by the notion despite her discomfort at being the subject of so many
curious stares.

"Not even a pygmy one."

His face remained impassive, but Cecily was sure she
noticed a twinkle lurking in his eye. Still, his derision nee-
dled her.

"You are quite determined to prevent me from enjoying
my brief moment of popularity, aren't you?"

"If by popularity, you are referring to the fact that you
are now surrounded by witless, fashionable young men with
little more to occupy their time than flitting from pretty flower
to pretty flower," he said sourly, "then yes, I am determined

to prevent you from enjoying it. Besides," he continued, scowling, "I thought we had an agreement."

"I am well aware of our agreement, sir." Cecily narrowed her eyes at him. Was it her imagination, or was there a hint of jealousy in Winterson's frown?

Refraining from voicing her thoughts, she continued, "But our agreement does not stipulate that I must avoid contact with gentlemen all together. That would raise suspicions, surely? Especially given the fact that I was seen just the other evening making a concerted effort to launch myself from the ranks of the social outcasts into the fashionable set."

"Our agreement was that I would assist you in your quest for a husband if you would assist me in tracking down your father's travel journals."

Cecily watched in fascination as the muscles in his jaw clenched with his frustration, only realizing at the last minute that some reply was expected of her.

"Perhaps, Your Grace, I am doing just that."

He raised one dark brow. "How so?"

A sigh escaped her. "I have it on some authority that there is to be a meeting of the executive council of the Egyptian Club this very evening."

She watched his expression sharpen with some satisfaction. "Go on."

"Lord Willowbrook is a member of the executive council," she continued. "I know this because my father was also on the council before his . . . attack."

"Go on."

Though she would be hard-pressed to say what exactly had changed, Cecily was aware of an alertness in him that had not been present before. Being the focus of all that energy was at once invigorating and frightening. She fought to maintain eye contact with him, though her every instinct demanded she look away.

"Well, Lord Willowbrook visited Papa this afternoon. It was the first time he has done so since my father fell ill. And

I could not help but overhear him telling Papa about the meeting."

"You were eavesdropping."

It was a statement, not a question.

"Yes," Cecily replied, her voice low to keep her from being overheard. "But that should hardly be of concern to you when—"

"It is a concern to me," he interrupted, "because if you had been discovered, Willowbrook would have been alerted to the fact that you are interested in the goings-on at the Egyptian Club."

"Do you or do you not wish to know what I learned, Your Grace?"

He waved a hand that told her to proceed, though Cecily suspected he wanted to chide her further.

She smiled and nodded at Lord and Lady Fortescue, who took their seats two rows in front of them, before continuing. "The executive committee meets tonight," she said in a hushed tone.

Then in a louder voice she trilled, "Oh, Your Grace, you are such a rogue!" For authenticity, she rapped Winterson's forearm with her fan.

"Ah!" he yelped, clearly not expecting her gambit. "Ah . . . and you . . . Miss Hurston"—Winterson widened his eyes and raised his brows in silent rebuke—"are a delightful lady."

Cecily sniffed. *Delightful lady, indeed.* Ignoring his lame response, she whispered, "They meet tonight, after the first interval of the musicale, in the Red Room."

Aloud she said, "I don't know when I've laughed so much, Your Grace. I never knew what a sense of humor you have."

"I'll leave first," she whispered. "Then you follow a few minutes behind me."

"Absolutely not," he hissed. "You have no idea—"

But he was kept from continuing by the loud voice of their hostess, who had taken her place at the head of the room, and called everyone to order.

Cecily gave a silent prayer of thanks at the interruption. It would be much easier for her to simply do as she pleased instead of having to inform Winterson of her plans. But she had agreed to help him investigate William's disappearance, and there was a certain comfort to be derived from having a partner in her quest to find her father's journals. She'd been fending for herself for such a long time now that she'd forgotten what cooperation felt like. "I intend to observe this meeting myself," she hissed during the moment of applause that followed Lady Willowbrook's introduction.

The stiffness in his bearing told Cecily that he was not pleased, but he held his peace, holding open the program to point out the number of pieces before the interval.

Risking a glimpse at him from beneath her lashes, she was shocked into stillness when her gaze locked with his. This time she was the first to look away, and the accelerated beat of her heart told her the reaction had little to do with their power struggle over her plans to attend the secret meeting. He was entirely too handsome for his own good, this man.

Determined to maintain her poise, she turned all of her attention to the pianist, Miss Jessica Slaughter, a plain young woman who had a surprising talent for the instrument. Allowing herself to relax, Cecily tried to listen to the music, but found herself hyperaware of the man seated beside her. His arm was warm through the superfine of his coat, and it was difficult for her to concentrate when she could feel him brush against her with each breath.

Restless, she fidgeted in her seat, smoothing her skirts against her legs, folding and unfolding her hands. When Lucas turned his head in question, she shook her head slightly. One could hardly tell a gentleman in the middle of a musicale that his very presence next to her was making her skin feel too tight. Or that he was causing a curious dampness in regions of her person that she had hitherto not spent a great deal of time thinking about.

She didn't even hear the second soloist, and when the interval came, Cecily nearly leaped from her seat in her desire to remove herself from the Duke of Winterson's disturbing proximity. Perhaps if she were fast enough he wouldn't catch up to her in the Red Room.

The musician after Miss Slaughter was not nearly as talented, and it was with some relief that Lucas heard Lady Willowbrook announce that they would be taking a short break for refreshments.

Cecily must have taken that as her cue. Rising, with a speed that surprised him, she said with only a slightly raised voice, "There is something in my eye. Please excuse me." Lucas stared after her with a rising sense of frustration as she hurried to the doors at the back of the room, and slipped out into the hallway.

He wanted to follow her, but leaving the room together would draw even more attention to them than they had already done just by sitting together for the musicale. Already he had received several curious looks from both male and female attendees.

So, he waited a full five minutes before rising from his seat and walking briskly toward the exit, only to be interrupted by Miss Amelia Snowe as he neared the end of the neatly aligned rows of seats.

"Your Grace," she said, her speculative expression sounding an alarm in his head as he headed for the exit. "The music will resume in only a few more minutes. I should hate for you to miss it."

Biting back a sharp retort at the interruption, Lucas decided a half-truth would not go amiss here. "I fear that I have recalled another pressing engagement, Miss Snowe." Which was true. He had an appointment with Cecily. Besides, Amelia was hardly his personal confidante. He found her about as trustworthy as a hyena. Which was reinforced when she gave a perfectly constructed titter and popped him on the arm with her fan. "Oh, it is not necessary for you to deceive me, Lord Winterson. It is quite apparent that you are trailing after the . . ."—she paused as if searching her brain for just the right word—"memorable Miss Hurston."

Lucas scowled and rubbed his arm. What was it with ladies hitting him with their fans tonight? Before he could respond, she went on, "It has been quite a surprise to me to see her attract attention from a certain impressionable group of young gentlemen. I do hope her head has not been turned by their flattery. I fear it is a little game they play from time to time. They will single out a young lady for the season, bring her into fashion, and then when the season ends, they simply cut the connection. They mean nothing by it, of course. Just a little harmless fun."

Looking down at the pretty blonde, Lucas realized that she was even more conniving than he'd supposed. But nothing she said would make him see Cecily as anything other than what she was. A highly intelligent, if headstrong, young lady who was worth one hundred Amelias.

He wondered for a fleeting moment if the other attendees of the musicale would read his departure so soon after Cecily's in the same way that she had done. It was irrelevant, of course, given that he intended to follow her whether it caused talk or not. But he did not wish for Cecily's reputation to suffer as a result. So he decided to redirect Amelia's attention with a bit of flattery.

"We gentlemen can be a fickle lot, can we not?" he said in response to her dismissal of Cecily's newfound popularity. "Still, I thought it would be kind to show Miss Hurston a bit of attention this evening. She is, as you say, quite popular right now. And I hear her father is unwell. Let's keep this our little secret, shall we? Not everyone can be lucky enough to sit next to Miss Amelia Snowe, can they?"

With a conspiratorial wink, he stepped away from the soulless beauty and headed out the doors leading into the grand hallway.

Whereas the music room had been filled to capacity, with many of the ladies plying themselves diligently with their fans, the hallway was as empty as the proverbial tomb. A lady's laugh from somewhere down the north corridor, however, had Lucas striding purposefully across the black-and-white checked marble tiles.

He cursed inwardly when he realized he hadn't learned exactly where the Red Room was located. A friend lived in this same row of town homes, and rationalizing that the layouts of the two homes were probably similar, he headed for the second floor where the library should be located.

The first door he opened led into a small sitting room. It was well lit, but deserted, so Lucas closed the door and tried the next one. He had no luck until three doors farther down where he discovered a couple locked in a passionate embrace. As the lady was very clearly a redhead, Lucas ducked back out of the chamber and pulled the door closed. From the looks of things, he doubted the couple was even aware of his interruption.

Finally, as he neared the end of the hall, he heard more voices, male this time. Not wanting to broadcast his presence to the occupants of the room, he opened the door carefully and was pleased to note the Moroccan red of the walls. The gathering of men was hidden from the view of the door by a number of screens and potted trees that surrounded what appeared to be a large round table.

Thick Turkish carpets masked the sound of his footsteps as he crept farther into the room, which was a masterpiece of gilt and all things Egyptian. From the crocodile carvings that adorned the screens, to the golden pyramids that stood out in relief on the pots that held the trees, everything in the room was somehow linked to the ancient culture on the Nile.

Even the tall, evening-gowned figure hovering behind a particularly ugly wooden screen depicting Cleopatra wrestling with an oddly winsome asp.

When she felt a warm body press up against hers, and an arm snake around to cover her mouth, Cecily squealed in alarm.

"Shh," whispered Lucas, his warm breath sending a shiver that had nothing to do with fear through her. "It's just me. What have I missed?"

Thanks to the tall potted trees that were arranged just so, they were invisible to the men in the room.

Cecily breathed a sigh of relief as he removed his hand from her mouth, but it was impossible to ignore the feel of his strong body pressed against the length of hers. Not to mention his scent, clean and masculine and spicy, which made her want to turn around and burrow her face in his neck. And she had thought sitting next to him was uncomfortable. Her agitation of earlier was now increased tenfold.

Taking a deep breath, she concentrated on calming herself and shook her head to indicate that she couldn't answer his question yet. She didn't wish to alert the club members to their presence.

But Winterson wasn't satisfied with being put off.

Touching her chin with one long finger, he turned her face toward him, his lips only a fraction from hers, and mouthed, "Tell me."

Irritated by his high-handed demand, but unable to look away from him, she decided it would probably be faster and easier to just tell him. He didn't exactly strike her as the sort of man who would wait patiently for an answer.

"They are discussing the club's latest acquisitions," she hissed.

At his brisk nod, Cecily turned back to watch the proceedings in the room beyond them. To her delicious agony, instead of moving to stand next to her, he remained behind her and slipped an arm around her middle to pull her closer to his body.

She knew very well that such contact was highly improper. And if anyone were to catch them like this, they'd be betrothed faster than Lord Deveril went through cravats. A few kisses in the park was one thing, but now they were for all practical purposes embracing in a room full of potential witnesses. Even so, the mixture of comfort and agitation his closeness brought her was utterly irresistible. And besides, she rationalized, if she made a fuss she'd give them away to the club members.

"We have added to the club's collection this month alone," Lord Peterborough, a portly older gentleman, spoke to the group. "Three mummified cats, acquired from a merchant in Billingsgate, for the sum of . . ."

As Winterson shifted behind her, Cecily swallowed, hard. She turned to scowl at him, just for propriety's sake, but he appeared not to notice, his eyes fixed firmly on the scene before them. Could he really be unaffected by their closeness? she wondered. Was she the only one who felt the least bit of excitement here?

"A bejeweled figure of Horus, the falcon-headed god," Peterborough continued, "dating from the fourteenth century B.C., estimated value unknown . . ."

Behind the screen, Lucas began to absently caress her with the hand against her midriff. Up. Down. Up. Down. The movement of his hand beat in counterpoint to her heartbeat. Cecily tried to concentrate on what Lord Peterborough was saying, but it was nigh impossible to do so with six feet and then some of solid male pressed up against her back and a strong arm wrapped around her waist.

"A wood cylinder seal from the third century B.C., worth an estimated sum of one thousand pounds."

But enough was enough. If this continued much longer she would combust and surely the smell of burning flesh would call attention to their presence if nothing else did. Reluctantly turning her head to request that Lucas step back, Cecily was startled to find him watching her. Their gazes locked and Cecily knew without a doubt that she wasn't the only one who found their embrace stimulating. But the moment was broken when Winterson winked at her, then twirled his forefinger to indicate that she should turn back around.

Cecily's mouth fell open in disbelief, her enjoyment forgotten. Insufferable fellow! First he took her in a highly improper embrace, and then he took over her spying session. This was her clandestine observation. It was only because of her that he even knew about it! He had no right to tell her how she should—

Her indignant thoughts were interrupted by the tickle of his whispering lips at her ear.

"I am standing behind you so that you will be shielded should someone discover us here. But I am only human. Stop wiggling or I won't be answerable for the consequences."

She tried to turn fully around to look at him so that she might gauge his expression, but his forearm held her firmly in place. Cecily fumed, but couldn't very well protest aloud given their circumstances. Besides, she'd wasted too much time on distractions as it was. But when they were safely away from prying eyes, there were one or two choice words she would share with her noble partner.

He deserved a medal at the very least, Lucas told himself, trying and failing to ignore the press of sweet curves against his body.

Not only had he managed to hide Miss Cecily Hurston from any wandering musicale guests who might stumble into the room, but he had done so without taking a single liberty with her infinitely delectable person.

Well, unless one counted the way he held her firmly pressed against his . . . He stopped his mind from finishing the thought. Technically, he affirmed, that did not count. If he had not done so, she would surely have given their hiding place away. And protecting her good name was more important than whether or not her body happened to oh so gently rub against his.

Repeatedly.

Definitely such selfless behavior deserved accolades of some sort. A parade, perhaps? He closed his eyes as Cecily wiggled her bottom against him.

An estate. With lots and lots of beautiful land and sweet, luscious hills just the right size for a man's hands to . . .

"And now, gentlemen." Peterborough's voice, louder now, penetrated the lust-soaked fog of Lucas's thoughts. To his relief, Cecily stilled, listening intently to the older man's words.

"Now I come to the Egyptian Club's most valuable acquisition to date. As you all know, before his recent illness, one of the club's founding members, Lord Hurston, donated to the club not only the entirety of the artifacts he unearthed during his last trip to the Nile basin . . ."

Cecily must not have been informed of the gift to the club as Lucas felt her stiffen with anger at Peterborough's words.

"But his lordship has also, quite generously, donated all of his writings pertaining to that trip, as well as the right to publish them, with all proceeds going into the club treasury as funding for the club's next trip to Egypt."

Though Cecily had not made a sound, Lucas knew instinctively that she would not be able to hold back her outrage for long. Such moments demanded questions and answers, and though he knew that she longed to pose those questions now, alerting the club to their surveillance was likely to have far-reaching consequences for both of them.

Before she could speak, he half dragged, half carried her backward out the door and into the hallway, ducking them both into an empty parlor several doors down from the meeting.

"What are you doing?" she demanded as soon as the door was closed. The only light was from the fire, which had burned down and lent the room an otherworldly glow. Her dark hair gleamed with hints of mahogany and russet. Her eyes flashed with annoyance.

He gave her a look.

"I would never have approached them there," she protested haughtily.

"How could I be sure of that?" he asked, keeping his voice low. "It was quite clear to me that what Lord Peterborough just announced came as an unpleasant shock to you. Battle-worn soldiers have cut up rough over less."

She gave a hollow laugh. "Yes, well, no battle-worn soldier am I. Ladies aren't allowed there, either."

"That is not a disappointment to you, surely?"

Scholarly activities were one thing, but the battlefield was no place for females. Those who did end up there were either no better than they should be or the wives and daughters of military men who ventured onto the field after a battle to search for their loved ones' bodies. The thought of his vibrant, strong-willed Amazon in such a place sent a shard of panic stabbing into his heart. He'd die before he saw her in such a position.

"No," she responded, her ire seeming to seep out of her, only to be replaced with weariness so strong it was palpable. "That is one place where this lady has no desire to venture."

Cecily lifted her eyes to his. "Does that make me a hypocrite, do you think?"

He offered her a half smile and, without conscious thought, stepped closer to her. "Only if you have campaigned that ladies should become men. Which I am quite sure you have not."

She lowered her lashes, then looked up at him again. "No, I never have."

"I'm glad," Lucas said, unable to look away as her pink tongue darted out to lick her lips. "Because I think you make an exceptional lady."

"D-do you?" Cecily looked up, her eyes warm as they locked with his. And for the space of a moment they leaned closer, inexorably drawn together by a thread of mutual attraction that crackled between them. Lucas placed his hands on her shoulders to draw her closer to him.

But the loud pop of an ember in the fireplace startled them apart, ruining the moment.

They stood there for a moment, staring at one another, breathless. Lucas ran a hand through his artfully tousled curls.

Cecily pressed a hand against her bosom, putting him in mind of a scandalized governess. He hid a smile at the thought. It was somehow reassuring to know his Amazon wasn't immune to every sort of agitation.

That *he* was that sort of agitation just now was heady enough to make him lose his breath.

"I repeat," she said, firmly breaking into his thoughts—

eager to get the last few minutes of madness behind them, no doubt. "I would not have approached Peterborough."

At his snort of laughter, she amended her statement.

"All right, perhaps I would have. But the man just announced that my father donated not only his writings pertaining to his last trip, but also the publication rights! It's unthinkable."

She frowned, her outrage lending a stark beauty that put him in mind of Saint Joan of Arc heading into battle. "My father may well have been a founding member of the club, and he definitely has donated artifacts to the club in the past, but he has always, always overseen the publication of his writings."

"Could it be," he asked, "that your father somehow knew that his health was in jeopardy and granted the journals and their publication rights to the club because he knew he would be unable to see to them himself?"

"Absolutely not," she said, her lips pursed. "Aside from the fact that he wrote them in code, which no one in the club has the least notion of translating, my father has always been notoriously secretive about his excavation methods. He has even gone so far as to have each member of his expedition sign an agreement not to disclose his methods to anyone not part of the process."

"That does not sound like the sort of man who would wish to delegate the preparation of his papers for publication," Lucas agreed, idly rubbing his chin in thought.

"He wouldn't have. It's that simple."

"What about the artifacts?" he asked. "Were they delivered to your father's home, or did the club remove them to their own premises right from the docks?"

"Oh, the artifacts have always been taken directly to the club on Papa's return. With the competition between the club and the British Museum for such things, Papa was always intent on ensuring that the club received all of his finds."

"For a fee, of course."

"Of course." She nodded. "He might have been determined

to see the club best the museum, but he did need funds to continue his travels. It isn't widely known, however, given the *ton*'s attitude toward gentlemen who earn their fortunes rather than inherit them."

"Would the Egyptian Club not pay for his trips on their behalf?"

"Oh, no. They pay a small sum, of course, but nowhere near enough to cover the trip and the cost of the various people one must employ over the course of the journey. He also gained much of his travel money through sales of his travel memoirs. That is another reason I cannot fathom him giving away their rights to someone else."

The ormolu clock on the mantel chimed the hour, reminding them that they'd been closeted in this room for nearly a quarter of an hour.

"We'd best get you back into the musicale," he said firmly. "Both our disappearances cannot have gone unnoticed."

"But what will we do about the club?"

"I will call upon you tomorrow afternoon. I believe it's time we start questioning the men who accompanied your father and my brother on this expedition."

Cecily nodded. "We should start with Neddy Entwhistle."

"And who is this Entwhistle? A member of the club?"

Her eyes turned mischievous. "You'll see tomorrow," she said, pushing past him to the door. "Neddy is . . ." She peeked over her shoulder at him. "Let's just say I think you'll find Neddy to be quite . . . unusual."

He watched her slip from the room, ruthlessly suppressing a desire to trail after her. It would do neither of them any good to encourage gossip. Besides that, he reflected, pacing the room to burn off some of the nervous energy their encounter had conjured, his Amazon would likely cut up rough if she thought—

Lucas came to an abrupt halt.

"When the devil did she become *my* Amazon?" he demanded of the empty room.

With a muffled curse, he ran a finger beneath his suddenly suffocating cravat.

"Damn it," he said again. It was all well and good to engage in a bit of flirtation. But possessiveness meant something else entirely. Something dangerous.

Not caring if enough time had passed between their exits from the room or not, he stalked into the hallway and headed for home. He had a sudden pressing need to reacquaint himself with his brandy decanter.

Six

*W*hen he arrived to collect her for their outing the next day, Lucas was irritated to find Cecily surrounded by a small army of suitors.

"My dear Miss Hurston," Lord Deveril said, a grin rendering the blighter's handsome face even more so. "You are such an original. I cannot understand how you are as yet unmarried."

Instead of giving the crackbrain the set-down he deserved, Cecily rapped him on the arm with her fan. "It is quite simple, really, my lord," she said, wry humor infecting her voice. "No one has ever asked me."

Seeing that more than one of the crowd seemed eager to rectify the situation then and there, Lucas stepped forward, the Hurstons' elderly butler announcing him.

"Oh, Your Grace," Cecily's stepmother fluttered, as Lucas bowed over her hand. "What an honor you do us."

"The honor is mine, Lady Hurston," he returned. "And may I inquire after the health of your husband, ma'am?"

The lady's famous violet eyes shadowed.

"I'm afraid Lord Hurston's condition has not changed," she said. "But I do thank you for your concern. Everyone has been quite kind to us since his illness began. Quite kind."

It was easy to see what had drawn Hurston to the lady. Not only was she incredibly beautiful, but there was an air of helplessness about her that called out to the protector in every male. The exact opposite, in fact, of her stepdaughter, he thought, looking over to where Cecily was trying to conduct a conversation with the hapless Lord Fortenbury in Latin. There was nothing weak about Cecily. And yet, he found himself wanting to rescue her all the same. Perhaps because she seemed so determined to hide the fact that she needed it. Bowing correctly over the hands of both Miss Juliet Shelby and Lady Madeline Essex, who were surrounded by their own, albeit smaller, cadres of suitors, Lucas cast an eye over the men surrounding Cecily. He'd hoped to find her ready to leave as soon as he arrived. Unfortunately, it would appear that she had other ideas.

"I was wondering, ma'am," he said to Lady Hurston, "if I might take Miss Cecily for a drive in my phaeton."

Lady Hurston exchanged a glance with her sister, clearly surprised by the request. But she agreed readily enough.

"Of course, you must ask Cecily," she added, looking at him with open speculation. Lucas had been a bachelor for long enough to know what the look meant.

Thanking his hostess, he wandered over to the corner where Cecily held court.

"What ho, Winterson," Lord Pennington said to the newcomer. "Didn't think you was in the petticoat line."

"Every man must succumb at some point, Pennington," he replied, his eyes on Cecily.

"Miss Hurston," he drawled. He may have imagined it, but her hand gave the slightest tremble as he pressed his lips to the back of it. "You are looking radiant today."

So quicksilver fast was the array of emotions that flitted through her eyes that Lucas was unsure he'd seen anything at all. Whatever had bothered her was gone again before he could remark upon it, and by the time she responded to his greeting she had returned to normal.

Though normal was not the way he supposed she would describe the crowd gathered around her.

"I'm afraid I must leave you, gentlemen," she announced when Winterson reminded her of her promise to drive with him. "His Grace has kindly offered to take me for a ride in his high-perch phaeton."

The chorus of disappointed groans that met her announcement was gratifying, if a bit jarring. Still unused to being the center of so much masculine attention, she had not yet come to terms with the fact that she was, no matter how she still viewed herself, a social success.

"Come, come, gentlemen," she chided, taking Winterson's arm, steeling herself not to show the way her body responded to his proximity. "I leave you in good company. My cousins and my aunt and stepmama are here to lend you their support."

Though Pennington looked as if he might argue, Lord Deveril, perhaps remembering his manners, smiled. "Indeed you are right, Miss Hurston," he said heartily. "We could not have asked for lovelier hostesses to make us welcome."

Cecily allowed Winterson to lead her to the door and help her on with her pelisse, a rich royal blue that went nicely with her light blue morning gown. Was it just accidental, the way his hands lingered on her shoulders once her outer garment was in place?

Still thrumming with awareness, within minutes she found herself several feet off the ground, seated in Winterson's bright yellow high-perch phaeton. But when she looked down, all thoughts of attraction fled.

"Are you comfortable?" he asked, leaping into the seat beside her and taking the reins from his tiger, before sending the lad on his way.

"Why shouldn't I be?" Cecily asked, trying to maintain an expression of nonchalance while gripping the side of the carriage like a woman overboard with a life preserver. "Just because this phaeton is higher off the ground than one is normally accustomed to does not mean that I am in any way feeling anxious."

"No indeed," Winterson said, giving her a quick look before turning his attention to the horses while he guided them into the street. "Though I think you might feel more comfortable if you move a bit closer to me on the seat."

Cecily narrowed her eyes. She had enough trouble ignoring the maelstrom of feelings he set off in her without having him plastered to her side . . .

Perhaps reading her suspicions, he gave her a guileless grin. "You might feel . . . ahem . . . more secure if you're nearer to the center."

"Hmmph," she returned, sliding closer to him all the same. And he was correct. She did feel less precarious in the middle of the seat. Though now she was faced with the discomfort of feeling his warm body pressed up against her own. She wasn't sure which situation was more disturbing to her equilibrium.

"Where are we going?" Winterson asked after they had driven in silence through the streets of Mayfair for a block or so.

"Neddy lives in Bloomsbury," she said, trying not to reveal just how disconcerted she was both by his proximity and the height of the phaeton.

"Blue becomes you." Winterson kept his gaze on the horses even as he delivered the compliment.

Cecily sighed. She had a very familiar acquaintance with her looking glass, and what it told her every morning was that she was passable at best. No amount of wardrobe changes could alter that. His insistence on paying her false coin was both unnecessary and foolish.

He turned to look at her more closely. "What? Am I not allowed to mention it when I notice such a thing?"

"Your Grace, you need not attempt to turn me up sweet with empty flattery. I have agreed to assist you in your quest to learn more about your brother's disappearance, and that is that. I keep my word."

Winterson gave a low laugh. "I do not know whether to be offended that you would think me such an unprincipled fellow as to give you false praise simply to ensure your assistance, or to be angry on your behalf."

"I meant no offense," Cecily was quick to say. "I simply thought you were—"

"You thought I was lying to you. Because that is what we

men do? Is that it?" His tone was curious, but underlying it Cecily heard a note of bitterness.

Before she could respond, he went on.

"Miss Hurston, whether you believe me or not I must needs inform you that when I remark upon your appearance, I do indeed mean it. You are quite a pretty girl. You have the sort of figure that men enjoy looking at. Surely that lot of preening peacocks who have surrounded you for the past several days have intimated as much."

"Oh, they do not mean their compliments, either." Cecily waved a hand to dismiss the notion, forgetting for a moment that she was terrified at being so high up off the ground.

"They have simply taken me up as their newest fashion because they saw me dancing with a couple of smart young gentlemen at the Bewle ball," she explained. "I believe they see me as something out of the common way and are diverted by the novelty of conversing with a sensible creature for a change. They certainly are not doing so because they find me attractive. I *am* an Ugly Duckling, after all."

"I beg your pardon, Miss Hurston," he replied, shaking his head as if in sorrow for what he was about to say. "But as a gentleman . . . as a man," he corrected himself, "let me be the first to inform you that you are utterly, splendidly wrong."

"So you would deny the fact that my cousins and I have for the past three seasons been known as the Ugly Ducklings?" she asked. "You, sir, are mad."

"Oh, I do not dispute that silly nickname that's been inflicted upon the three of you for so many years. I simply am informing you that as a man, I know what men hold up as standards of feminine beauty, and you, my dear, are dam . . . er . . . dashed close to the ideal."

He turned to look fully at her. Meeting her eyes in a manner that sent a thrill of excitement down her spine.

"This is a most improper conversation, Your Grace," she said, for once falling back on the social niceties that she normally found so annoying.

Lucas laughed, his full, rich baritone sending another shiver down the same path as the last one.

"My dear Miss Hurston," he said, a wicked grin bringing forth the dimples she'd found so enticing on the day they met. "I thought never to hear you accuse anyone of impropriety. I must have become very scandalous indeed."

"Perhaps not scandalous," she offered, unwilling to be thought overly prim, "but definitely less than absolutely proper."

He grunted. "Then pray accept my apologies for offending your delicate sensibilities. Do, however, know that despite your despicable nickname, you are quite fetching when you choose to be. Indeed, I have heard more than one gentleman remark upon it."

"Oh—"

"No, no," he interrupted. "It is quite true, I assure you. And also remember that the proper response when a gentleman gives one a compliment is a simple thank-you. Anything else smacks of false modesty. Something I am all too sure you would not wish to be accused of."

Cecily shook her head in disbelief. She wondered briefly what her cousins would have to say to such a notion. She was well aware that she was no beauty, no matter what the Duke of Winterson said. Still, she found his indignation on her part to be comforting.

"Then I suppose I should say 'thank you,' Your Grace, for your pretty compliments," she said, still bemused by his words.

"You are quite welcome, Miss Hurston," he responded, with exaggerated courtesy. "There, now. That was not so difficult, was it?"

"I suppose not," she allowed, still reluctant to believe him. "But I take leave to tell you, Your Grace, that you are a most peculiar man."

"I shall take that as a compliment."

To Lucas's surprise, after being ushered into Number 6 Bedford Square by a very proper butler, they were shown into a room that could only be described as extraordinary. There was, in fact, nothing whatsoever ordinary about Neddy Entwhistle's drawing room.

The walls were draped with brightly colored fabrics in exotic patterns, the reds and purples and golds giving the room a richness and a warmth that was unlike any respectable home he'd ever been in.

Every stick of furniture, every bit of open wall space, every surface was occupied by what he could only presume were mementos and keepsakes from Neddy's travels. Carvings, statues, bits of pottery, elaborately designed boxes—even, he was fascinated to observe, a stuffed monkey wearing a small cap. The chamber was like a museum of sorts, with a small, pantaloon-clad woman presiding over the whole affair from a pile of silken pillows, the makeshift bower draped tentlike with yet more colorful fabric.

"The Duke of Winterson, and Miss Hurston," the butler announced them, just as if it were a proper drawing room in a proper English home.

The odd little woman took a last puff from the hookah in her hand, and rose from the floor, her movements languid, as if she were moving through water.

"Cecily, my dear," she said warmly, embracing Miss Hurston, "how lovely to see you. And who is this elegant gentleman? Never say you have succumbed to the pressures of convention and become betrothed!"

"Goodness, no." Cecily laughed. "Neddy, please allow me to introduce the Duke of Winterson. Your Grace, may I present Lady Nedra Entwhistle?"

This fey creature was Neddy Entwhistle? Winterson fought to control his astonishment. But Cecily's next words brought him back to the real reason for their presence in Lady Entwhistle's home.

"He is the elder brother of Mr. William Dalton."

A shadow crossed the tiny lady's countenance at the words.

"Oh, how very sorry I am for your family, dear man," she said with some feeling. Grasping his hands with the familiarity of an old friend, she continued. "William was a dear, dear boy and his loss was felt keenly by all of us on the expedition with him."

"Thank you, Lady Entwhistle," Lucas said with a small bow. "It is heartening to hear you say so. Though I would remind you that there is nothing to lead me to believe that my brother should be spoken of in the past tense."

"Of course, Your Grace," she said, her expression contrite. "Of course, you are correct. We have no confirmation of anything, have we?"

Turning to ring the bellpull, she said, "Let me offer you both some refreshment." Facing them again, she gestured for her guests to be seated on the pillows.

"Wilton," she said to the butler, "fetch us some tea, please. And some of those ginger biscuits, if there are any left."

She turned back to Cecily and Lucas, who had carefully lowered themselves to the floor onto the cushions. It was difficult for him with his leg injury, but he doubted the pain was any worse than the deprivation his brother had endured in the Egyptian desert.

"I'm afraid that when I am in town," Neddy was saying, "I am apt to overindulge in those vices unavailable to me in the course of my travels. Ginger biscuits most especially."

When Neddy had resumed her seat on the floor, Cecily broke the silence.

"Neddy," she began, "we have come with ulterior motives, I'm afraid. His Grace is in search of any clues or suggestions you might have regarding William's disappearance."

"I have, of course, dispatched an investigator to look for my brother in Alexandria and Cairo," Lucas interjected, "but until I have word back from him, I am conducting an investigation of my own."

Lady Entwhistle nodded. "As any man of sense would do," she said approvingly.

They were interrupted by the arrival of Wilton with the tea, and for a few moments they were occupied with the ritual associated with the drink.

"I am not sure what help I can be to you," Lady Entwhistle said, after they had all been served. "I spent a good deal of the expedition dealing with the transport of our finds from the excavation site back to Lord Hurston's warehouse in Cairo."

"But you were there," Lucas said. "Even small details will be much appreciated."

"I'm afraid I have very little to tell you, however, Your Grace." Lady Entwhistle would not meet their eyes. Lucas was certain she was hiding something.

Cecily must have thought so too, for she reached out to grasp the older woman's hand and said, "Neddy, I know you would do anything to protect me, but if there is something you can tell us . . . even something that might portray Papa in a less than flattering light . . ."

Cecily paused, letting her words sink in. "I am well aware that Papa is no saint. Please tell us what you know."

Lady Entwhistle met Cecily's gaze with the hint of a rueful smile. "You always were more perceptive than your father gave you credit for," she said fondly.

Squaring her shoulders, she went on. "There is something, but Cecily, I'm afraid it will be more than just unflattering to your father."

Lucas turned to Cecily, gauging her response, praying she would be willing to hear what the other woman had to say. To his relief, she gave him a reassuring nod.

"I am willing to hear it," she said.

Lady Entwhistle nodded. "Very well, then, my dear." Her gaze was troubled as she continued. "For the two weeks preceding William's disappearance, he and your father were engaged in a rather heated argument over how the artifacts unearthed during the excavation were to be disbursed once they were brought back to London."

"But I assumed that everything would go to the Egyptian Club just like everything else?" Cecily said, her brow furrowed.

"That was true for all the things your father himself discovered," Neddy agreed, "but the largest cache of treasures found up to that point in the dig were uncovered not by your father, but by William, who had decided that he wished for the artifacts to remain in the country where they were found.

He'd even spoken with a gentleman in Cairo who planned to open a museum there that would rival the British Museum with its splendor."

This was new, Lucas thought, listening with growing unease. Such idealism sounded just like Will. They had often been at loggerheads over their differing perspectives on human nature. Whereas Lucas was a realist, with a healthy skepticism of his fellow man's motives and an eye out for practical consideration, William had ever been an idealist, his actions influenced by what he thought conditions should be rather than what they actually were. Had his reluctance to betray his own moral code led to his death or injury?

"But surely, as Father's secretary," Cecily said thoughtfully, "William cannot have done something so contrary to Papa's wishes without losing his post. I know my father can be indulgent at times, but he wouldn't countenance such subordination for very long."

"Oh, by that point William had quit your father's employ and struck out on his own."

Neddy's pronouncement was met with astonishment.

"How did my brother stay on with the expedition then?" Lucas did nothing to hide the incredulity in his voice. If Will had left Hurston's employment, this was the first he'd heard of it. He made a mental note to question other members of the expedition so that they might verify her story.

"Your brother and Lord Hurston reached an agreement, Your Grace," Lady Entwhistle said. "Though Lord Hurston was not best pleased with Mr. Dalton's perspective, he was still in need of a secretary. And Mr. Dalton was so proficient at recording their finds, even while he himself was participating in the excavation, that Lord Hurston agreed to keep him on. Though they both agreed that insofar as their hunt for artifacts went, they were nothing more than fellow explorers. Once they returned to London, Mr. Dalton's employment with Lord Hurston would be at an end."

"Extraordinary." Cecily shook her head in disbelief at Neddy's story. "I cannot imagine my father agreeing to such a thing."

"I was shocked as well, you may be certain," Lady Entwhistle replied. "I have never known your father to be so accommodating. But he was so desperate to finish the excavation before the French team we'd met in Cairo learned of the dig's location that he was willing to put his uneasiness about Mr. Dalton aside."

"Yes," Cecily agreed. "Papa is nothing if not competitive."

"But how does this conflict between my brother and Lord Hurston reflect on my brother's disappearance?" Lucas knew there must be something more to it than what Lady Entwhistle had told them.

The frown that crossed the lady's face confirmed his suspicion.

"On the evening before William went missing, he and Lord Hurston had a particularly explosive falling-out. William had informed us at supper that he was donating the extraordinary death mask he'd unearthed earlier that day to his friend with the plan for an Egyptian museum. Hurston was furious, of course. I'd seen his eyes when Dalton showed us his find. He wanted that mask for the Egyptian Club. We all knew it.

"Dalton, of course, would hear nothing of Lord Hurston's protests. He held firm to his notion that whatever treasures we found should remain in the country of their origin. They fought over the piece like two dogs after the same bone. I'm afraid Lord Hurston made certain threats regarding Mr. Dalton's future in both the *ton* and the world of Egyptian exploration, vowing that he would never be able to find another position again."

She paused. "Your brother was angry, Your Grace. But when Lord Hurston threatened his livelihood, his face lost all its color. I don't really think it occurred to him before that moment that crossing Lord Hurston would be quite so dangerous."

Though Lucas had encouraged his brother to accept an allowance from him when he inherited the dukedom, Will had been adamant about making his own way. Was he really so hell-bent on self-sufficiency that he'd face the loss of his position as if Lucas had never offered him an income in the first place? It was hard to believe, but if there was another man in the world who was more pigheaded, Lucas had yet to meet him. Then again, the loss of his position might not have been so alarming as the loss of his entrée into the world of Egyptian exploration. Lucas knew that his brother had fallen in love with the land of the pharaohs, and perhaps that was what had so unsettled him about Lord Hurston's threats.

"When Lord Hurston alerted the camp later," Neddy continued, her eyes shrouded with concern, "that his dueling pistols were missing, well, it did nothing to settle our nerves. Mr. Dalton had stalked off in an angry huff a few hours before, and I think we all suspected he was the one who had taken the pistols, though no one would admit to it aloud."

It made Lucas cringe to think of his baby brother as the subject of such fear, and he had to stop himself from hotly denying the older woman's concern. But he supposed things were different when one was deep in the desert with only one's fellow excavators to rely on.

Unaware of the duke's defensiveness on the part of his brother, Neddy continued her story. "We all retired that night with both the quarrel and the missing pistols on our minds." She shook her head at the memory. "I woke up for every little sound, convinced that someone was going to be shot before the night was through."

"But when dawn came and Mr. Dalton and the death mask were missing . . ." she continued, "well, I feel sure I'm not the only one who wondered if your brother had simply taken the mask and the pistols and run back to Cairo. One of the pack ponies was missing as well, so it wasn't out of the question."

"When did you decide he had not simply returned to the city?" Lucas asked, his tone as hard as granite. If these people hadn't just assumed his brother was a thief and a liar, his disappearance might not have been dismissed so easily.

"One morning a few days later I had need of Hurston's penknife," Neddy explained. "He was down at the dig site while I was back at camp writing a letter. I knew he kept such things in a little pouch with his things. So I ventured into his tent in search of it."

"Did you find it?" Cecily asked.

Lady Entwhistle's eyes gleamed with apology. "Oh, yes," she said sadly. "I found the penknife, but I also found something else much more alarming."

"What was it?" Winterson bit the words out, the desire to shake the words from Neddy making him close and unclose his fists.

"I found the missing pistols," she said with an apologetic glance at Cecily. "They were sitting there, open in their case, atop your brother's things. All of them, including the small bag he carried with him wherever he went." She looked from one to the other of them with a frown. "But that was not the most troubling of my discoveries."

Lucas felt Cecily stiffen beside him. Her body was as taut as a bowstring, and he could hardly blame her. Still, when Neddy continued, he almost wanted to stop her from saying what he knew would be bad news. Just as he and Will had done when they were children in the nursery, pretending that bedtime was still hours away, he wanted now to retreat into that place where nothing mattered but banter with Cecily and the cut of his coat.

Still, just as bedtime could not be ignored, neither could Neddy's tale, which he knew would change everything.

"The most troubling of my findings," their hostess went on, "was the fact that your brother's bag was covered with reddish-brown stains that could only be one thing."

Lucas was unable to remain sitting at the words. He needed to move, to pace, even for a moment to escape the news. Ignoring the protests of his leg, he stood.

"What was it?" Cecily demanded, climbing to her feet beside him, grasping his arm as she looked from Neddy to Lucas and back again

"Blood," Lucas said bitterly. "It was covered with my brother's blood."

* * *

Her attempts at conversation on the ride back to Hurston House were met with monosyllables and a clenched jaw. Cecily had grown to appreciate Lucas's easygoing but dependable personality, so seeing him in the grips of such a dark mood was unnerving. She was accustomed to being the more solemn one in their partnership, and his bleak expression made her want nothing more than to take him in her arms and offer him the comfort he seemed to need.

When they arrived at Hurston House barely having spoken twenty words to one another, Cecily made one last attempt to draw him out as he assisted her from the phaeton.

"We don't know that it's blood, you know. It might be any number of substances. Dirt, claret, even excrement," she said, dipping her head to look at his face.

He turned to face her and Cecily was reminded of a painting she'd once seen of an avenging angel. His eyes were just as fierce and there was a beautiful darkness about him that seemed to elevate him from the realm of the everyday.

To her surprise, his gaze softened when he saw her. And he blinked as if waking from a nightmare.

"Don't fret so," he said with a rueful smile. "I don't hold you responsible for anything your father might have done."

His words sent a stab of panic through her. She'd assumed he'd taken Neddy's details about her father's behavior in Egypt in the same way Cecily had—as Neddy's typical embellishment. But it belatedly occurred to her that Lucas had no idea what typical Neddy conversation was like.

She opened her mouth to tell him, but he raised a hand to stop her from speaking.

"Let's not talk about it right now," he said, his eyes still troubled, but no longer so bleak. She hoped he was not hiding his fears for her benefit. But men were often foolish about such things, so she did not press him.

"Thank you for driving with me," Lucas continued, bowing over her hand. "I hope that I will see you tonight at the Cranston rout?"

"Yes," Cecily said, her chest constricting at the look of genuine pleasure in his eyes.

"Then until tonight, Miss Hurston," he said, stepping back to watch her ascend the steps.

She would have looked back once she reached the door, but the butler informed her that her cousins were waiting for her in the sitting room and, bursting to tell them everything about their visit to Neddy's, she hurried to find them.

"Well?" Juliet demanded, having led the other two to a delicate inlaid table surrounded by three overstuffed chairs. "What did you learn?"

"Give her a moment to catch her breath, Jules," Maddie admonished, pouring Cecily a cup of tea. "But really, dearest, we have been dying for you to return so you could tell us everything."

Uncomfortable discussing what she and Winterson had learned from Lady Entwhistle in a room full of visitors, Cecily waved away the cup of tea and asked Juliet, "Is your carriage still here?"

At her cousin's nod, Cecily rose. "Let's go for a drive and I'll tell you everything."

All three ladies donned their hats and gloves and headed back outside to climb into the Essex carriage, where Cecily related what Neddy had said about her father and Will Dalton's altercations.

"There you have it, I'm afraid," she told her cousins, her fears beginning to wear on her. "It does sound, from Neddy's story, as if Papa had something to do with Mr. Dalton's disappearance. He was seen threatening Mr. Dalton in front of any number of people. And I, of all people, know how intense Papa can be about his work."

Juliet's eyes narrowed. "The blood is definitely suspicious. But who's to say it was William's blood at all? Perhaps someone planted the bag there to make your father look guilty."

"But why?" Cecily demanded. "I realize he is not the most agreeable man, but surely he is not so hated that someone would wish him hanged for murder?"

"You've complained about his drive for success often enough, Cecily," Madeline said kindly. "Perhaps he simply crossed the wrong person this time?" Staring out the carriage window, Cecily tried to imagine someone killing William Dalton and then framing her father for it. The very idea was enough to make her ill. As she spoke, she'd begun to understand just how damning her father's threats against Mr. Dalton were. She would have sworn that her father's passion for his work wasn't so powerful that he'd be prepared to perpetrate violence on another man over it. The matter of the missing pistols did muddy the waters a bit. Her first thought when listening to Neddy's tale was that Mr. Dalton had taken them in order to kill himself and lay the blame on Lord Hurston. But there was nothing to indicate that Mr. Dalton was so desperate as to take that sort of action. An alternate theory could be that her father had used the pistols to kill Mr. Dalton, but she had difficulty believing he'd make such a foolish mistake as letting Neddy find him with the pistols.

Pinching the bridge of her nose, Cecily fought down panic as she realized their task had now increased tenfold. She'd begun this journey wishing to obtain her father's journals simply to ensure that they were preserved for posterity. Now, with Neddy's revelations of this afternoon, the journals had become a sort of Pandora's box that held the key to proving her father's guilt or innocence. And to her horror, she was no longer so sure which she expected to find. She even wondered if she ought to be looking for the journals at all.

Then the vision of Lucas's worried expression when he left her earlier reminded her that she wasn't the only one in this situation with a family member's life at stake. What a coil.

When they'd climbed into the carriage, Juliet had instructed the coachman to drive them to the British Museum. It was one of the few places their mamas would allow them to go with only a footman for an escort. As the carriage slowed on the narrowing street, Cecily became aware of her surroundings and realized that they were already in Bloomsbury, on Lady Entwhistle's street, in fact. Determined to speak to her godmother again, she rapped on the roof of the carriage to request the coachman to stop.

"What is it?" Madeline's blond brows arched over the top of her spectacles.

"I need to see Neddy again," Cecily said, her mouth set in determination. "I need to know more about Papa's argument with Will Dalton."

When the carriage came to a stop she waited impatiently for the footman to hand her down. When Madeline and Juliet started to follow her, she made a noise of impatience.

"There is no need for you to come with me. I will have Neddy send me home in her carriage."

Juliet shook her auburn curls as she stepped down to the street. "If you think for one minute that we are staying behind, then you know nothing of us at all."

"Besides," Madeline added, "I need to ask Lady Entwhistle's cook just what she uses to flavor her macaroons. There is a spice in them that I can't quite place."

Since Madeline had been known to go into the kitchens of some of England's finest homes to confer with their chefs, it was quite possible that she was telling the truth. With Juliet, it was likely mere curiosity that motivated her. Either way, Cecily knew she had their company whether she wished it or not.

If he thought it odd to find Miss Cecily Hurston in his mistress's entrance hall twice in one afternoon, Lady Entwhistle's butler did not betray himself with so much as a twitching eyelid. Instead he asked the three young ladies to wait while he conveyed their cards to her.

Cecily felt a pang of guilt at having kept her relationship with Lady Entwhistle from Winterson. But she had been so nervous on the ride to her godmother's home, she had found it difficult to speak of anything at all, much less divulge that yet another person she'd known from infancy had been present on the expedition from which his brother had disappeared. And on the ride back to Hurston House they had both been so lost in thought over Neddy's revelations that Cecily had found herself being handed down before her father's town house before she had a chance to say anything at all.

If she learned anything new from Neddy this afternoon, she would most certainly inform Winterson of it. And if he should learn from someone other than herself of her relationship with Lady Entwhistle, then so be it. She was under no obligation to divulge her every connection to the fellow, after all. Besides, she was quite certain that her godmother had nothing whatsoever to do with William Dalton's disappearance.

Lady Entwhistle had been her mother's dearest friend, and it was she who saw to it that in addition to the genteel upbringing Lord Hurston intended for his daughter, Cecily received instruction in everything her mother had studied, and more.

A notorious bluestocking, Lady Entwhistle was reputed to be as dedicated a scholar as the most educated dons at Oxford or Cambridge. When no London publisher would print her translations of the various writings she had obtained during her travels to the land of the pharaohs, Lady Entwhistle, whose late husband had left her a tidy fortune, had simply bought a small publisher and had them published herself.

It was at the behest of Lady Entwhistle that Cecily explored her affinity for cryptography, and under that lady's tutelage, Cecily had become a scholar in her own right. She had always been good at working through puzzles. And when she'd begun to study Greek and stumbled onto the writings of Polybius, with his substitution cipher that used numbers in the place of letters, she'd found to her delight that she was quite good at working through the translations from numbers to letters. When she'd been inspired to create her own code systems, Cecily had soon found herself corresponding with some of the most brilliant minds in Europe. And from time to time, her colleagues had even asked for her help with their own puzzles.

Though her father had forbidden her to see Lady Entwhistle anymore when he learned of her role in introducing

Cecily to the other scholars, Lady Entwhistle had always managed to convince him otherwise. What hold that lady had over her father Cecily could not say, but whatever it might be, she was grateful for it. Without Lady Entwhistle, Cecily very much suspected that her childhood would have been as empty as a plundered tomb.

Thoughts of Egypt brought her mind back to the topic of Mr. Dalton's disappearance. What could possibly have happened to him? And what role had her father played in it? Though she had always had a troubled relationship with her remaining parent, it was difficult for Cecily to imagine him doing violence to anyone. True, he had a temper. She herself had borne the brunt of it on more than one occasion. But at heart Lord Hurston was a peaceable man, a scholar who had acted out of love for his family—even when he had been at his most adamant in his insistence that his daughter not be allowed to follow in her mother's, and indeed his own, footsteps.

There must be some other explanation for the blood on Mr. Dalton's pack. A shaving accident, perhaps? Or a flesh wound from handling a piece of broken pottery? Perhaps Juliet was right in her suggestion that the bloody bag had been placed in Lord Hurston's tent to throw suspicion on him. But even to Cecily these sounded like what they were—thin excuses for what might very well have been violence perpetrated upon a man who had served at her father's side for years. She felt a pang of alarm at the thought of what Winterson might believe now. The notion that he might blame her for her father's actions affected her more than she cared to admit.

Her mood must have shown on her face, for as she and her cousins were shown into Lady Entwhistle's drawing room, her godmother gasped upon seeing her and hurried forward to take Cecily in a firm hug.

"My dear, you look as if someone has been walking on your grave! Whatever is the matter?" Lady Entwhistle leaned back to look more closely at her goddaughter's expression. "You father has not . . . the worst has not happened, surely?"

"No, no, nothing like that," Cecily hastened to assure her,

sinking gratefully into a plush settee—a scholar she might be, but Lady Entwhistle was also one who very much enjoyed material comforts, and every stick of furniture she owned was built for comfort as well as utility—a habit for which Cecily was grateful.

"My father's condition has not changed," she assured the older woman once her godmother had greeted Juliet and Madeline, who met the older woman with a mix of curiosity and fascination.

Lady Entwhistle had long been absent from respectable circles of the *ton* where the Featherstone sisters still held court. She had married the much older Lord Entwhistle the year before she was to make her debut, choosing to escape the restrictive confines of her father's home instead of undergoing the rigors of a season. A star in the diplomatic corps, Lord Entwhistle had carried his young bride away first to India, then to Africa, where he succumbed to a lung fever. Rather than return to the country of her birth, the young widow had stayed in Cairo and dedicated herself to the thoroughly unladylike study of ancient languages.

Establishing herself as a hostess to the European community in Egypt, she befriended Lady Hurston, herself a young bride accompanying her husband on his first expedition to the desert pyramids. The two had formed a fast friendship, and when Lady Entwhistle accompanied the Hurstons back to England, she had established herself as a leader of the intellectual set, who cared little for the rules and restrictions of society but instead dedicated themselves to academic debate. It was the sort of life Cecily would have enjoyed had her father not kept her on such a short leash.

"Then what is it, my dear?" she asked her goddaughter. "Why are you so pale? Has something else happened?"

"No, it is nothing like that," Cecily assured her. "But I did want to ask you, away from Winterson, I mean, if you know anything about Will Dalton's disappearance? Something you perhaps didn't want to say in front of the duke?"

Lady Enwhistle started, then glanced briefly from Cecily to Juliet and Madeline.

"Anything you say to me, you may say to my cousins as well," Cecily assured her. "They know what you told us this morning about the bloody satchel in Papa's tent."

Still frowning, their hostess took a seat in a wing chair opposite the divan upon which the three younger ladies perched. "I do wish you would not involve yourself in this business, Cecily. Already one man is missing and another is bedridden."

"I find it hard to believe that you, ma'am, would warn Cecily to let the gentlemen handle the matter," Juliet said from her position at Cecily's side. Though she often kept her own counsel, Juliet was loyal to a fault. And like Cecily, she did not take kindly to the notion that ladies should be seen and not heard.

Lady Entwhistle smiled. "You are right about that, Miss Shelby," she said. "I have never been one to leave things to the men. More often than not they make a muddle of things." Her expression sobered. "However, in this instance, when my goddaughter's well-being is at stake, I have every reason to wish for her to stay far away from whoever has stirred up this trouble. And before you ask, no, I do not believe in that ridiculous curse that is being bandied about."

"Godmama, I promise you," Cecily said, "I will not do anything to put myself in jeopardy. But you must know that your story earlier today of what you found in Papa's tent would have roused my curiosity. And my fear that Papa may have had something to do with Mr. Dalton's disappearance."

"I regret how my words must have seemed to you, Cecily," Lady Entwhistle assured her. "Your father and Mr. Dalton were quarreling, as I told you and Winterson earlier. But you will remember that I did not make any claim that the presence of either William Dalton's luggage, or his traveling bag, in your father's tent meant that he must then be guilty of killing him."

"But Winterson believed it," Cecily told her. "How can you have expected otherwise?"

"My dear," Lady Entwhistle said, with a shake of her head. "Your father is a great many things—a stubborn lout, for one—but I cannot imagine him killing a man, a friend, in cold blood and then refusing to allow the poor man's family to know what happened to him. There must be some other explanation."

"That is what I thought as well," Cecily said, accepting a cup of green tea from Madeline, who had taken up a position at the tea tray. "But there is something amiss here. Perhaps Mr. Dalton asked Papa to look after his luggage. If thefts were occurring with such frequency, it would stand to reason that William would not wish to leave his bags unattended. But that doesn't explain the blood. Or Papa's illness."

"I have heard it said that an apoplexy might be brought on by an emotional upset," Juliet suggested. "Papa's uncle Fenwick suffered an attack in the middle of a roaring argument with his . . . um . . . lady friend. One minute he was shouting at her about the modiste bills and the next he was incomprehensible and paralyzed down his entire right side."

Cecily stared at Juliet. "Why did you not tell us this before? What's more, why didn't your mama tell Violet?"

Juliet shrugged. "I didn't think of it before. And you know very well that Mama would never speak of anything so tawdry. She likes to pretend that Papa's side of the family is everything that the Featherstones are not."

"But what if Juliet is right, Cecily?" Lady Entwhistle said. "What if your father argued with someone on the voyage home? I admit that I was the one to find him, but it was the morning before we reached France. He might well have had an altercation the evening before with no one the wiser until I came to see why he had not come up on deck as was his habit."

"It need not have been an argument, though," Cecily said. "What if the knowledge that he'd killed his assistant preyed so heavily upon his mind that it caused his brain to simply . . . shut down?"

Lady Entwhistle reached for Cecily's hand. "My dear, you know as well as I do that your father has a temper. Recall for a moment the time he caught me sneaking you from

Hurston House so that we might attend the exhibition of those naughty marbles at the British Museum? I thought he would evaporate in a flash of fire. But I cannot believe that he killed Mr. Dalton in cold blood."

Cecily shook her head sadly. "When it comes to Papa's work he has no patience for anyone who stands in his way. He cannot have taken kindly to William's attack of conscience regarding the disposition of the artifacts. Papa put months of work into locating that particular tomb. For his own assistant to change his loyalties midway through the excavation must have been infuriating."

Though Cecily herself was more inclined to think the artifacts should remain in the nation where they were discovered, she did understand her father's reasons for removing them to England. If they weren't taken to England for further study, the French, or worse, simple treasure hunters, would remove them sooner or later. And whatever educational or historical value might have been gleaned from them would be lost.

"In truth, I cannot fathom Father showing the slightest bit of agreement with Will's plan. He would not have taken kindly to having his own artifacts stolen out from under him. Especially when the political situation in Egypt is so unstable right now. The French have only been gone from Cairo for a few years."

"And there is certainly nothing your father detests more than his French rivals," Lady Entwhistle said with a frown. "Still, I cannot imagine, even in righteous anger, your father behaving with violence toward someone with whom he had worked so closely. Nor can I believe he would put another family through the same hell of not knowing what happened to their loved one."

Cecily nodded. She had been so small when her mother died. She could remember little from the event itself, though she knew that Lady Hurston had disappeared from their country estate and no one had been able to find her. She'd been told about it later, of course. And there were flashes of memory, though she was often unsure if they were real or imagined, where she heard her father plead with her, Cecily, to tell him if she knew where her mama had gone. She recalled trying to make him happy again, to tell him something that would erase the stricken look from his face, but in the end all she could recall was that her mother had tucked her into the large trunk in her bedchamber and told Cecily to wait. That it was a game and that Papa would find her soon. She had waited and waited, growing more and more afraid, until finally her papa had come. Her mother had been found a week later, dead on the moors surrounding their Yorkshire estate.

She couldn't remember exactly what had happened, but the event had altered the course of her life just the same. And even now she feared enclosed spaces to such a degree that she sometimes had to leave a room if the walls began to feel too close.

"I agree," she said finally. "But if Papa was not responsible for Will Dalton's disappearance, then what did happen to him? Papa is the one who stood to lose the most from Will's attack of conscience. And now that Papa is unable to speak of it, I cannot help but wonder if whoever was responsible for Will's disappearance also had something to do with provoking Papa's apoplexy."

"It would make sense," Juliet agreed. "Especially if whoever triggered it feared that your father would reveal something about what really happened to William."

"It is a puzzle, no question," Cecily said, sitting back in her chair with a sigh. "I only wish there were something more I could do."

Lady Entwhistle reached out for Cecily's hand. "My dear, you are doing quite as much as any person can do. You are trying to find your father's journals, and you have joined forces with Winterson.

"Now, tell me more about the Duke of Winterson," she said, her gaze becoming far too knowing for Cecily's comfort. "I believe he is quite handsome. And a war hero, besides. It must be a great hardship for you to spend so much of your free time with him."

"Yes, Cecily," Madeline said, fixing her cousin with an innocent stare. "Do tell us more."

Cecily elbowed her cousin in the ribs, barely repressing a groan. For such an unconventional woman, Lady Entwhistle had a sad tendency for seeing possible romances for her dear friend's daughter around every corner. She had explained it once to Cecily thus: "I do not have children of my own, you know, so I must look to you if I wish to have grandchildren. And because I know that beneath your bookish exterior there lurks a young lady who is, despite all outward appearances, a rather conventional sort, I must pray for you to marry sooner rather than later."

Now, Cecily tried to dispel her godmother's hopes for her and Winterson by telling her about his agreement to assist her in choosing a possible suitor from among the Egyptian Club, a plan which Lady Entwhistle found sadly lacking in verve.

"For I do know you, my dear. You will choose the dullest of the lot and won't allow him to touch you above once a quarter at the most."

"But it is not so different," Cecily said with a blush, "from what you yourself did in marrying Lord Entwhistle. And it is also a means for me to assure that I need not depend on Cousin Rufus should the worst happen to Papa."

"Yes, I know," Lady Entwhistle said with a shake of her head. "But honestly, I do wish you would not condemn yourself to such a dismal life. Believe me, I know how tedious such a marriage can be. I wish I'd had someone to steer me away from such a match all those years ago."

She took Cecily's hand. "Simply because that foolish Lawrence boy broke your heart all those years ago is no reason for you to deny yourself all that a marriage of true minds—and yes, I will say it, bodies—has to offer."

Cecily felt her spine stiffen at the mention of David. Though ever since meeting Lucas, she found herself thinking about David more and more. Not from any unrequited emotion she might feel for him—it was difficult to remember the man who had broken her heart by compromising another woman with any real fondness—but because the feelings Lucas evoked made it imperative that she not forget how dangerous it would be for her to give her heart away again. Ever.

As a reminder, she thought back to that day again. The day that David Lawrence, whom she'd thought was her very own knight in shining armor, had stood before her begging her pardon for betraying her. And then he was gone. Just as her mama had left her by dying. Just as her papa had left her by traipsing to Egypt without her. Just as everyone she'd ever loved had done eventually. And when the tears had begun to flow she couldn't stop them. Not when her father found her on the floor. And not when Violet had chafed her wrists and called for a footman to carry her upstairs.

She had never seen David again, though they mixed with many of the same people because of their shared interest in antiquities. And when she emerged from her bedchamber three days later she had been calm and cool and detached. And she had remained that way ever since. Never again would she allow a man to bring her to her knees with grief. Not even her father, and most especially not her husband should she ever have one.

Aloud, to her godmother, she only said, "I do know you want what's best for me, Lady Entwhistle, but in this case, give me leave to know what I want. I will make a comfortable marriage, you may be sure. The Duke of Winterson is a handsome man, I will admit it. But he is not for me. We will work together to discover what happened to his brother and then we will part friends."

She could not help the laugh that escaped her before saying, "Indeed, I suspect that gentleman would prefer a much more comfortable wife than I should make him. He strikes me as the sort of fellow who wishes to be the dominant partner in his household. We cannot go three minutes without grousing over something or other. Imagine the indigestion the poor man would have to endure if he faced a quarrel over his breakfast every morning."

Besides, she thought, she had agreed to let him investigate which bachelor members of the Egyptian Club would make her the best husband. Surely he wouldn't have agreed to do so if he was interested in marrying her himself. The idea was absurd. No matter how her heart might beat faster when he entered a room. The subject passed, but having been reminded of her heartbreak over David, she made sure to remember the vow she'd made to herself all those years ago— to never let her heart become engaged by a gentleman again— and whenever Lucas's face rose in her imagination she'd make sure to tuck the idea of him away, in a mental strongbox marked "Off Limits."

Seven

After the uncomfortable trip back to Hurston House with Cecily, Lucas headed for White's where he could think about what he'd learned from Neddy and avoid his mother's questions about his progress in looking into Will's disappearance. He knew she was anxious for news, but it was becoming more and more difficult to face her disappointment. And what he'd learned this afternoon had done nothing to raise his hopes.

The situation was further complicated by his alliance with Cecily. What if her father was the one responsible for Will's disappearance? Would he be able to continue their acquaintance? He thought back to the way he'd walked away from her outside the Egyptian Club that day. At the time he had been more than ready to believe Lord Hurston capable of hurting Will. In his heart, he still did. In war he had seen men, good men, brought low by their baser instinct for survival. What if Lord Hurston and Will had been in the same sort of situation? He disliked the idea of seeing Cecily learn the truth about her father, but he disliked what the knowledge would do to his own family even more.

And what the hell had he been thinking when he agreed to be a matchmaker for her? Two minutes of seeing her being courted by that group of nodcocks in Lady Hurston's drawing room was enough to let him know that he'd sooner eat his boots than see her wed to one of them. He'd have to come up with some way to divert her attention from husband-hunting. Or find some other way to get the journals for her. A way that did not involve seeing her wed to some other man who wasn't . . .

He was saved from completing *that* disturbing thought when one of the nodcocks, the dandyish Lord Deveril, approached. Though he was slightly acquainted with the younger man, they had never run in the same circles, mostly because of their age difference, but also because Deveril, as heir to a viscountcy, was so far above Lucas socially. The fact that he now outranked Deveril amused him in some small way.

"Winterson." The viscount bowed slightly, his elaborately embellished bottle-green coat contrasting with the bright yellow of his waistcoat. "I wonder if I might have a word."

Lucas waved a casual hand toward the empty chair across from his, wondering what business the younger man might have with him.

"Deveril," he said when the other man was seated. "To what do I owe the pleasure?"

Nodding at the waiter who appeared as if by magic at his elbow, Deveril ordered a coffee, and turned to Lucas. "Your Grace, it has not escaped my notice that you have been seen of late showing a . . . partiality for a certain young lady."

Years of military discipline kept Lucas from reacting in any perceptible way to Deveril's statement, but every part of him went on alert. "I'm not sure I understand what business it is of yours what young ladies I do or do not pay attention to," he said in a deceptively languid tone. "Pray, explain it to me."

If he had expected Deveril to be intimidated by the underlying threat of his words, Lucas would have been disappointed. Instead the blond man simply shrugged. "You've hardly been at pains to hide it," he said. "At every social event the two of you attend you spend at least part of the evening in a tête-a-tête. Surely you are not unaware that there is talk.

"But," Deveril continued, "that is neither here nor there. I do wish to talk to you about Miss Hurston, but not about your . . . ahem—"

"Careful, man," Lucas warned with a raised brow, unable to stop himself from enjoying Deveril's discomfort. "You're nearing dangerous territory."

In an unexpected burst of nervousness, Deveril thrust a hand through his carefully coiffed blond curls. "Dammit, I am not trying to insult you. Either of you. I'm trying to warn you."

All amusement at the viscount's predicament fled. "Warn me about what?"

Moving his chair closer to the table, Deveril spoke in a low voice, as if afraid they'd be overheard. "You are aware, I think, that I am a member of the Egyptian Club."

When Lucas nodded, Deveril continued. "Your investigation into the disappearance of your brother has gotten the attention of the club."

"Has it indeed?" Lucas took a thoughtful sip of his brandy. "I should think they might have been interested when news of my brother's disappearance first broke, but then I suppose I am ignorant to the ways of the Egyptian Club." He made no attempt to soften the acidity of his words.

"Oh, there has been interest," Deveril assured him.

"Well, that is good news," Lucas returned, his voice sticky with false cheer.

"Your Grace," Deveril said, ignoring Lucas's sarcasm. "Though there are those in the club who have sought to discredit your brother as a thief and a liar, I am not one of them. I had some dealings with Will from Lord Hurston's previous expedition, and I believe that I can say with truthfulness that he and I were friends."

"But . . . ?"

"But there are those in the club, who, I am sure you suspect, have decided that it would be in the club's best interest to discredit both Will and Lord Hurston."

"Why?" Lucas demanded. "What possible motive could the club have for wanting to discredit the two men who have been almost single-handedly responsible for building the bulk of the club's current collection?"

Deveril shook his head slightly. "I know not," he said

regretfully. "But what I can say is that after Lord Hurston's return to England, the powers that be within the society made it abundantly clear that unless we wished to have our membership revoked, we should avoid any conversation regarding Hurston's last expedition. And though it was not ordered, it was strongly suggested that we do our part to see that Miss Hurston was married off by the end of the season. To someone who would . . ." His eyes grew hard. "Well, let's just say, someone who would keep her busy."

Only too aware of what the younger man must have sanitized for his benefit, Lucas tucked his anger over that tidbit away to mull over later. Telling himself that his concern for Cecily was merely that of a friend, since her father's possible involvement with Will's disappearance would make anything else between them impossible, he seized upon the other part of Deveril's revelation.

"So you are saying that the upper echelons of the Egyptian Club have no interest in determining what happened to my brother—a member in good standing of your blasted club, and someone who has overseen the excavation of countless artifacts, documents, and treasures for your damned club. Moreover, that in order to keep Miss Hurston quiet, they have ordered the entire club to work together in order to ensure that she marries the sort of man who will keep so tight a rein over her that she will have no opportunity to bother with her silly investigations and inquiries into the club, which her father founded. Do I have that right?"

"In a nutshell," Deveril responded, "yes. Though there is not nearly the level of compliance to these orders from on high as the powers that be would hope for."

"Why tell me all this?" Lucas wondered. "Why take the chance that I might leave here and shout this news from the nearest clock tower?"

"In part because of your . . . ahem . . . closeness to Miss Hurston," Deveril admitted. "It stands to reason that if you care for the girl at all, and one would suspect at least some remote affection for you to have spent so much time with her of late, that you would wish to either protect her from these machinations, or warn her against the plot. Either way, I imagine that you will do your part to counteract the attempts by the Egyptian Club members to see her bound to some man who will do his damnedest to snuff out the curiosity that makes her who she is."

"Oh, indeed, how noble of you, my good fellow." Lucas leaned back in his chair, stretching his long legs out before him.

"Well." The fair-haired man actually blushed and ran a nervous finger beneath his collar. "I have an interest in one of Miss Hurston's cousins."

Cecily was pensive when she returned to Hurston House some time later. Her conversation with Lady Entwhistle had given her much food for thought. Why had her father never written about his disagreement with William Dalton? And more importantly, who was putting it about that the members of the expedition were the victims of some silly curse?

She had done extensive research into the various warnings etched into the stones of the tombs that had been uncovered in Egypt thus far in the quest for knowledge about that ancient civilization, and the warnings ranged from the unsettling to the ridiculous. One in particular she'd always found amusing warned that whoever disturbed the eternal slumber of the pharaoh inside should have his face spat upon. So, it was clear to Cecily that whoever perpetuated the story that the tomb her father had unearthed on this latest expedition was dangerous had no notion of how these curses worked. They were intended to frighten would-be grave robbers, who were in all likelihood the superstitious and uneducated thieves of their own culture. She doubted that the ancient men who considered themselves gods had had any notion that their resting places would be disturbed hundreds of years later by men who viewed their beliefs with skepticism at best.

Seating herself behind her tidy writing desk, Cecily took out her personal journal and began to record her thoughts about the happenings of the past few days. Writing in her journal was an activity that never failed to calm her, and seeing the emotions she so often had to suppress in company written out on the page had a cathartic effect.

She was lost in her recounting when she heard a brisk knock on the door.

Violet, her luminous beauty framed perfectly in the doorway, stepped firmly into the room.

"I see you have returned," she said, an unaccustomed diffidence in her expression.

Wondering what could make her usually confident stepmother falter so, Cecily gestured for Violet to enter the room. Cecily was still grateful for Violet's help in transforming her appearance, but she knew that their relationship was still not as easy as that which her cousins enjoyed with their own mothers. For all that Violet had been a part of her life for nearly twenty years, the beauty had never quite understood how to handle her bookish stepdaughter.

"Yes," Cecily replied calmly, stepping out from behind her desk, thinking with some amusement of how their interactions now—she, behind the desk, Violet coming in with some petition or other—were the mirror image of the child entering the father's study in expectation of a set-down. "I went to see Lady Entwhistle not long after Winterson brought me home. You still had visitors and I did not wish to disturb you."

This seemed to placate Violet, but once they were both seated before the fire she spoke out.

"Cecily, it has been brought to my attention that you have been spending an inordinate amount of time in the company of the Duke of Winterson."

This gave Cecily pause. "I have, but it has been perfectly innocent, I assure you. He is simply concerned about his brother's disappearance. I have offered to introduce him to those members of the expedition with whom I have an acquaintance."

Violet nodded, though she still seemed agitated. "I do know this, and I did try to assure . . . them that you were merely being helpful, but since your change in hairstyle, and mode of dress, there has been some talk that perhaps you have set your cap at him. He is, after all, a handsome man, and it would not be unheard of for a lady to single him out for her attentions. Ever since he inherited the dukedom he has been the target of such schemes."

"I have not made him the object of a marriage scheme, I assure you." Cecily laughed. Though she had a marriage scheme, the Duke of Winterson was certainly not the object of it. "I have perhaps changed my mind about marriage. Papa's illness and the fear that I might have to live with Cousin Rufus for the rest of my days have done their part to ensure that. But that does not mean that I have chosen the Duke of Winterson as my intended groom. Why, I cannot think of anyone more unsuitable."

She did not add that that was because of the real possibility that her father might be responsible for the disappearance of Winterson's brother.

"I am relieved to hear you say so," Violet said, relaxing. "For I must tell you that some of the gossip that was whispered about you this afternoon during my at-home was quite alarming. The Duchess of Bewle was telling everyone who would listen that she saw you and Winterson looking like April and May in the park the other day. And that you had quite deliberately rebuffed that nice George Vinson in order to chase after Winterson for his title alone!"

"As I am not quite sure what April and May look like, I have nothing to say to the former accusation, but I vehemently deny the latter. I accepted Winterson's invitation to ride in his phaeton for no other reason than to escape Mr. Vinson's prattle. He is quite sweet, but hasn't much conversation. And though Winterson is a better conversationalist, I am most certainly not engaged in any sort of improper behavior with him."

"Then you will see no great hardship if I were to request that you do not see him quite as frequently as you have done of late? It must be done to safeguard your reputation."

"That is not possible," Cecily said with a frown. "I have

agreed to assist the duke, and I cannot do so if I do not see him."

"Cecily, you have a reputation to maintain." Violet clearly did not like rebuking her, but the determination on her countenance told her stepdaughter that she would not shy from her duty. "And as your father is unable to look after you now . . ."

"Violet, I am a grown woman of five and twenty. There is no need for anyone to 'look after me' as you put it. I am perfectly capable of keeping my own counsel and protecting my own reputation. Simply because Father is unable to do his usual policing of my every move is no reason for you to do the job for him."

"I am not . . ." Violet pursed her lips in agitation. It was the one expression she made that made her less than beautiful. "I am simply looking out for your well-being, my dear. I know that you have little use for the *ton* and its ways, but if you wish to make an acceptable marriage, then you must allow yourself to be led by me in this matter at the very least. It is all well and good to say that you have no designs upon becoming the next Duchess of Winterson, but that is not how the scandalmongers see it. There has already been speculation about the two of you in the scandal sheets. And my sister warned me today that there have been whispers of your name linked with his in that ridiculous betting book at White's.

"Please," she continued, her voice softening. "Do not let your dismissal of gossip trick you into assuming that it has no effect on your life. It does. Take it from someone who has been the subject of some very nasty rumors. If there is a way to spare you from such, I will do it."

This was not the first Cecily had heard of the whispers that had circulated about her stepmama and her newly widowed father; even so many years later, there were those members of society who thrived on ensuring that everyone who had missed such tales when they first were bandied about were apprised of them at the first opportunity. She had been told of her stepmama's campaign to win over her father's grieving heart on the night of her own come-out. She could still remember the gleam of pure malice in Lady Bedford's expression as she told the still-nervous debutante about the rumors that had made the rounds before her papa and Violet wed. The insinuation that she might learn a thing or two from Violet when it came to husband-hunting had been hurtful considering that her stepmama was a famed beauty while Cecily was a gawky, overtall bluestocking with a distrust of crows.

Now she said, "I do appreciate your fears, Violet. I do not wish to make you the object of talk any more than I wish for it for myself. But I have made a vow to the duke and I do not wish to renege on that promise. He and his family are, understandably, worried about the disappearance of his brother. And I know that Papa, as William Dalton's employer, would not wish for us to ignore that."

"All your papa ever wanted was for you to have the genteel and leisurely life of a lady. You know as well as I that he blames your mama's studies for her death. And though you have defied him time and again with your pursuit of an education, he has, I think, been proud even as he worried for you. I beg that you will not further dishonor his wishes for you by continuing your disregard for the society of which he so fervently wishes you to be a part."

It was the first time she had ever heard Violet voice Lord Hurston's fears that Cecily would endanger herself by following in her mother's footsteps. She had long ago, with the approval of her godmother, dismissed his fears for what they were—the overprotective posturing of a man searching for something to blame for the death of a loved one. And in Violet, he had chosen a second wife who would never worry him on that score. A scholar Violet was not. But she had shown herself to be as fine an interpreter of human emotion as the first Lady Hurston had been of dead languages. And there was a part of Cecily that wished she could have inherited that sort of mental acuity rather than her own.

But she knew where her talents lay. And she also knew that whatever her father had wished for her, she would honor him more by proving he had had nothing to do with Will Dalton's disappearance than she could ever do by simply sitting back and behaving like the simpering miss he so desperately wanted her to be.

"Violet, I appreciate your concerns," she said, squeezing her stepmama's hand. "But I hope you will not think me disrespectful when I tell you that I must continue my association with the Duke of Winterson, no matter what reservations you might have regarding the gossip going around. I cannot allow William's mother and wife to continue on in ignorance of what happened to him. There was a time when this family suffered from not knowing what had happened to my mother. And I cannot, in good conscience, step aside and do nothing while another family endures the same heartache of not knowing whether their loved one lives or dies."

She saw in Violet's eyes the recognition that she had made her point. And knowing Violet, she had likely been arguing against her own conscience in asking Cecily to give up her association with Winterson. For all her desire to avoid gossip, Violet had a very tender heart, and doubtless sympathized with Will Dalton's family more than she had let on in order to do as she thought her husband would wish.

"I had to try, you know," she said quietly. "For your father's sake."

"I know," Cecily returned, feeling a rush of affection for her.

Smiling, she said, "I vow, I have the only stepmama in London who wishes for her stepdaughter to spend less time with the handsome Duke of Winterson!"

Violet grinned. "I only wished to save you from tittle-tattle. I still have every hope that in the course of your time spent with him something will develop between the two of you."

This was not the time, Cecily saw, to inform Violet of her plans to make a marriage of convenience with an as-yet-unknown member of the Egyptian Club. For now, she would agree to be more circumspect with Winterson. That way her stepmama and the *ton* would not worry overmuch about their relationship, and Cecily would be able to get what she wanted as well: a marriage of convenience with a member of the club, and her father's journals.

Aloud she said, "There is no danger of that, I fear. He and I are at loggerheads more than we are not."

"That matters very little, my dear," Violet replied, her look of amusement reminding Cecily that for all her own scholarly knowledge, her stepmother was far more advanced in the study of the heart. "I have known many a happy match to be made between couples who started out with nothing but quarrels."

"But that makes no sense," Cecily objected. "What is there about quarreling that speaks of love?"

"Oh, it's not the quarrels that bring them together," Violet said with a knowing grin. "It's the making up."

The next morning, Cecily was scanning the social columns of the papers for any rumors hinting of her continued friendship with Winterson, and was dismayed to see there was an allusion to the so-called Egyptian Curse that was alleged to have stricken not only Lord Hurston, but also William Dalton.

This reporter has seen the noble Duke of W——— and the lately fashionable Miss H——— together on more than one occasion. It would appear that the curse affecting the members of a recent trip to the Dark Continent has done little to dampen the budding romance between these two. Let us hope that they continue to elude the dark forces at work here. It would be a shame if either His Grace or his little miss were to have something dire befall either of them—as has clearly happened to both their exploring family members.

Cecily stifled a very naughty expletive indeed as she finished reading the insinuations. Not only had the blackguard brought up the nonsensical curse, he had also connected her father and William Dalton to it. She only hoped that Winterson's mama and his sister-in-law did not stumble upon the column. She would do her best to see to it that Violet was not exposed to it, either. Seeing it in print would only further cement her concern.

Having lost her appetite, Cecily pushed her half-full plate of breakfast back and prepared to rise from the table when a footman appeared in the doorway.

"Miss Hurston," he said, "this letter was just delivered for you."

Cecily took the missive from him and broke open the seal. A key fell from the folded paper, and a hastily scrawled note within explained its purpose.

To the Egyptian Club. Use it to find what you need.

Eight

*W*hy must you force me to suffer along with you?" Monteith complained as he followed Lucas out onto the terrace of Lady Mulsington's house.

"Because you need a bit of culture in your life, my friend," was Lucas's heartless reply. "If it were up to you, you'd spend your days in nothing but sporting pursuits and gambling away your inheritance. At least when I request your company at these damnable social gatherings you get to chat with someone besides pugilists and croupiers."

"I happen to enjoy conversation with pugilists and croupiers, old son. And what's more, you did too once upon a time yourself." He took a glass of champagne from a passing footman. "I believe your little arrangement with Miss Hurston threatens to make you forget just who your friends are."

Lucas rolled his eyes, taking a sip from his own champagne while he scanned the throng of partygoers for his Amazon. Their association had thus far led to more clues to his brother's fate than he had gathered on his own before their chance meeting in front of the Egyptian Club. If they raised expectations among polite society for a match between them, that would be put to rest just as soon as she chose one or another of the imbeciles from the list burning a hole in his pocket. His animosity toward those men he put down to a dislike of seeing such an intelligent lady saddled for life to her intellectual inferior. It certainly had nothing to do with their kiss in the park. At least, that's what he told himself. "I am well and truly aware of whom I may count as friend," he said to Monteith, turning his thoughts back to his present company. "But even you must admit that Miss Hurston is much more pleasing to the eye than Gentleman Jackson ever was."

Monteith choked on his drink. "Thank you for providing me with the distressing portrait of Jackson in a gown," he wheezed once the coughing fit had passed. "I will never witness him planting a facer in the same way again."

"Glad to be of use," Lucas said, hiding a grin.

He drained his glass and handed it to his friend. "Now, I must leave you and search out my befrocked nemesis."

"You cannot mean to leave me here! What if I am accosted by a wandering band of marriage-minded mamas? You cannot be so cruel!"

"I can indeed," Lucas said, giving Monteith a hearty cuff on the shoulder. "There comes a time in every man's life when he must strike out on his own. Now is that time. Besides, you might find yourself in need of a wife one of these days."

"Shhh! Do not let them hear you say it! They have very sensitive hearing when they are on the hunt for a mate!"

Leaving his friend to face his fate, Lucas wended his way through the attendees, keeping his gaze open for Cecily's dark curls.

He was apologizing to an older lady for stepping on her gown, when another woman plowed right into him. Looking down, he recognized Lady Violet Hurston, Cecily's stepmama.

"Your Grace!" she said, her lovely expression oddly cool. "Just the person I was hoping to see. You will escort me to the punch bowl."

It was a command, not an invitation, and Lucas felt a slight prickle on the back of his neck.

Still, he offered his arm, and together they made their way to the table where a footman presided over the beverages. The line was extended, and one look at his compan-

ion's expression was enough to inform Lucas that she had no
wish for punch.

"Over here," she said, leading him to a rose arbor with a
small bench. She did not sit down, but made as if to look at
the roses, turning her back slightly to him.

"I will be brief since I do not wish to add to the talk already surrounding your association with my stepdaughter,"
she said, her tone brisk, like a nanny informing her charge
of the rules of the house. "It has not escaped my notice that
you have shown a marked partiality for my Cecily."

He opened his mouth to defend himself, but she silenced
him with a raised hand. "I know that you two are searching
for the cause of your brother's disappearance. I speak instead
of the way your gaze follows her when you are in a room
together. The manner in which you speak to her, as if she
were the only lady you can see."

As she did not appear willing to give him a say, Lucas
simply nodded.

"You are hopeful of finding out news regarding your
brother. I do not doubt that. But I know the ways of men,
Your Grace. And I do not doubt that you have an attraction
for Cecily that goes beyond an appreciation for her reason-
ing skills. She has never been particularly concerned about
her looks or lack thereof, but I believe beneath her bluster
she cares very much what others think. She has already had
her heart broken once before and I will not allow that to
happen to her again. Her father may be incapable of defend-
ing her honor, sir, but I am not."

Lucas was silent. That he was attracted to Cecily went
without saying. As a gentleman he had never intended to act
upon that attraction, however, and to be accused of nefarious
intent with regard to her person would have been, in a man,
an offense worth dueling over. He suspected that Lady Hurston knew this all too well and was taking advantage of her
sex and her husband's illness to say her mind without fear of
retribution.

But more enlightening was her divulgence that Cecily
had once suffered a heartbreak. It was foolish to believe that

a woman would reach her age without some entanglement of the heart, of course, but he wished to hunt down the bastard who had broken her heart and thrash him soundly, anyway.

Aloud, he said in a dry tone, "I am pleased to know that my heart is such an open book, my lady. I shall stop playing cards immediately so as to save myself the distress of costing my partners every hand."

"Do not play the bored aristocrat with me, Your Grace," she said tartly. "I know very well that you were not born to wear the coronet and I admire you for it. You have handled it much better than David Lawrence would have done if he'd been in the same situation. A career in the army does much to mold a man into something of worth. If I thought you were just another fool with a title I would simply have warned Cecily away from you and that would have ended it."

Lucas filed away the name David Lawrence for further investigation later. Now, with Lady Hurston pinning him in place with her gaze, reminding Lucas of his most exacting tutor at Eton, he was forced to keep his thoughts on the matter at hand.

"But it's because you are who you are that she is in danger from you," she went on. "You are just the blend of charming and clever that is irresistible to a young woman like her. She is able to dismiss fortune hunters and raffish young bucks out of hand, but you, sir, I do not mind telling you that you are dangerous! Add in your noble quest to find your missing brother and you are damned near impossible to resist."

"Are you actually suggesting that I am using my brother's disappearance as a means to seduce your stepdaughter, my lady?" he demanded with a frown.

"No, of course not!" Lady Hurston's eyes widened in chagrin. "What I am trying to do . . . and am doubtless making a mull of it . . . is to ask your intentions. For I will tell you in no uncertain terms, should you in the course of your association with my stepdaughter compromise her reputation in any way, you will pay for it with your hand."

Weary of being raked over the coals for something of which he was not guilty, Lucas finally snapped, "Ma'am,

I must beg leave to tell you that if you were a man I would have called you out by now. Your stepdaughter is of age and, as I daresay she has already told you, perfectly capable of taking care of herself. But lest you fear that I am not a gentleman, which I will add I have never given you cause to suspect, rest assured that if, in the course of our acquaintance, Miss Hurston is compromised by me in any way, I will make up for that fact by marrying her out of hand."

Rather than being cowed by his show of temper, however, Lady Hurston laughed.

Lucas felt a headache coming on.

"There now," she said cryptically. "That was not so hard, was it? I knew Amelia Snowe was lying about you!"

Before he could reply, however, Cecily appeared at their side.

"Whatever are the two of you discussing?" Cecily asked, looking curiously from one to the other. "It cannot have been very pleasant, for Winterson looks in need of a tooth drawer."

Lady Hurston patted Cecily affectionately on the arm. "Oh, nothing of import. I'll leave you to cheer him up, dearest. I see Lady Ellis is here and I must ask her where she found that delightful hat she was wearing yesterday."

Cecily watched her stepmama walk away with bemusement. Was she not the woman who had warned her only yesterday that she must guard her reputation by spending less time with Winterson? Either Violet was much more featherbrained than Cecily had imagined, or she had some plot to throw Cecily and Winterson together in the hopes that they would make a match. She was inclined to believe the latter since her stepmother seemed to think that Cecily's sartorial transformation would lead her straight from the wallflower seats to wedded bliss.

She stole a look at Winterson, who did look rather splendid today in a bottle-green coat that fit his broad shoulders to an inch. Still, she had no intention of allowing herself to fall under the spell of any gentleman, much less one who could not give her what she needed—access to her father's journals. Which led her back to their plan.

"Have you made any progress on the list of possible candidates for my hand?" she asked, careful to keep her expression neutral, as if they were discussing something unobjectionable like the weather.

Unfazed by her direct question, Winterson shrugged. "It takes time to assess the various assets and deficits of the numerous candidates."

"Yes," she said, trying to keep her temper, though his lack of initiative bothered her. "But surely you have had time to come up with a preliminary slate of possibilities. Were you not the one who claimed to know more than I could because you are a gentleman? If you continue to shirk your duty, I shall be forced to rely on the dance card!"

"I did not misrepresent myself," Lucas began before her words brought him up short. "What dance card?"

Realizing what she'd said, Cecily inwardly cursed in five languages. "Nothing, Your Grace. Nothing that need concern you," she said hurriedly. "We were speaking of you and your obligation to me."

But he'd obviously noted her discomfort and pressed on. "That won't work, Cecily," he said firmly. "Tell me about this dance card."

She knew she owed him no explanation, but Cecily said in a low voice, "I found Amelia Snowe's dance card at the Bewle ball, if you must know. And it has been signed mostly by members of the Egyptian Club. Single ones."

His eyes narrowed. "So you've been using Miss Snowe's dance card under false pretenses?"

"Keep your voice down," she hissed. "I don't want everyone in the *ton* to know about it!"

"I should think not," he said, lowering his voice. His eyes narrowed. "So you've been pressing me to investigate these men *and* using this pilfered dance card? Miss Hurston, you have a more deceptive nature than I had guessed."

"It's because I am desperate," she said sharply. "If your father were being accused of murder, I have little doubt you'd do whatever it took to see his name cleared. I do not understand how you can be so patient given that we need those notebooks to learn more about your brother's disappearance."

"I did not say that I do not have a list, nor that I blame you for using the dance card—Miss Snowe is hardly my favorite person," he said, clearly unperturbed by her agitation. "But it may not be necessary for you to sacrifice yourself upon the altar of matrimony in order to procure your father's journals. There may be another way to obtain them."

She did not bother alerting him to the fact that she might be sacrificed upon the altar of matrimony regardless. As the days passed with no marked improvement in her father's condition, it seemed more and more likely that she would be forced to marry in order to remove herself from Cousin Rufus's meddlesome care. A husband of her own choosing—even if he turned out to be a not-quite-appealing one—would be far preferable to one Rufus chose for her. But she was shy of telling Winterson any of this. He was worried about his brother, and she did not wish for him to do something noble like offer to marry her himself. Something about the idea of him marrying her for duty made her stomach ache.

"What do you mean 'another way'?" she asked, unwilling to mention the key until she heard his plan.

Taking her arm, Winterson moved them away from the arbor, following the picturesque path that wound about the perimeter of the Mulsington gardens. Though they were not the only couple taking advantage of the privacy afforded by the trees, there was chatter enough to keep their conversation from being overheard, and company enough for them to remain perfectly respectable.

"I mean a way to get your father's journals that will not trap you in marriage with a member of the club that very well may have had something to do with my brother's disappearance."

"There is no way. We've been through this, and short of outright theft—of the notebooks, I mean—I cannot imagine what plan you might have to breach their defenses and retrieve the journals."

"Yes," Winterson said, nodding at her with approval. "You've hit on it."

She stopped, pulling him to a halt beside her.

"Theft?" she asked in a high-pitched voice. "You mean to *steal* them?"

"It worked for you with the dance card," he said with a raised brow.

"But I found the dance card. I didn't actually set out to take it," she argued, thinking of a myriad of reasons why the idea had no merit. It was ludicrous to imagine a peer of the realm, a duke, no less, stooping to outright thievery. She thought of that key sent to her by some unknown benefactor. The notion of using the key to get into the club after hours had occurred to her before, of course. Sneaking into the Egyptian Club alone had seemed like more adventure than she could manage on her own. With a partner, however . . .

"It's the only way," he said simply. "I cannot allow you to marry on the off chance that your husband may be so good as to allow you into the club. What if he disapproves of scholarly females? What if he takes you to live at his country estate, never to return to London again? It's a ridiculous plan and I will not be a party to it."

"Well, you did not think so before! Else why would you have even considered helping me?" She thought again of Cousin Rufus and the life she might be forced to endure should her father succumb to his illness. If she did not marry soon, she might lose any opportunity to make a choice on her own terms.

"I was humoring you," he said baldly. "And now that I've discovered another way to get the journals, it's entirely unnecessary."

He paused. She kept her expression bland, but inside she struggled to decide what to do next. What would she do without his assistance? She had gained a sort of popularity in the past few days, thanks to the dance card, but nothing like what she needed to attract a real suitor. And his earlier revelations about the proclivities of certain gentlemen she

had considered as possible husbands before had convinced
her that there was quite a bit that even Violet did not know
about what men got up to when left to their own devices.

"Tell me what you are thinking," Winterson demanded,
his blue eyes searching. "I thought you'd be pleased."

"Oh," she said, making a determined effort to steady her
features. "I am quite pleased to hear you've found another
way. I simply . . ." She searched for an excuse for her chagrin. "I do not like the idea of you risking your own reputation," she finished lamely.

He waved off her worries, and looked relieved that she
did not appear to have any other objections.

"I have found that there's actually very little a duke can
do to truly damage his reputation. I'm afraid you ladies have
a great deal more to worry about on that front." He cleared
his throat. "Which is why you are to have nothing to do with
this new plan of mine to retrieve the journals."

She'd been afraid he'd do something like this. "I will not
allow you to take over this endeavor," she hissed. "The journals belong to my papa, after all. And without me to translate them, they'll simply be gibberish to you! Or have you
found someone else to do the translation as well?"

"Do not fly into the boughs, Miss Hurston," Winterson replied mildly. "I am not proposing to cut you out of the investigation. I simply do not wish for you to risk your already—let's
be honest here—shaky reputation by breaking into the Egyptian Club with me. As soon as I have them I will bring them to
you at once."

Cecily pulled her arm out of his and faced him. "No."

"What do you mean, 'no'?" he asked, tilting his head in
puzzlement.

"Just what I said," she said, arms akimbo. "I do not choose
to let you take all the risk."

"Miss Hurston," Winterson said, his face a study in patience, "I cannot, as a gentleman, let you risk your person in
this way. I will simply nip into the Egyptian Club one evening, retrieve the notebooks, and then nip out again. The

next morning I will promptly deliver them to you and allow you to use your language skills to decode them. Nothing could be simpler."

"Yes." She nodded. "It will be quite simple, only I will accompany you."

"No you will not."

"Yes I will."

"No you will not."

"Yes I—"

He pressed a finger to her lips, surprising them both. Even gloved, his touch had the power to make her pulse race. And his darkening eyes, intent upon her mouth, sent a throb of awareness straight to her belly.

"I fear there is an echo," he said at last, drawing his finger across the sensitive skin of her mouth. "Let us stop this bickering and talk sense."

When she did not argue, he dropped his hand, though it was clear they had both been rattled by the jolt of attraction between them.

"I do appreciate that you wish to go inside the Egyptian Club," Lucas continued. "Believe me, I do. I promise to take note of every last detail, from the carpets on the floor to the décor on the ceiling."

"I believe you have forgotten one key thing, Your Grace," Cecily said, desperately trying to dispel the lingering sensuality.

"And what is that?" His slight smile revealed he was well aware of her discomfort.

She lifted her chin in defiance. "You have no idea what my father's journals look like."

"No, that is true, I do not." He nodded to acknowledge the point.

"And without that knowledge you will have no notion of just which—of what I can only assume is an extensive library of texts—books you seek."

"But you will tell me," he said quietly. "Won't you."

It was not a question, and Cecily felt the beginnings of a

blush creep into her cheeks. Lucas stepped forward, his height putting her at a disadvantage to which she was unaccustomed.

"Won't you," he repeated.

"I will not," she said, schooling her features to give no hint of how his nearness affected her. "You will take me with you."

"I will not," he said, parroting her. "So, it would appear that we are at an impasse."

"Not if you would simply agree to let me accompany you," she said, turning her persuasive powers, such as they were, on him. She lowered her voice, though no one seemed particularly interested in what they were saying. "I may even be able to obtain a key."

Lucas felt his resolve wavering. It would be a damned sight easier to get into the club if they had a key. He had been forced upon occasion in his military career to use various methods of skullduggery. He could, in fact, pick a lock with a great deal of success in most cases. However, the vulnerability in Cecily's eyes, coupled with her sensible assertion that he did not know what her father's journals looked like, served to tip the balance slightly in her favor. In addition, now that he considered it, even if he were familiar with the general appearance of said journals, he could not—being unfamiliar with her father's secret language—be certain that he could read the bloody things to make certain that he was taking the right ones!

"Tell me more about this key," he said, deciding to give her a chance to plead her case.

Her answering smile hit him like a right hook to the jaw. He'd better keep his wits about him in her company, he thought, stepping back and tucking her hand back into the crook of his arm. Too many more smiles like that and he'd find himself making a public spectacle of them both, which would do neither of them any good if they planned to become thieves in the night.

Nine

I cannot believe I allowed you to talk me into this," Lucas hissed as he followed Cecily into the basement entrance of the building that housed the Egyptian Club.

It was madness enough that he'd agreed to her ridiculous scheme to dress as a boy—the view of her backside in a pair of his worn breeches alone was enough to fever his blood— but that he had allowed her to accompany him was an indication of just how susceptible he was to a pair of beseeching blue eyes.

For two and thirty years he had toed the line. When his peers had gotten up to mischief in school, Lucas had been the one to dissuade them from taking things too far. When his brother had hit upon the capital idea for them to romance a pair of barmaids who were unfortunately possessed of two brothers with quick tempers and quicker fists, Lucas had been the one to smooth things over before anyone suffered any broken limbs. But for some untold reason, when faced with the pleading eyes and quivering lip of one Miss Cecily Hurston, the man who had previously been capable of talking himself out of any scrape turned to complete and utter blancmange. His heretofore iron backbone swayed like a windblown poplar tree.

No matter how many times he reminded himself that she might be the daughter of his brother's murderer, some part of him always seemed to give her the benefit of the doubt.

Maybe because she seemed just as determined as he was to find out the truth of what had happened to Will. Even if it meant learning that her own father was responsible in some way. For all her stubbornness and determination, he sensed that she was constitutionally incapable of covering up the truth. Perhaps it was because as a scholar, she had made it her mission to tell the truth. Whatever the case, he trusted her. And it was about more than just beauty.

She *was* beautiful. Not in the classic sense of beauty as her exquisite stepmother and her equally captivating Featherstone sisters, mind you, but in a subtler, more sophisticated manner. For it was not just her figure alone, though it certainly could entice the male gaze, but her mind that lured him. And while it was possible to control a woman's body for a short period of time, he was damned if he knew how to capture her mind.

Not that he would wish to control either her body or her mind, he reminded himself. One of the things that made both so enticing was the knowledge that either could surprise him at any moment. From the feeling of her long, nimble fingers playing along his jawline to the quicksilver turns that steered her every thought, being with Cecily was a constant struggle to keep up. And he liked it that way. To control either her mental or physical presence would be as cruel a deed as caging a lion meant to roam the wild.

However, he had to figure out a way to keep himself from turning into a babbling fool in her presence. For both their sakes. Until this issue with William was resolved, he could do nothing about the growing attraction between them. And if her continued push for his assessment of possible suitors was anything to go by, she was just as determined as he was to keep whatever it was between them on a strictly friendly basis.

Still, every time he attempted to inform his libido of the fact, he was met with stubborn disagreement. He was afraid his body cared little for convenience or the gentleman's code.

"Come on," Cecily hissed from inside the darkened cellar. "What is taking you so long?"

"Nothing," Lucas returned morosely, grateful that the dim lighting of the club would protect him from the view of her in those damned breeches. "Where are you?"

"Here," came her reply, closer than he'd supposed. As he stepped toward her voice, he smelled her clean rose-water scent, and followed it.

"The stairs are this way," she said, waiting for him to catch up.

When he reached her, she slipped her hand into his. "This is strictly for safety's sake," she warned him. Though he could not read her expression in the dark, he suspected that she'd adopted what he thought of as her "high priestess" look. It was the way she always looked when she did not wish to hear argument.

He made a noise of assent, though he could not help but enjoy the feeling of her soft hand in his. Silently, he followed along behind her toward the shadowy staircase. The full moon gave a slight glow of light through the window at the base of the stairs, though the farther they moved up the stairs the darker it got.

Lucas carried a candle and flint in the pocket of his coat, but they had both agreed not to use the light until absolutely necessary, neither of them wishing to alert the watch to their presence in the supposedly empty building.

They moved in eerie silence to the top of the stairs and into the main hallway on the ground floor. "I believe we are nearing the door to the club," he said as they passed first one then another door to the other organizations that took rooms in the building.

Finally, at the third entrance, they stopped, and when he tried the door handle, Lucas was not surprised to find it locked. Without a word, Cecily handed him the key she'd used to open the cellar door. Though she'd kept secret the means she'd used to obtain it, Lucas was grateful that she'd chosen to share the acquisition with him, rather than attempting to enter the building after hours herself. He dreaded to think what sort of mischief she might have gotten into on her own.

"My lady," he whispered, motioning her into the dark rooms.

Once inside, he removed the candle and worked the flint until he was able to light the wick. The candlelight flickered over Cecily's face, her dark eyes appearing even larger as she looked round the crowded rooms.

She had seen countless Egyptian relics in her father's house, of course. But the artifacts that had been so fascinating to her in the daylight now seemed to exude menace and foreboding. A death mask that had been recovered from the tomb of a minor prince hung on the wall, the jewels embedded in the eyes flickering eerily at her.

"I believe the library is this way," Lucas said, taking her hand in his. This time Cecily was glad to feel his strong clasp, though she would have preferred the strong clasp of her father's dueling pistol instead.

"How do you know where everything is?" she asked him, curious despite the flutters that ran down her spine. "I supposed you had never actually been here."

"I haven't," he returned. "But a friend gave me a diagram of how the rooms and artifacts are laid out."

"What friend?" Cecily demanded.

"I will tell you if you tell me where you got the key," he returned, with a smile in his voice. At her huff of annoyance, he nodded. "I thought not. Let us simply agree that there are some things best kept to ourselves."

"You are sneakier than I gave you credit for," she said finally.

"I am smarter than you gave me credit for too."

"I've never said you were unintelligent," she said a bit defensively. "One of the first things that impressed me about you was your wit. And one must have a certain level of mental acumen to run a ducal estate. Or so I am told."

She disliked the idea that he thought she found him stupid. Though, in all truth, she had met a number of people in her lifetime who might be described thus, but he was not one of them. She was unable to consider the matter further, however, because he pulled her along behind him.

"Come on," he said, moving forward, then stopping before a doorway and opening it. "Here, I believe, is where we need to be."

Cecily stepped forward into the interior and waited for him to follow with the candle. When he stepped forward the light did come with him, but as he moved ahead, her heart stopped and she gave a little scream.

For not three feet away, the light revealed the figure of a man.

Cecily's yelp of fear turned into a groan as she realized what she'd seen was not a man, but a sarcophagus tilted against the far wall.

"Fortunate that our friend there no longer has working ears," he said dryly.

"Sorry, I thought it was real."

"No matter," Lucas said, shaking his head. Taking the candle with him, he moved to the first row of bookshelves just inside the door. "Better stay close to me, though. It's not safe to wander through this room with no light to guide you. There are several displays of weaponry that could cause serious damage if you were to stumble into them."

Cecily fought a shiver. The enveloping darkness of the room, which was on the interior of the building and therefore had no windows to let the moonlight in, was disturbing to her on a primitive level. It wasn't that she'd never been in a darkened room. Of course everyone had been at one time or another. But the pitch-blackness coupled with the knowledge that the artifacts and manuscripts housed in this room held the secrets of multitudes of long-dead pharaohs and slaves and scribes imbued the dark with a sinister, portentous air that played havoc with her rattled nerves.

Moving closer to Lucas's side, she gazed at the rows of bound manuscripts and attempted to determine the organization principle used to shelve them.

"Alphabetical by author," she said firmly, comforted by the familiar task.

Lucas said nothing, obviously content to let her lead this task.

"Which should put Papa's journals—" Cecily stopped midway through the shelves to the left of the door. "Here," she said triumphantly, running a finger down the shelves to follow the names.

"Horner, Horton, Howington, Hulme, Hume, Hunter . . ." She stopped, puzzled. "Hussey?"

"What's wrong?" Lucas asked.

"They aren't here," she said with a frown. "Perhaps they've just been shelved out of place."

But when they began again and looked at every shelf, every row, they came to the same conclusion. Lord Hurston's journals were not on these shelves.

"How long has it been since the journals were taken from Hurston House to the club, exactly?" Lucas asked, crouched near the floor as he placed a manuscript back on the last shelf.

"Two months," Cecily answered, holding the candle closer to the shelf where her father's journals should have been. "Certainly more than enough time to add them to the collection. Though we really have no way of knowing what their process is for such things. Perhaps they are being examined by an expert of some sort?"

"Perhaps," said Lucas, coming to stand beside her. Together they looked at the shelf that should have housed the missing journals. As if staring at it long enough would conjure the books from thin air.

"Cecily, what is different about this shelf?" he finally asked, gesturing to the offending bookshelf. "Look at the others and then back at this one. What do you see that's out of place? Besides your father's books, I mean."

She stepped back, surveyed row after row of oddly sized bindings. Some were leather-bound, some simply sheaves of paper fastened together between thin boards and tied with string. But what made her father's shelf different was not the items on the shelf, but the missing items. Or rather the place where the missing items should have been. Every other row was filled from one side to the other with books, manuscripts, and so on. Only her father's row had a gap between the last book and the right side.

"The gap," she said finally. "At the end, where Papa's journals should have been."

"Exactly," Lucas said grimly. "So we know that your father's books were there at one time. Which means we know they were here, in this room. But there's something else about this shelf. Notice this bit of ornamental woodwork," he said, pointing to a decorative cornice at the corner of the shelf.

Every corner was decorated with an intricately crafted scarab beetle. All but one. Because there at the top edge of the Hurston shelf was carved, just as intricately crafted, an alligator, its snout and tail protruding from the cornice like tiny handholds.

Cecily stood on her toes to touch the alligator tail, but before Lucas could caution or catch her, she lost her balance and instinctively grabbed hold of the thing, pulling it down with an audible click. And to their great surprise, the shelf at the end of the row swung silently open, like a very wide, very heavy door.

"How did you know?" Cecily asked, looking from the darkened doorway to her partner in crime.

"I didn't know precisely what the alligator signified, of course, but we've got a priest's hole at Winterhaven with a lock triggered in a similar fashion. It's much more subtle than this one, however," Lucas replied. "If we were to see this room in daylight I feel sure the alligator would catch our attention at once. And if you are really aiming to hide something, the cleverest method is to place it in plain sight."

"So you don't think Father's journals are in here?" Cecily asked, peering into the darkened passage beyond the door.

"Oh, I didn't say that," Lucas said, gesturing her behind him as he began to descend the narrow stairway behind the shelves. "In fact," he said, his voice echoing to reach her as she followed behind him, "I wouldn't be at all surprised if we found the journals and many other valuable items down here. Whoever built this room had a distinctive flair for the dramatic. And what could be more theatrical than hiding one's most precious possessions in a secret room?"

Ten

*W*hat they found at the foot of the stairs was a long hallway that echoed the one on the floor above. There were three doors to the right and three doors to the left, and between each of the doors was placed a wall sconce holding an unlit torch.

Cecily asked if they shouldn't light the sconces so that they could see their surroundings more fully, but Lucas was not convinced that they would remain undiscovered, so in the end, the torches remained unlit.

"This is just a storage room, I think," said Lucas as he peered into the first door on the left, Cecily standing close behind him. He raised the candle to illuminate the interior, but all it revealed were neat rows of wooden crates, which upon further inspection contained nothing more noteworthy than unglazed pottery that Cecily pronounced of recent origin, and various other imported goods, none of them particularly valuable.

"I suppose someone brought these back from an expedition. It's typical for a traveler to purchase cheap goods to bring back as gifts for friends and relatives. Or to sell to London merchants. Especially with the current craze for all things Egyptian," Cecily noted. "Which is rather frustrating for actual scholars, of course, because it allows charlatans to pass off cheaply made modern goods as ancient artifacts."

"One would hope the members of the Egyptian Club would be above such schemes," Lucas said wryly.

"Indeed," she returned. "Though even true scholars are prone to exaggeration from time to time. Papa once complained about an acquaintance who attempted to pass off a shard of pottery from a broken bowl he'd purchased from a costermonger as the remains of an Egyptian water jug from the time of Ramses the Second. I believe in this case the fraud was caught out, but it's difficult for people who haven't spent their formative years engrossed in all things Egyptian."

"Like you?" he asked, with a raised brow.

"Precisely like me," she said with a frown "Though I suppose I did spend some of my formative years engaged in other pastimes. Such as learning to paint watercolors badly and to stitch a very uneven row indeed."

"I can't stitch worth a damn either." Lucas shrugged.

Cecily couldn't help herself. She laughed. There was something about his deadpan drollery that brought out her appreciation of the absurd. "Then I shan't ask you to show me your watercolors anytime soon," she said wryly.

"Too bad," Lucas said with mock sadness. "I do have some etchings you might be interested in, however." They continued on from room to room in companionable silence after that, finding nothing more incriminating than a scandalous sketch of an ancient couple engaged in a very naughty act.

"I don't understand it," she said finally, having stared down at the image for several minutes.

"I suspect that's because you're holding it upside down," Lucas said wryly, his voice pitched low to prevent them from being heard.

"Oh, you," she said, dropping the paper onto a table as if it were made of fire. "I didn't mean the drawing. I don't understand why they would bother with all these hidden rooms and not put anything of real value in them. What's the point? We've already decided this person has a flair for the dramatic; why then no hidden treasure?"

"It's a good question," Lucas said, closing the door of the

fourth room behind them. "We haven't checked all of them, but the ones so far have been underwhelming to say the least. No treasure, no manuscripts, no books of any kind."

He gripped her hand in his and led her to the other side of the hallway so that they could search the remaining rooms. As they had stepped from room to room, Lucas became more and more aware of the fact that they were utterly and completely alone. How easy it would be to simply pull her against him and kiss her as he had wanted to do since their encounter in the park.

He wondered if she had thought at all about that kiss or if he was alone in thinking that there was something between them.

As he opened the second but last door, the scent of decay filled his nostrils, and as he lifted the candle higher he saw why.

"Mummies," Cecily said matter-of-factly as they stepped into the room and surveyed the shriveled, wrapped figure laid out on the table that dominated the room. "I wondered if they housed any. Especially given the sarcophagus upstairs."

She moved forward until she reached the other side of the table and saw an empty sarcophagus on the floor. She clasped her hands against her, rubbing her arms as if to ward off the chill of seeing the dead bodies.

"They are dead, Cecily," Lucas said, putting a comforting arm around her shoulder. "They can't hurt you."

"Oh, it's not that," she assured him. "I've been around artifacts and even a few mummies before. I was just imagining how awful it would be to get locked in a sarcophagus. I am not altogether comfortable with small spaces," she admitted. "Though the dark isn't among my favorite experiences, either."

"I should have known," he said with mock despair. "I am in a room full of mummies with the only lady in the world without any fear of them. I suppose I shall have to find some other small room to lure you into so that I may take advantage of your fear for my own licentious machinations."

No sooner were the words out of his mouth, however,

than they heard a decisive *snick* as the door to the crowded room swung shut and the resulting breeze snuffed out the candle.

"Very funny," Cecily said with a wry tone. "I suppose you tied the door to a string or some other nonsense to shut the door from over here? There is no hope for you, my lord. I have a veritable army of male cousins who enjoyed nothing better than trying to frighten me out of my wits when I was a child. Though I will admit that this trick is particularly impressive. Tell me how you managed it."

"Cecily," Lucas said as he fumbled in his pocket for the flint, his voice impressively steady as he realized what must have just happened. "I'm afraid I have some very bad news."

As he stepped away from her and reached for the doorknob, the tiny flicker of light he'd conjured with the flint grew stronger as it burned down the wick.

"Do not try to gammon me, Lucas," she said with an air of confidence in him that he wished were not so very misplaced. "I know you did it, now tell me how."

"I had nothing to do with it," he said emphatically as he turned the doorknob and met with only resistance. "And I am very much afraid that not only did I not shut the door, but it is now locked from the outside."

At her gasp, he stepped back to let her try the door herself. When she also was unable to open it, he bit back an oath.

"Now, you may scream all you like."

Eleven

*B*ut Cecily did not scream. That would have taken too much air, and from the moment she'd realized the door was shut she'd begun to feel a distinct loss of breath.

"I am not fond of enclosed spaces," she said carefully, trying in vain to resist the urge to raise her hand to her throat in a gesture of panic. Why was the simply tied cravat she'd donned as part of her boy's disguise suddenly so unbearably tight?

"Do not worry," Lucas said from his kneeling position before the door, "I only heard the click of the lock sliding into place, without the sound of the key being removed. If we are lucky, he left it in the lock."

"I'm not worried," Cecily said, hearing her voice as if it came from some other person in the room with them. The floor shifted beneath her feet and she grabbed onto the table, not wanting to jostle the mummy, but not really capable of controlling her movements, either.

Lucas must have heard her for he was suddenly at her back, easing her gently down into a sitting position on the floor.

"Easy," she heard him say. "I've got you. I won't let you fall."

And he didn't.

His strong arms supporting her, taking over for her, were at once comforting and stifling. Unable to stand under her own strength, however, she let herself go, and gave in to the shamefully comforting feeling of knowing that, for just this moment, someone else would be in charge. For just this whisper of a second, she would not have to carry the burden of self-sufficiency alone.

"There now," he said, easing to the carpeted floor next to her. "Just breathe. Maybe you'd better put your head down between your knees." His tones were soothing, as if he spoke to a skittish colt or a frightened child. But instead of being insulted by his condescension, she simply fought to do as he asked. She ignored the indignity of the position he suggested and followed his suggestion, drawing her knees up before her and leaning forward to place her head between them, feeling his surprisingly gentle hand move in even strokes over her back.

"Would you like to talk about it?" he asked, finally allowing her to raise her head and lean back against the pedestal of the long table. "I assume there is a reason why you turn pale at the thought of being locked in a small room with such a handsome fellow?"

Still ill at ease, though thankfully not as panicked as she had been, Cecily scoffed. "You hold as high an opinion of yourself as ever, I see?"

"I was speaking of him," Lucas returned, gesturing up at the mummy. Cecily could barely see his expression, but she knew his raised brow meant he was joking.

"Of course you were," she returned, rolling her eyes, though the jest had produced the desired effect, breaking the air of seriousness that had invaded the room at her collapse.

She was quiet, thinking back over the shadowy memories of her childhood.

"Surely it can't be so dreadful," he said, reaching out toward her hand, but evidently changing his mind at the last minute, as he simply tucked a wayward strand of hair behind her ear.

"No," Cecily returned. "Or, rather, I'm not entirely sure. I have been fearful of close quarters since I was a child and I've never really been able to understand what happened to cause it. I know my mother was there—though I do not know in what capacity—and I remember crying for my favorite doll and having her bring it to me. I do remember a box of some sort and Mama telling me it was a game. But when I wanted to get out she wouldn't let me. She told me that I must be very quiet. But I wanted out."

She could feel the beads of sweat gathering on her brow as she remembered the incident. But it was impossible to know what parts she truly remembered and what parts she had fabricated in her imagination in the years that followed as a way to explain what had truly happened.

"Were you in danger?" Lucas asked, his voice neutral. "Did you get that sense from her?"

"I do not know," she answered truthfully. "The memories are so faded now. It's almost as if the only thing left is this illogical fear. Obviously I did not suffer for it. I am here to tell the tale, after all," she said.

"You do suffer," he said harshly. "Every time that terror grips you, you suffer. Even if, as you say, it does not happen very often."

She supposed he was right, though having him here with her alleviated her nervousness in a way that she could not explain. It was as if suddenly being greeted by a loved one after a long journey. The sense of relief and belonging was inexplicable, really. Certainly there was no logical reason her fear should lessen because he was with her. Having others around had never mattered before, and certainly she'd never been talked down in such a calm, efficient manner. In the past everyone had either become upset for her, or become upset themselves because her plight made them notice something that had not bothered them before.

But she would tell him none of this. Bad enough that she should have lost her composure in his presence, no matter how out of control her response had been. Informing him that his very presence in the tiny room with her had calmed her in some way would perhaps give him a hint of the power he had over her. And she was not ready to admit that any man, let alone this one, could possibly affect her in such a way.

Aloud she said, "Yes, I suppose I do suffer, a bit. But I am righted again soon enough. And I certainly do not endure any lasting effects. Certainly nothing like the limp you carried with you from the war."

"Nicely done," he said in a wry tone, referring to the way she had turned the subject from herself to him. "Only I am well aware that not all wounds have lasting *physical* effects."

"What do you mean?" she asked warily, worried that in some way she was about to be hoist by her own petard.

"Just that my leg injury was the least of my wounds when I returned to England from Waterloo," he said. "There are any number of ways that war changes a man, and not all of them can be seen on his person. In the same way that you dislike enclosed spaces, I dislike crowds. Neither of these symptoms are evident in our persons. I cannot look at you and know you become faint in small rooms. And you cannot look at me and know I would rather walk over hot coals than attend a crush in an overheated assembly room. But the wounds are there all the same."

Cecily was silent for a moment. Then said, "Can you really not stand a crush, Your Grace?"

"I cannot," he responded, reaching for her hand, which she gave to him willingly. "It's nothing to be ashamed of, you know," he said gently. "We all have flaws and weaknesses."

"Yes," she said, "but not all weaknesses keep one from doing their life's work. Even if Papa would have allowed it, I couldn't bear to go on an expedition because I'd never be able to enter the tombs. Or forget the tombs, I'd not be able to endure the closeness of the journey by sea."

It was the first time she'd ever openly admitted the fact. Over the years it had become easier to lay the blame for her inability to travel on her father. But something about the privacy afforded them by the small room gave her the space she needed to admit the truth she'd been hiding from herself for so long.

"What a pair we are," Lucas said with a rueful shake of

his head. "You cannot go to Egypt, the one place in the world you wish to go. And I cannot go back to war, the one thing in the world I am trained for."

"Misery loves company, I suppose," Cecily said, with a lightness she did not feel.

"Speak for yourself, my dear," he said dryly. "I am far from miserable just now."

Cecily felt her breath quicken at his words. Truth be told, she was far from miserable at the moment too. There was something about the duke's company that made her feel . . . safe. And safety was something she'd not felt for a long, long time.

Feeling an urgent need to change the subject, Cecily asked, "How did it happen? Your leg injury, I mean?"

He was quiet for so long that she was forming an apology when he finally spoke.

"I know you've probably read newspaper accounts of Waterloo," he said quietly. "Or heard stories from people who were there. But nothing—no amount of description— can convey just how chaotic and dreadful it was. The closest thing to hell on earth I've ever seen. I won't go into detail because even I cannot bear to go back there, even if only in memory. But I received my injury when my horse—Malvolio, a solid cavalry horse who'd been with me through several battles—was shot out from under me. I was fighting off a Frenchman at the time, and had already been winged. My strength was waning, otherwise I wouldn't have been taken by surprise. But I was, and by the time Mal was on his way down it was too late. I didn't make it out of the stirrups in time and my leg was crushed and I was trapped."

Cecily bit back a cry, too shocked to stop herself from asking, "Surely you weren't trapped beneath him for long . . . ?" But she knew as soon as the words left her mouth what the answer would be.

"I'm not actually sure how long I lay there before Monteith found me," he said quietly, running a weary hand over his eyes. "The French took me for dead, thank God, else I'd have been run through where I lay. In any event, Mal saved my life. And Monteith was able to round up a couple of men with less serious wounds to get him off me.

"My leg may pain me some days," Lucas continued, "but there is never a day that goes by that I don't appreciate the sacrifice Malvolio made for me."

She couldn't help it. Cecily reached out and clasped Lucas's hand. "I am so glad you survived," she said, meaning it with all her heart. The idea of this vital man, so full of life, lying dead on a Belgian field was unthinkable.

"Me too," he said with a lopsided grin. "Now, I've answered your question, so it's time you answered one of mine."

Cecily frowned, but nodded in assent. Fair was fair, after all.

"Tell me about David Lawrence," Lucas said firmly.

She felt her frown deepen. "What about Mr. Lawrence?" she asked frostily.

"It's hardly a secret, is it?" he asked, seemingly oblivious to her annoyed tone. "You told me about him yourself. The announcement was posted in the *Times*."

Some of the rigidity left her spine. He was right, of course. Any number of people must remember her engagement. She had told him about it herself. Still, there was no reason for him to know the extent to which David had hurt her.

"What do you wish to know?" she asked, trying to sound less wary, and failing miserably.

Lucas's tone was easy. "Let's start with why you aren't married to the man."

"It's . . . complicated," Cecily said stiffly.

"I believe we have time," Lucas said with a wryness that would have brought a smile to her lips if she weren't so uncomfortable.

"All right," she said, trying to maintain an even tone. "If you must know, David had the bad taste to fall in love with someone else. Under the circumstances I released him from our engagement."

"Just like that?" he asked, his tone suspicious. "You make it sound exceedingly uncomplicated. And falling in love with someone else is hardly reason enough for an honorable man to break his engagement."

"Well, it was perhaps a bit more . . . dramatic than I let on," she admitted carefully. "He asked to be released from our engagement because the other lady . . . well, to put it bluntly, she was with child, and David had to marry her."

Lucas said a word that Cecily had never actually heard spoken aloud before.

"So, he broke off his engagement with you so he could marry his lover," he said bluntly. "Dare I hope that she was penniless and he married her out of true love?"

Cecily lifted her chin. "She was a wealthy heiress whose father is a board member of the British Museum, where David had been angling for a position for years," she admitted. "But I was hardly crushed to break things off with a man who cared so little for me that he would dangle after another woman while he courted me. In the end, I realized that he'd probably sought me out in an effort to gain favor with my father."

"I hope your father thrashed the bastard," Lucas said, sounding more bloodthirsty than Cecily had ever heard him.

"Hardly," Cecily said with a bitter laugh. "Papa thought, still thinks, the world of David. Though he did promise to expel him from the Egyptian Club, he never really followed through on the threat. And in his defense, David is a good connection to have in the world of Egyptology. The British Museum houses the foremost collection of Egyptian antiquities in England. Papa could hardly cut off so valuable a resource."

Lucas would have said more, Cecily was certain, but something made him stop. Perhaps her extreme discomfort.

He rose to his feet. "If you are sufficiently recovered, I will attempt once more to retrieve the key."

Cecily waved him onward. The sooner they were able to leave the tiny locked room the better. Standing, she moved closer to him, not wanting to remain in the darkened center of the chamber since he had taken the candle with him.

"Good," he said as she crept in next to him. "Hold the

light, please, so that I can see if the key is indeed in the lock."

She maneuvered the candle, supressing a gasp when he took her hand in his firm grasp and moved the light where he needed it to be.

"I think I see the key there. Hold still for a moment while I attempt to dislodge it."

He took the lock pick that he brought for just such an emergency, and maneuvered it this way and that until Cecily heard the satisfying jingle of metal on metal followed by the heavy thud as the key fell to the carpet on the other side of the heavy mahogany door.

"Got it," he said with a grin of satisfaction. "Now we need to find a way to retrieve it. What we need is something thin enough to fit beneath the door, but long enough that we will be able to keep hold of it without fear of losing our grip."

Lucas stood and, taking the candle from her, peered into the darkness, raising the light from shelf to shelf, surface to surface, looking for something that would suit his task. But nothing seemed to fit their purpose.

"Let me look at your hand," Lucas said, reaching out to grasp her fingers. He took her hand in his, ignoring the little zing of pleasure as he held her thin hand in his strong one.

"Will it fit?" she asked.

"I suppose we won't know until we try it," he said, motioning her onto the floor, and following her down.

Carefully Cecily lowered herself to the floor and experimentally tried to insert just her fingers into the narrow gap between the bottom of the door and the floor. Her fingers cleared the opening, so she pulled her hand back out, moved into a sitting position, then carefully lowered herself onto her stomach, stretching her legs out behind her.

"Do not try to force it," Lucas said, leaning so closely above her that she could feel his warm breath on her neck. It sent a shiver down her spine that had nothing whatsoever to do with fright. "We don't want you to be injured."

* * *

Lucas tried to keep his distance from her, but the space they occupied was simply too small. As he sat with one knee bent, his arm draped casually over his knee, for all the world like they were having a picnic or playing at spillikins, he fought the urge to caress the delectable rearview of the woman before him. If such medals were awarded, he mused silently, then he certainly deserved one for Most Restraint Under Pressure. For never had a man been so provoked as he had during this midnight escapade.

Biting back a groan as she wiggled her bottom as she tried to work her hand more fully beneath the door, Lucas asked, "Are you able to reach it?"

"Not quite," Cecily returned, not looking up from her task. "My middle finger barely brushes the edge of the key, but if I can just manage to fit a little more of my hand here, I think I could work it toward me."

As she worked, Lucas recited Latin conjugations in his head, trying with all his might to keep himself from falling on her like a starving man at the sight of a beef roast. He couldn't remember ever feeling this way about any other woman, let alone a headstrong virago with a flair for danger. It was so entirely out of character for him that Lucas briefly wondered if he were suffering from some sort of brain fever.

Deep in his heart, however, he knew that the only explanation had nothing to do with fevers and everything to do with his burgeoning affection for the woman laid out like a Christmas feast on the floor before him. It was at once thrilling and utterly, utterly terrifying.

"Pardon? My lo-ord?" The sound of her voice, singsong and insistent, broke into his thoughts. "I require your assistance, please."

"Right," he said casually, as if he'd been paying attention the entire time. "What do you need, Miss Hurston?"

She craned her head as far as she could, looking up at him from the corner of her eye.

"I need you to help me turn my body a bit so that I can reach farther. I've almost got it, but if I can gain another smidgeon of reach I think I'll be able to maneuver the key toward me."

When he did not answer immediately, she said quickly, "Never mind. I'll do it myself. I simply didn't want to remove my hand or I'd lose the little bit of ground I've already gained. But I can—"

"Don't . . ." he interrupted her, putting a staying hand on the small of her back. "Don't get up. I'll do it, I was just . . . er . . . trying to determine the most effective manner of . . . um . . . moving you."

He ran a finger under his suddenly too-tight collar and shook his head a little to bring his focus back to the matter at hand.

Moving to his knees, he realized with an inward groan that the most expedient means of moving her would entail him straddling her legs on his knees, then gripping her hips to lift and slide her into a position parallel with the door.

How the bloody, cursed, damned, fucking hell did I manage to get myself into this ridiculous situation?

His jaw clenched, and looking down at his companion, he said, "All right, I'm going to need to lean over you a bit."

Lean over her.

He rolled his eyes at the euphemism. What he was about to do was quite a bit more than leaning, though he was damned if he'd tell an unmarried lady to prepare to be covered. Which was technically what he would be doing. Minus the actual . . . covering.

Lifting his left leg, he brought it over to kneel on the floor on the outside of her right knee, and deciding to simply jump in, Lucas leaned forward and grasped her by the hips. Ignoring her gasp at his touch, he lifted her up and simultaneously moved on his knees toward the door on his left, and moved her in the same direction.

"There," he said, removing himself from his precarious position and leaping to his feet. "That should do it."

Cecily cleared her throat, not sure she'd be able to speak beyond a croak even if she wanted to. When she had felt his presence, his heat, leaning over her backside, she had found herself fighting the instinct to press her bottom upward to meet his groin. Imagined what it would feel like if he had abandoned all propriety and reached down and caressed her breasts from his position leaning over her.

Finally, willing herself to stop her thoughts and concentrate on the business at hand, she said in what she hoped was a normal tone, "Thank you, I believe that will do it."

She reached around under the door again, patting the floor in the hall outside, searching for the key. It had been there a moment ago.

"I'm sorry, Your Grace," she said at last. "But would you mind terribly bringing the light down here? I seem to have lost the key."

"Stop 'Your Gracing' me," he said irritably. "And how on earth am I to shine the light under the door without setting the carpet on fire?"

"All right, then, Lucas," she snapped. "Will you bring the candle down here? Just hold your hand behind the flame so that it doesn't touch the carpeting. It's not that difficult a concept."

"I understand the concept perfectly, Miss Hurston," he replied sweetly. "But it will mean having me lie on the floor beside you. Is that something you are comfortable with?"

"Call me Cecily," she said finally. "And just get down here. The sooner I find this key the sooner we can get out of this horrible room. I will need to wash my hair four times to get the stench of mummy out of it."

He could have told her that she smelled like roses, as she always did, but thought that would try her patience.

"Ready or not, here I come," he said, once more dropping to his knees, then stretching forward to brace himself on one arm and thrusting out his legs behind him to lie flat on his stomach. Turning his head toward Cecily, he found himself facing her hair.

"Here," he said, purposely speaking into her neck, sending the stray curls at her nape into a flutter. Holding the candle, he stretched his arm out over her back, and turned the candle sideways, careful not to touch the flame to the carpeted floor.

"Just a little to the right," she instructed, resuming her sweeping hand motions under the door. "There, I see it!"

Propping his head up on his right arm, Lucas watched as she stretched as far as she could to reach under the door.

"Almost there," she said, biting her lip. "Almost there . . ."

Lucas smiled in spite of the almost physical pain of being so close to her without being able to touch her. The look of concentration on her face was so intent. He thought she was more beautiful than he'd ever seen her.

"Got it!" she cried, removing her hand from under the door.

Scrambling to remove himself from his hovering position, Lucas was too late, and instead of being the one to step back, he found himself in the novel position of having a woman thrust herself into his arms as Cecily flipped over onto her back and moved into a sitting position within the circle of an awkward embrace.

"Oh," she said, the soft whisper of her exhalation touching his face like a caress.

The key forgotten in the surge of desire that coursed through him, Lucas saw her eyes darken as her gaze dropped to his mouth. He snuffed the candle, leaned forward, and took her mouth in a searing and possessive kiss.

When Lucas kissed her, the lights went out.

Or so it seemed to Cecily, who was overwhelmed by both. Though they had kissed before, there was an intensity to Lucas's embrace now—due, perhaps, to the darkness—that both excited and frightened her. For all of her vaunted independence and defiance of her father, Cecily was ultimately rather sheltered. In the past fortnight she had experienced her first waltz and her first kiss with any sort of passion in it. And now she was to experience her first seduction. She did not intend to miss a moment of it.

His mouth traveled from her lips to her ear, to an incredibly sensitive point just at the crook of her neck. The hot caress of his tongue there had her reflexively arching into him, her breath escaping in a moan of pleasure. On her knees, Cecily lifted herself higher, exposing the bare patch of skin just above her breastbone to his lips, her fingers impatiently working to unknot the cravat at her throat.

"Easy," Lucas murmured against her, the rumble of his deep voice reverberating through her. His busy hands worked to untuck her overlarge shirt, and caressed up her sides as he lifted it above her head, baring her upper body to his plundering mouth.

Shielded from view by the darkness, Cecily reveled in the freedom it afforded her. No longer required to play the role of scholar or wallflower or debutante, she was here, in this room, with this man, simply a woman, with a woman's need for a man's caress.

His strong hands grasped her by the hips even as his mouth sought and found the peak of her breast, sucking it to hardness as he settled her legs to straddle his lap. She felt the press of his erection against her most sensitive place, and instinctively rocked once, twice against him.

Lucas muttered an oath against her as he lifted his mouth to hers again, his hands working the placket of her breeches even as hers fumbled with his. In one swift movement, he lifted her slightly and whisked them down to her knees and coaxed her knees upward to take them off entirely. While he was undoing her breeches, she had been undoing his. He bit back a tortured groan as he felt her tentative hand on him. What was it about this woman that drove him to lose control? He had escaped his legendary sense of duty exactly two times in his life, and both had been with this woman. But even as he moved to the precipice of dishonor again, he could not help himself.

"This will be over far too quickly if you go on like that," he said, his voice rough. "Let's try this instead," he continued, taking her mouth again as he caressed her hip and thigh. Then, gently but firmly, he stroked his index finger over the moist heat at her center.

The shudder that jolted through her brought her breasts up against his chest, and her pelvis thrust her sweet spot against his hard length. *So much for alternative plans,* he thought wryly, even as he touched her core again, this time slipping his finger inside her. Her sharp intake of breath spurred him on, and on the second stroke he thrust two fingers, then three, as she rode his hand in desperation.

"I want . . ." she exhaled. "I want . . ."

"What?" he demanded, his voice foreign to his own ears. "What do you need, sweet Cecily? What is it you need?"

She rocked against his hand, moving closer to her release, he knew, because he felt the grasp of her inner muscles on his wet fingers.

"More," she panted. "Just. More."

Her breathless words were to his desire like brandy spilled on flames, the intensity of his need for her threatening to consume him in fiery heat. Lucas knew she would regret it if he gave her everything she demanded. As a virgin she could have no concept of what she asked of him. It would mean marriage at best, a ruined reputation at worst. Neither was a course he thought she'd accept easily.

But when he only continued to thrust his fingers into her, Cecily took matters into her own hands. Literally. When he felt her close her fingers around the erection he'd been trying so valiantly to save her from, he gave a startled hiss.

"Cecily," he said between gritted teeth, "you don't know what you're doing."

Not letting go of him, she leaned up to kiss him, still rocking against his fingers. "I want you, Lucas," she exhaled. "I know there is more. I've seen pictures. Artifacts. Please."

For a brief moment, he managed to hold back, but the combination of the darknesss, her touch, her smell, all of it obliterated his defenses, and almost without thought, he reached for the fall of his breeches and finished undoing the buttons, setting his aching cock free.

The feel of her moist opening against the tip of his erection and her soft thighs cradling his own was enough to make him doubt his ability to stop if she balked. Still, he would try his damnedest if she changed her mind. "This might hurt," he whispered against her throat, praying she wouldn't.

"Want you," she sighed, rocking against him, obliterating anything besides a desperate need to be inside her from his mind.

"Then have me," he said, pressing up against her, feeling the tight grasp of her envelop the sensitive head of his prick. He bit back an oath at the sensation of her inner walls swallowing him inch by slow inch.

Cecily drew in a ragged breath at the brief flash of pain as his hardness broke through the barrier of her innocence. But it was gone in an instant, replaced by need. She raised herself to her knees and lowered herself onto his achingly hard shaft, taking a bit more each time she lifted and came down again. The fullness was like nothing she'd ever known—she simply knew that she had to keep going or die trying. Any worries over the loss of her virginity were lost in the sensations of the moment, the demands of her awakened sensuality.

"You are killing me," Lucas said, his hands lightly holding on to her hips as she rocked down onto him, taking a bit more of him before lifting off to begin again.

Her only response was a gasp as her body took him in, her stomach fluttering as she brought him closer and closer inside her.

As he finally felt himself fully seated within her, Lucas bit back a groan. He had never felt anything more blissful in his life. Lifting her bottom to raise her, reveling in the sweet friction of her soft, wet grasp around him, he held still for several moments, letting her adjust to the intrusion.

Then, instincts taking over, they both began to move. Lucas thrusting up, Cecily pressing down, their bodies sliding together in a dance more ancient than even the artifacts there in the room with them.

"Oh," Cecily cried out, her fingers digging into his shoulders as she fought against the sensations flooding through her.

"Let go, Cecily," he ordered, nipping her chin with his teeth, pulling her sharply onto his cock. "Let yourself feel it. Let your body tell you what to do. Trust yourself."

Cecily shook her head, not understanding or not wanting to, she only knew that this feeling inside her was excruciating and exquisite at the same time. She was afraid of it. Afraid of what it might do to her. She felt as if she would explode into a million tiny pieces. That there would be nothing left of her if she let this force, whatever it was, course through her.

"Cecily." Lucas's voice was strained, as if he were in pain. "Don't fight it, just follow it. You won't be alone. I'll be with you. Trust me."

And in that moment, she did trust him. Whatever they were to each other. Wherever this led, she trusted him. And with a gasp she clasped her inner muscles one last time, and then simply let go.

She was flooded by a wave of euphoria the likes of which she had never imagined. Her hands grasped Lucas close to her, and she felt the heat of his breath against her shoulder, her breast, and felt him thrust into her again and again, and moved without thought or feeling against him in a frenzy of need, all the while aware and not aware of her body. Herself. Until it all peaked in an explosion of light and feeling and sensation. Like the fireworks at Vauxhall and every exhilaration imaginable wrapped together into one blissful net, to capture both of them together like this. As close as two people were capable of being.

And then she was floating. Falling. Her body felt heavy, even as Lucas continued to thrust up and into her. And then he was kissing her. And murmuring against her mouth, just before he cried out and gave one last hard thrust. And she felt something warm flooding her. Inside, as he slowed his movements. Stilled. Gasped against her neck and whispered soothing words again.

"So sweet," he said. "So good."

Her mind and body filled with an overwhelming lassitude, she allowed herself to rest there in his arms. Allowed him to gently lower her to the floor. The darkness once again enveloping them, after the bright blazing light of their lovemaking.

Lucas drowsed for a few moments before he felt Cecily stirring against him, her movements inspiring thoughts of repeat performances. But the panic in her voice snapped him out of his postcoital sense of well-being.

"Lucas," she hissed, pushing her hands against his chest and sitting up. "We're still locked in."

With a sigh, and a quick kiss, he lifted her off him and wordlessly handed her his handkerchief, which she took with a soft, "Oh. Thank you."

They would have much to discuss tomorrow, he knew, but right now, they needed to get out of this damned place before someone found them and ruined Cecily's reputation. More so than a hasty marriage to him would do in a few days' time.

He buttoned the fall of his breeches as he listened to the sound of her setting her clothing to rights. His eyes having long ago adjusted to the darkness, he stood and made his way to the doorway. Though they'd started out just inside the doorway, they'd managed to move quite a bit away from it in the heat of the moment.

Lucas grinned into the darkness.

Knowing her passionate approach to life in general, he had not been at all surprised to find that Cecily was equally demanding as a lover. Though she'd been an innocent, her knowledge of what she wanted was never once in question. She had nearly slain him with her artless caresses. Touches that had aroused him more than Europe's most experienced courtesan's could. If one were to judge the future success of their match based solely on tonight's experience, then they would most certainly have a most excellent marriage.

"We have to get out of here," she said, moving to stand beside him. There was that demanding nature again, he thought wryly.

"Easy," he said, laying a reassuring hand on the small of

her back, and trying the door again. To his surprise, the door-knob turned easily. *What the hell?*

"It's unlocked," he said in disbelief, his mind searching for an explanation.

"What?" she demanded, moving past him to try the door for herself.

She opened the door and stepped out into the hallway.

"Wait," he said in an undertone. "He might still be out there."

Immediately, she stepped back into the room. They were both silent for a time as they strained to hear any hint of movement or sound in the building. But there was nothing save for the hiss of their own breathing.

When he was sure no one else was in the building, Lucas took her hand and led her into the hallway and quietly up the stairs and out the way they had come in.

They were in the carriage bound for the Hurston town house before she voiced the very question that had been plaguing him since they'd found the door unlocked.

"Do you think he . . ."—she stumbled over the words—"listened?"

From his position beside her, Lucas wondered that as well. Aloud he said simply, "Surely not." But as he tightened his arm around Cecily, he reflected that he wasn't convinced.

Just another in a long line of grievances he had against this bastard, he reflected.

"I'll call on you tomorrow," he told Cecily when they arrived at the mews behind her father's house. "Get some sleep."

But when he reached his own bed, sleep was not so easy to come by.

Twelve

The next morning, Lucas was disappointed to find his mother and Clarissa tucked into the small sitting room the ladies had chosen to use in lieu of the enormous drawing room where the previous duke and duchess had entertained their afternoon guests.

He'd arrived home sometime after two in the morning, having seen Cecily safely into Hurston House through the terrace door she'd left unlocked. They had both been quiet on the journey there, and they had parted with an awkward exchange of curtsy and bow.

Now, however, in the cold light of dawn, he knew what he had to do. And before he could make the trip across Mayfair to do the thing, he would first need to inform his mother and sister-in-law.

"Ah, Lucas," his mother greeted him, looking up from her needlepoint frame. "This is an unexpected surprise. I thought you went riding in the park most mornings."

He stepped forward and kissed his mother on the cheek, and exchanged an awkward nod with Clarissa, who had kept away from him since their last discussion about Will's disappearance.

"You are looking haggard," she noted somewhat waspishly, looking up briefly from her own needlework. "I suppose the pleasures of London have been keeping you up late."

Lucas ignored her, and sat awkwardly in a wing chair opposite.

"I have come for a particular reason," he told them both, hoping against hope that they would not ask any impertinent questions.

When both women looked up in surprise, he stood up again, preferring to pace as he spoke rather than sit in the direct line of their inquisitive eyes.

"I wanted to let you both know that I will be asking Miss Cecily Hurston to marry me today."

The silence that followed was so profound that Lucas heard only his own heart beating in his ears. Then, the quiet was shattered by Clarissa's angry hiss.

"How could you?" she demanded, leaping up from the sofa and stalking toward him. "The daughter of your own brother's murderer? All this time you have professed to care about learning the truth of what happened to William, but it has been nothing more than a lie. Your father would be ashamed."

"I will thank you not to assume, Clarissa, what my late husband would have thought of these circumstances," Winifred snapped. "You have let your worry about Will turn you sour, I fear. Lucas has every right to marry whomever he chooses and if this Miss Hurston is the woman he chooses, then there is nothing you or I can say about the matter."

On a broken sob, Clarissa stormed from the room.

Her words were supportive, but Lucas suspected his mother was less than pleased with his news as well. Still, he was thankful for her defense.

"What do you really think?" he asked her, sitting next to her on the sofa.

"I meant what I said," his mother told him, grasping his hand in hers, as if he were a small boy again needing her comfort. "Besides, you do not need my permission."

"No," he agreed. "But I'm afraid there's more to it than simply marriage."

At her frown, he said, feeling oddly sheepish, "The wedding will need to be . . . soon."

"Oh, Lucas," she said with disappointment. "I had hoped that you at least would have a love match like your father and I did."

"There is every possibility that I will," he said, surprised to find he was speaking the truth. "We are well suited, I think. More so than Will and Clarissa, at any rate."

"That would not take much," she returned dryly. "And do you believe that Miss Hurston's father is blameless in your brother's disappearance?"

"I do not know," he said. "We have found nothing that says he is and nothing that says he isn't. But regardless, Mama, we will marry, so if it does turn out that Lord Hurston is to blame, then there will be talk. More talk than there has been already."

"I do not pay attention to gossip," she said with a frown, her eyes fierce with loyalty. "You know that. What matters to me is your happiness."

Rising, he leaned down to kiss her cheek.

"Thank you for understanding," he said. "I believe you will like Cecily once you meet her. She is an independent lady, to be sure, but she also has a very generous heart. Like someone else I know."

And with that bit of flattery, he left her.

Lucas arrived at Hurston House in Grosvenor Square impeccably dressed and determined. He requested an audience with Lady Violet Hurston, and was shown promptly into the lady's sitting room within moments of his arrival.

"What brings you here, Winterson?" asked Lady Violet, gesturing him toward the chair across from her own perch on a chintz-covered settee. An embroidery frame was arranged neatly beside her seat, and he did not miss her glance toward it, as if she were eager to get back to her project.

"My lady," he said baldly, "I have come on a matter of some delicacy." He cleared his throat, suddenly more nervous than he could remember being in years. "About Miss Hurston."

One delicate brow rose in query. "Oh, indeed. Do go on." Her voice was calm, but Winterston detected a hint of steel in her tone.

He swallowed. "I have come to ask for Miss Hurston's hand in marriage. I know that her father is currently indisposed, so I have come to you in your position as her stepmother, though she is past her majority and might marry me without your consent."

Lady Hurston studied his face for a moment, as if trying to read what he had not said. "You have compromised her," she said without malice. "Even after my warning."

Refusing to be cowed, he inclined his head in assent. "Yes. Discretion prevents me from going into more detail, but suffice it to say that we should be married. Soon."

The viscountess nodded. "I see. Well, then, let me be the first to wish you happy." She rose, and smiled at him. "Though you will, of course, need to procure Cecily's assent."

Lucas grinned, grateful that she had chosen not to upbraid him for his actions, though she would have been well within her purview to do so. "I would appreciate your best wishes for that endeavor as well," he said. "In fact, I suspect it may be more difficult to gain Cecily's consent than yours."

"Oh, undoubtedly," Cecily's stepmama responded, also grinning, "but then that is what we love about her."

Knowing better than to fall into that trap, Lucas simply nodded and began to pace before the fireplace as Violet excused herself to summon Cecily.

What would she say? he wondered. Surely she would not be surprised to find him here.

Last night had changed things between them irrevocably, and the knowledge that she might even now be carrying his child filled him with a resolve unlike he'd ever felt. Whatever it took, whatever he had to promise her, he would leave Hurston House today with her acceptance, or he'd throw her over his shoulder and carry her off to Gretna Green whether she consented or no.

He was still frowning at the imaginary Cecily in his head, the one who had refused his proposal and forced him to kidnap her, when the real Cecily entered the room.

Their late night had left purple shadows beneath her eyes. And though she had, of late, worn more fashionable clothing than was usual for her, today she had chosen a pale rose-colored gown that only accentuated her pallor.

Yet, from her simply dressed hair, which was once again working to escape its pins, to her plain but serviceable slippers, she was, to Lucas, more beautiful than he had ever seen her.

"Miss Hurston," he greeted her with a very proper bow.

"Your Grace," she said, dropping into a graceful curtsy.

"I trust you have not suffered any ill effects from our . . . adventure last evening?" he asked politely. Searching her face for signs of upset or tears, he saw only weariness.

"I am perfectly well, thank you," she said, her tone calm, controlled. Only her eyes flashed with the knowledge that their "adventure," as he called it, had been something more than just a youthful escapade.

Still, her mouth quirked with a smile as she asked, "And you? Did you suffer any ill effects?"

Lucas hid his amusement at her inquiry. It was just like her to offer his solicitude back to him, emphasizing her rejection of the notion of the female as the weaker sex.

"Miss Hurston, there is something which—"

"Your Grace, if I might speak to you regarding the events of—"

They both stopped, the aborted attempt at conversation breaking the awkwardness between them in a way their prettily rehearsed words could not have done.

"I will speak first, if I may, Miss Hurston," Lucas said, leading her to an overstuffed sofa near the window.

Waiting for her to be seated, he remained standing, restless energy preventing him from any sort of relaxation.

"Miss Hurston," he said, stopping before her. "Cecily."

Lucas found himself nervous in a way that he had not experienced since he was a raw youth asking a debutante for a dance at the village assembly. And for her part, Cecily kept her gaze fastened on her hands, clasped tightly in her lap. The knowledge that he was not the only one suffering pangs of trepidation soothed his agitation somewhat.

"Our . . . encounter of last evening makes it imperative that we wed without delay." Lucas spoke decisively. His words emphasized the seriousness of their situation.

Seeing her head snap up at his words, he continued, "Before you object to my proposal, I beg you to hear me out."

"How do you know I was going to object?" she asked, two furrows appearing between her brows. "Am I not allowed to speak?"

"Come now, Miss . . . Cecily, I had not known you above ten minutes before I realized your most common response to any sort of declarative statement is an immediate questioning of its validity."

Before she could object again, he raised a staying hand. "It is not a bad thing," he said, trying to explain more thoroughly. "I suspect it has something to do with your being the daughter of a scholar. They have, as I was able to determine during my years at Oxford, a tendency to ponder the whys and wherefores of everything from the most mundane to the most complex concepts. It is certainly nothing to be ashamed of. I see it as a mark of your inquisitive nature."

"Yes, well," she answered wryly, "I doubt there are very many members of either my family or the *ton* who will agree with you on that point."

"Indeed," he said, unable to make small talk in the present circumstances.

"I have already obtained your stepmama's consent," he forged on.

"Ah," she said, her eyes shadowed, perhaps because her father was unable to perform that office now. "I am not surprised she agreed. I believe she thinks you are a good catch."

That surprised a laugh from him. "I wouldn't go so far as that," he said. Then, growing serious again, "But I did inform her that given the circumstances we should probably be wed sooner rather than later. And, given the precarious state of your father's health," he went on, "I believe you could count it a good thing to know that should the worst happen, you will not be forced to throw yourself on your cousin's mercy. I believe that was one of your reasons for wishing to marry a member of the Egyptian Club?"

Cecily nodded. "Yes, it was." Still, she was quiet for a moment, thinking.

When her presence was requested in the drawing room, she had not been at all surprised. Since they had parted the evening before, she had expected just such a summons every hour on the hour.

It was not Lucas's proposal itself to which she objected. Last night's removal of the final barrier between them— both literally and figuratively—had been tantamount to a marriage proposal in and of itself. The fact that she simply did not accept every dictum dreamed up by society regarding what did and did not constitute a woman's ruin was simply another hurdle for him to leap over in his pursuit of her.

No, what kept her from accepting him outright was something far more selfish, and more immediate.

"I do, in fact, wish for a home of my own. I even, though you will be surprised to hear me admit it, wish for a family, a husband, children. But it has never been my objective to marry for those things alone. I had hoped to marry someone with whom I could share my scholarly pursuits. A man who would encourage me in my work, rather than object to it outright, as my father did with my mother."

Cecily twisted the handkerchief she clutched in her hands, nervous energy coursing through her as she tried to keep her voice level and to conceal her agitation. She searched Lucas's face for some clue to his thoughts, but it was as impassive as her own.

"And you think that I would not encourage you?" he asked, his blue eyes sharp, cutting into her like an accusation. "That I would resent your mental acumen? Your skill with languages and your translation abilities?"

"I do not know," she answered truthfully. "I know very little about you at all."

"I should think you know me well enough after our activities of last evening," he said, one dark brow arching in accusation.

Cecily felt a blush creep into her cheeks but she said nothing.

"Even if we are not so closely acquainted as to sense one another's every thought, we 'know' one another in the biblical sense at the very least," Lucas said pointedly. "And that, if nothing else, makes it imperative that we marry. I daresay there are some couples in the Beau Monde who have been married for as long as you have been alive who remain incognizant of even how their spouse takes their tea. But they are married still and rub along together well enough."

Cecily stood, and began to pace the floor while Lucas was now the one who remained stationary.

She stopped before him, her face set in lines of determination.

"But that is just it," she said. "I do not want a typical *ton* marriage. I want more than just conversation over the breakfast table and bodies occasionally joined. I want the sort of marriage Miss Wollstonecraft speaks of. A marriage of partnership and mutual understanding."

"And you do not believe you could have that with me?"

"I do not know if I might or not," she said. "But I must confess that the idea of marriage at all strikes fear in my heart. I have seen what the imprisonment of an unhappy marriage can do to a woman, my lord. And I do not wish to be sacrificed on the altar of propriety merely because we were unwise in our actions during a time of great duress."

"I see," he said, his expression stark. "So it is not me you object to but the institution?"

She nodded.

"And how, pray, did you intend to overcome your objections when you planned to marry one of the men on your stolen dance card?"

Cecily waved a hand at his question. "Those gentlemen would have been easy enough to manage. I doubt Lord Fortenbury would have batted an eyelash over my pursuits so long as he had possession of my dowry. And Mr. Vinson is notoriously silly. He would not care what I got up to so long as I maintained a fashionable enough wardrobe and played a hand of whist at his card parties once a fortnight."

Lucas's jaw dropped. Finally, she had succeeded in shaking his calm. "Do you mean to tell me that you do not wish to marry me because I am *not* a simpleton? Because I am not easily managed?"

"I would not have put the matter so bluntly," Cecily said, refusing to look away. "But, in effect, yes. You are a duke. You are used to having your own way. You would wish me to curtail my scholarly activities to maintain my position in society as your duchess. And I should not blame you. Really, it is because I hold you in some esteem that I would not wish to saddle you with a wife such as I will make."

"And what if that decision is not up to you? What if I am somewhat in awe of your scholarly pursuits and would have no objection to your quest to edit your father's journals? What if, so long as you were able to maintain a nominal presence in the *ton,* I don't give a royal damn whether you play whist or not?"

He leaned forward, placing his lips close to her ear, so that he could whisper, "What if I will do anything to put you in my bed and keep you there?" Cecily felt a shiver run through her as his tongue flicked out and swept up the whorl of her ear.

"What if I won't take no for an answer, sweet Cecily?" he asked, turning his head to kiss a path down her jaw toward her mouth.

"What then?" he murmured.

By the time he pressed his mouth to hers, Cecily was on fire with longing. All the places where he had touched her last night seemed to pulse in readiness, to draw her body toward his in an effort to bring that sweet friction that had brought her so much pleasure before.

She did not hesitate to return his kiss, to open her mouth and welcome him into her, match his tongue thrust for thrust. Her hands crept from his shoulder to grasp him closer, pulling him more tightly against her even as they thrust into the soft waves of the slightly overlong hair at his nape.

Wordlessly, he pulled her against him, relishing the feel of her soft curves against his hardness. He had thought perhaps she would deny the power of the attraction between them, but instead she had given in to it.

With reluctance, Lucas pulled back from her. Stepped away, made no attempt to conceal the evidence of his desire for her. Needing to keep his hands busy so that he could resist reaching for her, he straightened his waistcoat, smoothed his hair back down.

"You cannot deny what is between us, Cecily," he said quietly. "An attraction like this cannot be suppressed or denied."

"But attraction does not last, Winterson. I have seen marriages based on passion. Once it is gone there is little else to recommend the married state."

Her gray eyes were bleak, stirring a protective instinct in him that he had thought gone long ago. He wanted to reach out to her, but knew that if they were to settle the matter, he had best keep his hands to himself until his cause was won.

"I cannot, I will not, profess an undying love for you, Cecily," Lucas said with more severity than he intended. "I will not flatter you or tell you what you want to hear. I am drawn to you, however. I have been since I saw you that day in front of the club.

"Now, circumstance and fate have brought us together, and by God I will not be denied. You say you wish for a marriage based on partnership? Then you shall have it. I told the truth before: I do find the quickness of your mind, your facility with languages, fascinating. I am not a scholar myself, but that does not mean that I will begrudge you your own pursuits."

Unable to continue without touching her, he stepped forward. Took her hand in his. "Cecily, you were prepared to marry men for whom you had little affection and even less attraction. I do not offer you the sort of partnership you crave—I am not even sure I know what you mean when you speak of it. But is it not foolish to refuse me when we are both intent on the same goal? When I can offer you more than those other men can?"

He took her other hand, was encouraged when she did not pull away.

"You are a practical being above all else. If you refuse me, there is a chance that your cousin will make life in Hurston House even more unbearable for you than I suspect it already has been. If you were to find yourself with child, the scandal alone would send both Hurston and his wife into the vapors for a month.

"And even if these reasons do not persuade you, I beg of you to remember that we have been seen in company together a great deal over the past few weeks. I very much doubt we could continue to do so without raising suspicions among both the *ton* and whoever it is who has taken your father's journals. And if we are forced to look for them separately it will be difficult to share information as we have done up to now. It is in both our interests to continue our partnership. A couple newly married are afforded a great deal more eccentricities than an unmarried lady and gentleman with no discernible ties to one another."

He waited in silence for her to say something, anything, in response to his argument.

Unable to see her eyes, he caught his breath in longing as her pink tongue darted out against her upper lip.

"Do you really not find my facility with languages off-putting?" she asked quietly.

Inwardly he cheered. Aloud he said, "On the contrary. I find it quite alluring."

"And do you honestly believe we will have a better chance of finding Father's journals if we are married?"

"I do," he said.

"I would like to try to visit Egypt sometime in the near future, despite my fear of enclosed spaces," Cecily said, lifting her chin in defiance. "My father refused to allow me to go. If this is something you would find objectionable I should like to know now before I give you my answer."

"I do not foresee any reason why we should not be able to take such a voyage," Lucas responded, not surprised in the least by her demand. He had expected her to mention it earlier. "Though I would suggest we postpone it until we have found your father's journals."

Cecily looked up at him, her eyes searching his, for what, he did not know. But she seemed to find whatever it was she sought, for she nodded as if coming to a decision, and said, "Then, my lord, I accept your proposal of marriage."

"Excellent," he said, taking her mouth in a kiss that left them both breathless with the memory of the passion they had shared only last night. Before he succumbed to the need in them both, he pulled back.

"You will not be sorry, Cecily," he said, looking into her eyes, and pleased to see the flush in her cheeks. He reached out to caress her lower lip with his thumb. "I promise you, you will not."

"I know that," she returned, smiling ruefully at him. "I believe I must have known it already when I gave myself to you last night. Though I suspect I did not realize it until just now."

The heat that her words generated in his groin, Lucas understood. What surprised him more was the constriction in his chest. Now that she had acceded he felt both relief and a vague sense of being on the cusp of something. Something important.

Badly needing to find some occupation, Lucas kissed her briefly on the cheek, told her he would inform her stepmama of their impending nuptials and would go in search of a special license. To Cecily he left the details such as where they would be married. He would brook no objections to the time, which would be the end of the week at the latest. When she objected to his haste, Lucas shook his head.

"I know you would perhaps like more time, but I will not take the chance. The members of society are perhaps mentally deficient in many ways, but they are all, to my knowledge, capable of counting to nine. I will not have you or our child exposed to the censure of polite society."

Wordlessly, Cecily nodded. Watched him leave the room with a sense of unreality. She had awakened this morning knowing that he would propose. But now, having accepted him, she had the uncanny sensation of being on a runaway coach. No matter how she pulled on the reins, she realized, there was no stopping now.

She only hoped that her faith in Lucas would not flag once the vows were said. Because she very much feared he was the sort of man she could fall in love with.

And that, she realized, had been her real objection to the match all along.

She was resting in her bedchamber from the whirlwind that was Violet with a project, having spent the better part of the day being fitted for a wedding dress that she would wear in three days' time, when Cecily heard a light knock at her door, followed by the sound of her cousins entering the room.

"Cecily?" she heard Juliet call. "Are you sleeping?"

"Of course she's not sleeping," Maddie retorted. "I just saw her twitch. She's faking so that we'll leave her alone."

"That's not very sporting of you, dearest," Juliet chided. "Especially when you've got such news as this to tell."

Knowing that resistance was futile, Cecily opened her eyes. "From the sound of it you already know the news, so there's no need for me to tell it."

"But there's every need," Juliet argued, tucking a lock of red hair behind her ear. "We've only heard the bare bones of the story. You must tell us the rest, with the pertinent details added in."

"Then let us call for the tea tray first," Cecily said briskly, leading them into the small sitting room adjacent to her bedchamber. "For it is quite a long story."

When they were all seated, with the tea tray and a generous number of ginger biscuits laid out before them, she told them about her visit to the Egyptian Club the night before with Winterson. With certain details omitted, of course.

"But I don't understand," Juliet said with a frown. "If no one discovered you'd been there, then why is there any need for you to marry? It's not as if you—"

A pointed look from Cecily stopped her in mid-sentence.

"Oh," she said, her green eyes widening.

"Oh, indeed," Maddie said wryly. "I should never have thought you'd be the one to compromise yourself, Cecily. I am quite impressed."

Cecily rolled her eyes. "I hardly did it on my own, Maddie. Before you go leaping to the duke's defense, he was quite a willing participant."

"Oh, I don't doubt it," Maddie retorted. "He does not strike me as the timid sort."

"No, he's certainly . . ." Cecily stopped, her face turning red, much to her cousin's delight. "Oh, do be quiet, Maddie."

"But what was it like, Cecily?" Juliet demanded, her own face turning pink even as she asked the question. At the poke in the ribs Maddie gave her, she protested, "You know you wanted to ask the same thing, Maddie, so don't look at me like that."

Affection for her cousins overwhelming her, Cecily couldn't help grinning at them. "I am so lucky to have you two, no matter how unsettling your questions might be."

But Maddie and Juliet would have none of it.

"Stop trying to change the subject and talk," Maddie said, crossing her arms over her chest. "We want details."

"Not details so much," Juliet said with a frown at Maddie. "But rather, confirmation of a few things. For instance, is it lovely? Or horrid, like we overheard Mama telling Lady Stepney?"

"Lovely," Cecily said with a blush, remembering just what it had been like to lie in Lucas's arms, to feel all that strength pressed against her softness. "Definitely lovely."

"Oh, you were definitely compromised, then," Maddie said with a brisk nod. "I had wondered if perhaps you hadn't just kissed him, but now I know."

"How do you know?" Cecily asked, frowning. Was it really that clear just from her expression?

"You've got that glow about you. Remember when Lavinia Parman was forced to marry Lord Langham after he compromised her at Vauxhall?" At Cecily's nod, she continued, "Well, I saw her that evening just before her parents hustled her away. You've got that same dazed and knowing look."

Since Lavinia had been dangling after Langham for the entire season before they wed, Cecily rather thought their circumstances were different, but she didn't argue the point. The sooner she turned Maddie's and Juliet's minds to another subject, the better.

"Well, I think you look lovely," Juliet said, reaching out to squeeze Cecily's hand. "And I couldn't be happier for you. Winterson is charming. And it's obvious from the way his eyes follow you when you're in the same room that he is besotted with you."

"Well, I wouldn't say that," Cecily said with a wry smile. "But I think we will get along well enough together."

"But you love *him,* don't you?" Juliet asked with a frown. "I mean, you wouldn't have let him—"

"I am fond of him, of course," Cecily began, "but I don't really—"

"Of course she loves him," Maddie interrupted before Cecily could finish her denial. Her eyes flashed a warning that made Cecily regret her words. She did think that Juliet had a little too much sensibility about such matters, but it would be cruel for her to dash her cousin's hopes in such a cold fashion. "Now, tell us all about the wedding details, Cecily."

Juliet looked as if she wished to question Cecily further, but she followed along without demurral into the conversation about the wedding plans.

When they were ready to leave, Cecily followed her cousins downstairs to see them out.

"I do wish you happy," Juliet said, giving her an impulsive hug. "Even if you don't love one another."

At Cecily's startled look, her cousin smiled. "I'm not quite so naïve as you and Maddie seem to think me," she said. "I just wish for you to have a happy marriage. Happier than the other marriages of convenience I am familiar with."

Knowing she spoke about her own parents, Cecily felt a rush of affection for her cousin.

"Thank you, dearest," she said, with a squeeze of the other girl's hand. "I wish that too."

More than she was willing to admit. Even to herself.

Thirteen

*I*t was with a sense of unreality that Lucas stood before the bishop in St. George's Hanover Square three days later, Cecily standing tall beside him.

Though he had assumed planning so hasty a wedding would be at least a little trouble, once Cecily's stepmother and aunts and cousins had become involved, the small ceremony he had in mind had transformed into a church full of friends, relatives, and curious onlookers.

But when he saw Cecily enter from the rear of the church, he had been proud to stand before them all and claim her as his bride.

A hush fell over the congregation as she walked up the aisle on Lord Geoffrey Brighton's arm, looking lovelier than he'd ever seen her. Her gown was a pink satiny fabric under some sort of silver tissue material. He wasn't sure what the style was called, but he loved the way it showcased her long-limbed beauty and her creamy white skin. When he took her gloved hand in his, he was startled to feel it tremble.

Something about the vulnerability in her eyes as she looked up at him made him want to lift her into his arms and run away with her. But instead, he squeezed her hand in his before placing it firmly in the crook of his arm. Nothing, not even an uncommon bout of nerves from his bride, would convince him to delay the ceremony that would make her his.

When the time came, however, she said her vows in a loud and clear voice, as did he. And when he slipped his grandmother's sapphire that so reminded him of her eyes onto her finger, she gave a sigh that sounded very much like relief. That made two of them, he thought, grinning down at her. Not caring if the entire world knew how pleased he was to call her his at last.

Once the ceremony was at an end, there was the registry to sign, and in a very short time he was handing her into his crested carriage, where they rode the short distance to the Hurston town house, where their wedding breakfast would take place.

"The ring is lovely," Cecily said, holding out her hand to admire the sapphire flanked by two diamonds set in a filigree band. "Was it your mother's?"

"Grandmother's," he replied, watching her turn her hand this way and that to see the stones sparkle. "I would not have imagined you to be impressed by jewels," he teased.

She blushed, and immediately dropped her hand into her lap. "I am not, particularly," she said primly. "But anyone can have an appreciation for a thing of beauty."

"Indeed," he said, looking his fill of the thing of beauty that sat before him in the person of his new wife.

The carefully arranged curls that had been gathered in a knot at the back of her head, a rose pink silk ribbon threaded through them, gave her the look of a fairy princess or a wood nymph. Small eardrops dangled from her lobes, swaying against the soft spot of skin beneath her ear, a spot he himself had kissed not three nights earlier and knew from experience to be sweet with the mixture of rose water and a scent that was all Cecily.

Her eyes were bright, though a hint of shadow lingered beneath them, as if she had not slept well the night before. Lucas could certainly understand that. He felt as if he hadn't slept since their encounter in the Egyptian Club. All the days since had been spent getting his affairs in order and preparing Winterson House and his various family and servants for the arrival of a new mistress in their midst.

"I have sent a footman to Hurston House to retrieve your things," Lucas said, breaking the silence that had fallen between them.

"Excellent," Cecily returned with more enthusiasm than the announcement warranted. Lucas stifled a smile at her forced cheerfulness. It was unusual to see Cecily made nervous by anything, he thought, remembering that trembling hand at the altar. He found some strange comfort in the notion that she was just as nervous about their new marriage as he was.

"I have a bit of other news as well," he told her, watching as she twisted her handkerchief into a knot and then unwound it again. "Lord Peter Naughton is one of the nation's foremost collectors of Egyptian artifacts, and I have it on good authority that he has been boasting of late about a particularly important find that gives the whereabouts of quite an important bit of pottery from the tomb of Ramses the Second."

Cecily's eyes lit up. "Father's journals! There was a rumor that he'd found the tomb of Ramses, though since he was unable to verify the story himself I wasn't quite sure how true it could be."

"Yes," Lucas said. "If Naughton knows where the journals are, then we might be able to persuade him that telling us would be infinitely safer than divulging the information to the other members of the society. At least with you and me he will not need to worry that we would steal the information and go in search of the treasure ourselves."

"Speak for yourself," Cecily said with a grimace. "If I were able to do so I would embark tomorrow on the first ship bound for Cairo in order to follow in my father's footsteps."

Seeing the mulish set to her new husband's jaw, she continued, "Not that I have any intention of doing so anytime soon. I was merely expressing a dream, not one upon which I plan to act."

Lucas hummphed, and continued, "With any luck we will have found your father's journals by this time tomorrow. And you will be able to start the translation of them as soon as possible."

But Cecily was not so optimistic. Ever since they'd been unable to find the journals in the Egyptian Club, she had begun to wonder if there were not some more powerful forces at work in this instance.

But, not wishing to press Lucas, on this morning of all mornings, she held her tongue and decided to ask him for more information later. When they were alone. The very idea of which sent a thrill of anticipation through her and a blush to her cheeks. Which was noted, doubtlessly, by the well-wishers who greeted them as they alighted from the carriage in Grosvenor Square.

"My dear," Violet said as Cecily stepped into the dining room, "I have never seen you look lovelier."

"Your mama would be so proud," Lady Entwhistle added, kissing Cecily on the cheek before she linked her arm in Lucas's and led him away to greet the other guests.

He glanced over his shoulder and winked at his new bride before he disappeared into the crowd.

The room was already filling up with both those who had attended the wedding and the dozens more who were invited to the breakfast only. Though Cecily and Lucas had thought to keep the celebration small, Violet had insisted that in order to appease the gossipmongers they must invite as many prominent members of the *ton* as possible. "Thank you, Violet," Cecily returned, giving her stepmother an affectionate hug. "And thank you so much for your help in planning the event itself. I would not have known where to begin."

Violet was saved a reply by the appearance of Cecily's new mother-in-law, Lady Michael Dalton, and William Dalton's wife, Mrs. Clarissa Dalton.

"Congratulations, my dear," Winifred said warmly, kissing Cecily on the cheek.

They had only met a few days before the wedding, but Cecily had found Lucas's mother to be a practical, good-natured sort of woman, who, while pleased about her son's inheritance of the dukedom, was not the least bit interested in using it to elevate her own standing with the *ton*.

"For all that my husband was the son of a duke," she

confided in Cecily over tea in Violet's drawing room, "he never put on the sort of airs one would expect of one of such high birth. He was a clergyman first and foremost. And I knew that when I married him.

"Not," she added, her eyes intent upon Cecily, "that I would expect you or Lucas to deny yourselves the comforts that the dukedom affords, of course."

Her expression seemed to imply otherwise, as if she were testing Cecily to see just what her reaction to such a proposal might be. She might have objected to such a test if she had been the mercenary sort of woman Lady Michael must have suspected her to be. But since she was marrying him out of necessity rather than a desire to become a duchess, she was comfortable in dispelling his mother's fears.

"To be honest, Lady Michael," she said, "I haven't actually considered just what Lucas's status might entitle me to."

While Lady Michael seemed to believe her, William Dalton's wife, Clarissa, scoffed. "You'll forgive me if I doubt you, Miss Hurston, but I find the notion of such selflessness to be implausible at best."

"And at worst?" Cecily asked, feeling an intense dislike for the other woman. She did understand how difficult her lot must be with Will missing, but it gave her no right to be rude to Cecily.

"At worst," she replied with a frown, "it is a bald untruth meant to win over the goodwill of Winterson's mama so that she will leave you to your own devices once you are the duchess."

"Clarissa," Lady Michael said with a sharpness Cecily doubted was usual with her. "You are here at my request. And I now request that you wait for me in the carriage."

A mutinous set to Mrs. Dalton's mouth told Cecily that she did not particularly wish to adhere to her mother-in-law's request, but perhaps seeing that she risked alienating her further, Clarissa muttered some inane good-bye and left the room.

"I do apologize for my daughter-in-law, my dear," Lady

Michael said with a sigh. "She has never been the most pleasant person, but my son William's disappearance has brought out the worst in Clarissa, I fear."

"Think nothing of it, my lady," Cecily reassured her. "I know it must be difficult for both of you dealing with Mr. Dalton's absence."

"If we knew something," Lady Michael said, her pain evident in her voice, "anything at all, I think we would all feel a great deal better. Not knowing is . . ."

Knowing from her own experience with her father that there was nothing she could say that would alleviate the other woman's pain, Cecily reached out and took the older lady's hand in hers and squeezed it.

"But what am I thinking?" Lady Michael said with a shake of her head. "We are here because of a happy occasion."

"But the sad occasions make the happy ones that much more satisfying, do they not?" Cecily asked with a smile.

"They do indeed, Miss Hurston," Winterson's mother said with a smile of her own. "I do wish my Michael were still here to meet you. He'd like you very much, I think."

Pleased by the compliment, Cecily allowed her to steer the conversation toward wedding details and less serious matters. She found she liked Lady Michael very much, and when the older woman rose to take her leave it was with a real sense of fondness that Cecily wished her good-bye.

Now, standing before Lady Michael and Clarissa, her vows to Winterson having been solemnized, Cecily reached out her hands to both women. "Congratulations, Your Grace," Clarissa said with what looked more like a grimace than a smile. "I can only hope that your marriage will be a happy one, like mine to my dearest William has been."

Since Cecily knew now that Clarissa and William had been far from happily wed, she realized that the woman's good wishes were worth little; still she thanked the woman prettily, and offered her hope that William Dalton might be found alive very soon.

"For your husband was always a great favorite of my

father's," Cecily assured her. "Indeed, he was a favorite with me as well. Mr. Dalton was unfailingly cheerful in the face of my father's temper and they worked quite well together."

"Yes." Clarissa frowned. "William worked quite well with everyone except for his family." Then, perhaps realizing she had said too much, Clarissa excused herself to adjourn to the ladies' retiring room.

Lucas's mother shook her head sadly as she, Violet, and Cecily watched her walk from the room. "She was always a difficult young woman, but since William's disappearance she has become positively unpleasant."

"Have no fear, Lady Michael," Cecily assured her. "I know it has been a trying time for her."

Lady Michael gave a sad smile. "Well, she and I will be taking ourselves away to Bath for the next few weeks in order to give you and my eldest some privacy in these first few days of your marriage."

When Cecily protested, the older lady raised her hand in a forestalling motion. "Pray, my dear, do not speak of it any further. Marriage is difficult enough without having one's dour sister-in-law and a busybody mother-in-law meddling in one's business."

"I must admit," Violet said on a laugh, "I was quite fortunate that when I married Hurston his mother had already passed away. Not that I don't believe she was a delightful lady, of course."

"There," Winifred said, nodding, "listen to your stepmama. Besides, we will have more than enough time to become better acquainted once you and Lucas are settled in together."

Before she could move further into the room, Cecily was stopped by Amelia Snowe, who had come with her parents. She had already come through the receiving line, so Cecily wasn't sure what else the beauty could want with her.

"Cecily," she said haughtily, looking the new bride up and down, "I didn't get to say so before, but you are looking quite well. Much better than I'd have thought you could in such a short time. You are quite transformed."

Reminding herself that she was to be on her best behavior, Cecily bit back the retort she wished to give Amelia, and replaced it with a brisk thanks.

"I shouldn't have thought you'd be able to bring Winterson up to scratch," the other girl continued, a nasty gleam in her eye, "but I suppose when one is willing to compromise oneself, one's odds of contracting a match are raised considerably."

Cecily had thought she knew what depths Amelia was willing to sink to in order to further her spiteful agenda, but this was beyond even Cecily's comprehension. Was Amelia actually insulting her to her face at her wedding breakfast?

"Amelia," she said, her anger belied by her calm voice, "you are a—"

She was interrupted by the arrival of Lucas, who slipped a proprietary arm around her waist.

"I see you've come to wish us happy, Miss Snowe," he said to the blonde, his manner pleasant but firm. "It's quite kind of you to take time out of your busy social schedule to attend our nuptials. Some have suggested that you only came for the opportunity to gather gossip and to snub my new bride, but I told them that you weren't that ill-mannered."

Cecily watched with burgeoning satisfaction as Amelia's face turned from slightly pink to rose red as Lucas continued. "You won't make a liar out of me, will you, Miss Snowe?" Amelia's mouth opened and closed, once, twice, three times, before she shut it with an audible snap as her teeth came together.

Finally, she plastered a patently false expression of sincerity on her face, clearly unwilling to offend Lucas despite her enmity toward his new wife, and said, "Of course not, Your Grace. I . . . I thank you."

And, desperate to get away from the newlyweds, she made an inarticulate sound and hurried away.

"That," Cecily said, laying her head on her husband's shoulder, "was marvelous. I don't think I've ever seen her speechless before."

"She's lucky I only gave her a set-down," Lucas said with

a frown. "If she were a man I would have called her out for insulting you. As it is, I think words and her fear of social ostracism should work in our favor from now on."

Cecily felt a rush of warmth for this man who had known her for only a few weeks but was ready to come to her defense so readily, with no questions asked.

"Now," he said, reaching down to give her hand a squeeze, "I must go hunt down Monteith. Will you be all right?"

"Yes," she said with a laugh. "I don't think I'll have any more trouble with her. At least not today. Besides, I need to tell Maddie and Juliet about how you just routed our mortal enemy."

"Excellent," he said with a grin. "I like slaying dragons for you. I think I'll enjoy this husbanding business."

At the thought of what else this husbanding business would entail, Cecily felt a blush rising, and hurried away to join her cousins, who were stationed near a large potted palm.

As Cecily's bridesmaids, both of them were dressed in green, though in shades that complemented their individual coloring. They were meant to be the leaves and stems to Cecily's bloom. Madeline was quietly pretty in a pale green gown—with puffed sleeves and a contrasting dark green ribbon gathered beneath the bosom—that emphasized her hazel eyes and light blond hair. And Juliet, in a deep green gown of similar cut, wore her red tresses in the same style twist as Maddie's, and was looking better than Cecily had ever seen her.

"What's amiss?" Madeline said, taking Cecily's hand. "It can be nothing to do with your appearance. I don't think I've ever seen a lovelier bride."

"She's right." Juliet grinned, taking her other hand. "You are quite transformed."

"Careful," Cecily warned, taking her cousin's words for the dry jest they were. "That"s what Amelia Snowe told me just before she was given a spectacular set-down by my new husband."

"Oh, I'm so sorry we missed it!" Madeline said, her eyes lighting with glee. "Was she very angry?"

As Cecily recounted the incident to them, her cousins grew more and more animated.

"I'll bet she was furious," Juliet said with a grin.

"I just wish the rest of polite society could see her for what she is," Maddie said with a frown. "A vain and spiteful bully."

"Yes, well, the *ton* rarely if ever does what it should," Cecily said ruefully. "Though perhaps now she will stop making us the object of her derision."

"We can but hope," Maddie said. "But let's not let Amelia ruin our morning. Though one does wonder how she ended up receiving an invitation."

"I'm sure it was Violet's doing," Cecily said with a sigh. "She is forever going on to me about how I should try to make peace with Amelia, if only to ensure that she ends her 'Ugly Duckling' campaign. Though I have a feeling Winterson's slight will have more effect on her than anything I could possibly do."

"Indeed," Juliet agreed. "Though it is lowering to know that a gentleman has been more effective on this score than we have."

"So," Maddie said, changing the topic, "tell us where you are going on your wedding journey. Are we to be dreadfully jealous?"

"We are staying here in London," Cecily replied, her mood growing somber. "Neither of us wants to be too far in the event that there is some change in Papa's condition, or some news comes regarding Winterson's brother."

"Very sensible." Juliet nodded in approval. "I don't suppose there has been any change with Lord Hurston, has there?"

"No." Cecily frowned. "He is still insensible. I worry that he may never recover, though the physician assures us that there have been cases where men much older than Papa have gone on to make a full recovery."

Their conversation was interrupted by the approach of Mr. George Vinson, whose customary bluff humor was marred by a look of reproach.

"You are a beautiful bride, Your Grace," he said, bowing over her hand. "Winterson is a lucky fellow. First Knighton's bays and now you. If I didn't know better I'd suspect the fellow was trying to ape my dashing style."

As jests went it was a lame one, but then Vinson was not known for his wit.

"Thank you, Mr. Vinson," Cecily acknowledged. "I daresay there are much worse men for Winterson to emulate. Though I suspect in this case the connection is mere coincidence."

"What's this I've heard about a curse, Miss . . . er . . . Your Grace?" Vinson asked. "Miss Snowe sounded quite serious about it."

"It is nonsense, of course," Maddie said, coming to her cousin's defense. "Miss Snowe is obviously overreacting, as she does with any number of things."

"Yes," Juliet said, her usual retiring demeanor replaced with a ferocity that surprised and humbled Cecily. "There has been a lot of talk—by people with nothing better to discuss. I suspect that the story has been fueled by those who wish to discredit both the Hurston and Winterson families. Surely you would not choose to ally yourself with those blackguards."

Vinson ran a finger under his collar in discomfort. "Dashed sorry to bring it up, Your Grace," he said. "I meant no offense, of course. Certainly wouldn't want to . . . er . . . I think I see my cousin Chester talking with Lord Darlington. There is a pressing matter we must discuss. Your humble servants, ladies."

With that, Mr. Vinson hurried off as if he were being pursued by Sally Jersey on a broom.

"Spiteful cat," Juliet hissed, referring to the absent Amelia, who had revived talk of the curse. "She's simply jealous because you removed an eligible duke from the marriage market."

"And married before she did, despite her popularity," Maddie added with vehemence. "I do not think there is a charitable bone in Amelia Snowe's body."

"Well," Cecily said, shaking her head, "I wish Amelia were our only worry. With Papa's continued illness, Will's disappearance, and now the speculation among the *ton,* even I am beginning to wonder if there is some truth to the curse."

"Nonsense," Juliet said bracingly. "You are merely feeling overwhelmed. Do not give Amelia the satisfaction of seeing her poisoned words hit their mark."

The new Duchess of Winterson nodded, shaking off the dark mood Amelia's insinuations had brought.

"Tell me what goes on with you two," she said brightly. "Maddie, I see that James is not here. Is he off on some sporting adventure once again?"

James was Madeline's scapegrace elder brother who showed no signs of settling down as he neared his thirtieth birthday.

His put-upon sister frowned. "I believe he is in town," she said with exasperation. "He did promise to send his regrets, Cecily. But you know as well as I do how nervous a wedding can make a single gentleman. And I fear my brother is more skittish than most about such events."

"It is shabby of him not to at least make an appearance, though," Juliet pronounced. "He and Cecily may not be blood relatives, but that has never mattered before."

"Fear not," Cecily said. "I am not in the least offended. Though I am curious at what could possibly keep him in town in prime hunting season."

"I believe he mentioned cards," Madeline said with a weary sigh. "At Lord Peter Naughton's house. It is rather tedious to have a brother with such a wild reputation. It does nothing but make Mother worry and certainly has no positive effects on the family reputation at large. It is no wonder I haven't had an offer for the three years since my debut. No man in London would be foolish enough to saddle themselves to such a brother-in-law."

Cecily and Juliet squeezed her hands in commiseration.

"Is Lord Peter known to be a gambler, then?" Cecily asked, careful not to show her interest in the man. Lucas had told her only yesterday that there were rumors circulating that

Lord Peter had added some newly discovered artifacts to his extensive collection of Egyptian treasures. "I confess I had not heard much beyond his penchant for antiquities."

"Oh," Madeline said with a wave of her hand. "He is your typical rakish type. He does everything to excess—gambling, women. The men in Jamie's set are forever going on about what a capital fellow Lord Naughton is. How he bested them all when they raced their curricles from Ascot to London. How he blackened Gentleman Jackson's eye in a bout of fisticuffs."

Madeline made a noise of disgust. "I have grown quite weary of hearing about him. If I were ever lucky enough to be in his company I would tell him so. Alas, that is unlikely given that the man also abhors polite society and would rather dine on his boots than set foot in Almack's. That last is a direct quote, by the way. I heard him once when he came to visit Jamie at Essex Grange."

"It sounds like you have made a study of the man, Mads," Juliet said, her tone sly. "One would almost imagine you are drawn to him yourself."

Cecily was intrigued to see a faint blush rise in Madeline's cheeks. She would take special note of the man when she and Lucas visited him. Though she would not mention her knowledge of the house party. Her husband doubtless knew of the man's tarnished reputation, but she would not remind him lest he decide to exert his authority as her husband and forbid her to accompany him.

If Lord Naughton were as competitive as Madeline claimed, it was entirely possible that his possession of artifacts obtained during her father's last expedition was more about besting some other collector than simple joy in the object itself.

Called away from her conversation with her cousins, she spent the rest of the wedding breakfast accepting congratulations and chatting with other guests. To her surprise, she enjoyed herself more than she had at any other gathering of the *ton* in years. Whether that could be owed to the fact that she was one of the guests of honor, or some change in her own degree of self-assurance, she could not say. But when she and Lucas left to make the short journey to his town house, she was both tired and, to her surprise, happy.

When the carriage stopped in Grosvenor Square, Cecily had a sense of being out of place. As if she should be going back to Hurston House instead of stopping at Lucas's home. But she shook the feeling off as the normal consequence of so life-altering a change.

They were greeted by the butler, Watkins, and every servant of the house had lined up to greet their new mistress. It hammered home her new position as nothing to this point had done, and as she neared the end of the procession, the enormity of what she had taken on descended upon her and she was at once exhausted.

Perhaps seeing her weariness, Lucas took her arm and ordered baths and supper for both of them.

"There was not time to redecorate, of course," Lucas said when they reached the duchess's chamber. "But you are free to do so as you see fit."

Cecily could only nod as she took in the surprisingly comfortable rooms. Furnished in fabrics and papers of pale blue and cream, the rooms were not so lavish as she had expected. For which she was grateful.

"There is a connecting door, here," he said, gesturing toward the far wall. "There is a sitting room between our two dressing rooms. I will join you there for dinner in an hour or so."

His voice sounded suddenly formal, and it occurred to her that perhaps her new husband felt every bit as awkward as she did in their newfound intimacy.

Before he could step through the doorway, Cecily pressed a staying hand to his arm. "Your Grace, wait."

Lucas turned, his brows raised in question, but he slid his hand down to hers, carelessly rubbing a thumb over her clasped fingers.

"We are wed now," he said quietly. "I should like it very much if you would call me Lucas."

She felt a heat suffuse her cheeks. "Very well, Lucas,"

she said, feeling a sudden shyness. "I . . . I was hoping, that is . . . please stay."

One dark brow rose in query. His gaze flicked to the bed, then back at her. He raised their clasped hands to his mouth and kissed her hand. "I had thought to allow you some rest. If your sleep was as fitful as mine was last evening, then you undoubtedly need a nap."

"Might we sleep . . . together?"

So many things had changed in her life in the past few days that the idea of remaining in her new chamber alone filled her with trepidation.

His eyes widened in surprise, but he nodded.

"Come."

His fingers still linked with hers, he led her through her dressing room, the sitting room, and finally through the connecting door to his bedchamber.

It was the mirror image of her own, albeit the décor was more masculine, with darker furnishings of deep blue. The bed, a large, imposing affair, dominated the room.

Stopping at the bedside, he indicated that she should sit, and to Cecily's bemusement, he began to undress her, beginning with her shoes and stockings.

"Lucas," she protested. "I had only meant . . . that is to say . . . It is still daylight. Surely we cannot engage in . . ."

Her implication was clear, even if she could not bring herself to say the words. On any other day she would have had no qualms about speaking her mind, but her fatigue coupled with Lucas's gentleness had sparked an uncharacteristic diffidence in her.

Unperturbed by her objection, however, he continued rolling down her left stocking and paused to place a brief kiss on her knee.

"We will only sleep, Cecily." She read nothing but honesty in his eyes and she was struck again by how honorable he was. How *kind*. For the first time in her life she felt complete and utter trust in another person. It was at once comforting and dangerously disturbing.

"You are exhausted and so am I," he continued.

Lucas rose and began unbuttoning his coat. It was something she felt sure he would have done with his valet's assistance had she not been present, but as he did not wear his coat as tight as fashion dictated, he soon had it off.

It was the first time she had seen him in just his shirtsleeves and the sight made her breath catch in her throat. Amazing that something so simple could be so exciting, she mused. As he began to unwind his cravat, she found herself waiting with anticipation to see the naked skin beneath it.

Throughout the process, Lucas's eyes never left hers, and warmth began to rise in her belly and farther below. Without prompting she tucked her feet beneath her and lay back on the pillows, feeling as decadent as a harem girl.

When he climbed up beside her and tucked her against his side, she reveled in the warmth of his skin through the thin barrier of his shirt. Her senses warred between arousal and languor.

"Sleep," he whispered against the top of her head. "There will be time enough for us to feed our other hungers later."

She was still formulating her protest when she drifted off in his arms.

Lucas came awake slowly, though he was fully aware of where he was and with whom he had just slept. He could not recall another time when he had shared his bed with a woman for the purpose of sleep only. But then there were apparently to be many such firsts with Cecily. For a brief moment of panic he wondered at her absence, but then the murmurs of sound coming from the adjoining room, one of the voices clearly hers, reassured him. He would not have been shocked if she had made a rope from the bedsheets and made her escape, but he was relieved to know she had not, all the same.

A faint hunger pang prompted him to leave his bed in search of her. They would dine in the sitting room, and if she was hungry also he would order the servants, whom he had instructed not to disturb them, to bring a light supper.

But padding on bare feet to the sitting room, he saw it was empty. When no one answered his sharp rap on the door to Cecily's sitting room, he turned the knob and stepped inside. Already the room smelled of his wife and roses, and he smiled at the change. He wondered idly what other alterations her presence in his household would bring.

A light beamed from beneath the door of her dressing room and he crossed and silently turned the handle. The sight of his new wife, resting languidly in the deep bath his predecessor had installed, snatched the breath from him.

Her delicately arched feet resting on the tub's edge, her eyes closed in utter relaxation, Cecily was Aphrodite come to life. Allowing his gaze free rein, he drank in the sight of her—his eyes caressing the pale, perfect skin of her long legs, lingering for a moment at the dark profusion of curls at the juncture of her thighs, skirting up to the dusky nipples that pebbled just above the surface of the water, resting at last on the dusky lashes that fanned out against her cheeks.

No goddess had ever been more enticing, and Lucas was struck suddenly by the knowledge that this sight, Cecily in all her glory, belonged to him now.

Only to him.

It was at once humbling and invigorating. He made a silent vow that as long as there was breath in his body he would do whatever it took to ensure that she never had reason to regret their hasty marriage. That he would prove himself worthy of her.

Still silent, he stepped carefully until he sank down on his haunches behind her head and leaned forward to kiss her ear.

Startled, she dropped her feet into the bath with a splash.

"Are you in the habit of sneaking up on ladies in their baths?" she asked, reflexively covering her breasts with her folded arms, scowling up at him. "Because I warn you now that I will not countenance it."

He listened to her scold without succumbing to the urge to laugh.

"Yes, ma'am," he said without a hint of contrition, moving his lips from her ear to her neck. "Have you ever been told how magnificently lovely you are?"

She leaned back, suspicion shining in her eyes. "Not in so many words, no," she said. "Ugly ducklings do not normally find themselves recipients of compliments."

This last was said with a hint of resentment that she seemed immediately to regret, for she added, "Not that it matters, of course. Empty flattery is something ladies like Amelia Snowe thrive on. I have no need of such folderol."

They were the words of a woman who for too long had been subjected to the cutting remarks of the *ton*'s less pleasant denizens. And, he suspected, hid a great deal of self-doubt. Cecily might be assured in her cerebral acumen, but as a woman she was as unschooled as a newborn foal trying to find its balance.

He felt a surge of protectiveness for this beautiful, prickly woman he'd married. Turning her head with a gentle hand beneath her chin, he looked into her eyes, speaking softly, earnestly. "Believe me when I tell you that you are exquisite. I do not flatter. I do not fawn. I will tell you the truth. Always."

He kissed her, allowing his mouth to linger as she relaxed into him, opening herself to the caress. Pulling back, when she would have looked away, he held her chin and looked directly into her eyes.

"I will tell you a secret," he said. "It is difficult for a man to hide his reaction to a beautiful woman."

A furrow appeared between her brows. "What do you mean?"

He let go of her chin and took her hand, guiding it down to brush against the evidence of his reaction to her particular form of ugliness. "This is what you do to me," he said, his voice growing rough. "And though you will never have reason to test the theory, I daresay I am not alone in my appreciation of your charms."

Twin flags of color rose in her cheeks, even as she opened her hand to cup his erection, curiosity overcoming missishness.

"Careful," he hissed, lifting her hand away from the front of his breeches and lifting her palm to kiss it. "You may explore me as much as you wish later. For now I should like not to disgrace myself on our wedding night. So I respectfully request that you refrain from your explorations until afterward."

A wrinkle of puzzlement appeared between her brows.

"How long afterward?" she demanded. "Tomorrow? I thought gentlemen were able to do this sort of thing again and again."

"They are . . . that is to say, we are . . . or rather, I . . ." Lucas resisted the urge to run his hands through his hair. "Perhaps we should save this chat for later, once we have . . ." He paused, allowing the unsaid words to linger.

"But . . ." Cecily sat up straighter in the tub, and once again his gaze was drawn to her bosom. Through a haze of lust, he heard her ask diffidently, "Did we not already . . . ? That is to say, have we not . . . ?"

With effort, he stood, thankful for the cover his banyan provided. "Yes, we have already . . . er, consummated the marriage," he said, "but I am . . ." He wondered how best to phrase it, and cursed the heat he felt rising in his cheeks. "Somewhat eager and do not wish to rush my fences."

Cecily nodded, as if such conversations were an everyday occurrence. "I see," she said, staring down into the bathwater, seeming to take a sudden interest in her left knee. "However, I . . . I rather liked it when you . . . um . . . rushed things in the Egyptian Club."

At his strangled sound she swung her gaze upward. "What? Have I said something wrong?"

"No, my dear," he assured her, wishing like mad that this conversation would end before one of them expired from embarrassment. But he thought it best if they spoke frankly about the issue, given that they had a whole lifetime of such conversations ahead of them, and the more they discussed, the less embarrassing they would seem.

"It is just that . . . well, there is a sort of code that demands that a gentleman waits to rush things until after the lady has already . . ."

He circled his hand in the air, employing the universal sign of unspoken conclusions.

"Already . . . ?" Then, understanding dawned in Cecily's eyes. "Oh! You are afraid that you will disappoint me. Well, let me be the first to tell you that you have nothing to fear on that score."

Dammit! He felt the blush creep into his cheeks again. But her next words had him staring openmouthed at her like a surprised trout.

"I mean, I really have nothing to compare your performance to," she went on guilelessly. "You could be utterly unimpressive on that score and I'd be none the wiser."

"Yes, well, we should perhaps have supper now," Lucas said quickly, suddenly eager to change the subject. "I'll ring for your maid."

"I gave her the evening off," Cecily said, however. "I thought perhaps you could help me."

The gleam in her eye told him that she knew exactly what she was doing. And when she gripped the sides of the tub and stood, rivulets of water gleaming as they slid over her luscious curves, he lost the ability to breathe.

Again.

At this rate, he'd lose all lung function before the evening ended. Though on a positive note, he'd certainly die happy.

Cecily waited with apprehension for Lucas to say something, anything, in response to her boldness. She had no idea what had come over her. While she'd always been comfortable in her scholarly pursuits, she was a bit more reserved when it came to matters of her appearance.

She knew of course that she was hardly an antidote, no matter what Amelia Snowe said. Though she had never been particularly successful in social settings, she had been courted by one or two gentlemen, including the faithless David. If Lucas's test were to be employed there, she was indeed capable of alluring men. Still, her years with the spinsters and wallflowers had left her with a bruised notion of her own attractiveness. And as a result it was with some trepidation that she stood boldly before her husband now, conscious of every tiny defect, every blemish, every mark that might make her less than beautiful in his eyes.

"You are . . ." she heard him say, not daring to look up and see the disappointment in his eyes, "exquisite."

"There is no need to lie," she said faintly, though his words were like balm to her wounded *amour propre*. "I know I am not beautiful."

She felt him move toward her, aware of a shift in the air as much as anything else. It was odd how she could sense him entering a room, drawing near to her. Almost as if they were bound together with some invisible force, like the pull between two magnets of opposing poles.

"I do not lie, Cecily," he said, tilting his head to make sure she met his gaze. "You are exquisite. Beautiful even if it comes to that. I fear you have been too long without a compliment and have lost the knack for receiving them."

He dipped his head to take her mouth with his, his lips feathering hers with a touch as light as down. "Repeat after me," he whispered, leaning back to watch her. "Thank you, Lucas."

She raised her gaze to his, noting the tiny flecks of green that circled around the dark centers of his eyes, fighting the urge to look away from the understanding she saw there.

"Th-thank you, Lucas," she repeated, suddenly shy in the face of his open admiration.

Smiling, he ran his hands down her arms to take both her hands in his.

"There, now," he said, "that wasn't so bad, was it? I must warn you, you must get used to this sort of thing. For I mean to pay you a goodly number of compliments."

Cecily only nodded, unsure what the best response to that announcement would be. She was unused to being the focus of such intense scrutiny, and if truth be told it was somewhat unsettling. Still, she supposed having one's husband find one attractive was better than being completely ignored.

She was spared further time for reflection when Lucas leaned in again and took her mouth in a much more thorough kiss. Turning her, he pulled her still dripping body to press against his, the sensation of his hard muscles against her soft curves filling her with an ache she longed to assuage.

His tongue swept into her mouth, conquering, claiming, and for a brief moment she was lost to the sheer pleasure of the feelings he incited in her. Unable to remain passive for long, however, she ran her own tongue against the length of his and soon they sparred, their mouth fused together in a wicked dance. Accepting his thrusting tongue, she sucked gently, gasping when she felt his hand sweep up her side and palm her breast, her nipple aching as it cried out for the attention of his fingers.

She almost cried out her frustration as she felt him draw away, then inhaled sharply as he grasped her behind the knees and swept her up into his arms, carrying her dripping through the dressing room door and into his darkened bedroom beyond.

The bedclothes were still mussed from their nap earlier, but Lucas paid no heed, depositing her onto the sheet, and drawing the rest of the covers back down to the foot of the bed.

He untied the sash of his banyan, and shrugged out of it, his haste at once flattering and frustrating her.

"Wait," she said, lifting a staying hand to his chest. "I want to see you."

She knew of course, from drawings and some of the more salacious books that her father kept in his library, what an unclothed man looked like, but with the exception of that one night in the club, she had never been at liberty to gaze on a flesh-and-blood specimen. And, if truth were told, for all her boldness, she was feeling a little bit overwhelmed by the pace of their lovemaking thus far. She had gone from lounging alone in the bath, to naked and trembling in the nuptial bower in a rather brief span of time.

"Please," she added, allowing her fingers to gently caress the crisp dark hair that covered his chest.

For a flash she saw what looked like pain in his gaze, but then with a brisk nod, he brought his knee back off the mattress and stood before her, his arms open to the sides as if he were a merchant selling a particularly enticing side of beef.

Determined to stifle her propensity to blush, Cecily instead leaned forward, comfortable in her own nudity now that she was not the only unclothed person in the room. Though she made a valiant effort to look at the rest of him— and from what she glimpsed the rest of him was very handsome indeed—her eyes were drawn to the ridge of flesh that tilted proudly before him, straining toward his flat stomach.

From the arrow of dark hair that drew the eye downward, to the sharp slashes of his hipbones that pointed inward, it was as if he'd been designed with the sole intention of advertising the splendidness of his male member. To Cecily's mind it was rather a shame that he was forced to hide such an impressive specimen under clothing. Though she could understand that perhaps it might get in the way during day-to-day activities.

When he coughed, she realized that she'd been staring silently for some time.

Striving for nonchalance, she nodded sagely. "Very well."

"That is all you have to say?" he asked, one brow arched. "You do not perhaps wish to tell me more?"

Unable to lift her eyes from crotch level, she watched in fascination as it twitched under her gaze. "Oh! I . . . that is . . ." She struggled to come up with suitable words. Perhaps he wished a compliment?

"Your . . . er . . . appendage is very elegant, Your Grace." There.

She tore her eyes from his middle and met his gaze. Which twinkled with mirth.

"Elegant?" he demanded. "I have had my cock called many things by many . . ." His ears reddened as if he realized that his words were leading him toward danger.

Now it was her turn to raise a brow.

"That is to say," he rumbled, climbing back up onto the bed, bracing his back against the headboard. "Thank you, Your Grace."

"You are welcome," Cecily responded, feeling suddenly shy again. "Thank you for letting me look."

Lucas shook his head, sliding his hand down her arm from shoulder to fingertips. "Cecily, I have had the oddest sorts of conversations since I met you," he said, pulling her to straddle him, then taking both her hands in his and kissing her full on the mouth.

"I am merely thanking you," she muttered as he caressed her jaw with his lips, making his way up to a particularly sensitive spot below her ear. She dipped down to caress his chest with her breasts and was pleased to hear his sharp intake of breath, her own breath catching at the pull of sensation that the friction created between her breasts and that ache between her legs. "Never let it be said that I am not polite."

Lucas fought for control as he luxuriated in the feel of her nipples against his chest, mentally cursed himself for allowing her gaze. Her eyes on his cock had been as arousing as if she had taken him in hand. And what he had planned as a slow seduction was rapidly taking on a momentum he was powerless to stop.

What was it about her that made him lose every last semblance of gentlemanly grace and revert to some sort of ravening beast? From the moment he spied her outside the Egyptian Club he'd been drawn to her like a compass to true north. And now that he had her, he would make damn sure she never wanted for anything again.

"Good manners are always important." He kissed his way down her neck to her bosom, worshipping first one, then the other with his mouth.

She moaned, and wriggled against him, the inadvertent friction between her bottom and his arousal causing beads of perspiration to break out on his forehead.

With a muttered curse, he flipped her neatly onto her back and drew her hands above her head with one hand.

"I want you to hold on to this," he said, placing her hands on the ornate headboard and bracing himself above her.

"But wh—" she started to ask, but he silenced her with a hard kiss.

"Next time," he said briskly, looking into her puzzled eyes, "I promise you may do whatever you like, but for now, I want to give you pleasure."

She frowned. "But what about you?"

He blew out a long sigh. "The thing is, gentlemen enjoy this sort of thing no matter what. It takes very little effort on your part for me to climax. It's just the way we were made."

Cecily bit her lip. "So, I should do nothing?"

Dammit. He was making a mull of it.

"Not at all." He kissed her neck to soothe her obvious discomfort. "You must do what comes naturally, whatever that may be. But what I'm trying to say, and failing at miserably, is that because I have the easier time of it, I wish to make sure that you enjoy yourself thoroughly. And—"

"Winterson," she interrupted. "Lucas."

He leaned back to see her smiling indulgently at him.

"Just do what comes naturally." She brought one arm down to rub a caressing hand along his jawline. "I feel sure I'll enjoy things no matter what you do."

He closed his eyes. Perhaps he *was* being overly conscientious.

"You're sure?"

"Absolutely."

"Well, then." He ran his hand lightly over the concave plane of her stomach. "I suppose we might try it your way for a bit."

He dipped one finger into the molten heat at her core, was surprised to find her already wet with wanting. "Watch me," he whispered into her ear, taking the lobe between his teeth. "Watch me stroke you here, ready you for our joining."

Cecily looked down to see his long, nimble fingers against her mound, bit back a moan as sight and sensation joined to create a wave of need within her. She felt the press of his manhood against her belly, and instinct urged her to move her hips, to open herself to him.

He drew his forefinger away from her, her own moisture glistening on his hand in the candlelight. "See how your body responds to mine," he whispered, settling himself between her thighs, running one hand down the outside of her leg, to bend it at the knee.

"Lucas," she hissed as he teased her opening with the head of his erection. "Please." She wanted, no, needed him there. Inside her, thrusting into her like he had on the floor of the club.

At her use of his given name, something in him seemed to shatter, and Cecily felt the muscles of his back tense beneath her hands that sought only to press him more fully into her.

One arm leveraging himself above her, Lucas used the other to guide himself into place, then with one steady push, he seated himself fully within her.

The fullness, at once overwhelming and deeply satisfying, stole Cecily's breath. When she looked up, the planes of his face, only inches from her own, were stone hard, his eyes closed as if he were in pain.

Just then, his long lashes rose, and she was arrested by the intensity of his gaze.

"Hold on to me," he ordered, his customary grin replaced with a serious expression that made her stomach leap.

He dipped his head and took her mouth. Her hands slid down to grasp his hard buttocks as he began to move within her, mouths and bodies working in tandem as they rocked together.

Cecily lifted her hips to meet his thrusts, digging her heels into the bed as she fought for purchase against the power of his penetration.

Lucas broke their kiss to bury his face in her neck. "Wrap your legs around me," he said, his breath hot against her skin. Cecily was too far gone with feeling to mind his continued orders. It no longer mattered who was in charge or whether she might embarrass herself. Giving herself up to the demands of her body, and her husband, she drew her legs up to grasp him to her and was rewarded with a few more precious inches of fullness.

"Oh God." The words escaped her as the feel of him sliding into her channel radiated through her in a wave of pleasure that nearly brought her to tears. And all the while she felt it building within her, urging her toward that same nameless pinnacle that she'd briefly reached the last time she and Lucas came together.

"Sorry," he breathed into her skin. "Can't wait."

And as he spoke, he slipped both hands beneath her bottom, bringing her closer to him as he began to move harder, more erratically in and out, in and out. The increased momentum added to the need Cecily felt rising within her.

Of its own volition her body moved, rising to meet his pumping flesh in a feverish race toward ecstasy. Then, as if sensing how close she was to shattering, Lucas reached one hand down between their bodies and, with a flick of his thumb, sent her spiraling into wave after wave of mindless, wanton release.

Almost against her will she felt a rush of emotion as she plummeted over the edge of some invisible precipice, her chest filling with affection for this man who even now cradled her body as he found his own pleasure, bit lightly at the apex of her shoulder while he shuddered his own climax within her.

Fourteen

Cecily awoke to find herself alone in the enormous bed. Only a light indentation in the pillow beside her indicated that she'd not spent the night alone as she had done every other night of her life. A slight soreness, however, reminded her of last evening's novel activities, and a flash of Lucas's face as he held himself over her brought back a physical memory of what they'd done.

It had been much more pleasurable than the night in the club. Though that had been pleasant enough. She smiled to herself at the memory of his whispered words during their second coupling in the night. Who would have guessed Lucas to be such a romantic? It would be a struggle to keep herself from falling in love with him. She saw that now.

Maintaining a certain distance was crucial to the success of their marriage. Which meant that she must guard against such unfettered joinings as they had enjoyed last night. Part of her mourned for what might have been, had they been different people, free to act as they wished. But she had known the pain of losing a loved one before and only she could guard against exposing herself to such pain again. Lucas was a kind man, and she could not imagine him casting her aside as David had done, but who knew what might happen in the right circumstances? Even kind men could cause pain.

She dressed quickly and found her way downstairs to the breakfast room without incident. Though the house was much larger than Hurston House, it was well ordered. And though she was disappointed to find the chamber empty, she decided it was for the best. They should not live in one another's pockets, after all.

She'd just accepted a second cup of tea from the footman when she heard what could only be her husband's confident stride pass by the door.

Wiping her mouth, she hurried out into the hall, only to see his back as he took the stairs down to the floor below.

"Winterson," she called to him, noting with a certain feminine satisfaction the way his broad shoulders filled out the dark blue coat. "Are you going out?"

He glanced behind him in surprise. Almost as if he were a small boy caught engaging in some activity his governess had strictly forbidden. But the look was gone in seconds, replaced with what looked suspiciously like pleasure at seeing her.

"Good morning, my dear."

As it always did, his deep voice sent a little thrill down her spine. She steeled herself against her body's reaction. It would not do for her to melt into a puddle of desire every time he bid her good morning. She'd never get a thing done at all.

"Good morning," she answered, irritated when instead of sounding sophisticated, her own voice sounded breathy.

"Are you going out?" she asked again.

"Just out to White's for a bit," he said, taking her hand and drawing her down to the entrance hall, where the butler awaited them.

Lucas pulled her with him into a small parlor and shut the door firmly behind him. Before she could protest he pressed her against the door and took her mouth in a scorching kiss that sent currents of pleasure through her, reminding her in explicit detail of just where that mouth of his had been last evening.

"Good morning," he whispered, against her lips. She opened her eyes, now drowsy with passion, to see his smiling down at her. "Now that is a proper greeting. I hope you will learn these small things I teach you about how a wife behaves with her husband."

"Indeed." She smiled, unable to keep the joy that suffused her at bay. "And how does a heretofore single gentleman like yourself learn all these details of marriage etiquette? Is there a book, perhaps?"

He kissed her nose and stepped back. "As a matter of fact, there is a book. However, I do not believe it gives rules per se. In fact there are rather more pictures than words. To illustrate the activities that most contribute to spousal happiness, I suspect."

She reached out to return his cravat to something similar to what his valet had achieved, but it would never be the same, she feared.

"I look forward to your showing me this book."

"Oh, fear not." He grinned. "I will."

He reached down to straighten his cuffs, "Now, madam wife," he said, "I dislike leaving you here with all that pent-up energy, but I must be off."

"Must you?"

"I'm afraid so," he said. "I'm off to the club."

"That's all right, then," she said. "I thought for a moment that you were off to visit Lord Peter Naughton without me."

His eyes blinked, and it was enough to confirm her suspicion.

"You are!" she hissed. "I should have known you were trying to distract me with kisses. That is most unfair, Lucas!"

He had the grace to own his guilt. "I did genuinely wish to kiss you, my dear," he said. "But I do need to visit Naughton, and I need to do so alone. I had hoped to forestall this discussion."

"Oh, we will have this discussion now, Your Grace," she fumed, pacing further into the room. "I should have known better than to think you'd play fair when it came to this investigation."

"I am being reasonable, Cecily," he said, stepping further into the chamber to stop her pacing. "There are some things that a gentleman feels more comfortable discussing with another gentleman. You cannot think that Lord Peter Naughton will speak in front of you about artifacts he may have purchased on the black market? He would be a fool to do so. Especially the daughter of the man from whom they were stolen. I'll have a devil of a time getting him to speak to me, let alone to you."

"But without me you will have no way of knowing the value of the items. Or even ascertaining whether these are the items that were found in the Alexandria tomb."

"And with you, I will not be able to see the items at all," he countered. "Perhaps you can give me a brief description of what to look for."

Cecily stared. Could he be so foolish?

At her look, he nodded. "Yes, I see. It is absurd of me to think you could teach me in a few moments what it's taken you years to study. But surely there is something you could tell me to look out for."

"There is no way, Lucas. You are a quick study, but as you say it would be impossible."

She stared at him, her eyes appraising, before she stepped closer. He had the good sense to eye her with suspicion.

"What are you doing?" he asked her, as she stepped into his arms, and tilted her head so that she could press her lips against his.

"What do you think I'm doing?" she purred, kissing his cheek, and working her way down his neck.

"I suspect," he said wryly, "that you are trying to seduce me into letting you come along."

"As I said." She nipped his chin, darting her tongue out to touch the slight indentation there. "A quick study."

"Cecily." His voice was low, raspy. "I have made up my mind."

"Then you will just have to change it," she whispered, lifting his hand up to cup her breast. "I do so want to come with you."

"I know, my dear."

She gave a little jump as his thumbs rubbed against her straining nipples. As she'd said before. A quick study.

"Please, Lucas," she cooed. "You need me there. I promise that I will leave you to speak to him in peace so that you can have your man-to-man conversation. I will simply request to see his collection. I know his type. They are always eager to show off their most prized items. And he will be unable to resist letting the daughter of England's foremost Egyptian explorer view his finds."

Lucas nodded. He was clearly beginning to see some merit in the plan, though Cecily tried not to allow her triumph to show.

"All right," he said against her hair before setting her firmly away from him. "I will let you come with me. But I must warn you that you're playing with fire. If you intend to use this method to wheedle me around your little finger for the whole of this marriage you are very much mistaken. I have agreed to bring you along because you argued your point well. Any other inducements you offered, while pleasant, in no way affected my decision."

What a liar, she thought, grinning at him. She supposed she must allow him these little solaces to his pride. Still, a little doubt gathered within her. Had she misjudged her effect on him? She was not as confident in her lovemaking skills as she was in her language skills. And she did not like being a novice. At anything.

"You have grown quiet all of a sudden," he remarked as he assisted her into her pelisse, which had been brought forward by the household's newest footman. When Cecily gave the young man a smile of thanks, the lad turned as red as a beet. Lucas bit back a grin. His new wife would need to ration her smiles, else she'd have the entire household staff mooning after her, including young George.

Cecily did not respond until he handed her into the waiting carriage.

"I am merely thinking about strategy for questioning Lord Peter," she lied. She was thinking instead that she must guard against allowing her affection for him to turn into anything stronger. The last time she had succumbed to the wiles of a man she had lost all sense of perspective and dignity.

She would not let that happen again.

Once they were in the carriage, Lucas took her by the arm and seated her next to him, casually draping an arm around her shoulders. When she flinched away he looked down at her in surprise and removed it, nodding for her to return to her seat if she chose. With a heavy heart she did so.

"Apologies, my dear."

Her heart constricted at the hurt he quickly masked before turning his gaze to the carriage window. But it was for the best. If she allowed their easy relationship to develop into anything deeper, they both stood to lose all sense of perspective. And that would spell disaster for this marriage.

The journey to Lord Naughton's home in Kensington was brief and they were soon being shown into his lordship's opulent drawing room. The magnificence of the architecture coupled with the vivid colors on the walls, the carpets, and the upholstery made the room as enthralling as anything Cecily had even imagined.

As the child of an antiquarian she was no stranger to the collector's impulse to cover every available surface with bits and pieces of treasure. Her father had certainly done so with both his country and town houses. Lord Naughton, it would seem, had been unable to resist the impulse to show off his prize pieces as well.

"Remarkable," she said, leaning in closer to examine a frieze of the Furies that had long ago been broken into three separate pieces, and was now mounted on a red silk-covered wall. "I believe this must have been part of the Parthenon marbles. I wonder how he was able to convince Elgin to part with it."

"What, no date?" Lucas teased, his scent tickling her nostrils as he leaned over her shoulder to more closely inspect the piece. "I would have thought at the very least you could give an approximate value."

"Priceless, I should imagine," Cecily returned. Though she had long ago become accustomed to being around, and even working with, priceless artifacts, the notion that Lord Peter Naughton would place so valuable an item here in the open made her distinctly nervous. "Though there is no way of knowing, of course, without conducting a careful examination."

The butler returned and informed them that Lord Peter would see them in his study. Cecily and Lucas followed him through the black-and-white marble-tiled hallway and upstairs to a room overlooking the gardens.

It was a richly appointed library, with glass-fronted mahogany bookshelves lining every wall, plush oriental carpets covering every inch of floor. The room had clearly been influenced by the owner's love of antiquities and the Gothic, for the room itself was composed of a mixture of arches and curves and the mahogany-trimmed walls were adorned at regular intervals with exquisitely carved finials in the same finish. The walls—where they were not covered by artwork, sculptures, and floor-to-ceiling mirrors—were a rich, Moroccan red, at once arresting and warm.

"Your Graces," Lord Naughton said, stepping out from behind a massive desk to offer Lucas a bow and to kiss the air above Cecily's hand. "To what do I owe the pleasure of your visit?"

He was a devastatingly attractive man whose bright blond hair and wide shoulders put her in mind of a Viking warrior. She was not surprised that her cousin Madeline had found the viscount attractive. Especially if his manners were as handsome as his looks.

The man did not look as if he spent a great deal of time engaging in the sort of debauchery her cousin Jamie seemed to gravitate toward. His eyes were clear, and he did not sport any of the signs of dissipation she had come to expect from the more hardened rakes of the *ton*. Still, there was something about his eyes. Something jaded. He might not wear his sins upon his face, but he was clearly not a green youth.

"My lord," Lucas began once he and Cecily had been seated. "We are here on a rather urgent matter with which I hope you will be able to assist."

Naughton seemed surprised, but not unpleasantly so.

"Whatever it is, I hope that I may do so, Your Grace," he said, his brows raised in curiosity.

"It has come to my attention that you have recently purchased some items of Egyptian origin for your personal collection."

Lord Naughton's gaze shuttered. "And if I have?" he asked silkily.

Before Lucas could answer, Cecily said, "We suspect that they may have been stolen during my father's most recent expedition."

Lucas flashed her a look of exasperation but added nothing.

Naughton leaned back in his chair. "The expedition where your father fell victim to an apoplectic fit?" he asked. Then turning to Lucas, he added, "And where your brother went missing? That expedition?"

Cecily nodded.

"And is this theft a part of the curse, or is that strictly meant for the welfare of the expedition team and not the goods they retrieved from the angry Egyptian's tomb?" His words were mild, but Cecily couldn't miss the hint of sarcasm in the man's tone.

"I suspect that all three unfortunate circumstances can be blamed on all-too-human perpetrators instead of nameless Egyptian gods," Lucas responded dryly. "With the possible exception of Lord Hurston's illness. Though there is some debate over whether his distress at my brother's disappearance might have negatively affected his health."

His words startled Cecily, but she remembered just in time not to let Lord Naughton see her surprise.

"Yes, well," Naughton responded with an approving nod. "I have little use for superstitions, either, but one never can tell who will fall prey to such tales. I am sorry to hear about your father, Duchess," he said, nodding to Cecily in acknowledgment. "He has done much to promote the appreciation of Egyptian artistry in our nation. I wish him a speedy recovery."

"I beg your pardon, my lord," Cecily said, after thanking him for his well wishes, "but you have not answered my husband's question about your newest acquisition."

Lord Naughton threw back his head and laughed. "You are delightful, Your Grace." Turning to Lucas he asked, quite seriously, "Wherever did you find her, Winterson? I should very much like one myself."

"I'm afraid that she is unique," Lucas told the other man, before Cecily could voice her objection to being referred to as his possession. He thought wistfully of his earlier plan to call upon the collector alone, but chose not to dwell on it. "But she does raise a good point; please do tell us about your Egyptian pieces."

Naughton sighed. "I suppose it was too much to hope you would be easily led away from the subject." He ran a hand over the back of his neck, appearing to think over his next words carefully.

"The truth of the matter is this," he said with a sigh. "I did purchase several pieces from a dealer with whom I have had business in the past. He is not always, shall we say, nice, about the provenance of the items he brings to my attention. Some collectors are fastidious about having a clear line of past owners to ensure that their pieces are authentic."

Lucas watched him carefully, noting that he seemed defensive. Because he was lying? It was hard to say.

"I am not all that concerned with knowing precisely where an item comes from, because I have no intention of selling my collection. I purchase things that I want and I enjoy owning them. It's as simple as that." His eyes grew rueful. "I know it will sound absurd after my diatribe against superstition, but there is another, more . . . complicated reason for me to eschew more common methods of authentication. I have a certain talent for detecting whether a piece is genuine."

Lucas exchanged a look of puzzlement with Cecily.

"You are able to tell from looking at them whether they are from the period associated with them?" Lucas asked, intrigued.

"Not precisely," Naughton said, his ears growing pink. "I cannot say precisely how I know, but I know."

"I don't understand," Cecily said, frowning. "You must have some sort of method."

"Duchess," he said wearily, "believe me when I tell you that I wish I knew what allows me to determine a real item from a fake, but rest assured that I have tested my ability for all of my adult life and I have never been wrong."

The room was silent as the Duke and Duchess of Winterson stared at their host.

Lucas cleared his throat. "Then I suppose we must take you at your word. Regardless of how you ensure the validity of the items you acquire, we do wish to know from whom you received these Egyptian artifacts."

Looking more comfortable now that they had abandoned his odd gift, Naughton allowed his shoulders to relax. "I'm afraid that you will not be able to speak to the fellow for several weeks. He just left last week for an extended trip to the Continent."

"Indeed," Lucas said, surveying Naughton for signs that he was prevaricating. "We still would like to know the man's name if we might."

The viscount opened a drawer and withdrew a card, which he handed to Lucas. "His name is Giles Hunter. He keeps a shop at number 46 Bond Street. You may inquire from the clerk there when he can be expected back, though I presume he will be gone for some time. He has taken his sister, who is quite ill, to convalesce in Italy."

"The antiquities trade must be very profitable," Lucas remarked. Then, changing the subject, he asked, "Might we see some of the items you purchased from Mr. Hunter? Just so that we can determine for ourselves that they are the ones reported stolen from the expedition."

Naughton shook his head, looking sheepish again. "I'm afraid that won't be possible," he said.

"Why not?" Cecily's tone was sharp; it appeared to Lucas that his wife was also growing suspicious of Lord Naughton's excuses.

"I do not like to admit this. Especially given the measures I have taken to ensure the safety of my collection," the antiquarian said with a scowl, "but there was a burglary here just last week."

His jaw clenched as he spoke of the outrage.

"The only things the thieves took were the pieces you suspect came from Lord Hurston's expedition."

Fifteen

The next week, Lucas found himself escorting his wife to a small dinner party at Lord and Lady Shelby's house. Though they'd not spent a night apart since the wedding, he could not help but note the distance Cecily strived to put between them. At night she was passionate, even loving, but in the cold light of day she receded into a pleasant but reserved persona that no amount of cajoling on his part could break through. So, when they arrived at her aunt and uncle's house, he was not surprised to see her retreat with her cousins to the corner of the drawing room while the guests waited for the sound of the dinner bell.

They had come up with no leads on the artifacts that had been stolen from Lord Naughton's town house, and the whereabouts of Lord Hurston's diaries remained unknown. Which in turn meant that they were no closer to learning what had happened to his brother. In the face of so much disappointment, a simple evening gathering was a welcome diversion.

He fell into conversation with Lords Deveril and Monteith about their recent trip to Tattersall's, but was mildly surprised when Lord Geoffrey Brighton appeared at his elbow and asked if they might speak privately. Excusing himself from the other men, he followed Brighton to an empty spot near the fire.

"I beg your pardon for interrupting your conversation,

Your Grace," Brighton said, his pleasant features schooled into an expression of regret. "But I could not waste this opportunity to speak to you about your wife."

Though he knew Brighton had known Cecily since she was a small girl, there was something about the way Brighton spoke of Cecily that put him on alert.

Still, he managed to answer with a jovial enough tone. "I am most interested to hear what you have to say, sir. Though I must confess that I am at a loss for what it could be."

Brighton nodded. "Yes, you are right to be leery. I would not bring it up if it were not of the utmost importance."

Lucas nodded for the man to continue.

"It has been brought to my attention that your wife is looking into the disappearance of your brother, and possibly into what happened during that last expedition before he went missing." He paused, as if gauging Lucas's reaction to the news.

Lucas kept his features impassive. "I wonder who could have told you such a tale. I do not believe Cecily has had much time for anything but household matters since the wedding. There is a great deal for her to do as the Duchess of Winterson now. Though I can assure you that if she is doing so, it is with my full consent."

"Even when she places herself in harm's way?" Brighton demanded. "I must confess that I thought you cared more for Cecily's well-being than that. But I suppose your desire to find your brother must overshadow some of your solicitude for your new wife."

Lucas merely raised a brow in query at the other man's outburst, which was enough to force Brighton into a rather insincere apology.

"Forgive me, I am somewhat overwrought at the thought of seeing someone for whom I have great affection placed in harm's way. Of course you are taking every possible care of her."

"Indeed." Lucas inclined his head to accept the apology. "I do hope you realize that I would not allow my wife to endanger herself unduly."

"Of course, of course, Your Grace," he said with a smile that Lucas began to doubt was genuine. "I must beg the indulgence given to an old friend of the family."

"Ah, yes, but then as merely an old friend of the family," Lucas said with deadly charm, "you have no need to worry about such things. She is under my protection now. Though I must thank you for inquiring about the matter."

Seeing that he would be getting nothing further from Lucas, Brighton excused himself and wandered off to Violet's side. Winterston stayed where he was, looking after the other man with puzzlement.

"What was that all about?" Christian asked, coming to his side. "I looked over and saw him giving you a look that would slice you to ribbons were it a knife."

"Hm." Lucas nodded. "I believe Lord Brighton is less than pleased to learn that he is no longer as influential in Cecily's life as he once was."

"Well, what did the fellow expect?" Christian shook his head. "It's not as if she's going to listen to him now that she's married to you. As the Bible says . . . something about cleaving unto . . . someone."

"Ah, yes, you were ever the great biblical scholar, were you not?" Lucas clapped his friend heartily on the shoulder.

"Oh, stubble it, Winterson."

His reply was forestalled by Lady Shelby's calling them into dinner.

Cecily found herself seated between Lord Geoffrey on her right and Lord Deveril on her left. Though she tried to respond to Deveril's conversation, she found that more often than not Lord Geoffrey would not allow her to leave his attention for more than a moment at a time.

First he asked her about the changes in her life since her marriage. And since little more than a week had elapsed since that event, she had little enough to tell him. Especially given that most of the changes involved the fact that she now slept, most nights, with a naked man beside her—something she most definitely would not be discussing with Lord Geoffrey, or anyone else for that matter.

Then he queried her about her father's condition, and what news the physician was able to give them regarding his long-term prognosis. On this subject, she was, thankfully, able to speak at some length, though the details of her father's treatment were upsetting to her.

"For I cannot help but think, my lord," she said as the footman took away the plate of nearly untouched turbot in wine sauce, "that somewhere within that twisted countenance, my father is somehow aware of everything that goes on around him, and struggles to make himself understood."

"Surely that cannot be so, my dear," he returned, "for has not the physician said that he can hear none of what goes on around him?"

"Well, of course he says that," she said with some feeling, "but when I sit with him, sometimes I will speak to him of what has been going on in my life . . ." She smiled sheepishly. "I suppose it is silly of me, but I have found that if I tell him about mundane matters, or Winterson, or even sometimes you, he squeezes my hand in such a way that I cannot help but think that he does understand me."

Lord Geoffrey stopped with his spoon halfway to his mouth, putting it back down again. "You have spoken to him about me?" he asked, his gaze intense. "What did you say?"

"Just that you have been speaking of him, and how wonderful his last expedition was. Indeed, when I told him about your kind offer to write us a catalog of the items that were found in the final tomb, he squeezed my hand."

"Did he? Did he indeed?" Brighton's arrested expression sent a pang of sympathy through her. As her father's oldest and dearest friend it was probably difficult for him to see how Lord Hurston's fine mind and strong body had been affected by his illness.

She reached over and patted his hand. "He did." She nodded. "Furthermore, I know how much you have done to ensure that my father's legacy be preserved with the Egyptian

Club. And do not doubt for a moment that we are not grateful for all your assistance."

Lord Geoffrey nodded. "It is little enough, my dear," he said, turning his hand over to squeeze hers.

Cecily caught a glimpse of Lucas watching them from across the table, and hastily removed her hand from Lord Geoffrey's. Why she should feel embarrassed about the moment, she could not say. However, when Lady Shelby announced that dinner was finished, she rose to her feet with relief to follow the other ladies into the drawing room. Leaving her husband and Lord Geoffrey to work out that conflict between themselves.

After dinner, because the party was small enough to make it manageable, Juliet suggested that the younger couples engage in some parlor games. Lucas allowed himself to be cajoled into participating, though he felt foolish in the extreme. As a married couple, he and Cecily could just as easily have bowed out, but he could see that Cecily wished to play along, and where she was concerned, he found it almost impossible to think of his own wishes.

"The first game," Juliet said, once card tables had been set up, "is to be one of transpositions." She and Madeline, who was clearly her cousin's cohort in this scheme, passed out slips of paper and pencils to each of the eight couples.

"I will name the category, and then the ladies will have one minute to write down a word fitting that category, only rearranging the letters to make it unrecognizable. Once it is done, the gentleman will have to guess what word the lady has given him. If he cannot guess before two minutes have passed, then he will have to pay a forfeit. Then we will switch to gentlemen, then ladies and so on, until one half hour has passed. At which point, the couple who have paid the fewest forfeits wins."

"But first," Madeline said, "we must break into pairs. I have written down the numbers one though eight and put them into two piles. Each lady and each gentleman will choose a number from the appropriate pile. The lady with the number one and the gentleman with the number one will form a pair and so on."

Trying not to be a poor sport, Lucas duly waited his turn and chose a slip of paper. He unfolded it and looked. Seven.

The others were all milling about calling out their own numbers and finding their partners.

"Seven," he said dutifully, scanning the ladies who were not yet paired up. "Who has number seven?"

To his surprise and delight, Cecily, who had also been scanning the others, met his gaze.

"Seven," she said with a rueful smile. Her slightly exasperated expression seemed to indicate that she suspected her cousins of playing matchmaker. Though as they were already a match it seemed a bit beside the point.

"Everyone to their tables," Juliet directed them, following her own partner, Lord Christian Monteith, to the table with a place card reading "7/8."

Lord Geoffrey had been pressed into service as timekeeper, and had taken up a position at the head of the room with his pocket watch and a small sand-filled hourglass.

"The first category," Brighton announced, "in honor of our hostess and her sisters, is to be flowers. Each lady must rearrange the letters in a flower name with more than seven but less than ten letters."

He took the hourglass, and held it up. "Your time begins . . ." He turned the glass. "Now!"

Lucas watched with fascination as Cecily looked at some unknown point in the air as she searched her brain for a flower name. Finally, having arrived at something she found doable, she began to write, scribbling the letters as quickly as she could, then passing the slip of paper over to him.

He looked down at the paper and sighed. XATLODFA.

Next to him, Christian let out an audible sound of displeasure.

"Do you wish us to lose?" he demanded of Juliet.

"My thought exactly, old fellow," Lucas said.

Clearly the cousins were enjoying themselves, for they

both gave shrugs of indifference and sat back to watch their partners struggle to solve the puzzles.

The room was silent as all the males in the room got to work. One by one, cries of flower names rang out as gentlemen began to solve their puzzles.

"Daffodil!"

"Harebell!"

"Primrose!"

"Daisy" was disqualified as being composed of fewer than six letters, which annoyed Madeline greatly. The same fate befell Lucy Huntington's choice of "pasqueflower" for being too long.

Ignoring the din around him, Lucas got down to work and arranged the letters of his clue into some semblance of order. In the end he was only able to guess because he had just been conversing about this particular flower with his mama last week as it was also a bit of a nuisance and had taken root in the back garden at his London house.

"You are running out of time, Your Grace," Cecily warned in a singsong voice.

"I had no idea what a competitive creature you are, my dear," he returned as he quickly made sure his answer was correct. Finally, he looked up into her eyes and slapped his answer onto the table.

"Toadflax," he announced.

Though she had teased him, he could tell that Cecily was pleased that he had solved the puzzle.

Thinking to give her a taste of her own medicine, for his first clue to her, he gave her what he thought was a moderately difficult one: ECADNLAINE.

But she had solved it in seconds. "Celandine!"

When his next turn came around, he chose an even more complex flower name: OKDCSAYLM.

"Lady-smock!" she said with even less time remaining on the clock than before.

Again and again, Lucas tried to stump his wife, having long ago given up the restraints of the game and giving her clues that involved many more letters than ten, and again and again she unraveled the letters like a child pulling a thread in a scarf.

"How do you do it?" he demanded. He assumed it had something to do with her facility for languages, but was interested in knowing whether there was some sort of process she employed.

"I'm not quite sure," she said with a shrug. "I look at the letters and somehow I am able to see them forming the word, even when they are jumbled together without rhyme or reason."

"She's always been like that," Juliet added. "Maddie and I were always loath to play at any sort of games with her in the nursery, since she was always sure to win. Not that we minded, but there's not much sport in playing when you know you've no chance of winning."

"I did try to let you win sometimes," Cecily protested. "Many times!"

"Yes, but you were never very patient about it," the other girl said, her grin taking the sting from her words. "I know it cannot have been very pleasant for you to be forced to play with us, when we could never offer you any competition."

Lucas watched his wife and her cousin's exchange and imagined what she must have been like as a child. A grave, serious girl with an intellect that separated her from her peers. The very thought of it made his chest constrict.

As if sensing the mood had become too serious, Christian spoke up. "Well, I suppose Winterson knows what it's like to always lose to a superior opponent. The story of his whole childhood, he and Will being forced to bow to my overwhelming prowess at every possible sport. It's a wonder he survived at all."

Lucas flinched at the mention of Will, though he was grateful that his friend had drawn the conversation away from Cecily's difficult childhood. Still, the mention of his brother in that context reminded him that Will had always been a dab hand at word puzzles as well. Which triggered another memory—of Will's letters home from his last trip to Egypt, which were crossed and recrossed to conserve paper, but had seemed illegible to both Lucas and his mother. What if the letters weren't illegible? What if they were written in a cipher of sorts? Lord Hurston had been careful enough to write his journals in code. Well, what if Will, as his secretary, had employed a similar technique for recording his thoughts about the expedition? Only he sent them home to his mother rather than recording them into his personal diaries.

It made sense.

Perfect sense.

The party was breaking up, and as soon as it was possible he and Cecily said their good-nights and made their way to the waiting carriage.

"What was the hurry?" Cecily demanded once they were in the privacy of the carriage.

Lucas gathered her into his arms and gave her a thorough kiss.

"You'll see," he said with a grin.

The ride was maddening—mostly because though Cecily tried, she could not convince Lucas to tell her why he was so excited.

When they finally arrived at Winterson House, he bounded out of the carriage and bodily lifted Cecily down before the footman could even get the step down.

"Lucas," she said, struggling to keep up with him as he pulled her by the hand behind him into the house and up the stairs to his study. "What on earth is the matter?"

"I should have done this from the beginning," he said. "I see that now, though at the time I didn't make the connection between your father's journals and Will's letters. I was a fool not to consider it, though. Especially since you told me that very first day that you were able to interpret his blasted code."

Cecily shook her head in wonder as she watched him hunt through his desk drawers, clearly searching for something in particular.

At last, he extracted a bundle of letters and tossed them onto the desktop.

"Here," he said, gesturing for her to come and sit behind his desk.

She complied, but it felt odd to be seated in the place from which the Dukes of Winterson ruled. Metaphorically, at least. Still, she did as he asked, if only to see what he meant about Will's letters.

"These are all of them, I believe," he said, untying the dark ribbon that bound them together, leaning over her so that she felt the warmth of his body where he pressed against her. "There are only four in all. I forgot the bloody things existed until tonight when you raced through the flower names. Absurd that I should have, but there it is. If this turns out to have endangered his life in any way . . ."

He stopped there, shaking his head. Cecily glanced down at the papers on the desk. They were letters, from Will, she presumed.

"What does this mean?" she asked, needing some context for her husband's odd behavior.

Lucas took a deep breath, and as if needing to keep moving, he stepped around to the other side of the desk and began to pace.

"They're Will's letters to my mother, written during the damned expedition."

She did not take offense at his characterization of the dig, or the swearing. He was clearly overset by the idea that by forgetting about the letters he had somehow endangered his brother's life.

"And?"

"And they have some chicken scratch crossed through them. I thought at first that it was the foolish code we made up when we were boys. I was never very good at it, but I supposed that he might want to tell me something that he didn't want Mama or Clarissa to know about. But it was like nothing we'd ever worked on together. And it's certainly not any language I've ever studied. When I met you, I thought about asking you to look at them, but at first I wasn't sure if you were trustworthy enough to translate them—especially given that they might contain information that implicates your father in something unsavory. And then we became so focused on finding the journals that Will's letters fell by the wayside."

Cecily stared down at the letters, his mother's direction scrawled across them in Will's bold hand.

"Go ahead," he said to her, stopping his pacing before the desk. "See if you can figure out what it means."

The gravity of the situation hit Cecily just then. What would she do if they contained accusations against her father? Her father, who was even now bedridden and insensible. Could she learn damning information about him and convince her husband to keep the matter secret? Or worse, would her conscience compel her to reveal whatever it was Will Dalton had to say? She hoped against hope that the message was simply some confession of an indiscretion from one brother to another. But given the trouble Dalton had taken to encode the message she doubted it.

"Why would he send you a message in a code you did not know how to decipher?" she asked, picking up the first letter and opening the folded pages.

"I suspect he thought I'd be able to ask someone at the Home Office. Being a celebrated war hero has to be good for something," he said, with a rueful smile. "But I dared not take it to them without knowing what they actually say. If it contained something that would embarrass him, or worse, England, I would not be able to keep the news from becoming public knowledge. And whoever I asked to translate them would feel duty-bound as well. I assumed that he sent the coded messages to me for one of two reasons: either he was desperate to get the message out of Egypt and hoped I'd figure out a way to decipher it, or he thought I'd seek you out. He thought very highly of your language skills, you know. He even mentions you in one of these . . ."

He gestured to the letters.

Cecily nodded absently as she looked down at the page

and began to examine the letters crossed through the actual text of the first letter.

"Do you have a slate?" she asked. "Or perhaps some sheets of foolscap and a pen and ink?"

Lucas gathered the items for her, and soon she was silently working through possible substitutions for the letters in the first of Will's missives, losing herself in the beautiful patterns of letters.

Lucas finally gave up his pacing after an hour or so of it. Cecily had ceased to notice him at all after a few minutes of concentration, and he watched her work with a combination of fascination for her mind and frustration with his inability to help her.

He wondered for the millionth time how he'd forgotten about the letters. They'd been sitting here in his desk, moldering away, for nearly six months now. He should have considered asking for Cecily's help with them from the minute they met in front of the Egyptian Club.

He thrust a hand through his disarranged hair, and reached up to remove his neckcloth. Since it appeared that Cecily would not be asking for his help for a good while, he poured himself a brandy and dropped down into a chair before the fire. And waited.

Lucas was drifting into a light doze when he heard Cecily give a little squeak. Immediately he was on his feet.

"What is it? What have you learned?"

"I've broken the code," she said. "Now, I'll need to go through and decode the messages."

Seeing that he had resumed pacing, she said, "You can help with this part if you like."

He nodded, and pulling another chair around next to hers, he waited while she showed him the substitution code his brother had used. "Now you simply go through and replace the letters."

Within a few minutes they were finished. They took turns

reading the letters aloud, each one giving them more reason
to be anxious about Will's fate.

In the first of the letters, Will had written:

> *Am convinced that a member of our party is steal-
> ing artifacts and selling them to French encamped
> nearby. Hurston and I have hatched a plan to flush the
> thief out. We will pretend to have a falling-out, and I
> will accuse Hurston publicly of appropriating my finds
> as his own. Then I will ally myself with the group from
> the British Museum, making it known that I will act as
> go-between should any member of Hurston's team wish
> to sell their finds for more than Hurston is willing to
> pay. Hurston has heard from David Lawrence and the
> museum expedition in Alexandria that they are experi-
> encing thefts as well. Wish we could catch the black-
> guard.*

"So Papa and Mr. Dalton were not actually fighting,"
Cecily said when Lucas had finished reading. She hadn't
liked to think of her father and William at odds with one
another. Especially given how close they had been to one
another in the past. "But who could this thief have been?
Who would have the audacity to steal artifacts right out
from under Papa's nose?"

"I think if we knew that, we'd have unraveled this whole
puzzle by now," Lucas said with a weary sigh.

"True," Cecily said. "This next letter is dated three days
before your brother disappeared."

> *The ruse is working, thank God. But we are still un-
> able to catch the thief. It's as if our attempts to draw him
> out have simply made him more wary than ever of re-
> vealing his identity. Still, I have every faith that we will
> find the fellow soon.*

"The difference in tone between that letter and this one,"
Lucas said, holding up the next letter, "is extraordinary.

Something must have happened in the days between that made the situation seem more dire. Listen . . ."

> *Though it may seem foolish of me, I will ask you, brother, to take care of Mama and Clarissa should anything befall me that prevents my return home. I pray this letter finds you safe and well. And I beg that you not cast blame upon yourself should the worst happen. You were much better suited to the army than I ever could have been. And in the end I have found more joy with my position as Hurston's secretary than I ever would have discovered on the Continental battlefields. If I do not return, information about the thief's transactions may be found in the blue cat. Hurston will know what I mean. And if not Hurston, then David Lawrence at the British Museum.*

"It's as if he's in fear for his life," Lucas fumed, pushing his chair back from the table. "Bloody hell."

Cecily was silent, watching her husband's strong back as he stood staring into the fire. She rose to offer him comfort.

"We do not know that the thief discovered him," she said, taking him by the hand now, and leading him to the comfortable settee on the other side of the fire. "We know nothing now but that he and my father were engaged in a deception to flush out the thief."

"We know enough," he said. "We know that Will is missing and your father is unable to speak. I would not be at all surprised if somehow your father's apoplexy was brought on by this whole business. Whoever this man is, he has been clever enough to keep his identity a secret from even the people he did business with in Egypt."

"But now we have someone else to question, at least."

The thought of facing David Lawrence again made Cecily's stomach roil in protest, but if they were to find out what had happened to Will, then she would force herself to suffer through it.

"Under no circumstances will I let you question David

Lawrence. For all we know, he is the thief," Lucas said fiercely. "I'll speak to him myself."

Cecily shook her head. She appreciated Lucas's wish to shield her from contact with her former fiancé, but if they were to learn anything more regarding Will's disappearance, she would have to swallow her distaste. David wasn't honorable in the least, but as far as she knew he had never stooped to theft. "It is doubtful he's the thief. He has no reason to be. He has plenty of wealth of his own. And there is no way he will consent to speak to you alone. Besides, he owes me. I can use that to force him to reveal what we wish to know."

Lucas clenched his jaw, and looked as if he would argue, but finally, acknowledging her point, he nodded. "Then we will pay a call on him. I wonder if he knows about this blue cat. What the devil does Will mean by it?"

"Cats were worshiped as gods by the Egyptians. It sounds to me as if there were some artifact that they brought back with them that is either engraved with a blue cat or in some way resembles one. It may even be a sarcophagus. If I recall correctly a blue cat was on the list of items recently received by the Egyptian Club. The list they were reading from on the night of the secret meeting we spied on."

They were silent for a moment. Each lost in their own thoughts as they reflected on the news they'd gleaned from Will's letters and the implications their proposed visit to David Lawrence would have on their partnership.

Still, Cecily sensed there was something else on her husband's mind. Something that had nothing to do with Lawrence.

"It was supposed to be me, you know," Lucas said finally. "I was supposed to be your father's secretary. As a younger son, my father's fortunes were not so great that he could afford to pay our way. So Will and I knew early on that we would need to embark on some profession or other. The Duke of Winterson, my father's elder brother, was friends with your father and had secured the position of secretary for me."

The lines of his face were stark in the dim light, his eyes bleak.

"But I was full of my own importance then, and had my heart set on a career in the army. I'd saved just enough to purchase a commission. But Papa did not wish to anger his brother. He owed his own living to him, you see. And as the eldest I was expected to embrace the wonderful gift of the position with Hurston. We argued about it for weeks that year. Finally I'd had enough and bought the commission anyway. I didn't even have the decency to tell my father in person. The next thing I knew I was on the way to Portugal and Will was on his first expedition to Egypt."

"But he seemed so happy in his position," Cecily said, covering her husband's hand with her own. Wanting to offer him comfort, but unsure of how to do so. "I never once got the impression that he had not chosen it on his own."

Lucas smiled, though his eyes were still shadowed with guilt.

"It simply wasn't in him to be spiteful or bitter. He accepted the world for what it was. With all its flaws. I think he'd have been suited to the church if he'd only had the inclination." His lips quirked in a wry smile. "Alas, like his elder brother he was a bit too fond of the ladies and carousing for that."

Cecily stood. "Come, Your Grace. Let me take you to bed."

The flash of desire in his eyes sent an answering thrill zinging through her solar plexus.

Silent, he took her hand and led her upstairs.

Sixteen

*T*he next day Lucas sent a note round to David Lawrence at the museum requesting an appointment, but was informed that Mr. Lawrence was away on business and would not be back for a sennight.

Cecily, nervous about the coming meeting, spent the week unable to relax around Lucas for fear that he might guess her agitation stemmed from the fact that she'd soon be seeing David again. It wasn't that she feared falling under his spell again. It was more that she feared what David might say or do. And if she were completely honest with herself, dredging up the feelings she'd endured so long ago with David had reminded her just what she was risking if she allowed Lucas to take possession of her heart. She simply could not incur such a risk.

To spare herself the discomfort of Winterson's too-knowing gaze, and to gain some much-needed distance, the night after they had translated the letters, she pleaded a headache and requested that he allow her to sleep in her own bed.

Alone.

"For I am liable to toss and turn all night and keep you from your rest," she told him from the doorway that divided their chambers.

Barefoot and coatless, her husband had been preparing to bathe when she knocked on the door. His shirt gaped at the neck where he had already discarded his cravat, and Cecily could not help but let her gaze linger on the vee of exposed skin there. She knew from experience how hard the muscles of his chest would feel pressed against her own softness. Embarrassed at the wave of desire that coursed through her, she closed her eyes in what she hoped would seem like a reflex against the pain in her head.

When she looked up again, Lucas's brows were drawn together in concern. "Is there anything I might do to make you more comfortable?" he asked her, stepping forward, hand extended as if to caress her.

"N . . . no!" she stammered, taking a step back, which seemed to surprise him. "That is . . ." she amended, "I . . . a night's rest is all I need, Your Grace. I will be quite well tomorrow."

His expression was inscrutable for a moment, but then he offered her a crooked grin. "I suppose I haven't given you much opportunity for sleep of late."

Unable to suppress her answering smile, Cecily nodded. "Thank you, Lucas," she said softly, before closing the door between them.

Climbing into her empty bed, she sighed. Keeping her distance from him had not proved as easy as she had hoped it would be.

Unbidden, the memory of David Lawrence as he had looked at their last meeting rose in her mind. A little part of her brain insisted that Lucas was nothing like Lawrence, but she ignored it. She had loved and lost once before. She had no intention of behaving so foolishly again.

Cecily seemed to be over her headache the next day, even going shopping with her cousins that afternoon, so Lucas was surprised that evening when he found her once again standing at the connecting door, requesting another night to herself.

"For I'm afraid the headache has come back and I would

not care to keep you awake," she said, the shadows beneath her dark eyes attesting to the fact that she was indeed fatigued.

Still, there was something about her request that rang false. Suddenly an explanation occurred to him that brought *him* to the blush. They had been married nearly a month and she *was* a lady. He cursed himself for a fool for not thinking of it sooner. She was probably shy about speaking of such things with her husband.

"My dear," he began, wondering just how best to approach the subject, "there is no need . . . that is to say . . . I know nothing of such . . ."

He shifted from one foot to the other, suddenly wishing for the masculine comforts of his club and an enormous snifter of brandy.

Cecily's brows drew together at his discomfort, then crimson bloomed in her cheeks.

"Oh! No! That is to say . . ." She shook her head. "It is not that, um, time."

"Ah."

"Yes. Quite."

"Just a headache, then?"

"Indeed."

They both looked at the ground for a moment.

Dragging a hand through his hair, Lucas swallowed, then nodded. "All right, then. I bid you good night."

And promptly shut the door.

Still smarting the next day over his embarrassment of the night before, Lucas stayed clear of Cecily until later in the evening. He had dinner at White's and returned home to find her cozily tucked into the library, reading *The Odyssey* in the original Greek.

"How nice to find my own Penelope waiting patiently for me at the hearthside," he drawled, leaning over the back of her chair to kiss her.

To his surprise and chagrin, she leaped almost to the ceiling in surprise.

"Good Lord, Lucas, you startled me!" He watched in appreciation as her bosom heaved with her quick breaths.

"I am sorry, my dear," he said, stepping around the chair to lift her into a comforting embrace. "I did not mean to do so. I thought you had heard me come in."

He felt her relax into his arms and rest her head on his shoulder. They stood together like this for a moment before either of them spoke.

"I must have dozed off," she said into his neck. The soft tickle of her breath against him sent a frisson of lust straight to his groin.

As if sensing his reaction, she began to pull away from him.

"Stay," he murmured into her hair. He had missed her these past two nights. He had grown accustomed to her soft body pressed against his—so accustomed that he had found himself unable to rest properly in his bed alone.

"I have missed . . ." he began, but stopped when she tried harder to remove herself from his grasp.

"Let me go," she said, pressing her hands against his chest, shoving against his hold. "Lucas, let me go."

"What the devil?" he demanded, opening his arms so that she could step back.

He watched in baffled amazement as she tore to the other side of the room as if he were a hunter and she the hind. Her breath came in gasps and she was clearly in distress.

"Cecily, what's amiss?" he asked, his voice gentler now that he saw how upset she was. "Have I done something?"

She closed her eyes, and said in a clipped voice, "It's not your fault."

"What's not my fault?" he asked, stepping closer to her. The side of the room to which she'd fled was shadowed and he could not see her expression. But everything about her posture spoke of determination.

"I apologize, Your Grace," she said to him, her dark eyes luminous in the candlelight. "When I agreed to marry you I had thought that perhaps we would be able to rub along well enough together. But it has become increasingly clear to me that by allowing you certain liberties—"

"Liberties?" he asked, dumbfounded, stalking across the room to her like an angry jungle cat. "How can take liberties with one's own wife?"

She ignored his question, and when he came to stand before her she seemed unperturbed. The only clue to her nervousness was the flutter of her pulse in her soft neck.

"I have done both of us a disservice," she started again, unable to meet his gaze, "by allowing our relationship to become more physical than I had originally intended. I see now that was a mistake. And I ask you now to please allow me to return to my chamber alone, so that—"

Understanding dawned like an arrow in the back.

"There were no headaches," he said dully. "Damn me for a fool for not seeing it sooner."

"Please do not swear . . ."

"If I'm to be denied my conjugal rights, I'll swear as much as I bloody well please!" he said, his voice loud enough that even he was startled.

"Has this been your plan all along?" he asked, more softly now. "To fob me off with a few weeks of playing the dutiful wife, then cut me off completely?"

At this she blanched. "No! Nothing like that," she cried. "I thought I might be able to risk . . . to have some affection without . . ."

When she made no move to finish her thought, he shook his head.

"Well, fear not, wife," he said. "I won't bother you with any more of my unwanted affections. Not until you ask. And maybe not even then."

Turning on his heel, he left her looking as miserable as he felt.

Less than a week after their confrontation, Cecily dressed without any real enthusiasm for the meeting with David Lawrence. She chose one of her new, flattering gowns, and had her maid, Molly, arrange her hair into a fashionable twist. The result, when she examined herself in the long pier glass, was not breathtaking, but she knew she would not shame herself or her husband.

The thought of Lucas and their estrangement pulled sharply at her conscience. It was hardly her husband's fault that her former fiancé had been such a knave. But the thought of letting Lucas back in, of allowing him close enough that he had the potential to hurt her, sent such fear lancing through her that she could barely breathe. Her sense of preservation was too strong. If her reaction to losing David had been overwhelming, how much more devastating would the damage to her heart be if she allowed herself to grow attached to Lucas—a man who outshone David in every possible way? It had taken years for her to recover from David Lawrence's betrayal. But recover she had. Indeed, the only emotion she could call to mind when she thought about Mr. Lawrence as she dressed was embarrassment at her behavior when he'd broken things off. That she had broken down in tears before him filled her with shame even now. For Mr. Lawrence himself, however, she felt nothing aside from a natural curiosity to know how he went on, and to learn what he might be able to tell them about Mr. Dalton's disappearance.

As for Lucas, his behavior to her since their fight had been scrupulously polite. He was courteous, kind, and every bit as solicitous as he had been since their marriage. The only difference was that he no longer made any effort to come to her bedchamber. If she was disappointed at his lack of interest, she reminded herself that it saved her heart the risk of being broken again. That must outweigh any temporary hurt feelings his diffidence might cause.

Thus it was that when Cecily and Lucas were shown into Mr. Lawrence's office at the museum, she was in complete control of herself. Mr. Lawrence, however, appeared to be overset by her appearance on his figurative doorstep.

"Miss Hurston!" he exclaimed, stepping around an enormous desk to greet them, and immediately taking her gloved hands between his own. "What a surprise this is!"

"She is the Duchess of Winterson now, Lawrence," her husband said, the sharp edge to his voice revealing just how much contempt he held for the other man.

Recalling himself, Lawrence flushed and turned to the taller man and gave a slight bow.

"Yes, of course," he said with a forced smile. "It is a pleasure to meet you, Your Grace."

He looked from Cecily to Lucas and then back at Cecily again, as if trying to figure out how the two of them could possibly have ended up married to one another.

"My apologies. I was caught up in the moment and forgot my manners." He spoke to Lucas, but his eyes were all for Cecily. So much so that she felt herself blush under his gaze. "It is good to see you, Your Grace," he said to her. "It has been too long."

Cecily pulled her hand back and gave him a cynical smile. "Yes, well, you have known my direction these past three years, Mr. Lawrence," she said tartly.

Rebuffed, but not particularly repentant, Lawrence gave a brisk nod and directed them to take seats before the fire. His office was small, but exquisitely furnished. Cecily had only been here once or twice in the past, but since then it would seem that he had grown plumper in the pocketbook. Probably as a result of his marriage, she thought darkly.

"What brings you to the museum, Your Graces?" he asked, once they were all seated. "An endowment, perhaps? Or can it be that you will finally be able to travel to Egypt, Cecily, now that you are married and out from under your father's thumb? Perhaps you wish to travel along with the museum's next expedition?"

As a trip to Egypt had been the intended destination of her wedding trip with him, despite her fear of tight spaces, she was not overly surprised to hear David ask if she and her new husband intended to travel with the museum. What did surprise her, however, was the ease with which he spoke of such a topic. Especially considering that he'd met his wife on such a trip. Still, he had never been the most considerate of men. And he had always said that men like him made their own luck. He would see her marriage to Lucas not as it related to her, but insofar as he might make use of it himself.

"Her Grace," Lucas said through clenched teeth, before Cecily could formulate a response, "and her travels are not of concern to you, Lawrence. We are here to discuss your last trip to Egypt and to learn what you can tell us about the theft of several items from both your own group's finds, and from those in Lord Hurston's camp."

He didn't seem particularly worried by the duke's disdain, but at the mention of the theft, Lawrence blanched. "I do not know what you are talking about, Your Grace; someone has obviously been trying to—"

"Do cut line, David," Cecily said, tiring of his lies. "We know there were thefts on the trip. That is not in question. What is in question is whether you were working with my father and Mr. Dalton, who also happens to be Winterson's brother, to discover who the culprit was."

Lucas gave her an inscrutable look, not revealing whether he was annoyed at her taking over the questioning, or pleased at her lack of deference to her former fiancé. Whatever the case, he seemed willing enough to let her lead now.

"Before I say anything," Lawrence began, "I want your assurance that my colleagues here will not learn about my role in your father's little scheme. If it were known that a member of the museum staff was working together with a member of the Egyptian Club there might be serious repercussions."

"Go on," Lucas said curtly.

Cecily watched as her former suitor prepared to tell his story. It was the first time she'd been given an unobstructed view of the man since their engagement had been dissolved three years ago so that he could marry another. There was no comparison between his looks and Lucas's. That hadn't been his appeal. It had been David's mind that made her heart beat faster. He had a clever way with words, and a keen mind that he used to work himself up through the ranks of the museum. And, she suspected now, he'd used her own facility for learning ancient languages to assist him in his climb to the top. What she had seen as their mutual interest in ancient culture, he had seen as nothing more than a tool to help him achieve success. And when he was finished with her, he'd broken their engagement and married another woman whose wealth could take him higher still.

Rather than sorrow or upset, she felt as if a heavy burden had been removed from her heart. She would never again need to feel the guilt of having done the wrong thing, or reacted in the wrong way in response to his easy dismissal of her. Instead, she knew that short of possessing a dowry of eight hundred pounds a year, there had been nothing she could have done to keep him by her side.

"Your father and I had begun speaking again shortly after his party arrived in Cairo," Lawrence explained. "His anger over what happened between us . . ."

Cecily fought her annoyance at his terminology for what had been, in essence, his jilting of her.

". . . had dissipated, and though we were not on the same intimate footing as before, Lord Hurston and I were able to discuss matters pertaining to his expedition and mine that would be of use to both of us."

Lawrence looked at some faraway point over both Cecily and Lucas's heads, his voice warming to the story.

"Since our two expeditions would be only some twenty miles or so from one another, we made an agreement to trade information should the need arise. Both our groups had been at it for only a week or so when we noticed items, mostly smaller, easily transportable relics, were disappearing from our collection of finds. We wondered at first if the guards we had hired in Cairo to accompany our groups were responsible. They were, after all, the only people at our dig sites whom we had not handpicked for the digs."

"But you discovered you were wrong." It was a statement from Lucas, not a question.

"Yes." Lawrence nodded. "It turned out that my guard was the brother of Lord Hurston's guard. And they were both called away for one evening because of a family illness. While they were gone, I went to store that day's finds—in this case several pieces of lapis-lazuli-and-sapphire-encrusted jewelry that had been buried along with the pharaoh's wife—in the artifact tent that morning. By the evening, before either man had returned from Cairo, one of the smaller pieces was missing. Whoever had stolen it had perhaps chosen that particular piece because he hoped its absence would not be missed. Especially given that it had been stored near a larger, and much more precious and valuable, piece."

"And had you any idea who might have gone into the tent during the day while the rest of your party worked?" Lucas asked. "I assume you've accounted in some way for the whereabouts of the rest of your party during the hours in which the piece might have been taken."

"Of course," Lawrence affirmed. "And none was out of sight of the rest of the party during any point in time. I asked my valet to watch the tent while the rest of us were at the tomb, but there was a short period of time when he came to inform me of the note he'd received from the guards, telling us that they were on their way. He went back to the tent with all possible haste, but I suspect that that was the time during which the piece was stolen."

"But surely a stolen artifact would not be enough to convince a man such as yourself to risk his employment by joining forces with a member of the club that has made public threats against the museum? No man with any sense of self-preservation would do so."

The notion that Mr. Lawrence was not exempt from that group hung in the air like the smell of day-old fish. Lucas clearly had no use for Lawrence and men like him who ruthlessly cut down anyone who stepped in the way of their rise to power. But for all that there was an air of combativeness between the two men, Cecily was relieved to see that they would use only words as their weapons of choice today. She did not like the idea of her husband engaging in any violent acts, regardless of how satisfying she herself might consider the notion of seeing Mr. Lawrence's smug expression forcibly removed from his face.

"Of course not," Lawrence agreed. "But when I discovered

that Hurston's party was also experiencing losses from some unknown thief, it occurred to me that for us to quibble over our own personal institutional affiliations could put our very empire at risk. For all that we pursued our separate goals, both Lord Hurston and myself explored these ancient wonders for the good of king and country."

"Quite." If there was any irony in that one word from her husband, Cecily could not detect it.

"So, we began to plan. Lord Hurston, Mr. Dalton, and myself. The three of us decided that we would not let word of our alliance reach the other members of our party. And since there was no indication that outsiders had been sneaking into our encampments and stealing from us, we came to the rather upsetting conclusion that the thief must be a member of one or both of our parties."

"Could not the thief have simply paid off your guards or sneaked into the tents holding your finds while the rest of your party was sleeping or away?" Cecily asked. She had always assumed that her father's expeditions had traveled with trunks with sturdy locks to prevent theft, but instead she learned that they were kept in open and vulnerable tents with nothing more than a flap and an all-too-human guard to keep the treasure hunters out. It was most disconcerting to imagine the temptation such a situation must have presented to a thief.

"It is possible, I suppose," Lawrence acknowledged. "God knows the native people of Egypt are without the sort of ethical code or morality that we English hold ourselves to."

Cecily forbore from pointing out that he himself had not held to any sort of moral code when he decided to jilt her and marry someone else.

"But," he went on, "it seems unlikely given that we were already paying the guards exorbitantly to stay on duty with us, and though there was no way of locking the tents, we did rig up a crude means of alerting us should some unannounced visitor enter the storage areas. And no one was ever heard coming or going from the storage tents."

"What sort of plan did you, Lord Hurston, and my brother

devise to smoke out the thief?" Lucas asked. He sat up straight in his chair and his eyes did not leave the other man's face.

"Mr. Dalton and Lord Hurston would stage a very public falling-out. Mr. Dalton would break away from Lord Hurston's group, but he would continue to work alongside them. Lord Hurston would explain that while he and Dalton could no longer be employer and employee, he had come too far to do without Mr. Dalton's expertise when it came to languages and excavation. Mr. Dalton would be allowed to keep a certain percentage of his finds, but agreed to pay Lord Hurston a sum for his permission to continue his exploration of the site."

"And what happened?"

"Well, at first it all worked as we had planned. Hurston and Dalton fought in front of the rest of their party about the proper way to read a hieroglyph, and soon enough Dalton was striking out on his own. His every find was cataloged with the others, but he let it be known to the rest of the party that he would not be averse to selling those items he found in order to pay for his passage back to England. Almost immediately he was approached by a member of the party—neither he nor Hurston would tell me who—who wished to purchase one piece in particular. A lovely lapis lazuli sculpture of a cat."

"And did he sell it to them?" Cecily asked, careful not to let on that his mention of the lapis cat had caught her attention.

"I do not know," he said. "For the very next day Mr. Dalton was discovered missing. And so was the cat statue."

"Both of them went missing?" Lucas demanded. "It stands to reason that whoever wanted the statue was responsible for my brother's disappearance. Why did Lord Hurston not act?"

"Well, I raised that same concern with him, Your Grace." Lawrence's expression was troubled. "But he assured me that the person who wanted the cat and the person who made Mr. Dalton disappear could not possibly be the same person."

"How could he possibly know?" Cecily asked, surprised that her father would make such an assurance given the way he'd suspected members of his own party of stealing from him.

"He could not," Lucas said, "unless he either knew what happened to Will, or he knew where the person who wanted the cat had been during the time that Will went missing."

"But he disappeared in the night," Cecily objected. "He cannot have known . . ."

A possibility hit her, and made her stomach leap with angst.

"Oh," she said, unable to keep the disappointment from her voice.

Lucas took Cecily's hand, but remained seated.

Looking uncomfortable, Lawrence cleared his throat. "It was Lady Entwhistle, of course. She had tried to buy the blue cat for her own collection. I have no idea if she succeeded in persuading Mr. Dalton or not. But Lord Hurston assured me that she had been with him on the night in question and so could not have had anything to do with Dalton's disappearance."

Cecily struggled with her feelings of betrayal. She had known Neddy since she was a small child and the idea of Neddy and her father together—well, it changed everything she had thought about both of them. She put her feelings about their relationship away, however, and concentrated on what that relationship meant in the investigation of Will's disappearance.

"Will had a bag," she said to her former fiancé. "Neddy claimed to have seen it in my father's possession. Do you know anything about it?"

Lawrence shook his head. "I never even entered your father's tent, so I would not know of such things. I wonder, however, if it was included in the items your father had shipped with the artifacts from the museum's excavation."

Cecily felt Lucas tighten his grip on her hand.

"What items? Why would Lord Hurston have items that

were meant for the Egyptian Club shipped with the museum finds?" Lucas's whole body had tensed beside her.

"Because . . ." Lawrence flushed. "If you must know, we had made an agreement between ourselves that certain items pertaining to the Dynasty of Ramses the Second would go to the museum, while items from the Dynasty of Seti the First would go to the club."

"For a price." Lucas's words were a statement, not a question.

"It is not unheard of," the other man said, his voice rising in defense of himself. "Deals such as ours are struck all the time among fellow collectors. The members of the Egyptian Club can well afford . . ."

"I don't give a damn about your trade practices, Lawrence," Lucas snapped. "I want to see these artifacts that came from the Hurston dig. Where are they?"

"We store newly acquired items in a warehouse near the East India docks," Lawrence said. "We keep them there until we have devised a scheme for working them into the existing collection."

"Will you take us there?"

"I'm afraid I cannot, Your Grace," Lawrence demurred, "but I can have one of the clerks take you this afternoon. He knows the location and can accompany you."

"That will be acceptable," Lucas said, his expression grim.

They waited a few moments for the arrival of the clerk, a young bespectacled man named Mr. Hornby.

Within minutes they were on their way.

When Cecily and Lucas arrived at the warehouse, the sky had darkened with the threat of an approaching storm. The wind had just begun to swirl around them, stirring the smell of the river and the surrounding streets into the foul stench of an odiferous perfume. The first drops of rain had just begun to fall as Lucas handed Cecily down and Mr. Hornby went about unlocking the massive door of the ramshackle building.

The three of them hurried inside as the shower turned into a deluge, and Hornby set about lighting the lantern he'd found just inside the door.

"The goods from Mr. Lawrence's last trip are there, Your Graces," the young man said, his formerly erect shirt points wilting from the humidity. He pointed to several large crates stacked neatly against the far wall. "We try to keep some semblance of order here. Organizing the boxes by the dates of acquisition."

Uninterested in the organizational schemes of the museum, Lucas pulled Cecily along with him to the boxes, and spotting a sturdy stick against the wall, he picked it up and got to work opening the first of the boxes.

"Your Grace, I beg you," Hornby said, hurrying over to them. "I have a list here detailing what each box contains. If you will just let me know what you are—"

"We do not know what we are searching for, Mr. Hornby," Cecily said, laying a placating hand on the young man's arm. Lucas knew he should probably wait, but he was tired of waiting. Tired of holding back when the clues to his brother's whereabouts might have been here all along.

He heard Cecily speaking to the clerk behind him as he fitted the bar into the seam between the box and its lid and began to work it free. "But would you be so kind as to see if there is any mention of a blue cat in your inventory?"

"Yes, Your Grace, of course."

When he had wrenched the top from the box, Lucas asked for the lantern and held it up so that he could get a clearer view of the box's contents.

"This is Box E-2," Hornby said. "It should contain various small pieces from the tomb of Prince Al-Kameli."

It was ironic to Lucas that the gem-encrusted masks and ornaments in the box could be described as simply "various small pieces." But he supposed that calling them what they were—a priceless fortune in emeralds—would be an invitation to thievery.

He moved on to the next box, reveling in the strain of his muscles as he worked to get the lid off. For so long he had been using only his mind to puzzle out what had happened to Will. It was a relief to be expending physical energy in the search for a change.

Three boxes later, they still had seen no sign of the blue cat. Cecily had glanced through the inventory pages and found no mention of cats of any kind. And the sixth box, which Lucas had managed to move slightly out from behind another, smaller one, was described as having only a sarcophagus and a small statue inside. Despite the pain in his leg, which had begun to weaken under the strain of his physical labors, he pressed on, needing to do whatever it took to find his brother.

"Winterson," his wife chided, "I can see that you are beginning to tire. Perhaps we should come back—"

"We will not come back," he almost growled, knowing he was being unreasonable, but unable to stop himself. "If you two would render your assistance, we might be able to get to this one."

Shaking her head at his stubbornness, Cecily nevertheless followed Mr. Hornby through the maze of crates toward the large one that Lucas had already slightly edged out from behind another one.

Cecily moved alongside Lucas, gestured for Hornby to step onto her other side, and then the three of them used their collective weight to slide the crate over so that its end was facing the empty row between two towers of crates.

Beads of perspiration had broken out on Lucas's forehead, and the stench, which they had all become accustomed to after several minutes in the warehouse, grew fouler.

"Goodness," Cecily said with a moue of distaste as she watched her husband wield the lever to remove the crate's lid. "This is worse than the mummy room at the club."

"The odor usually subsides after a while," Hornby said

apologetically, as if he were responsible for the sins of the decomposing flesh in the crate. "I suspect that it has simply built up over time after being trapped for so long in the box."

Lucas said nothing, for the smell had reminded him suddenly of the stench of the battlefield after Waterloo, and it took every ounce of concentration on his part to keep from fleeing the warehouse altogether. Instead, he wrenched the lid off and gestured for Cecily to bring the lantern. Later he would castigate himself for exposing her to this ugliness, but for now, he had to keep his thoughts on the task at hand or risk succumbing to his own disgust.

"Lucas, look!" she said as the lantern illuminated the contents of the box. "There is a blue cat."

He squinted into the light, and saw that she was correct. They were looking at the bottom of a sarcophagus that had been placed lengthwise in the oblong crate. And there, carved into the foot of the piece, was an ornately detailed blue cat.

"Help me," he said to Hornby, who had stepped forward to see what they were speaking about. Together, the two of them managed to grab hold of the foot of the decorated casket and pull it from the box.

For a few minutes, there was only the sound of the men's gasps of air, both of them panting from exertion.

"It should not be . . ." Hornby gasped, "so heavy."

He pulled out a handkerchief and mopped his brow.

"There must be quite a bit of statuary or jewelry buried with this one," he said. "Or perhaps the blue cat is larger than we thought."

Cecily had already moved to the side of the sarcophagus and was feeling along it for a mechanism that would unlock the lid. At last, she found it. "There," she said. And with an audible click, she worked it free and, with her husband's help, raised the ornately carved front of the casket.

She looked over her shoulder to gesture that Mr. Hornby should come closer. "After all . . ." she said to him, turning to look down into the sarcophagus.

But whatever she might was said was cut short by her scream.

They had found the blue cat.

But they had also found Mr. William Dalton.

Seventeen

$\mathcal{B}$y the time they arrived home that evening it was well past midnight. Lucas had revealed the news to his mother and sister-in-law in a calm, soothing tone, offering each of them in turn a shoulder to cry on and assurances that it seemed likely that death had been swift and merciful.

Only Cecily could know, having seen the body for herself, that such matters were impossible to determine. It may well have been that Will did not suffer, but it was just as likely, as the Bow Street runner had told them baldly, that he may well have spent his last moments clawing for air in a darkened tomb.

Still, she said nothing to contradict her husband, and when they were finally alone in the quiet of their own chamber, she watched him go through the motions of undressing and washing with a mechanical stoicism that broke her heart.

It had been years since her mother's death, but the misery she had felt on hearing the news still lingered in her memory, and she knew now with the wisdom of adulthood that though her grief had been real, it was oh so much more painful to feel the loss of a loved one without the shielding barrier of childhood innocence to protect one. Children, she knew now, were remarkably selfish beings. They did not experience the same sort of empathy that now prompted her to wonder just what those final moments had been like for Will. And if she, who had only been slightly acquainted with the man, were prompted to wonder, she could only imagine what sort of wrenching emotion must now be pressing upon her husband.

While Lucas undressed, she hurried through the connecting door into her own room, allowing her maid to assist her to undress. In a haste born of concern, she allowed the woman to drop the filmy nightgown over her head and dismissed her.

She noticed that someone had shut the door while she was in her own chamber, and for a moment she wondered if Lucas might wish to be alone tonight. Never having been in a position to offer comfort to a husband, she wondered if perhaps she ought to allow him his privacy. Yet, the memory of his expression as he held his mother earlier that evening, the bleakness that had suffused his face while he offered her comfort, made Cecily turn the knob and step inside.

His valet was gone, and Lucas stood alone, his naked back to her as he stared down into the fire. He had one arm braced against the mantel, and his broad shoulders tapered in a graceful line down to his waist, where his lower half was still covered by his buff breeches.

She stared a moment at the glorious specimen before her, grateful for the rare opportunity to look upon him without fear of being observed. The crackle of the fire and her own breathing were the only sounds as they stood there. Together, but apart. Unsure of whether to announce herself, Cecily was about to speak up when she saw a shudder run through him, and a soft, low sound rent the air.

He was weeping, she realized, a sob rising in her own throat at the notion of this strong, gentle man, who earlier tonight had held his mother and sister-in-law as they cried out their own grief, now giving vent to his own feelings in his chamber alone. The notion nearly brought her to her knees for him, but rather than succumbing herself, she strode across the room, careful not to startle him.

She touched him gingerly on his back, and though he jumped a little, he did not immediately turn and order her from the room. Instead, he kept his back to her, and said,

"Cecily, if you will forgive me, I should like to be alone to-night."

"Would you?" she asked softly. "Would you really, or do you think to spare me witnessing you in your grief? For I can assure you, Your Grace, nothing you can say or do tonight will make me think less of you."

He seemed to take in a deep breath. "Please," he said, his voice strained. "Please just leave me in peace."

"Lucas," she said, "please don't shut me out. I want to help."

At this he turned, his eyes blazing. "You have the temerity to ask me not to shut you out? You who hold yourself at a distance even as we are joined in the most intimate way possible? You who refuse to give me one fraction of affection more than is absolutely necessary for fear that you'll find yourself in love with the man who just so happens to be your husband? You will pardon me, madam, if I do not leap with joy at your kind offer. But I would just as soon endure my grief alone as share it with you only to have you draw back into your cocoon again in the morning."

She was startled by the vehemence of his outburst, but the substance of what he said was nothing more than the truth. She had been keeping herself removed from him in an effort to protect her heart. But she could no more have left him alone tonight to grieve than she could have ignored an injured animal left for dead on the side of a carriageway. Like it or not, some inexorable force had drawn them together, and even as she listened to his angry words, she found herself moving closer to him.

"I am sorry," she said simply, for it was what she felt, and it was the truth. She was sorry for having let him down. Sorry for having led him to believe they might have a real marriage, then pulling away from him night after night. And most of all she was sorry that he had lost his brother. "So sorry," she said, wrapping her arms around him, offering him the comfort of her body even as he trembled against her.

"There will be no going back tonight, Cecily," he said harshly. "If you stay with me tonight, then that is how we will continue to go on. No more retreating to your own chamber when you do not wish to discuss something. No more running away."

She looked into his intense blue eyes, at the residual moisture that glittered in his lashes, and knew she had no choice. He had given her so much since their marriage and she was compelled tonight to return the favor.

"Yes," she said, her decision making her bold. "I promise."

He gave a brisk nod, and as he had done on their wedding night, he lifted her into his arms and carried her to the bed. But unlike that night, there was no time for talk, only pleasure.

With a hunger born of grief, he took her mouth with a ferocious intent that left her breathless, lowering her to the bed and unfastening his breeches at the same time. Not even taking the time to remove her gown, he pulled her to the edge of the bed, and lifted the sheer fabric to her hips.

Cecily was overwhelmed by the strength of his ardor, and when he flipped her over so that her bottom and legs dangled over the side of the bed, she felt a jolt of fear along with the excitement that his mastery inspired.

"No going back," he whispered into her ear as he covered her back with his body, curving his front into her back and gripping both of her hands together over her head with one hand while with his other he guided his erection to that part of her weeping for him to fill it.

With one sharp plunge he drove himself fully into her, the slide of their bodies together making both of them cry out in pleasure. Again and again, Lucas flexed his cock into the warmth of her, and again and again her body gripped his as he slid back out. He lost himself in the rhythm of their coupling, the drive to find his release making him forget anything but the bliss of feeling Cecily's softness devouring his cock.

The noises she made, something between a moan and a sigh, only added to the intensity of his pleasure, and before long he felt himself nearing his peak. Thrusting once, twice, he reached a hand around and touched her just above where their bodies merged, and he was rewarded with a sharp cry from Cecily as she plummeted over, her pulsing center drawing him to his own fulfillment. Like a stallion covering a mare, he bit her lightly on the neck, his hands gripping her hips as he pistoned into her.

Much later, when Cecily was curved into the warmth of his body, both of them drowsy from spent passion, she asked, "Would you like to talk about him?"

She felt the sigh of weariness run through him. He was silent for some moments, while he traced circles on her back with his fingers.

"He was my younger brother," he said simply. "I can still remember his baby voice, begging me to take him up with me on my pony. I must have been seven or so, and he was four. He was always begging me to take him along."

Her heart aching for him, Cecily said nothing. Only held him.

"I loved him." His voice was quiet now, as if saying the words aloud would somehow bring more pain. "And now he's gone."

She tried not to feel the guilt that lanced through her at his words. Though he had whispered words of love to her in the heat of passion, she still had not been able to say the same to him. Now, knowing how vulnerable he was, she wanted to assure him that she returned his affection, but part of her still held back. In part because she knew that giving him her heart might in some way bring her to the same sort of grief he endured now.

He buried his face in the curve of her shoulder. Cecily felt the wetness of tears against her skin.

"Why couldn't I," he whispered, his voice breaking a little, "just have let him ride that damned pony?"

Cecily turned and kissed him. Not a kiss of passion, but one of comfort. She hoped it was enough.

For now, it was all she had to give him.

* * *

The next week passed in a blur of activity, from the notification of Bow Street about how they suspected Will had died, to informing his mother and Will's wife, to traveling to the Winterson estate in Kent for the funeral services and subsequent burial.

Since the night they'd found Will's body, when he'd broken down and revealed the true extent of his grief to her, Lucas had returned to the polite but distant demeanor of the days leading up to their awful discovery. He rose before dawn to ride over the estate with his steward, and did not return home until nearly suppertime.

One morning, a week after William's funeral, she looked up from a translation of Herodotus to find him watching her from the doorway of her private sitting room.

Dressed for the country in buckskin breeches and a loose-fitting coat, he was every inch the country gentleman. His leg had grown stronger since that first day outside the Egyptian Club and he walked with little trace of the limp that had kept him from waltzing with her at the Bewle ball. And he was the most handsome man she'd ever seen.

"I did not mean to disturb you," he said, thrusting one hand into the pocket of his coat and looking just as ill at ease as she felt. "But I thought perhaps you'd like to see what I found in the barn."

Her heart racing, she stood quickly, knocking her book to the floor in the process. "Oh, bother," she cried, stooping to pick it up.

He stepped closer to help, but she was already crouched on the floor beside the desk when he reached her. When she looked up, she was at eye level with his coat pocket. Which, oddly, had begun to undulate.

"Good Lord!" she said, staring at his moving jacket. "What in the world have you got in there?"

This startled a laugh from her husband, which quickly turned into a cough.

"Don't be lewd," she said quickly, knowing from the gleam in his eye that the direction of his thoughts was decidedly improper.

"Oh, all right," he huffed, though his grin dispelled any real pique.

Reaching into his pocket, he grasped hold of something inside and carefully drew it back out.

"Mew," said the tiny ginger kitten blinking in the bright glare of the afternoon sun.

"Oh." Cecily stared at the fuzzy little cat that barely fit in the palm of Lucas's hand. "What a little darling."

"I think its mother abandonded it," Lucas said, sending a silent apology to the tabby mama cat and her brood from whom he'd appropriated this little fellow. "Thought maybe you might want to have him for a pet."

She still hadn't even touched the kitten, just stood staring at the tiny creature.

"If you don't want him I might ask one of the tenants if he needs a mouser," he said, suddenly uneasy. He had thought all women liked baby animals. Though he knew Cecily hadn't reacted like all women with regard to anything else, so maybe he shouldn't have presumed.

"Don't you dare!" she said, grabbing him by the arm with such ferocity, he suspected she'd left a mark. "Don't you dare give my kitten away!"

Lucas suppressed a smile at her words. "Then why don't you pick him up?"

Cecily swallowed. "I . . . I've never had a pet," she said. "I'm not sure what to do."

Her expression was such a mix of awe and chagrin that he wanted to hold her. He had decided not long after they arrived in Kent that if his marriage was to have any chance at success, he would need to woo her with every bit as much finesse as he would have used had they not been compromised into marriage. Though there was no doubt that the hard shell Cecily customarily wore around her heart had grown weaker in the past weeks, she was still too intent upon self-preservation to let him in.

So now, remembering his plan to draw her to him in stages, he kept his hands to himself. Instead, showing her how to cup her hands, he carefully placed the mewling kitten into her keeping.

"Oh," she said softly. "He's so soft. And light."

The look in her eyes was something Lucas would never forget as long as he lived. And he made a vow that he'd do whatever it took to make sure he put that look in them as often as possible.

After the look she made when he was buried inside her, of course.

Suddenly feeling like a lecherous brute for thinking about sex while his wife held a kitten, he cleared his throat. Which made the kitten jump.

"Oh, you've frightened him," Cecily chided. "It's all right, little one," she crooned to the kitten.

Excellent, Lucas thought, they've joined forces against me.

"Lucas," Cecily said quietly. "Thank you. No one has ever given me a better gift."

Unable to speak around the lump in his throat, Lucas merely nodded.

They stood there looking down at the kitten for a few minutes before Cecily spoke again.

"If," she began, "if you would like to come to my bed-chamber this evening . . ."

They were the words he'd been desperate to hear for weeks now. And it took every ounce of resolve he had to keep from shouting his assent to the rooftops. Instead, he shook his head.

"I thank you, my dear," he said carefully, not wanting to let on how much he hated to deny her, but utterly committed to telling her the truth, "but I'm afraid that I've discovered I want something more from you than just affection."

He saw her wince at his use of the term she'd fobbed him off with before. He hadn't meant to throw her words up in her face, but it was as good a name as any for the easy relationship they shared. It was only after the discovery of his brother's body, when he'd realized just how fleeting their time together might be, that he had known exactly what it was he wanted from Cecily.

It wasn't affection.

It wasn't camaraderie.

"Love, Cecily," he told her now. "I want your love. And until you are ready to give it to me, I won't be coming to your bedchamber."

He left her staring openmouthed after him, the kitten curled up in the cradle of her hands, blissfully unaware of the human drama unfolding around him.

In the days that followed, true to his word, Lucas stayed out of Cecily's bedchamber. When he had made his declaration that day in the library, she had wanted nothing more than to give him exactly what he asked for. It would be so easy to let herself fall in love with him. She was already halfway there, she knew. But the memory of how much she had hurt when David left her kept her from succumbing. She had wanted nothing more than to offer him the sort of comfort that he himself had offered her from the beginning of their association with one another. And she knew that with very little coaxing on her part, she'd have been able to persuade him.

But instead, out of respect for his wishes, she had held herself back. Most days she didn't see him until the dinner hour anyway, since he spent much of his time laboring over estate business, like repairs to the tenants' cottages. And at night, they each retired to their separate beds. If she wished for someone more substantial to curl up with besides little Ginger? Well, she would endeavor to forget the passion she'd felt beneath her husband's hands and would instead concentrate on figuring out who had killed Will Dalton.

Thus it was that she found herself standing on the steps of Winterhaven with her husband, Ginger curled up in his basket that was draped over her arm.

"I will send for you at once if I learn anything more about the cat," she told him, both of them staring out at the parkland beyond, not daring to make eye contact. "The blue cat, I mean."

"Cecily," he said, turning to face her, "while I am here, I wish to have your promise that you will not proceed with any sort of investigation into Will's death."

She frowned. "Yes, of course, but you must know that—"

"Promise me, Cecily," he said sternly, his eyes shadowed from lack of sleep and fatigue. She wished that he would allow her to take care of him through this miserable time. It weighed on her conscience that she might have eased his burden in one respect, but in the end she knew that it would be kinder not to offer him false hope.

Aloud she said, "I promise. And you must promise me to look after yourself, Your Grace."

But he waved off her concern. "I am well enough. Once I can convince my mama to go to her sister in Bath, and the repairs to the tenant cottages are completed, I will return to London with all haste."

She knew that his mother was uncomfortable in the opulence of Winterhaven, especially given her past residence in the modest parsonage that served the nearby village of Snowden. It had taken no persuasion at all to ensure that William's wife, Clarissa, had gone back to live with her family, but it seemed that Lucas's mama had taken it into her head that she owed it to her son to stay with him at the country estate. Even after Cecily had announced her intention of going back to London.

"After all, my dear," she had told her newest daughter-in-law, "you must surely be missing your own family. And since Lucas is forced to remain here, I will see to it that he is made comfortable."

If Cecily had not known better, she would have thought her mother-in-law was trying to make her son choose between his wife and his mother. She knew, however, that such a consideration had never crossed Lady Michael's mind. Instead, she was simply clinging to the one man in her life that was still living. With both her husband and her younger son gone, she was feeling vulnerable to the capricious nature of fate. And having experienced such worries herself, especially given her mother's death when she was a child, Cecily could not blame her for it.

"Please do return to us in London as soon as you wish," she told the older woman as she accepted a heartfelt hug. "If you find anything at all unpleasant about your sister's household in Bath I will be only too glad to welcome you back to Winterson House."

Lady Michael laughed at that. "I shall manage my sister, my dear. Do not mind that. Besides, I must leave the two of you alone so that I may hold a grandchild before too much longer has passed."

Cecily gave a brisk laugh and hurried downstairs. Where she currently stood in her husband's arms. She inhaled the scent of him and gave him a quick kiss on the cheek, which made him smile. Keeping his arms around her, he lowered his mouth to hers and took her lips with a tenderness and longing that had her eyes welling up.

"I will see you soon," he said, letting her out of his arms as he handed her into the carriage.

From the carriage window, Cecily watched him there—a tall figure dressed in unrelieved black, dwarfed by the enormous Doric columns that flanked the front door of the neoclassically designed estate. The image stayed with her; visible in her mind's eye as she closed her eyes and let the exhaustion that had threatened to overtake her earlier finally claim her.

And she slept.

Lucas pulled the collar of his drab greatcoat higher and the hat he'd borrowed from his groom lower as he pushed into the Sergeant's Arms, a dark, dank tavern on the edge of Whitechapel. The clientele of the establishment was made up of the impoverished, desperate people who lived in the surrounding neighborhood, but the owner had been one of his men at Waterloo and given an arm in service to his country. Sam had been more than ready to offer his former commanding officer a room and a pint, and needing a place to stay while he conducted his investigation, Lucas had taken him up on it.

He had been back in London for three days now, and being so close to Cecily without being able to see or hold her was maddening. But it was for her sake that he had embarked on this solitary quest. Now that he knew Will had been murdered to protect the thief's identity, Lucas had no doubt that such a person would have little compunction about killing anyone who got in his way. And, though she would be loath to admit it, Cecily was more vulnerable than he was to an attack. Just the thought of anything untoward happening to her sent a chill through him, and though he knew she would not thank him for it, he was determined to keep her out of harm's way until this murderer was caught.

Thus it was that he found himself hurrying through the taproom of Sam's tavern, his eyes skimming the tables for one face in particular. In the corner table, his back to the wall, he finally saw him.

Plunking down his mug of ale, Christian looked up and offered a slight wave to him.

As Lucas took the seat opposite, he felt his friend's scrutiny. "What?" he asked, after he had told the scrawny little barmaid he'd also have ale.

"Just wondering what would make a peer of the realm hide out like a common criminal when he has a nice comfy bed and a sweet little wife to keep him warm in it."

"Who says I'm not going back to that warm bed every night?"

"Well, your sweet little wife, for starters," Christian said, raising one blond brow in mimicry of Lucas's. "She says that you have been detained in the country on estate business."

"Yes, I disliked telling that bouncer, but you know how she is. Too smart for her own good."

"Ah, then you are hiding from her?"

"Not precisely," he began, but then with a noise of impatience, he added, "Yes, I am hiding from her. Though again it's for her own damn good. Do you know how difficult it is to keep any secrets from a clever woman?"

Christian laughed. "Well, yes, that is why I only offer my favors to silly ones. Though they're devilishly bright when they need to be at times."

"You have no idea what a bright woman can do until you've crossed wits with Cecily," Lucas said with a frown. "It's as if the woman has some sort of sixth sense and can read my bloody mind. It makes it dashed difficult to do anything on one's own."

"And what are you doing on your own? You who have only been married a month or so?" Christian demanded. "And do not tell me that you've got some other woman on hand for I will not believe you. You're not the type."

"Nothing like that," Lucas said dismissively. "Cecily is more than . . . well, just no, there is no other woman."

His friend smothered a laugh. "Then what?"

"I am looking for Will's killer." He watched as all the humor fled from his friend's expression. "And I do not want to put Cecily in any danger. If something were to happen to her, I'd never forgive myself."

The other man nodded. He sat back as the barmaid brought them more ale.

"I'm getting close, Christian," Lucas continued, grateful for the noise in the room that kept their conversation relatively private. "Whoever this bastard is, he's been damned smart, but I am smarter, and more determined."

Christian listened as Lucas explained what he and Cecily had learned up until this point. Ending with the discovery of Will's body and the blue cat.

"So you're looking for this blue cat. But you don't even know what it is?"

Lucas nodded. "It's got to be some sort of statue or hollow box or something that will allow one to hide papers inside. At least that is my guess. I have been to every secondhand and antiquities shop in London and none of them has any record of a blue cat ever passing through their hands."

"I don't suppose it's occurred to you that the blue cat is in storage at the Egyptian Club," Christian said, his brow furrowed in thought. "Which you cannot possibly have access to given that you are not a member."

"Yes," Lucas said. "But it's not there either. Or, it wasn't a few weeks ago. Cecily and I . . . ahem . . . well, I just know, that's all."

His friend's eyes brightened with mischief. "Winterson, you do lead such an exciting life, I must say."

Turning serious, he continued. "So, what is your next move? While you are away from your wife, I suppose you had best do all that you can to unravel this puzzle. You cannot pretend to be in the country forever, you know."

"Yes, and that is why I need you, Christian. I need you to distract Mr. David Lawrence while I search his office for the blue cat."

"What? You mean the fellow at the British Museum?"

"Yes, that's the one. I got the feeling when Cecily and I were questioning him that he knows more than he's telling about this business. He was already lying to his employers at the museum. What's to stop him from lying to me or Cecily?"

"Are you sure this has nothing to do with the fact that he jilted your wife?"

"Certainly not. I am grateful to him for doing it, else I'd not be married to her myself." Lucas smiled. "But I will not deny that I would like very much to catch him out in a lie, just on the off chance that she still harbors any sort of feelings for the man. And if he should discover me searching his rooms and become violent? Well, let us just say that I would not be sorry if my fist were to accidentally smash into his smug face a few times."

Christian shook his head in wonder. "I had no idea you were capable of all this . . . this passion, Winterson. You were always the most levelheaded of us all. I don't know what's come over you!"

But Lucas had a suspicion about that. And it had everything

to do with his love for a certain dark-haired Amazon with a sharp tongue and a tendency to high-handedness. He was well and truly hooked. He only hoped that she was not the sort of angler to throw her biggest catch back into the pond.

Eighteen

Cecily had fallen back into her own routine at Hurston House with shocking ease. Violet had put it about that, still overcome by her brother-in-law's death, she had returned to her father's home while her husband stayed behind in the country. Which was the truth, of course, but that did not stop the more biting of the *ton* wits from speculating as to the real reason for Cecily and Lucas to be living apart.

Being back home had afforded her the opportunity to spend some time with her father as well. He was improving bit by slow bit, but there was little chance of him returning to the active life he had enjoyed before his attack. It was difficult for Cecily to see him in such a humbled state, though there was something tender and vulnerable about him that had been missing before. Perhaps it had something to do with the way that his every emotion lay so close to the surface now. His speech had not returned, nor had his ability to write, and his frustration about those failures often left him in tears. Something that she was certain he would not have wished others to see, were he in his right mind.

What astonished her about her father in his present incarnation, however, was the ease with which he showed affection. Whenever she visited, he was quick to take her hand in his and squeeze it. And there was a wealth of feeling in that small gesture. Something that had been missing from their relationship since her mother's death so many years ago.

Now, when she read aloud to him from the newspapers, and even from his own travel diaries, she spent the entire time with one hand firmly clasped in his.

He had just fallen into a fitful sleep, the third day she'd been back in London, when she saw his chamber door open to admit Lord Geoffrey Brighton. He was a frequent visitor, and often timed his arrival to coincide with the conclusion of Cecily's time with Lord Hurston. She was not sure if he did it to relieve her or so that he might have a word. It was difficult to know what motivated her father's old friend, but she was nonetheless grateful to him for the reprieve. Spending time in her father's company often left her exhausted and she was always grateful for the break.

Today, however, Lord Geoffrey did not come to his old friend's side as he normally did, but gestured for Cecily to follow him into the hallway outside.

"Good morning, my lord," she said, once they had shut the door to her father's room so as not to disturb his sleep.

"Good morning, Cecily," he returned. His normally tidy appearance was a bit disheveled today, with his shirt points slightly wilting and his cravat tied in a simple knot that seemed to suggest he had tied it himself, rather than allowing his valet to do so. "There is something I must discuss with you. And I hope you will hear me out."

"Of course," she replied, wondering what this could possibly be regarding. "Please feel free to discuss whatever you wish."

"Cecily," he said with a sternness she had never heard from him before. "It has come to my attention that your husband has been seen in a rather disreputable part of town."

This was so ludicrous as to make her laugh. "My lord, you must be mistaken. Winterson is still in the country dealing with some estate business. And when he is in town he might visit such areas. I believe he goes there to visit those of his men who have been down on their luck since the end of the war. But it is certainly nothing to cause you such concern."

"My dear." Lord Geoffrey's eyes were kind. "He has been seen with a woman."

Cecily tried to make sense of what Lord Geoffrey was saying. "Who?"

"It is Neddy Entwhistle, I'm afraid."

Cecily could not stop her gasp. "What?"

"I know he told you that he would be in the country this week, but even this morning I saw him emerge from her house in Bloomsbury."

It was absurd, of course. Cecily did not believe for one minute that Lucas was involved in any sort of amorous liaison with Neddy, but he could very well be questioning Neddy about her relationship with Lord Hurston. She was furious! How dare he sneak back to London and conduct an investigation behind her back!

Misinterpreting her anger, Lord Geoffrey patted her on the shoulder. "Now, my dear, do not fault him too much. Young men will have their little peccadilloes."

Unable to remain while Lord Geoffrey heaped consolation upon her, she quickly excused herself and raced upstairs to her room, and instructed her startled abigail to begin packing for their return to Winterson House at once. If Lucas was indeed back in London, then he could very well deal with having his own wife in the house with him.

She was trying to decide what to tell Violet when George, the fresh-faced lad who had only recently begun as a footman at Winterson House, scratched on the door.

"A note for you, Your Grace," he said, his expression far too open and expressive to make a proper footman. Though she knew Violet would never stand for such an unprofessional servant, Cecily preferred to give the young man a chance. After all, one of the responsibilities of running a ducal household was to provide gainful employment to those who needed it. Besides, she liked the young man.

Taking the note, she broke the seal and was disappointed when she saw it was not her husband's handwriting. She had hoped that he would contact her and let her know that he had returned to town on his own. But the message in her hand made all thoughts of her husband's perfidy fly from her mind.

*I know you seek your father's travel diaries. I know
where you can find them. Meet me at half past three
at the magazine to the northwest of the Serpentine.
Come alone.*

Cecily stood staring down at the missive, thinking. It
would serve Lucas right if she procured her father's journals
on her own, while he pursued his own investigation without
her. She was still quite annoyed with him over that, and it
would take many apologies on his part to set the matter right
with her.

Still, she knew that to follow the instructions in this
anonymous note would be foolhardy in the extreme. One
man had already lost his life in this business, and she had no
intention of doing the same. No, she would go to the park for
this meeting, and she would see who this mysterious person
was. But she would not go alone.

Quickly, she went to the escritoire and scrawled a note of
her own, which she hurriedly sanded and sealed. She handed
it to George.

"Wait for a reply," she told him. "And ask Molly to come
to me at once."

Two hours later, Cecily allowed her husband's best friend,
Colonel Lord Christian Monteith, to hand her from the hired
hack, just on the other side of the Serpentine from Rotten
Row.

She had chosen one of her old gowns, from the days before her fashionable transformation. And by wearing one of
her old bonnets she hoped that she was unassuming enough
to be mistaken for a less-than-prosperous merchant's wife.

It had taken a bit of doing to convince Monteith to accompany her on her errand. At first his response to her request
had been an adamant and resounding, "No!"

Chief among his reasons was his friendship with her
husband.

"I can tell you now that if your husband were to find out

I'd accompanied you on such a fool's errand he would thrash me within a hairbreadth of my life," he said, shaking his head to add emphasis to his denial. "And I would let him, because a gentleman does not come between a husband and wife. It is simply not done, ma'am.

"I will," he added, doing his best to placate her, "however, go and meet this mysterious person myself and report back to you immediately. You have my word."

"The note says that I am to be the one to meet him," Cecily said calmly. "If you show up in my stead this person is very likely to disappear into the mist. Surely you can see why. We have no idea who this person is. For all I know it could be a maid who works in the Egyptian Club, or a young boy in the employ of whoever it was that took the diaries. I cannot risk this opportunity for answers simply because you are too chicken-hearted to accompany me."

After much wrangling, during which Christian tried his damnedest to talk her out of it, Cecily found herself riding along in a hack with a much-put-upon Colonel Lord Monteith.

"I do not mind telling you, Your Grace," he informed her when they began to near the Serpentine, "that while you may be accounted a rare intelligence when it comes to scholarly thingummys, you are thoroughly lacking in common sense. If you had simply let me come here on my own I could have easily gained your father's journals for you with a little persuasion. Now, of course, we'll have to explain all of this to Winterson when he comes."

Cecily turned to stare at him. "What do you mean 'when he comes'? My husband knows nothing of this. And you will not tell him of it. I forbid you."

"With all due respect, Your Grace, what did you think he would say when he discovered you had your father's journals?"

"Well, I hadn't thought that far ahead."

Monteith merely gave a noncommittal grunt. To which she would have responded, if they had not at that very moment rolled to a stop. Her escort leaped to the ground and handed her out of the hackney. Before she could object, he paid the driver, who drove off at a rather fast clip.

"My lord," she hissed, "I had hoped to ask him to wait for us."

"Don't need him" was the curt reply. And to her annoyance, the colonel took her elbow and led her to the powder magazine, where the Four in Hand Club was often to be found showing off their latest tricks and maneuvers. Today the area surrounding the small building was thin of company, with only a couple of young men in a phaeton who seemed intent upon testing their own driving skills. Perhaps hoping to gain some sort of wisdom from doing so where the most acclaimed driving club in London was often to be found.

"Don't see anyone yet," Monteith said in a low voice.

Cecily felt a little chill run up her spine as she tried to keep watch for her mysterious messenger. Of course, it was difficult to know what to look for, given that he'd told her nothing about himself. She hoped that she and Christian looked nondescript enough to keep from alarming her note writer. She was opening her mouth to request that he step away from her so that the person with the diaries didn't run away when he saw that she wasn't alone when all hell broke loose.

A loud blast sounded from somewhere behind and to the right of her, followed quickly by a burning sensation in her right shoulder. At which point, first Christian, then someone else both leaped upon her, bringing her down to the ground with a thump. A shout rang out as the horses pulling the phaeton nearby reared up in response to the blast.

It all happened within the same few moments, but to Cecily, it felt as if time stood still. And even as she found herself thudding into the ground under the weight of not one, but two rather large men, she was relieved of one of them almost before she hit the ground.

"Cecily," she heard her husband say, "dammit, answer me!"

And as he hauled her against his very solid chest, Cecily did something she'd never in all her life thought she'd do.

The foremost English scholar of Egyptian hieroglyphics, that bluestocking-turned-fashion-plate who had only recently married the Duke of Winterson, who had faced mummies and the patronesses at Almack's with the same degree of calm, took one look at the blood pouring from her shoulder and fainted dead away.

Lucas got Christian's note when he returned from a fruitless search through Lawrence's lodgings. His friend had lured the fellow from his rooms with a cock-and-bull story about needing him to appraise a statue his grandfather had left him. A statue Lucas had borrowed from Neddy Entwhistle that afternoon. A statue that both Winterson's and Monteith's fortunes combined would be unable to pay for should something untoward happen to it. Which he'd reminded Monteith of several times before he'd headed off to find Lawrence.

Lucas knew that Lawrence was hiding something, but he was damned if he could find precisely what. Whatever it was, he must have it in his office at the museum. Which would prove slightly more difficult to gain access to, given that many more people tended to congregate there than at the Albany.

Of course when he read his friend's note, he wondered whether Lawrence had been the one to request this meeting with Cecily. Putting his hat back on and shrugging back into his greatcoat, he tore out of the hotel and took one of their stable horses.

He saw Cecily and Christian alight from a hackney some distance from the magazine, probably in the hopes that whoever had summoned her would not see them together. Of course, if he were watching their approach as Lucas had, that hope was a fruitless one. His wife's inclination to go alone had been sound from a tactical standpoint, but he was glad Christian had refused to let her do it all the same. It was unclear whether the person who called this meeting was the same one who had killed Will, but if having Christian along meant that Cecily remained unharmed, Lucas was willing to do without whatever it was this person had promised her.

Striding through the trees at the edge of the park, he had

just watched Christian pay the hackney driver, and was nearly close enough to touch Cecily, when a shot rang out. He saw Cecily flinch, and with the automatic reaction he'd honed on the battlefield, Lucas flew through the air and took her to the ground even as he felt Christian slam into him with the same goal in mind.

His friend, seeing that Lucas had Cecily, took off in the direction from which the shot had come. Still wary that more shots might come, Lucas covered his wife's body with his own.

He'd expected her to object in some manner, but when no protest was forthcoming, and with no further shots fired, he lifted himself up and realized that she'd fainted. Easing her over onto her back, he saw a singed flap of fabric at the shoulder of her drab-colored pelisse, and a darkening spot where blood rose to the surface.

He tore through her garments, rending them with his bare hands in order to see whether there was much damage. Fortunately she had escaped with only a flesh wound, but if the shot had been even a few inches lower . . . well, he did not care to think about the possibility.

"Lucas?" Cecily murmured as he made a pad from the sleeve of her now-ruined outer garment. "Did you get him? Did you see?"

"Shhh," he told her. "Christian has gone after whoever it was. And no, I didn't see anything, save you." He did not add that he'd seen her *recoiling from a gunshot*.

"My shoulder hurts," she said, as if just feeling her injury. "What happened?"

"The bastard shot you," he said through clenched teeth. "That's what happened."

"The diaries," she said, becoming restless and trying to sit up. "Did you get them?"

"No," he said, pushing her back to lie down. "Now lie still. We'll talk about this at home."

Something he said must have jarred her memory because he saw her expression clear and she frowned at him.

"Home," she said. "I hope you mean Hurston House, because I will not be returning to Winterson House."

"What do you mean? Of course you're coming back to Winterson House. You're the duchess."

"Yes, I am, aren't I?" she asked. "Then I suppose that means that I should be informed when the duke returns to town. Wouldn't you agree?"

She tried to sit up again, and this time, he let her.

"Not," he said, "if the duke has very good reasons for keeping his return to town a secret."

"Indeed? And what very good reason could that be? Perhaps to keep the duchess from getting in the way of his secret investigation into a matter that heretofore has been something that both of them worked on together?"

"Dammit, it's not like that. The duke—" He stopped and ran a hand through his disheveled hair.

"I," he began again, "wanted to protect you from this blackguard who has already killed my brother and might very well wish to kill you."

She shook her head. "Not good enough. Do you know what my father's argument against my becoming involved in scholarship has always been?"

Her eyes were clear, all traces of her earlier fainting spell removed in light of their very serious discussion.

"He always said," she continued, "that he could not allow me to stress my brain in such a way, because he feared that it would endanger my health, as my mother's health had suffered from her own studies."

"That's not the same thing," he said. "Your father's worries were unfounded, and were based on fear of some nebulous threat. This is real, Cecily. The danger here is very, very real. This person has killed, and today has tried to do so again."

"Yes, and who is to say that he wasn't driven to shooting at me today because he saw both you and Lord Monteith here with me when he expressly said that I should come alone."

"But you're the one who asked Christian to go with you!"

"Yes, and it was my intention to make sure he moved away from me as soon as I found a spot to wait for the message writer."

He was saved from saying something he would come to regret by the reappearance of Christian, who was out of breath, and looking most put out.

"Damned snake got away from me," he said, panting. "He had a horse hidden on the other side of the footbridge and was swinging into the saddle before I could get a decent look at his face."

He looked up at his friend, his expression serious. "I shouldn't have—"

But Lucas forestalled him. "We'll discuss things later. Now I need to get Cecily home and examined by a physician."

His wife was being unaccountably quiet, which he worried was due to her injuries. "I'd offer you a lift, Monteith, but I've only brought the phaeton."

"I'll find a hack," Christian replied, nodding to his friend. He made his bow to Cecily and trotted off in the direction from which he'd just come.

The duke handed his wife into the open carriage, careful not to jar her injured shoulder, and vaulted into the seat beside her. They made the trip back to Mayfair in silence, arriving at Winterson House in record time.

"I do not wish to stay here," Cecily said when she realized he was not taking her to Hurston House.

"We will discuss the matter indoors like civilized people," he returned, steering his horses to a stop before the entrance to his town house.

She opened her mouth to protest, but perhaps seeing that he was in no mood for argument, she shut it again and allowed him to lift her by the waist and carry her up the front steps and into the house.

It took a great deal of self-control to keep from protesting his high-handed behavior, but one look at his countenance told her that her husband was not ready for discussion.

Once they were inside, he barked an order to Watkins to

send for a physician, and then made the arduous climb of two flights up the stairs to the duchess's rooms. Cecily knew she was not a lightweight, but as he seemed not to notice that she was heavier than the average lady, she had no intention of telling him.

Finally, he opened the door to her sitting room and deposited her onto a settee that was arranged at a jaunty angle before the fire.

"Thank you, Your Grace." Cecily could hear the distance in her voice, but was unable to stop it. She was angry with him for a variety of reasons and was unprepared to behave as if nothing had happened when in fact something had happened. Something that vexed her in the extreme.

"You are welcome," he said stiffly.

"Now," he went on, "perhaps you will tell me what exactly made you endanger yourself in such a foolish manner. If Christian hadn't sent for me—"

"Oh." She stopped him. "Yes, let's discuss how Christian knew to send for you! Explain to me why your friend was aware that you had returned to the metropolis, but your wife was not."

"I do not need to explain myself to you, madam," was his harsh reply. "But your actions today are certainly part of the reason."

"What do you mean?" she demanded, clenching her fists at her side.

"Can you deny that you would have been unable to keep from insinuating yourself into my investigation?"

"I do not insinuate myself," she huffed. "But if there was some role I thought I would be able to play in your search for Will's killer, then why should I not inform you of it?"

"Cecily, you do not simply inform. You take over. When you have an idea, you leap from thought to action with frightening speed. That is all well and good when you are working with scholarly notions, but in the real world that can get a person killed."

"Oh, I beg your pardon," she said with exaggerated courtesy, "I thought I was living in the real world. I had no notion that I was destined to remain in the fanciful world where only scholars with outlandish notions live."

"Do not be a child," he snapped. "I am not trying to hurt your feelings, I am trying to keep you safe."

"You said that before. That you are only trying to protect me. What you haven't said is why. My father always said he did it because he loved me. A ridiculous notion, to be sure." She said the words with a sneer. "But what of you, Lucas? If I am such a head-in-the-clouds simpleton who must be protected from her own impulsive actions, then why on earth do you even care? Surely it would be easier for you if I got myself killed and left you free to marry some timid flower who would never cause you a moment's trouble."

"Because I love you, dammit!" he roared, hauling her up against him, completely unmindful of her shoulder and kissing her with a ferocity that made her knees go weak. And not just from blood loss.

A hesitant cough from the doorway broke the spell.

"I do not wish to disturb, Your Grace," the footman, George, said with a nervous laugh. Clearly he was embarrassed at having witnessed their embrace. "But D-Dr. Tillby is here."

Lucas stepped back from Cecily, both of them breathing heavily and staring at one another.

"Show him in," Lucas said, never taking his eyes from her. Cecily allowed him to hand her back down onto the settee, and dropped his hand as if it were made of fire as soon as she was seated.

"Your Grace," the physician said with an admirable calm. "What seems to be the trouble?"

It was some twenty minutes before the doctor ordered Cecily to take a bit of laudanum for the pain and saw her bandaged and settled into her bed. When he was gone, Lucas was left, seated at her bedside, her slim hand clasped in his large, strong one.

"I have more to say," Cecily said, fighting her heavy eyelids to keep focused on him, the opiate already beginning to have its effect on her. "Do not think you've won."

Lucas gave a sharp laugh. "Never fear, my dear," he said, bringing her hand to his lips. "I look forward to hearing you shout at me like a fishwife again soon."

She shook her head, as if trying to shake off the sleep that was slowly claiming her. "Why did you say it?" she asked, her voice getting softer. "Not fair. Not fair at all."

He grinned. "You know what they say about love and war," he told her.

"Can't," she said, her lids dropping against her will. "Can't let you . . ."

Watching over her as she lost her fight to stay awake, Lucas leaned forward and pressed a kiss onto her forehead. "I'm afraid you can't stop me, Duchess," he said softly. "I will love you whether you allow me to or not."

Nineteen

The next morning, Cecily awoke alone, and feeling surprisingly refreshed given that she'd been shot the day before. Dressing quickly, she stepped out the door of the duchess's chamber to discover that three large footmen were guarding her.

Lucas's doing, she decided, and moved down the hallway. To her annoyance, the footmen seemed to have been instructed to follow her.

"James," she said to the senior among them, "why are you following me?" She tried to keep her voice as calm as possible. It was not the footmen's fault that their master was an overprotective fool, after all.

"If you please, Your Grace," the young man returned, "the duke told us that we're to go wherever you go today. At least until the man who tried to shoot you yesterday is caught."

"He told us you were not to be left alone at any time," the fresh-faced one, George, added.

"Did he indeed?" She knew her husband meant well, but really, it was annoying in the extreme to see that none of her explanations she'd given him yesterday had had any effect at all. Not only had he continued to treat her like a person without the sense to protect herself, but he couched his argument within the mantle of protecting her. "Well, I hope you gentlemen are prepared for a great deal of walking today, for I'm engaged to go shopping with my cousins this afternoon."

"Of course, Your Grace," James said, keeping his face expressionless. "We will accompany you wherever you like."

"Excellent," she said with false brightness. "First I will have some breakfast, and while I do so you will perhaps ask for the coach to be brought around."

And some twenty minutes later, Cecily was inside the carriage with Maddie and Juliet, on the way to Bond Street in search of the perfect gift for Violet's upcoming birthday. Both young ladies gave her hard hugs with deference to her injured shoulder as soon as she climbed in.

"You could have been killed," Juliet said, her brows drawn in concern. "You must promise me that you won't take any more risks like that."

But Cecily waved her concern away. "If it were up to you and Winterson I'd never leave the house again."

"Well, I think it's perfectly lovely that he wishes to protect you," Maddie said with feeling. "There are any number of wives whose husbands wouldn't care a fig whether or not they were attacked by some maniac."

"I'd wager there are some who would greatly appreciate it," Juliet said, unable to remain serious for long. "With the state of marriage in the *ton* these days it's a wonder someone hasn't offered it as a service to the unhappy spouse."

"It's not that I do not appreciate the sentiment," Cecily said, squeezing her cousin's hand. "But I've spent my entire life resisting the strictures society places on young ladies. I had hoped now that I am married I'd be allowed more freedom rather than less. Isn't that how it's supposed to be?"

"This is hardly a usual situation, though, Cecily," Juliet argued. "Someone did shoot you yesterday, after all. I would hardly equate your father's fears that your following in your mother's scholarly footsteps would cause you to suffer a decline with Winterson's very sensible attempts to protect you from some madman with a gun. Your mama's death was caused by a fever. And there's nothing of any real consequence one can do to protect against that. Whereas there are steps that can be taken to protect one from being murdered."

"I suspect that you're right in some ways," Cecily

conceded, "but it is so utterly frustrating not to be in charge of one's own destiny. First we are children who are lorded over by our fathers, then we are wives who are lorded over by our husbands."

"What a trial it must be for you." Juliet's smile took the sting out of her words.

A flush rose in Cecily's cheeks. "I suppose I was being a bit insufferable, wasn't I? I am sorry. I do not wish to sound ungrateful."

"Is there something else bothering you?" Maddie asked, her brow furrowed with concern. "I mean, aside from the fact that someone is trying to have you killed."

The wry addendum provoked laughter from all three of them. "Yes, Cecily," Juliet said, her eyes merry. "Do tell us if something else has eclipsed the all-consuming terror of being faced down by a killer. The peas at dinner last night were too soft, perhaps? Or your favorite pair of boots have been scratched?"

"Oh, pooh," Maddie said with mock severity. "You know what I meant. After all, there is more to life than the quest for Lord Hurston's journals. What about Winterson? Is everything well with the two of you?"

The question caught Cecily by surprise, and she paused a moment to frame her answer. Finally, deciding to empty her budget, she said baldly, "Winterson told me he loved me last night."

Madeline squealed happily and clapped her hands. "I knew it! I knew he loved you! From the first moment I saw you together at the Bewle ball I saw how suitable the two of you are for one another." She took a breath. "Tell us all about it."

At a raised brow from Juliet, she hastily amended, "Within reason, of course."

"Well," Cecily began, "there's nothing to tell. He told me, I told him thank you, and we went to sleep."

"You were in the bedchamber?" Maddie gasped. "How lovely!"

"Not for that." A blush suffused Cecily's cheeks. "We don't always . . . that is to say . . . we weren't . . ."

"No need to explain," Juliet said, saving her cousin's modesty. "So, he told you he loved you. What did you tell him?"

"Thank you."

Madeline and Juliet stared.

"What?" Cecily demanded. "Is 'thank you' not an appropriate response? I suppose you would have had me declaring my unending adoration?"

"Not necessarily," Juliet said, her lips pursed. "But certainly something more positive than 'thank you.'"

"What is wrong with 'thank you'?"

"Nothing is wrong precisely," Madeline said. "But it does lack a certain . . ."

"Romance," Juliet supplied. "'Thank you' is what you say in response to 'that's a nice hat you're wearing.'"

"Not what you tell the man who has just declared his love for you. Unless of course you do not love him. In which case . . ." Maddie's expression was sad.

"You would say 'thank you.'" Juliet nodded in disappointed agreement. "You really do not love him?"

Cecily shifted uncomfortably in her seat. "It's not that I do not love him. I am quite fond of him really. He is much more intelligent than I thought when we first met. And he is always doing sweet little things for me. Why, the other evening he . . ." She began to blush again. "Well, never mind that. He is very sweet."

"But?" Juliet prompted.

"But, I do not know if I love him. Or rather, I do not know if I am ready to tell him such a thing. Or to give him anything more than simple admiration and affection. What if he decides to leave me? Or go traveling without me?"

"He is your husband, Cecily." Madeline squeezed her hand. "He cannot leave you. Not really."

"My father left my mother home alone in London while he traveled the Continent and Africa in search of fame and fortune. Just because a man marries does not guarantee that he will stay with her forever."

"Winterson is nothing like your father." The adamancy of Juliet's statement brought Cecily up short.

"How can you know that? How can you know that he won't declare himself to be my eternal love and then board the next ship bound for America a week later?"

"I can't know it. But I know you. And I know Winterson. And neither one of you would do such a thing to the other. If Winterson tells you that he loves you, then you can believe him. Honor is not just another byword with him. He lives by it. I have been out long enough to know which gentlemen are to be trusted and which are not. And your husband is definitely an honorable man. Even if he did not love you he would never simply leave you, his wife, to deal with the vagaries of life on your own. He would no more do that than you would."

"That is what I thought about David," Cecily said quietly. "I thought he was an honorable man. He was well mannered, graceful, affectionate. He was everything I thought I desired in a husband, and he also told me he loved me."

"I hope you will not let that toad David Lawrence ruin what you have with Winterson," Juliet said with a frown. "Lawrence is half the man Winterson is, and if it were not for the fact that your father was away at the time, he would have been called to account for jilting you. If I didn't think I'd be laughed off the field, I'd have put a bullet in the bounder myself."

"So would I," Madeline added. "David Lawrence can make no comparison with Winterson. And for you to fear Winterson because of what Lawrence did is unfair to both you and Winterson."

"I know," Cecily conceded. "It's just that I . . . I am afraid. Afraid of having my heart broken again. I did not think I would survive the last time. If it were to happen to me with Winterson, I fear I'd never recover."

"But isn't that the risk of falling in love?"

She was saved from answering by the slowing of the carriage. She didn't know how the conversation had turned, and though she was grateful to have her cousins' counsel, it was trying to be the focus of their attention. She looked forward to the day when they were married so that the tables would turn.

The three ladies allowed the coachman to hand them down and soon they were in Bond Street, browsing the shop windows. After a stop in the stationer's, the glover's, and the haberdasher's, they simply wandered from shop window to shop window, occasionally stepping inside to sample the merchant's wares, from confections to perfume. All the while being followed at a discreet distance by three sturdy footmen. Despite being slightly annoyed at Lucas's high-handedness, Cecily did feel more secure knowing that should anything untoward happen she would be well protected.

Maddie and Juliet had walked on ahead to look at the printer's shop window when Cecily stopped to examine a particularly fine bit of jade carving on display in a jeweler's window. As with many less prosperous shops, this one seemed to have added to their inventory by purchasing decorative odds and ends, some of which were likely to have been obtained through questionable channels. Still, there were some lovely pieces to be had, and Cecily had always made it a practice to search for wares that might have made their way from Egypt or India or some other foreign land. She had found many pretty pieces this way, including a scarab that might well belong in a museum.

Allowing her gaze to wander over the small bits of scrimshaw, the odd candlestick, the carved figures, Cecily was just about ready to move on to the next window when a flash of blue near the bottom of the window caught her eye. Her heart began to beat faster as she recognized an oblong object lying on its side—it was a sarcophagus, the likes of which she'd seen many times before. Small because it was not for a human being, but a cat. In this case, the cat still held the pale sheen of the blue paint some ancient Egyptian had used to decorate the final resting place of this small sleek animal with the powers of a god. And more important still, it was an exact replica of the blue cat that had been carved into the side of the casket where they'd found Will's body.

She had found the blue cat.

* * *

Maddie and Juliet had come hurrying to her side when they heard Cecily's squeal of delight. When she told them what had so overset her, they followed her into the shop and waited patiently while she asked the clerk if she might speak to the proprietor.

Conscious of nobility when he saw it, the young man nearly hit his head on the floor from bowing so low. And when he disappeared into the back room to fetch his employer, Cecily and her cousins waited with barely concealed impatience.

At last a tall man, whose limbs resembled nothing so much as walking sticks stuffed into fabric, stepped into the room, smoothing down his oily hair, clearly hoping to make a good impression on the Duchess of Winterson.

"Adolphus Hogg, at your service, Your Grace," he said, lowering his thin frame into a deep bow. "I understand you are interested in the Egyptian death box."

Cecily only just succeeded in keeping her eyes still. She was beginning to understand why Lucas had been so leery of meeting her that first day. It was pleasant, of course, to be accorded a certain amount of condescension because of one's station. She would be disingenuous if she were to declare otherwise. There were, however, those who granted such liberties to her simply because of her title, so that she feared very much that one day she would puff up like a hot air balloon she'd seen in Green Park once, and fly away into the sky never to be heard from again.

"The sarcophagus, yes," she answered, careful to offer her correction as an alternative rather than as an outright dismissal of her colorfully termed "death box." "Could you tell me where you acquired the piece?"

His eyes narrowed as he tried to determine whether her interest was sincere, and wondered whether he ought not to charge extra for the information he gave her. After a moment, he must have made up his mind, however, for he gave an almost imperceptible nod and moved toward the window to remove the cat carving.

"I'm afraid I'm not sure where this item came from, Your

Grace," he said, the fatuous smile not losing any of its falseness. "We have gotten in quite a bit of new inventory of late, so it is difficult to know."

Ah, Cecily thought. So he wants to play that game, does he?

"Surely you are more careful about the provenance of your wares, sir. I cannot believe for one moment that you do not know where each and every item in this shop hails from."

At his sharp intake of breath, she gave him a frown. "Just because I am a lady," she warned him, "does not mean that I am mentally deficient."

She gave a slight smile at Juliet's and Madeline's nearly inaudible cheers.

"Now," Cecily snapped. "Let's begin again. Where did you acquire this piece?"

Clearly overset at being caught out in a lie by a duchess—a duchess who might consider spending quite a large sum of money in his shop—Hogg smiled again, this time in an obviously placating manner.

"Oh," he said, as if he'd only just now remembered her question. "I believe that piece was obtained from the collection of a gentleman who has just recently returned from a trip to Africa."

"Indeed." Cecily tried and failed to keep her impatience from showing. "And why did he sell it?"

"I believe he was . . . that is to say . . . he . . ."

"Had pockets to let?" she supplied.

"Yes."

Finally, she thought. Aloud she continued, "And do you know whether the piece is genuine?"

"It would appear so to me, Your Grace," he said, shifting from one foot to the other like a naughty schoolboy.

"Might I see your loupe?" she asked, nodding at the tiny magnifying tool he wore on a string around his neck.

"But of course, Your Grace," he said, his forehead breaking out with beads of sweat. He handed the little glass to her and she held it up to her eye, adjusting it so that she might see the sarcophagus properly. Carefully, she looked at the casket, searching the slightly bumpy wooden surface for some sign that it might be opened using a secret latch of sorts. But if there was such a latch, it was invisible.

"I'll take it," she told the proprietor, handing back his eyepiece.

"But madam." He hesitated. "Do you not wish to know the price? To consult your husband?"

"Uh-oh," Juliet said under her breath.

"He's in for it now," Maddie whispered back.

And sure enough, Cecily stared at the man as if horns had begun growing from his forehead. "My husband?" she asked with a deceptive purr. "What would my husband have to say about matters?"

Perhaps realizing that he trod on thin ice, the man tried to retract his statement. "N . . . nothing, Your Grace." He gave a high-pitched girlish laugh. "Nothing at all. It was silly of me to think of it."

"Indeed it was." Cecily nodded agreeably. "Now, hadn't you best take my blue cat back there and wrap it up? I should like to take it with me."

Twenty

Lucas was in the study when Cecily returned to Berkeley Square with her cat sarcophagus.

To her surprise, she found him examining a specimen that seemed remarkably similar to her own.

"Where did you find that?" she demanded, handing her hat and gloves to Watkins, who stood hovering behind her. She ignored the man's look of reproach as she took the mummified cat back from him. He was put out with her because she'd refused to allow either himself or a footman to carry it into the house for her.

"Good afternoon to you too, my dear," her husband said, stepping aside to allow her to place her sarcophagus next to his own, and leaning in to give her a quick kiss on the cheek.

"Do not 'good afternoon' me, Winterson," she huffed. "I supposed that this was the only Egyptian blue cat in London and now I've come home to find you with one exactly like it. This is not the time for pleasantries."

"Well, I should think it would be perfectly obvious to you that I found this mummy in the same place where yours came from."

"From Mr. Hogg's shop in Bond Street?"

"No, my dear bluestocking," he said with a laugh, stepping back from the desk to look at the two pieces lying side by side. "From your friend Lawrence's warehouse of things he brought back for the museum."

The news nonplussed her. "Oh, Lucas," she said, looking up at him. "Do not tell me that you went back there alone."

"No," he assured her, "I did not. This was among the things that Bow Street brought to me that they suspected belonged to William that were found with his body. What with the burial and seeing to Mama and Clarissa, and that madman trying to shoot you, its presence here escaped my notice until this morning, when I decided to box up the rest of William's things to send to Clarissa."

She searched his face but all she saw was grief.

As if sensing her worry, he smiled sadly at her. "Do not worry, wife," he said. "I have decided that his death is too large a burden to carry with me for the rest of my days. I know that Will would not have wished that for me. And even if I will always feel a sense of sorrow for what might have been, I have decided that the best way to honor my brother will be to live my own life to the fullest. After, of course, I learn who is responsible for his death and see that he is punished to the fullest extent of the law."

Cecily smiled. "That is good to hear."

"Now," he said, changing the subject, "tell me where you came upon your mummified cat. I know that these are not all that uncommon, but it seems strange to note that these two are so remarkably similar."

He turned his own mummy onto its right side, then did the same thing with hers. He pointed to a particular mark on the underside of the wooden casket's carved cat head. It was a small mark of about an inch in length and appeared to be a flaw in the wood. Only that very same flaw was there on both of the carvings.

Cecily leaned forward to get a closer look at the indention. The marks were remarkably similar. And of course, the thing that set the pieces apart from the genuine pieces she'd examined from the most recent batch of items brought back from her father's last trip was the one thing she herself was most confident in using to debunk the two mummies.

The hieroglyphs.

Unlike the pieces she had examined in the past, there

was nothing on either of these two sarcophagi that intimated in the least that they were genuine artifacts from Egypt. First of all, there was nothing at all to indicate the status or position of the man who had owned the cat. If it were genuine, she'd have expected to find invocations to the various deities imploring them to care for the beloved pet in the hereafter. What language there was, was disjointed and made no sense. There was nothing to be discerned from the juxtaposition of "water," "hand," and "hill slope." No, she was quite sure that both of the items before her were not only fakes, but also were simply two of a number of others. There was something about the sameness that seemed to mark these two pieces that made her imagine a long line of workers adding bit by painstaking bit these trappings of Egyptian culture—and having no notion of just how far off the mark their forgeries were.

"I found it in the shop of one Adolphus Hogg, in Bond Street. He said that he'd purchased it from a gentleman who was down on his luck and had been forced to sell off his valuables. One of which happened to be, according to Hogg, at least, a priceless Egyptian relic."

"Well, clearly," Lucas said with some asperity, "your Mr. Hogg has been misinformed. I find it utterly alarming to know that there can be such a lack of forthrightness among the pawn trade these days."

"Indeed," she said, moving to examine the other sarcophagus. "I suppose the creator of these two items never expected to be so unlucky as to have them both examined by an expert in Egyptian hieroglyphics."

"The thought probably never occurred to the fellow," her husband returned. "I would imagine that most items like this are snatched up by true collectors—who lock their prizes away from the prying eyes of the hoi polloi—and of course museums and such establishments as the Egyptian Club."

"Oh, I suspect whoever created these had no intention of them ever making it to either a museum or the club. It would be far too risky to allow them to be seen by those with the ability to discern their falseness."

"Indeed." Lucas's brow furrowed.

"What is it?" Cecily wondered, looking up from her examination. "Are you wondering why this piece was found buried with William?"

"Yes," he said with a frown. "I cannot help but think that William stumbled upon whoever was responsible for creating these two forgeries, and in doing so got himself killed."

She slipped her hand into his, and leaned into his body with her own. She might not yet be comfortable returning his love, but she would not flinch from offering him comfort when she could.

"Suppose it's true," she said. "What then? Could it be that someone on that trip was engaged in creating forgeries of Egyptian artifacts? If that is the case, then there could be a panic among both the people working in the museum and among the members of the Egyptian Club."

Lucas sat in the massive chair behind his desk and pulled a protesting Cecily into his lap.

"I wonder," he said. Gazing down at his mummified cat, he ran his fingers over the base of it. "Do not be alarmed," he said, then to her surprise, he grasped a small lip of plaster and pulled.

"Oh, no!" she said, unable to stop herself from crying out at the destruction of the piece. But to her astonishment, the piece did not begin to unravel. Rather a circular plug came away from the base, revealing a small recess within the piece.

"You'd better take it out," he said to a gaping Cecily. "Your fingers are smaller than mine."

She shook her head in exasperation at him. "How did you know that would happen?" she asked. "It could just as easily have disintegrated in your hands."

"I had a hunch," he replied, watching as she pulled a rolled-up piece of foolscap from within the mummy. "Besides, you've already established that it is not actually an ancient Egyptian artifact. Even if this one had disintegrated we still have another to show to the authorities."

Unrolling the paper, Cecily held it before them so that they could both read it.

"It's an inventory of the items from the excavation of the—tomb," she said. "Why would it be hidden here? Surely Papa would have kept this in order to check it against the actual cargo he brought back."

"I've got another idea," he said, and proceeded to pick up Cecily's mummy and began to pull on the identical lip of plaster at the base. Sure enough, the same sort of plaster plug came away and he wordlessly handed it back to his wife and watched as she removed another piece of foolscap.

"It's another inventory."

They spread the two sheets out side by side on the desktop, scanning the two documents for similarities and differences.

"Lucas," she said, pointing to the first sheet, "look here where it lists the scarabs. Why are there twelve on the first sheet, but only six on the second? Both of these inventories seem to have the same types of items, but the numbers are half as small on the first page as on the second."

"I'm afraid, my dear," he said, "that we've found something that is definitely worth killing for."

"You mean someone was stealing these items?" she asked.

"No," he said. "Remember I looked around the warehouse for a bit before we found the sarcophagus with Will in it? Do you remember there being nearly as many items there as are listed on this first page?"

Cecily thought back to their visit to the warehouse. That whole day had been so traumatic she'd tried to put the memory of that warehouse, of the sights and smells she'd been exposed to, from her mind. But she closed her eyes and visualized the room. Tried to remember what impression she'd gotten of the volume of antiquities housed there.

"No," she answered, opening her eyes to meet his. "There were not nearly as many items in that warehouse as there are on this list. But perhaps that's just because the second list is the correct one."

He shook his head. "Why go to the trouble of writing out two lists if only one is correct?"

"Good point," she said, pursing her lips in concentration.

Then, she snapped her fingers. "I've got it! Do you remember something odd about the warehouse?"

"You mean aside from its location? Not particularly."

"I recall thinking when we entered the building that it appeared much larger on the outside than it appeared to be from the inside. Items from the expedition were lined up all along the back wall of the room, and if there was another door back there, I certainly did not see it."

Lucas rubbed a hand thoughtfully along his jaw. "Nor did I," he said.

"What if whoever oversaw the shipment of the artifacts from Egypt to England kept two sets of cargo? With two sets of inventories? One, the smaller inventory sheet, would be shown to the customs agents when they arrived back in port. The other, he hid inside of the mummified cat, thinking to remove it once he got back to England."

"How did they manage to get the extra artifacts into the country without the customs officials noticing?"

"It is not all that difficult to create a false bottom in a wooden crate," she said. "The extra artifacts would be stored within the false bottom, and the top part would appear to be filled with whatever artifacts appeared on the label and perhaps sawdust or some other filler material to make it seem as if whoever packed the items simply did not know how to do it properly. And I am afraid that the agents who check those sorts of things are rather notorious for being quite easy to pay to look the other way when necessary."

"Then once the artifacts were unloaded they were divided into two groups—one of smuggled items that were to be sold off as quickly and quietly as possible so that the members of the club and the museum did not discover that their pieces were not as unique as they seemed, and one to go to the club and the museum."

"But which lot was real and which lot was forged?" Cecily demanded. "I cannot believe that Papa would knowingly pass off forgeries as genuine. Especially not after staking his career on his reputation. And what of Will?"

"I'm afraid that both your father and my brother must

have discovered what was going on. And Will paid the ultimate price for his knowledge."

Cecily dropped into the chair. "But how on earth could someone have provoked Papa to apoplexy?"

He went down onto his haunches next to her, and chafed her hand between his. "I don't know. I wonder if there is not some sort of medicine or herb that might bring an attack on. In someone of your father's age I would imagine it wouldn't be too difficult to do."

Her eyes were bleak when she raised them to him. "All of this—murder and mayhem—all of it to protect someone who wanted to use my father's expedition as a means to make more money than was possible with the actual artifacts."

"I would venture a step further," he said. "And posit that whoever it was, was not entitled to the profits from the original excavation, and managed to hire someone in Cairo to create cheap replicas that might be taken back to England with them and sold at a profit."

"I never thought I'd say this," Cecily said sorrowfully. "But if I do not see another hieroglyphic or Egyptian artifact again it will be too soon."

Lucas kissed the back of her hand. "Don't say that, sweetheart. It is neither your fault, nor the fault of the ancient Egyptians, that this happened. It may all be heaped upon the head of a murdering, lying snake, who will be stopped soon enough. Just you wait."

She smiled sadly. "I know you are right," she said, "but I cannot help but think of all the people who might still be alive if none of us had ever even heard of the ancient Egyptians. Papa and your brother, Will. How many more have been cursed by the gods?"

"Surely you do not believe in that curse nonsense," he said with a frown. Being a little down was understandable. Actually believing that the gods had placed a curse on all who dared disturb their tombs was another thing entirely.

A sigh escaped her. "No. I do not believe the curse. Though Uncle Geoffrey has worked hard enough to make me heed it. If I didn't know he was such a rational being I'd wonder if he weren't beginning to lose his mind to age a bit."

"Indeed," her husband returned. "Now, I suppose we had best request the Bow Street runners to come for a visit so that we may inform them of our theory. If nothing else, they may wish to examine the warehouse for themselves."

Twenty-one

$\mathcal{W}$hile Lucas spoke with the Bow Street runners, Cecily traveled the short distance to Hurston House, hoping to spend a bit of time with her father before his afternoon session with the latest physician.

Though she could not forgive him for his attempts to keep her away from the studies that had given her such a sense of purpose, her relationship with Lucas had shown her that her father's relationship with her mother had likely been more complex than she had been able to understand as a child. In addition, she now understood Lord Hurston's reasons for wishing to shield his daughter from the dangers that his travels abroad could bring. She didn't agree with him, but given that one man had died, and another had almost done so, she was willing to concede that there were perhaps some elements of her father's work that were indeed more dangerous than she could have imagined.

And, perhaps most importantly, she had seen her husband's cordial interactions with his mother and she understood in a way she had never done before that there was much to be gained from such a relationship. For all of Lord Hurston's faults, she did love him, and for whatever time he had left on this earth she would do whatever she could to ensure that he knew it.

She was handing her hat to the butler when she spied Violet descending the staircase, her eyes red-rimmed.

"Violet, what is it?" Cecily rushed forward to grasp her stepmother's hands. "Is Papa worse?"

Lady Hurston struggled to regain her composure, and shook her head. "No, no, there is no change, my dear," she said at last, having taken a deep breath to calm herself. "I was merely trying to come to a decision about something."

The two walked arm in arm into the little sitting room that Violet called her own. It was a cheery room, decorated in yellow chintz and bright patterns, which glowed in the afternoon sun.

When they were seated, with a pot of tea on the table between them, Cecily asked, "Now, if it will help, please tell me what troubles you."

Her stepmama smiled. "Do you know, Cecily," she said, her smile fond, but her eyes still shadowed, "I believe that marriage suits you. You have seemed a great deal more content with life since your match with Winterson."

Cecily felt a telltale flush creep into her cheeks. "I suppose you may be correct," she said, attempting to appear blasé about the matter. "Winterson is a good husband, I believe."

"Oh, come now, dearest. It is there for anyone who really knows you to see written plainly on your face. You are glowing. Even if you refuse to admit to the man that you adore him as much as he adores you."

"How did you . . . ?" Really, it was too trying to be read so easily. There had been a time when she fancied herself perfectly inscrutable. A time that had clearly passed.

Violet gave a little tsk, then took a sip of her tea. "I have known you since you were four years old, Cecily. If I know one thing about you it is that you are stubborn."

At her stepdaughter's protest, the viscountess merely shook her head. "I also know how devastated you were when David Lawrence broke your engagement all those years ago."

Before Cecily could ask, Violet raised a hand to forestall her question. "There was no way on earth that I would believe that you were the one to release him. I knew how desperately in love with him you were, and I also knew that Millie Pilkington came with four thousand a year. He might have been flattered by your attentions—enough to propose—but in the end, I knew that he would do what was best for him."

"I had no idea you knew," Cecily said with shake of her head. "I thought I was so clever to make it seem as if I were the one who cried off. If I'd known you and Father—"

"Oh, heavens, your father had no idea!" Violet told her with surprise. "If he'd known that Lawrence jilted you he would have called the fellow out the next morning. And I did not wish for you to bear the scandal of it. So I let him believe the story you wished him to believe.

"That wasn't wrong of me," she asked, a frown line appearing between her brows, "was it?"

Cecily was surprised, but not shocked, she supposed. It had been a long time ago. And she had been trying to keep the scandal to a minimum. As much for David as for herself. And if her father had discovered the truth, there was no doubt in her mind that it would have been pistols at dawn and damn the consequences.

"No," she said aloud. "It was exactly the right thing to do. Otherwise I'd have been forced to marry David, and though at the time I thought that was what I wished, I know now that it would have been a mistake."

"Well, there is another matter which I need to confess to you, Cecily," Violet said, her expression remaining serious. "I fear that you will not be able to forgive this action of mine so easily. There is a small possibility that you may even decide to cut yourself off from me altogether."

"Do not be foolish, Violet," she said with a laugh. "I doubt there is anything you could do or say that would cause me to break with you completely. Come now, confess and we will laugh about it together."

But Violet did not laugh; instead she looked down at her hands, as if unwilling to meet her stepdaughter's eyes. Cecily felt a sense of foreboding ripple through her.

"Cecily," Lady Hurston began, "do you remember when you asked me about your father's journals, and whether or not they'd been sent to the Egyptian Club?"

"Yes, of course."

"Well," the older lady said, "I may have told a tiny bit of a lie about that."

"What do you mean?"

"Well, I could not help but recall how adamant your papa had always been about keeping you from entangling yourself in the world of scholarly things. And how he tried again and again to ensure that you would not harm yourself with too much knowledge. And it was this that I was thinking of—so soon after your father had returned from his trip, and so very ill—when I told you that small, little fib."

"And?"

"And, I'm afraid your father's journals have been here in this house the whole time."

Silence descended upon the little parlor. Broken only by the sound of the fire burning merrily in the grate.

"Here?" Cecily finally asked. "The whole time?"

"Yes."

"But I looked," she said, aghast. "His study was the first place I searched for them."

"I moved them whenever I knew you were coming to search for them," was Violet's response.

"When I was sneaking into the Egyptian Club with Winterson? When I was compromising my reputation?" Cecily felt her voice rise in volume and pitch. "All that while, Papa's journals, which I wanted to translate for the perfectly altruistic purpose of presenting what might be his final voyage to the land he loved, all that time they were here in this house?"

"Yes."

As her stepmama was confessing what she had done, Cecily examined her heart for outrage, for anger, for feelings of betrayal. But to her surprise she felt none of these things. Rather than feeling hard done by, she felt relief at knowing where her father's journals were. At knowing they were within her reach at last. And suddenly, she realized what a gift Violet's lie had given her. And she was grateful. Grateful that her stepmother had so respected her own husband's wishes that she had lied to her stepdaughter. Grateful that she herself had taken matters into her own hands that day and gone to the Egyptian Club, hoping to get a glimpse of the journals. For without Violet's lie, there would be no marriage between her and Lucas at all. "You are not angry?" Violet asked, obviously stunned to see her stepdaughter grinning at her from across the tea table.

Cecily threw her arms around Lady Hurston and hugged her. "I am elated!" she said with a laugh. "Now, let us go get the journals at once." Her expression grew serious. "If there is any mention at all in Papa's journals about who might have been responsible for William's death, then we must find it at once."

The two ladies rose and Cecily followed Violet upstairs to her father's study.

To her surprise, Lord Geoffrey was already there. He stood on the library ladder, his hand clasped around a red calfskin-bound volume, which Cecily recognized as the same sort of journal her father had been keeping for years.

"Geoffrey," Violet said, obviously startled to see her husband's old friend making free of the library. "Whatever are you doing here?"

"Cannot an old friend be allowed to borrow a book now and again?" the gentleman said, nimbly climbing down the ladder, careful not to drop the three volumes he had tucked beneath his other arm.

"What are you doing with Papa's journals, my lord?" Cecily asked, fear gathering in the pit of her stomach as she realized with a sinking heart that the man before her had as strong a motive as anyone to kill William Dalton. "I feel sure that if you would only ask Violet, she would give you whatever you wish."

"Is that right, Cecily?" he asked, putting the books down on the desk, and reaching a hand into his greatcoat to remove a small pistol. "I fear that you much mistake the matter. Though I have asked again and again since our return from Egypt just where your father's journals were hidden, Violet would only tell me that they were perfectly safe. Isn't that unaccommodating of her? To force me to look for them on my own?"

Though the hand that held the pistol was perfectly steady, Cecily noted that a faint tremor ran through his left arm.

"There is no need to threaten us, my lord," she said carefully, her mind racing as she tried to think of some means to draw the attention of the servants. "We will do whatever it is you wish."

"Will you indeed?" His expression turned nasty. "I highly doubt that you would so demean yourself as to do what I really wished of you, my dear."

His voice sent a chill racing down her spine as she realized she knew nothing about this man whom she had called uncle from the time she was a small child. His lascivious gaze chilled her, but she managed to control the rising bile in her throat. If both she and Violet were to get out of this situation alive and intact, she would need to keep her wits about her.

"G-G-Geoffrey," Violet stammered, her face paler than Cecily had ever seen it. "You mustn't harm us. You know that Hurston would never forgive you."

He barked a laugh at Violet's warning. "As if Hurston has any say in the matter now," he said, sneering. "Surely you don't think I'd allow him to live now that I've gotten what I wanted."

Thinking to distract him, Cecily said, "You must have been trying for quite some time to get Papa's diaries. Since before you left Egypt."

His eyes narrowed in suspicion, but unable to pass up an opportunity for self-aggrandizement, he nodded. "I planted the blood-soaked bag in his tent after Dalton's disappearance, thinking I might kill two birds with one stone, as it were. If Hurston found himself under suspicion, perhaps he'd give his journals to me for safekeeping. Of course no one believed that Saint Hurston could possibly kill a man he'd loved as a son."

The description of Will's relationship with her father stung, but it was obvious that in this instance Brighton hadn't purposely been trying to wound.

"When that didn't work," he went on, "once we'd set sail for England, I thought there might be some way to coax him into telling me what he did with the journals, but after his unfortunate attack, that was impossible. My little elixir worked a bit too well, I'm afraid. He was writhing on the floor before I even got the chance to ask him. When I heard they'd been donated to the club, I was elated, of course. But it would seem that your bitch of a stepmama couldn't part with them after all."

He meant to punish Violet for her transgression, Cecily was certain of it. She swallowed back bile at the thought.

"Now you'll never be able to reconcile with your dear papa, will you, Cecily?" Geoffrey's expression held just the right note of empathy, but he was unable to keep a straight face for long. His mouth twisted with mirthful scorn. "What a pity."

"What have you done to him?" Cecily demanded. "What did you give him?"

"Oh, do not pretend alarm, my dear." He sneered. "The dutiful daughter role does not suit you. You are too independent-minded for such a thing. Too intelligent by half to be so trite. No, I know what you really think, and you would be wise to remember it."

"Just tell me what poison you used to subdue him." Cecily's voice was hard, unflinching. "I know that he would never have allowed you to subjugate him willingly."

"Well, it would appear that you hold him in some affection after all," Lord Geoffrey said, laughing. "I must admit that it was always difficult for me to understand just the right words to use to keep the two of you apart. Thank goodness that you, Cecily, are so quick to take offense. And that your papa is so easily led. It took little enough persuasion on my part to convince him that your mother's death was the result of overstimulation of her poor little brain. Hah! If you could have seen the look on his face when I told him that. Convincing him that following in your parents' footsteps would do you grave injury could not have been easier. It was just the thing to ensure he never allowed you to travel abroad as you wanted to. I couldn't have you traveling with us to Egypt and ruining my little side business, now could I?"

Oh, God, Cecily thought. He had been there all along. All her life she'd known this man. He'd dandled her on his knee, for pity's sake. And now, layer by layer, he peeled back the veil to reveal the illusions that her entire existence had been built upon.

"Winterson will find us," Cecily said with a conviction she wished she felt. "He is on his way to me this minute."

"Now, you should know better than to tell a lie, Cecily," Geoffrey said with an unsettling grin. "Your husband is just where I left him, holed up in his study waiting for the Bow Street runners he sent for. Unfortunate for him that they will never come. I took very great care to ensure that his little summons was, shall we say, misdirected . . . By the time he realizes they are not coming you will be long gone from Hurston House, and England."

"What do you mean?" She tried to keep him talking. The more time they spent in conversation the more likely Lucas would be to come for her.

"I rather fancy," he went on, rubbing his chin in thought, "sending you on that Egyptian holiday you've been wishing for all these years. What say you?"

"I say that you are liar and a thief, Lord Brighton," Cecily said coldly. "And my husband will be most unhappy to hear that you've been holding his wife, the Duchess of Winterson, hostage in her own father's home."

"Tsk, tsk, Cecily," he said. "Have you no understanding of men? The Duke of Winterson might well be unhappy, but it will be because of the note you left for him telling him that you cannot go on with your sham of a marriage any longer, and are running away with your one true love, David Lawrence."

"What?"

"Well, you did not think that I could simply sit by and watch when you marched purposefully to your father's house with the information you'd learned from the inventories hidden in the cat mummies. Really, it would have been foolish of me indeed to sit by while you told your stepmama all about the plot to manufacture fake antiquities and sell them on the black market. I worked for decades to set up the relationship with the manufacturer in Cairo. It would have wrecked years of careful work on my part if I'd let you tell the world about my little artistic pastime."

"I believe you're mistaken, Lord Brighton. Winterson knows me well enough to discount any lies you tell him about my feelings for him."

His expression hardened. "You're the one who is mistaken, Cecily," he said with a growl. "I know everything you and your husband discuss in that house." He raised one lip in a sneer. "Everything.

"Did you think I'd let you marry that man," he asked, "and not have one of my people looking out for you at all times?"

"George!" Cecily said before she could stop herself.

Now she understood why the footman had hovered in the background so many times, why he seemed so clumsy. Her stomach knotted as she thought back to some of the more personal words she and her husband had exchanged in Winterson House. Had George been listening to them the whole time? Even their most intimate exchanges?

Not wishing to let Lord Brighton know how much the knowledge revolted her, Cecily kept her back straight.

"So, you've had George in our home. Spying for you."

"Yes, indeed." He smiled at her like an indulgent schoolmaster. "The boy has always been ready to do whatever his father asks of him. A pity I couldn't marry his mother, the poor penniless slut. I could hardly saddle myself to her for the rest of my days. And once your father stole your dear mother from me, I couldn't marry anyone, could I? It would be disloyal."

"What do you mean 'stole her'?" Cecily asked, hoping that if she distracted him for long enough there might be time for the servants to intervene.

"I saw her first, you see." Brighton's mouth was white with rage. "I saw her first but Hurston got there before me. Damn him. So I had to step aside. But I waited. Hoping she would realize her mistake in marrying him. But after four years,

I couldn't hold my tongue anymore. But he had already poisoned her against me.

"He made me kill her." Brighton's tone was conversational. "You see that, don't you? You are so like her, you know. So very much like her."

The change in his gaze, as if he were caressing her with his eyes, sickened Cecily.

"Stop it, Geoffrey," Violet said harshly, stepping closer to her stepdaughter. "Stop it this instant."

Before Cecily could prevent him, Lord Brighton reached out and hit Violet across the jaw with his closed fist. "Silence!"

With a cry at the impact of his hand against her face, Violet slumped to the ground.

"You are vile," Cecily said coldly, dropping to her knees beside her stepmother. "My mother was right to reject you."

"Yes, well, that doesn't matter now," Brighton said with equal coldness. "You'll be quite dead before the night ends. But I plan to have a bit of fun with your adoring husband first."

Twenty-two

*L*ucas stood staring out the study window into the back garden, waiting for the arrival of the Bow Street runners. He was feeling restless and was unable to concentrate upon any of the numerous tasks his private secretary had stacked neatly on the corner of his desk. Until this business about Will's death was settled, he feared that his attention would be difficult to engage. His years in the army had accustomed him to taking action when the need arose, and his inability to determine just who was responsible for Will's murder and punish the perpetrator left him with a feeling of helplessness that he did not like at all.

A brisk knock on the study door broke through his reverie and he turned to find Christian and Lord Alec Deveril stepping into the room.

"We thought you might care for some company," Christian explained, lowering his tall form into a low wing chair.

Deveril nodded, carefully ensuring that he did not wrinkle his splendid velvet coat as he took a seat across from Monteith. "And we have news."

This caught Lucas's attention. "What news?"

"It would seem," Christian drawled, stretching his long legs out before him, "that you have a traitor in your midst."

"A traitor to the crown?"

"Oh, fear not." Deveril raised a placating hand. "You will not be guillotined by the teeming masses. This traitor is far more mundane than that. He is, instead, someone planted in your household for the purpose of gathering information about you and your wife. And your search for her father's journals in particular."

"Who the hell is it?" Lucas demanded, his blood running cold at the idea of someone in his own household carrying tales. "And who is he reporting to?"

"Whom he reports to, I do not know," Deveril said, "but as to who has been carrying tales, I fear it is your new footman, the fresh-faced young George."

Lucas stalked to the door and threw it open, intending to summon the butler, but he was forestalled by the sight of the footman being held between two hulking fellows he recognized to be from Bow Street.

The taller of the two runners, his lank hair pressed down into his head by a porkpie hat, tugged what bit of his forelock he could grip, like a country lad meeting the squire. "Your Grace," he said, his voice raspy, "Mr. Winehouse sent us to apprehend this here lad. Colonel Lord Monteith swore out a warrant."

Deveril and Monteith stood.

"Bring him in here for a moment, Harker," Deveril instructed the man. Clearly he and Christian were on friendly terms with the fellows.

"Something didn't sit right with me the day Cecily was shot," Christian explained, as if reading Lucas's thoughts. "I was speaking of it with Deveril at White's, and we decided to do a bit of digging."

The three men stepped back as the two men from Bow Street half dragged, half led the scowling footman into the room.

"What bothered me," Monteith explained, "was that when I arrived at Winterson House in response to Cecily's note, that footman seemed a bit too interested in her comings and goings. He rather . . . hovered . . . as if he were listening for information."

"Go on." Lucas glanced at the man they spoke of and noted that his expression now was as impassive as a statue.

His gawking attitude must have been part of the ruse, he decided.

"Well, when we got out of the hack at the footbridge, I could have sworn I saw the same fellow ducking behind the magazine. But then when the shots were fired from the other direction I decided I'd been seeing things." Christian shook his head ruefully. "But I couldn't let it go. When I talked to Deveril about it, we decided to do a bit of checking on the fellow."

Before Lucas could ask, Deveril added, "We knew you had other things on your mind. And besides, there're only so many *ton* activities a man can stomach before he begins to think that all tea must be weak and all biscuits stale."

"And," Christian went on, "with the help of our own servants—who really do have the best understanding of what goes on upstairs and downstairs—we discovered that before he decided to become a footman, young George Grimly worked as a clerk for—"

"The Egyptian Club," Deveril finished.

Lucas shook his head in disbelief. "I cannot thank you enough," he told his friends. The thought of the sour-faced man before him in the same house with Cecily, watching over her, for God's sake, chilled him to the bone.

"Your Grace," the shorter, stouter runner said, "we should be taking this fellow in to the magistrate."

"I beg your pardon, gentlemen," Lucas told the two men. "But I would like to question this man before you take him in. He may have valuable information about who ordered the shooting of my wife."

Attempted murder of a peeress was no joking matter, so when the duke suggested they retire to the kitchens for a bit of ale and one of cook's famous blueberry tarts, they were quick to abandon their charge to the three gentlemen and retire below.

"Now, George," Lucas said, his voice deadly soft. "Why don't you tell me how a young man goes from clerking at the Egyptian Club to taking a position as a lowly footman in a ducal household."

It was not a question but an order, but the young man

slumped in the chair before them only tightened his jaw, refusing to answer.

"Why don't I give it a try," Christian said, leaning back against Lucas's massive desk. "It seems to me that a young man such as yourself, growing up at the edge of poverty, might be tempted, should he find himself working in a place like the Egyptian Club, to help himself to one or two of the baubles that come across his desk."

"And perhaps a club member discovered your little thefts. And maybe in exchange for keeping your crimes a secret, he made you try to get a position at Winterson House?" Deveril's voice was light, as if he were merely making a friendly inquiry. But the friendliness in his tone did not match the deadly seriousness of his eyes. "Is that what happened, son?"

"I don't have to say noth . . . anything," he corrected himself, "to you."

"No, indeed," Lucas agreed, "but I fear you are mistaken if you believe that your benefactor will get you out of this mess. After all, you are now implicated in the attempted murder of the Duchess of Winterson. That is a serious charge. A hanging offense. And unless your patron is the king himself, there is no way he will be able to save you."

But the boy sneered. "My father is a powerful man. He will protect me."

"Your father?" Lucas paused. "Who is your father that he can stop the hands of justice?"

They were interrupted by a knock at the door. It was the head footman, James.

"Your Grace," he said, his expression grave, "I have brought George's belongings. I thought perhaps they might help you find out more about him."

Lucas took the kit bag and dismissed the man.

In full view of the perfidious footman, as well as Monteith and Deveril, he unceremoniously dumped the bag's contents onto the surface of the desk. He looked up to see a flare of something in the young man's eyes. Fear, perhaps?

He pawed through the man's belongings. A penknife, a few letters, a marble. A journal with only a couple of pages used. *Does everybody in the kingdom keep a bloody journal?* Besides the journal, there was a three-volume set of books. Surprisingly enough, an account of Lord Geoffrey Brighton's travels in Africa.

Opening the first volume, he saw the inscription, and his blood ran cold.

"To my dearest son: One day all my worldly treasures will be yours."

It was signed *"Brighton."*

When they arrived at Hurston House, it was to find the establishment in an uproar.

Young George Grimly had been persuaded to tell them where his father could be found after Monteith casually made mention of the techniques the French had employed upon him during the time he'd spent as a prisoner of war. The three men neglected to inform the footman that Monteith's time in captivity had lasted all of two days, during which time he'd been completely unconscious. It seemed better that way.

And when the boy choked out that he was meant to watch Lucas while his father followed the young duchess to Hurston House, it had taken all of Lucas's willpower to keep from shaking the rest of the information from the boy. Deveril convinced him that however he might wish to throttle the erstwhile servant, it would go better for Cecily if they simply sprinted the short distance to Hurston House.

The butler showed the three men into the drawing room, where Violet lay prostrate on a settee, her maid holding a slab of beefsteak to her jaw, which already showed streaks of purple fanning out from it. Flanking their aunt were Miss Juliet Shelby, Lady Madeline Essex, and their respective mamas.

On seeing Lucas, Violet struggled to sit up.

"Thank heavens you are here, Winterson!" she cried, waving off her maid, who seemed willing to bodily restrain her mistress if necessary. "You must go after them at once. You may take as many footmen as you wish, only hurry."

"Hurry where, ma'am?" he demanded, dropping to bended knee beside her. "Where has he taken her?"

"It's Lord Geoffrey Brighton, of all people," she said, as if still coming to grips with the idea herself. "He has taken her to the Egyptian Club, I think. He keeps an office there, where he conducts research."

She pointed to her jaw. "He thought I was unconscious, but I was only feigning it. I heard everything he said to her. And I also heard him give the direction to Mixon, the butler. I sent a footman to find you; he must have just missed you."

"The bastard was confident he'd not be followed," Christian said. Then, realizing they were in mixed company, added, "Your pardon, of course, ladies."

But Violet was unconcerned with the proprieties. "He made Cecily write a note for you," she told Winterson, thrusting the paper at him.

"She meant none of it, I assure you," she continued as he scanned the words. "Cecily would never have written it if he hadn't insisted upon it."

His jaw clenched as he scanned the words. He knew better than to believe the content of the note itself. It was the nonsensical postscript at the bottom that made his heart stop. In the same code they had seen in his brother's letters, he read her real message to him: *He means to kill you. Do not risk it.*

If Cecily thought for one moment that he would sit by while she fought a madman, then she was mistaken. Crumpling the note, he strode from the room, leaving the others to follow behind him.

Twenty-three

$\mathcal{W}$hen Cecily and Lord Brighton arrived at the Egyptian Club in his closed carriage, instead of entering through the front door, he instructed the coachman to take them around back to the mews.

Her hands bound behind her back, Cecily was draped with a light cloak that hid her captive state. The gun, which Lord Geoffrey secreted in the folds of his greatcoat, never wavered from its aim at her, and she did not doubt for an instant that he would shoot if she tried to escape.

"Here now, my dear," he said, opening the carriage door and letting down the step. Like a courtly gentleman of old, he carefully helped her alight from the vehicle, his care in sharp contrast to his earlier sneers. But Cecily knew it was all part of his act for the servants. They did not know, after all, that their master was a madman who had already killed two people and had tried to kill two more. To them he was simply an indulgent uncle offering his beloved niece a tour of the club where he spent so much time.

Cecily considered raising a ruckus, but she would not put it past the man—she refused to think of him as her beloved uncle—to shoot anyone who got in his way. And so she allowed him to lead her up the back steps into the club without saying a word.

Seeing the Egyptian Club in the light of day, something she'd longed to do for so many years now, was bittersweet at best. All the affection she now held for the establishment was tied to the night she'd spent there in Lucas's embrace. The hallway Brighton now led her down was the same one that she and Lucas had traversed that night, a candle their only illumination. She thought about all they'd shared since that night, and prayed that if for some reason she was unable to save herself, he would not believe the vile letter Lord Brighton had left for him.

"Come this way," her captor said, leading her into the workroom where she and Lucas had been trapped. "Does it look familiar?" he asked.

"It was you?" Cecily demanded. How could she not have seen it? she wondered.

He gave a little bow. "Yes, indeed," he said. "I thought if you were married off to the young war hero, he would keep you from getting in my way. Were you not pleased? He is after all a handsome fellow, even if he is not quite so smart as he is pretty. And I'll wager he keeps you well enough entertained in the marriage bed, eh?"

His lascivious tone brought on another bout of nausea.

"Oh, do not be such a prude, my dear," he said, reading her revulsion correctly. "If you're anything like your mother you enjoy a good tupping well enough. Besides, you need not worry about that sort of thing anymore, anyway. When I'm through with you you'll be sleeping peacefully with your beloved Egyptians. Unfortunately, unlike them, you will begin the journey to the afterlife in the same way your dear brother-in-law did."

Cecily scanned the room, noticing that the implements and materials on the table were all that was needed to begin the mummification process. Understanding dawned, and swiftly behind it, horror.

"You . . . you . . . cannot!" she stammered. She had seen the twisted expression on the face of William Dalton, looked at his hands, which were flat as if they'd been pressing against the lid of his sarcophagus as he died.

"I'm afraid I can, my dear," Lord Geoffrey said, shutting the door of the workroom. "It is what happens to those who defy me. Even your dear mama, as beautiful as she was, made that mistake. Are you not pleased that I spared you? I am a hard man, true, but even I draw the line at murdering a child."

Suddenly, Cecily was assailed with memories of that long-ago day when her mother had begged her to hide in the trunk. She remembered hearing her mother's voice, and that of Unc . . . Geoffrey Brighton, raised in an argument. Ill, she remembered the sickening thud that had stopped her mother in mid-scream.

"You knew," she said, trying to force calm into her voice. "You knew I was there. Hiding."

He sneered. "Of course I knew, foolish girl." He laughed. "Allowing you to live has caused me a great deal of trouble. If I had it to do over again, I would have stifled my pangs of conscience and silenced you too. After all, how much more affecting it would have been to see mother and child dead together."

Cecily looked around the room, desperate to find a weapon of some kind. Swallowing, she realized that her mouth was dry. Perhaps she could ask for a glass of water and he'd be forced to untie her hands.

"I . . . I'm feeling faint, Uncle Geoffrey," she said suddenly, swaying on her feet a little.

He looked impatient, but stood up and helped her into a hard wooden chair just inside the door.

"I do not like that foolish nickname," he snapped. "Call me Father. Perhaps I would have been your father. If your mother hadn't abandoned me for Hurston."

She licked her lips. "F-Father, could I please have a drink of water? Please? I am so thirsty."

He shook his head in disgust, but moved to the table on the other side of the room, where a water pitcher and glass were arranged.

Plunking the glass down before her, he only rolled his eyes a bit when she lifted her tied wrists to remind him that she'd need help.

"I will untie you," he said, "but you must promise me not

to leave the room. If you leave, then I will make sure that your last moments are very bad indeed."

She nodded mutely, and when her hands were free she did not feign her eagerness to drink from the glass before her.

Moving back to his place on the other side of the table, Brighton began mixing various liquids and potions in a large vat near the window. He was careful always to keep her in his line of sight, but when he dropped a small vial of perfumed oil, he looked up at her, as if gauging whether he could trust her long enough to let him pick it up. Then a flash of an idea shone in his eyes.

"Come here, Cecily," he said, stepping aside so that there would be room for her on his side of the table.

She got up on shaking legs and walked toward him. When she stopped a few feet from him, he nodded to the bottle on the floor.

"Pick it up," he ordered, a gleam of malice glittering in his gaze.

She glanced down, wondering if it were some sort of trick. It made sense that he would ask her to retrieve the bottle, given that if he turned his back to her she was likely to attack. But if she angled herself in just the right way, she might be able to turn this into an opportunity for escape.

Carefully, she leaned forward, reaching down and grasping the bottle in her right hand. As she began to unbend herself upward, she paused when her head and shoulders were pointed at Lord Geoffrey's middle.

And shoved with all her might.

The move took him by surprise and gave her just enough time to slam the bottle as hard as she could into his nose. She heard a satisfying crunch and her hand was covered in warm liquid—whether it was blood or oil, she didn't know or care.

At that moment the door to the storeroom burst open and Lucas, Monteith, and Deveril, followed by several Bow Street runners, pushed into the room.

Cecily almost collapsed from relief as she watched the rescue party file in. Lord Geoffrey, furious at having been bested by a woman, growled even as he clasped his rapidly reddening handkerchief to his nose, the vat of potions forgotten in his pain and anger.

"Cecily!" Lucas cried, rushing toward his wife.

She allowed him to gather her into his arms, and for long minutes they just stood holding each other close.

"Thank God," he said against her hair. "Thank God you are safe."

"I love you," she said, not caring who heard her. "I am so sorry I didn't say it before. But I love you."

At a loud noise behind them, Cecily twisted to see if Brighton had been subdued and was relieved to see that two of the runners were holding his arms quite fast, while he screamed epithets about his "dose."

"Take me home, Lucas," she said to her husband once they had watched the runners lead their prisoner from the room. "I don't think I ever want to see this place again."

"But I thought getting into the Egyptian Club was your highest ambition?" he said, kissing her forehead.

Cecily did nothing to hide her shudder. "I have found, sir, that it did not live up to my expectations."

He shook his head, though a corner of his mouth kicked up in a slight grin. "But madam, what does?"

To her surprise and delight, before she could answer, he lifted her into his arms and proceeded to carry her from the building into the early summer sunshine.

"You," she said, tucking her head into the curve of his shoulder.

A hitch in his breath was the only clue that he'd heard her.

Once they were settled together in the carriage, Cecily sprawled across his lap, she spoke again.

"We must go to my father's house at once. Lord Brighton struck Violet quite hard."

"Hush, now," Lucas said against her hair. "Violet is well. She's the one who told us where to find you."

She sagged with relief, then stiffened again.

"Lucas," she said carefully, "did you read the letter I left for you at Hurston House?"

When she felt his arms tighten around her, Cecily's heart sank. "You did, didn't you? Lucas, I meant none of it! Brighton forced me to write it."

"Shh," he said, rubbing circles over her back with his hand. "I knew immediately that you hadn't written it of your own free will."

"But—" She stopped. "You believe me?"

Lucas chuckled, the noise reverberating through her. "My dear, I had not seen you and David Lawrence together for above a minute before realizing that there is no way in heaven or on earth that you would ever willingly abscond with the man. Your loathing for him is evident for anyone with eyes to see and I was able to decipher your message. Besides," he whispered into her ear, "you love me."

"Lucas." Cecily leaned back to look into his eyes. "When I thought I might never see you again, I was mad with regret for being so foolish. I thought that by refusing to confess my love to you I was somehow protecting myself from the pain I might feel if something should ever happen to part us. But when Lord Brighton told me that he was going to kill me, all I could think was that if the situation were reversed, then I would much rather have known you loved me before you were taken from me than not."

Her eyes welled at the thought that Lucas might never have known how she truly felt about him. "I love you. I think I've loved you since that first day on the steps of the Egyptian Club."

He took her face between his hands and kissed her with a tenderness that stole her breath.

"I love you too," he said, finally, his eyes smiling, his whole body radiating with joy. "God willing we will only be parted by death, and that when we are well into our dotage and surrounded by scores of grandchildren."

On the last word he brought his mouth down on hers and kissed her again.

Some minutes later, she asked, "Scores? Hadn't we best wait on predicting the number of our grandchildren until we have some actual children?"

His grin turned wolfish.

"Of course. But I'd better warn you. It is a project to which I plan to devote a great deal of time. Are you equal to the task?"

As he took her lips again, Cecily couldn't stop her grin.

"More than equal," she whispered.

This was one dance for which she and her duke were very well matched indeed.

Epilogue

Three weeks later

Cecily sat at her father's bedside, reading aloud to him from the latest issue of *Proceedings of the Royal Society,* though he had fallen asleep several pages ago.

At one time she would have rushed away as soon as she was able, but now that they had put many of their past difficulties behind them, Cecily cherished these moments with her father in a way she had never dreamed of before the events of the past few months. He was slowly regaining his ability to speak, though it was halting, and he still had difficulty at times recalling just which word he wished to use. But just that small bit of communication was a welcome relief to those who cared for him.

As with many who faced serious health problems, Lord Hurston was frustrated by his vulnerability, but he also seemed grateful to have his family around him. Especially Cecily.

Per the doctor's orders they had not yet told him about the perfidy of Lord Brighton, and since he did not seem to have any memory of the events leading up to his illness, there seemed no need. If Lord Hurston wondered at the absence of his old friend from his bedside, he did not remark upon it.

A soft knock on the door diverted her attention, and Cecily looked up to see Violet come to her side in a rustle of skirts.

"Juliet and Madeline are waiting for you in the sitting room. Do go see them," she whispered, so as not to disturb the now sleeping Lord Hurston.

Cecily nodded and stepped quietly from the room.

She found Juliet and Madeline tucked cozily into Violet's sitting room, chatting over the tea tray.

"When were you going to tell us?" Juliet demanded before Cecily could even be seated. "We had to learn from Amelia Snowe of all people!"

"Imagine!" Maddie said with a frown. "Having that horrid girl know your news before we did! It was most upsetting, I assure you."

Cecily was nonplussed. "How could Amelia possibly know about . . . ?"

She had only told Lucas yesterday, after all. And though he was quite pleased, she somehow did not think that would translate into him telling Amelia their good news.

"Wait," she said, eyes narrowed with suspicion. "What are you talking about?"

Mid-macaroon, Juliet paused. "The fact that you will be editing your father's journals, of course."

"Why?" Madeline asked, looking from Cecily to Juliet and back again. "What other news is there?"

Cecily felt her face redden under their scrutiny, but said nothing.

"Cecily!" Juliet cried. "Never say that you are enceinte!"

At her nod, Maddie clapped her hands, and then both cousins nearly smothered Cecily in a massive hug.

"A baby," Maddie said, once things had calmed back down a bit. "I can hardly imagine it. Especially since only a short time ago we, none of us, thought we'd ever marry at all."

"It is rather hard to fathom, isn't it?" Cecily asked. "But I have every faith that the two of you will be making equally promising matches very soon."

Juliet laughed. "I am very much afraid that even having our cousin the Duchess of Winterson on our side, Mads and I will still be spending our evenings with the other wallflowers."

Rising, Cecily stepped over to the console table near the fireplace, and retrieved her reticule.

"Here," she said, removing something and pressing it into Juliet's hand.

It was Amelia's dance card that she had used at the Bewle ball.

"Do you remember how we worked together that night to make sure that Amelia didn't know we were using her card?" she asked. "Well, the way I see it, Maddie and I will simply do the same thing again. And this time we will be even safer, because who on earth would dare suggest that a duchess had stolen a dance card? It's perfect."

"But why me?" Juliet asked, looking guiltily at Madeline. "Why me and not Mads?"

"You're older," Madeline said before Cecily could respond. "Cecily was oldest, then you, and then me. It makes perfect sense. After all, you have much less time before you are completely on the shelf and are doomed to be an ape-leader for all eternity."

"Very funny," Juliet complained. "So, I am to dance with all these tulips of the *ton* and then expect to find myself the latest toast? It worked for you, Cecily, but that doesn't mean it will work for me."

"Stop complaining and just take the dance card," Cecily told her with a laugh. "Lady Rawlins has a ball coming up next week. I believe that's ample time for us to transform you into a toast."

"This will be so much fun!" Madeline said with relish. "I get to choose her shoes!"

Juliet was saved a reply by Winterson's entrance.

"What are you doing here, dearest?" Cecily asked as he approached her. "I thought you were spending the afternoon at Tattersall's."

He leaned down to kiss her on the cheek. "We finished early and I thought I'd bring the carriage round to take you home."

A pucker formed between Cecily's brows.

"Why should I need the carriage?" she asked. "Winterson House is barely two streets away."

He raised one dark brow. "I thought we had agreed that you would rest a bit more. Because of . . . ahem . . ."

At his vague words she smiled. "They know, Lucas."

"Ah." He looked slightly disappointed. As if he enjoyed a bit of subterfuge. "Well, then, I thought we had agreed that you would rest a bit more because of your delicate condition."

His ears turned slightly red at the words "delicate condition," drawing smiles from Madeline and Juliet.

Cecily, however, was slightly annoyed.

"I am not a delicate flower, Lucas," she said with a frown. "I am perfectly capable of walking from here to—"

When he silenced her with a kiss, she sighed. "All right. I will take the carriage home. But I warn you that if you intend to do this for the entire nine months, you will have a very ill-tempered wife on your hands."

"My love," he said, winking at Juliet and Madeline, "I will count myself lucky to be upbraided by you."

Once they were safely ensconced within the carriage, Cecily asked, "Did you mean it? About feeling lucky, I mean."

He kissed her hard on the mouth. "My dear," he said, "I love you and I count the day you snubbed me outside the Egyptian Club as one of the luckiest of my life."

Cecily felt her eyes well up. "Truly?"

"Absolutely." Lucas kissed her eyelids and then the tip of her nose.

"And I love you. And I count the day you accosted me outside the Egyptian Club as one of the luckiest of *my* life," Cecily said.

"Then there's nothing for it, my dear," he said against her throat. "We must pool our resources and get lucky together."

Her reply, while enthusiastic, was unintelligible.

Read on for an excerpt from the next book
by Manda Collins

HOW TO ROMANCE A RAKE

Coming soon from St. Martin's Paperbacks

One

*F*rom his close-cropped golden curls to his gleaming dancing shoes, Lord Deveril was a man envied by men and adored by women.

And he was bloody tired of it.

A leader of the fashionable set, he was dressed tonight for his family's annual ball in a style slavish young fops had dubbed "Deverilish" which was marked by a blend of Brummell's simplicity and a hint of dash. His pristine neck cloth was skillfully tied in a knot called—what else—The Deveril. The cut of his black coat was looser than in Brummell's day, but the tailoring was exquisite.

It was not that he minded his popularity so much. Given the snubs he'd endured from the hypocritical *ton* when his father had still been drinking and whoring his way through London, the *ton*'s approval had been a welcome change at first.

It hadn't happened overnight, of course. He had been ruthless in his social campaign for those first few years. He'd worked hard to establish himself as a man of substance as well as style. He gambled, but only enough to prove himself honest. He had his share of liaisons with willing widows and even kept a few mistresses. But though he'd enjoyed the affairs while they lasted, always in the back of his mind was the memory that he was proving to the world just how different he was from his father.

And eventually, his diligence had paid off. Whereas he'd left university still in the shadow of his father's notoriety, now he was considered a good 'un by the gentlemen, and a catch by marriage-minded mamas.

Given what his social status might have been, then, Alec knew just how ungrateful it was for him to admit he was less than satisfied with it. His ennui sprang, he supposed, from the knowledge that if he so chose, this same pattern could continue on into his dotage. Breakfast at White's, horseflesh at Tattersall's, seeing and being seen in the park, followed up by some evening entertainment or other. The same people, the same food, the same conversation.

"Why so gloomy, Deveril?" Colonel Lord Christian Monteith asked from his usual post, one shoulder propped against a marble column. "Trouble with the old cravat? Champagne not shining your Hessians as bright as you'd like? Stickpin poking you in the . . . ?"

"Don't be an ass, Monteith." Alec raised his quizzing glass and a dark blond brow, channeling his annoyance through the eye-piece.

"Sorry, chap, that thingummy doesn't work on me," Monteith said apologetically. "My head's too thick. Its powers cannot penetrate to my brain."

With a sigh, Alec tucked the glass away. "Should have known you'd ignore it."

Taking up a position on the other side of Monteith's pillar, he nodded toward the ballroom floor. "Why aren't you dancing?" he asked.

"Already did."

"What, you danced once and having done your duty, retired here to this pillar?" It was unfair for Monteith to shirk his duty when Alec knew full well that there were plenty of ladies who would be without a partner. Ladies like his sisters. He ignored the fact that his own failure to marry someone who could serve as a chaperone for them might also impact their social success or lack thereof.

"For your information, Lord Hauteur," Monteith returned, "I danced with at least five ladies and now I am resting my tired bones, rather than sprinting to the card room as my less noble spirit would have me do."

Oh. "Where's Winterson?"

The Duke and Duchess of Winterson had become good friends with Alec earlier in the season through their investigation of the Egyptian Club, of which Alec had been a member. Theirs had been a rather hasty marriage, but to his delight they seemed blissfully happy together. Winterson and Monteith had served in the campaign against Napoleon together and were often to be seen surveying the crowds at these *ton* entertainments.

"Keeping watch over his lady wife," Monteith said with a frown, "and intimidating young swells into paying court to her cousins."

Alec felt an unfamiliar pang of jealousy. He'd been considering the possibility of marriage as a means of curing his ennui, and the Duchess of Winterson's cousin Lady Madeline Essex was high on his list of potential candidates. Curvy, blond, and quiet, Madeline would make an excellent Viscountess. And her easy manners would endear her to his sisters. But if Monteith beat him to the punch, it wouldn't matter whether his sisters liked her or not.

"How is that working?" he asked, careful to keep his tone neutral.

"Not too well." The taller man grinned. "I don't think Miss Shelby or Lady Madeline care for being managed by their cousin's husband. Took quite a bit of convincing to get Lady Madeline to dance with me, and that was only grudgingly done. I do not think the lady cares for me."

Something in Alec's gut unknotted. He had come to admire both ladies over the past few weeks. But he had no wish to compete with his friend as a rival for Lady Madeline's hand. He was quite sure he could hold his own, but Monteith could be charming when he set his mind to it. Things would be much better if Monteith set his sights on Miss Juliet Shelby, the Duchess of Winterson's other cousin.

Slim and fair of complexion with deep auburn hair, Miss Shelby could have been the toast of the *ton* were it not for an accident during her teens that had left her with a pronounced limp. Alec had been partnered with her at a card party some weeks ago and found her to be a sensible and witty young woman. She was not one to suffer fools gladly, and he could only imagine her annoyance at Winterson's interference. If he guessed right, she'd much rather have spent the evening at home working on one of her compositions for the pianoforte.

"On the other hand," Monteith continued, "Miss Shelby and I had a delightful conversation speculating over the identity of the artist everyone is chattering about. She thinks he's probably some unknown trying to gain the spotlight. I think it's probably some chap with a flagging career who wishes to raise speculation about his work."

"*Il Maestro*, you mean?"

All of London had been engrossed with learning the identity of the mysterious artist who had begun showing his controversial paintings a little over a month ago. The gallery owner claimed not to know, as did the few who had purchased pieces from the show. And it was generally agreed that the longer he kept his identity a secret, the more intrigued the public would become.

"Who else?" Monteith said with something like disgust. "I blame Byron for all of this ado. He swans about with his dark looks, spouting poetry and seducing women, and now every other fellow with the least bit of artistic inclination thinks a foreign sobriquet and risqué art are the shortcut to celebrity."

"Yes," Alec reasoned, "but Byron didn't keep his identity a secret. He makes sure everyone knows it's himself he's writing about."

The other man grimaced. "Just wait. *Il Maestro* will have a grand unmasking as soon as he's whipped the ladies into a sufficient frenzy of curiosity." He smiled. "All except for Miss Shelby, that is. I think a surfeit of chatter about that blighter is what sent her over the edge."

"What do you mean?" Alec asked, his brow furrowed. "Is she unwell?"

He did not like to think of Juliet ill. And it was the duty of a good host to ensure the comfort of all his guests, of course.

Monteith's glib tone turned serious. "I think her leg might be paining her a bit," he said. "And of course her harridan of a mother refused to allow her to take the carriage home."

On that point, Deveril and Monteith were in firm agreement. Lady Shelby was one of the most beautiful women to grace the *ton*. She and her two sisters had taken society by storm when they'd made their debuts some two and a half decades earlier. The daughters of an undistinguished Dorset squire, they'd been introduced to the *ton* by a distant cousin and within months married three of the most eligible bachelors in town. Of the three, Rose was the least admired. Not because of her looks, which had only improved with age, but because of her unpleasant nature.

"It would have surprised me to hear she had done so," he remarked. "Lady Shelby loves no one but herself. And even those feelings come with conditions."

The other man made a snort of agreement.

His respite from his guests over, Deveril took leave of his friend and wandered over to the line of chairs that had been set out for the matrons and those young ladies who either did not care to dance, or had not been asked. An empty seat next to Lady Madeline Essex beckoned, but as he glanced up, he saw a familiar figure slipping through the doors leading to a hallway off the family rooms. Changing direction, he threaded his way through chattering guests, and finally made his way to the exit.

When he reached the corridor, it was deserted except for a few wandering pairs taking advantage of the less crowded room for quiet conversation. Or perhaps for assignations. He was hardly one to judge.

Turning into a side hallway, he saw what he was looking for. A familiar man was turning a key in the door of Alec's office.

"Uncle," he said, making no effort to hush his approach. "Is there something I can help you with?"

Roderick Devenish gave a start at being caught, but quickly regained his composure.

"Nephew," he nodded, revealing the extent to which his graying hair had begun its slow retreat toward the back of his scalp. "I was just wondering if you had any of those Spanish cheroots you like so much."

Bollocks. But Alec did not challenge him.

"Were you, indeed?" he asked blandly, letting his eyes convey what he really thought of that falsehood. "I would have offered one if I knew you wanted one. Of course I didn't realize you had a key."

A pregnant silence fell between the two men. Alec marveled at his uncle's audacity. He was just like Alec's late father.

"A legacy of my youth, I'm afraid," Roderick said, fingering the key in his hand. "And I thank you for the offer, but I've decided I don't wish to indulge after all."

"Then I'll have to ask you to return to the ballroom," Deveril said, his voice still calm. "If the other guests find you wandering about in the family quarters, then they'll think we're actually family."

At the cut, Roderick let his urbane mask slip.

"You know as well as I do that the same poisonous blood runs in us both."

His sneer made him look every one of his fifty years.

Unwilling to be led down that path tonight, Alec shook his head. "Get out," he said simply. The steel in his tone was sharp and cold. "But first give me the key."

The naked hatred on his uncle's face was nothing new. It was akin to the look his own father had turned on him so many years ago. Grudgingly, he slapped the key into Alec's outstretched hand. Turning, he stalked back down the hallway in the direction from which Deveril had come.

When he was sure Roderick was gone, Alec let himself into the study to ensure that nothing had been disturbed. To his relief nothing had. He did find, however, a collar—the same sort worn by the housemaids. He had no illusions that it had been dropped in the course of her regular duties. Roderick, it seemed, was as ever, just like his late brother.

The same blood might run in both of them, but Deveril

was determined to ensure no woman he encountered would ever find herself a victim of it. He'd built his entire adult life upon that principle.

When he stepped back into the hall, he saw that the door to the music room three doors down was slightly ajar, and strode down the hall. Tonight, it seemed, the ballroom might be the least crowded room in Deveril House.

Hiding behind a screen was not how Miss Shelby had intended to spend the bulk of the Deveril ball.

When she'd arrived an hour earlier, she and her cousin Madeline had dutifully made their way to the side of the ballroom, where chairs had been set up for the chaperones and wallflowers. Though their other cousin, Cecily, had recently wed the Duke of Winterson, Juliet and Maddie had no illusions that they were now to be accepted among the elite of London society.

After an hour or so of chatting with Maddie, and later Colonel Lord Monteith, a friend of Winterson's, she'd felt the familiar sting of pain in her left leg. But it was the note in her reticule that made her less than eager to socialize. Pleading a headache, which showed every indication of becoming a real complaint, she excused herself to pore over the cryptic message in private.

Limping through the darkened corridors of Deveril House, she finally found the music room, which was, thankfully, deserted. She'd always admired the room, and had even played the magnificent pianoforte a time or two for the small musical evenings Viscount Deveril's sisters sometimes held. Though much younger than Juliet and her cousins, Lydia and Katherine Devenish were personable young ladies, and among the few friends the cousins could name amongst the more fashionable crowds of the *ton*.

She'd no sooner stepped into the music room when she heard familiar voices approaching in the hall. Cursing fate, she hurried as quickly as her painful leg would allow behind an elaborately decorated chinoiserie screen, where she lowered herself onto a tufted stool and waited for her unwelcome visitors to leave.

"I cannot account for it, Felicia," Miss Snowe complained. "It is bad enough that Cecily Hurston has stolen a march on every eligible female in London by marrying Winterson, but now she thinks to foist her ridiculous cousins on the *ton*. I had thought that Lydia and Katherine had more discernment than to allow such unfashionable people free rein in their ballroom. Or Lord Deveril for that matter. I am sorely disappointed in the Devenish family at the moment."

"Oh, I agree wholeheartedly," Amelia's bosom friend, Lady Felicia Downes said.

What a surprise. Juliet rolled her eyes.

"It's insulting to anyone of taste," Lady Felicia continued, "as if we've forgotten how the Ugly Ducklings languished with the rest of the ineligibles these past three years. Does Cecily Hurston really believe that her lucky marriage will erase Lady Madeline's plumpness or Miss Shelby's unfortunate limp?"

Juliet could hardly be surprised at Felicia's unkind words; hearing them aloud, however, stung. For the three years since their debut, when Amelia had dubbed the unfashionable cousins "the Ugly Ducklings," they'd been subjected to one unkindness or another from the blonde beauty and her friend. Though she had hoped that Cecily's marriage to the Duke of Winterson would give the cousins a much-needed social boost, it would appear with Amelia and Felicia the change in status for Cecily had barely registered. And it most certainly hadn't erased their derision for Madeline and Juliet.

"Cecily Hurston may have trapped Winterson into marriage," Amelia said, "but there is no way that Lady Madeline or Miss Shelby can possibly expect to make comparable matches. Why, the idea is preposterous."

"While it is certainly within the realm of possibility that Madeline will go on a strict reducing regimen," Amelia continued, warming to her topic, "there is certainly nothing that Juliet can do about her unfortunate limp. I had supposed that one such as she would be confined to her home and not be thrust upon genteel society. I wonder what her parents were thinking to bring her out as if she were any normal girl."

Juliet felt her cheeks redden with anger. It wasn't as if she had never heard such sentiments expressed before. Indeed, her own mother had at times said similar things, though she had the decency to keep her thoughts out of the public eye. So long as Juliet kept the true nature of her unfortunate injury secret, Lady Shelby had agreed that her daughter might attend as many society events as she wished. But to hear Amelia Snowe, who had fooled the gentlemen of the *ton* into believing her to be a sweet and nurturing angel, express such sentiments was infuriating.

"I daresay," Felicia responded, "they are hoping to marry her off to some aged lord who has already sired an heir. The idea of anyone else wishing to marry such an antidote is laughable. What man would possibly wish for the mother of his children to drag herself around with a walking stick?"

As she listened to the two girls share their mirth at her expense, Juliet vowed to "accidentally" trip Amelia at the first opportunity.

"You don't suppose they've already chosen someone, do you?" Amelia asked, once her giggles had subsided. "Because I would dearly love to be present at that wedding! How does one stumble down the aisle, do you think?"

"At least we would not be forced to see her dance at her own wedding! Imagine what a spectacle that would be! Carroty hair mixed with a halting gait. She will be as amusing as a performer at the circus." This came from Lady Felicia.

The laughing fit brought on by that bit of mean-spiritedness was interrupted by a cough. A gentleman's cough.

"Miss Snowe, Lady Felicia," she heard a deep voice say. "How is it that you are not on the dance floor?"

Juliet could all but hear Amelia's simpering smile slide back into place.

"Your lordship," she cooed, "what a delightful entertainment you've hosted this evening. Felicia and I were just taking a bit of a rest in between sets."

"I thank you for the compliment," Viscount Deveril said smoothly, though was that a hint of annoyance Juliet heard in his voice? "I must ask you to return to the festivities," he continued, his voice definitely cool. "This room is for family use only."

And you two are not family, his voice implied. Juliet bit back a cheer.

"We will leave at once," Amelia said, her voice thick with apology. Of course she would not wish to insult an eligible like Deveril, Juliet thought cynically.

"We apologize for the intrusion, my lord," Felicia cooed.

Juliet bit her lip to keep from laughing at the insincerity.

"There is no harm done, ladies," Deveril assured them with more generosity than they deserved. "And I pray you," he added, "try not to stumble down the hall. One would hate to see the two of you make a spectacle of yourselves. This isn't the circus, you know."

Behind the screen, Julie's mouth fell open in astonishment. Had the Viscount Deveril, leader of the fashionable set, just delivered a set down on her behalf? It was not to be believed!

In the room at large, an awkward silence fell, no doubt while Amelia tried to come up with a suitable response. Apparently she was unable to do so, because Juliet soon heard both ladies thank his lordship again for the warning and hurry away in a rustle of silk skirts and the firm click of the closing door.

Waiting a few minutes more to ensure the room really was empty, Juliet was making to rise from her seat behind the screen when she heard the Viscount's now-familiar voice.

"You may come out now, Miss Shelby. Your detractors have gone back to the ballroom."

Juliet dropped her head into her hands in frustration.

He had known she was there the whole time.

Damn. And double damn.

Schooling her features, she rose awkwardly from her seat and stepped out from behind the screen.